RAPTUROUS RECKONING

Morgan strode into the room and pulled her to him, his mouth crushing her soft lips in an impassioned kiss. He'd waited forever.

Hairpins fell to the floor like raindrops. The silky red twist of her hair came apart in his hands and tumbled down her back. A cry escaped her.

Norah was in his arms, returning kiss for passionate kiss. Her small, rounded body fit against his as if she'd been made for only him. Groaning, he pulled her closer. . . .

Also by Catriona Flynt

One Man's Treasure
Lost Treasure

Available from
HarperPaperbacks

Harper Monogram

Promise Me Tomorrow

⊰ CATRIONA FLYNT ⊱

HarperPaperbacks
A Division of HarperCollinsPublishers

This is a work of fiction. The characters, incidents, and dialogues are products of the author's imagination and are not to be construed as real. Any resemblance to actual events or persons, living or dead, is entirely coincidental.

HarperPaperbacks *A Division of* HarperCollins*Publishers*
10 East 53rd Street, New York, N.Y. 10022

Cover illustration by Jean Monti

First printing: December 1993

Printed in the United States of America

HarperPaperbacks, HarperMonogram, and colophon are trademarks of HarperCollins*Publishers*

❖ 10 9 8 7 6 5 4 3 2 1

This book is dedicated to two wonderful friends
without whom it could never have been written:

Virginia Probst

the Holbrook, Arizona, librarian who
introduced us and believed in our writing
abilities when no one else did

and

Garnett Franklin

artist and Holbrook historian

Prologue

October 1875
Indiana

Norah stood on the flagstone path studying the dirt caked on her tiny feet as she nudged a clump of dying grass with her toe. Her body trembled badly and her heart pounded in her thin chest. She heard her dad beating on the thick kitchen door, and heard people talking inside, but she didn't look up.

The farmhouse loomed in front of her, enormous, white, and terrifying. Norah clenched her fists tight, willing the pain of her ragged nails biting into her chapped skin to keep her from begging her father to take her back home. His temper scared her far more than her own uncertain future. A lump formed in her throat, and she swallowed hard, fighting for control. Dad would be mad if she shamed him.

The door swung open.

"What are you wantin', Tommy Kelly?" a chilly female voice asked. "It's too early for handouts."

Norah's eyes crept up to the pristine ruffle on the cook's starched apron. A hot flush of humiliation stained her young cheeks as she touched her own sackcloth dress. It wasn't Mam's best effort.

"I'll be speakin' to the lady o' the house, woman," Tommy answered contemptuously. "About me girl Norah a'workin' here."

"That little thing? She's but a wee babe!"

"What is it, Sadie? Who are you talking to? You're disturbing Mr. Robert's nap."

Norah saw the hem of a black skirt beside the gray one. The black skirt had no apron covering it, and the shoes that peeked from beneath it were shiny black leather with no patches or cracks.

"Miz Matthews," Tommy Kelly called, uncaring of disturbing Mr. Robert. "I brung ya me Norah ta do fer ya."

Norah's cheeks burned bright when she heard Mrs. Matthews's harsh whisper, "Who is that?"

The cook barely bothered to lower her voice. "That's the squatter what lives on Welsh's property. The one with all the babes."

"Oh," Mrs. Matthews said, "the *papist*." She made the word sound particularly loathsome. "I'll take care of it, Sadie. You can get back to the pudding."

Jean Matthews moved forward into the doorway, her long face set in a frown, and addressed Tommy sternly. "What do you want, man?"

Norah felt her father bristle beside her. Edging away from him, she waited for his explosion. Instead, she saw him pull the cap from his head.

"Me girl, here, wants ta work." He flashed his most winsome smile.

"That one?" Jean Matthews peered down at the little red-haired girl. "Good God, how old is she?"

"Nine, or so." His voice took on a wheedling tone.

"She can't be—she's much too little."

"She ain't but a little bit o' nuthin', but she works real hard. She allus has." His sharp finger poked Norah in the back.

Trying not to flinch, she spoke the words her father had told her to say. "I'll do good." They came out in a hoarse whisper.

Norah felt his flash of anger, and jerked her head up to meet Mrs. Matthews's steely blue eyes. "I promise I'll work very hard," she said solemnly.

For two cents Jean Matthews would have taken the broom to the odious Irish squatter! The very idea of putting such a small child out to work when he was too lazy to hold down a job himself made her blood fairly boil. But the mute appeal in the little girl's eyes—and the goose bumps on her bare arms—kept Jean from slamming the heavy door.

"What's your name, child?"

"Norah Kelly."

"And when's your birthday, Norah?"

"May first, ma'am. I'm nine and a half. And I's worked for Miz Welsh since I was five—puttin' by and cannin'. She'll tell ya." Another sharp poke in the back shut her up. She was talking too much, telling the biggest landowner in the area what her father didn't want known. Norah dropped her eyes, noticing she had a bloody toenail from where she'd stubbed it on a jagged rock down the lane.

In the distant meadow a fresh cow lowed softly. The autumn wind rustled a pile of multicolored maple leaves, scattering a few from the neat mound they'd been raked into, and stirred the crimson and gold chrysanthemums near the door. A duck waddled into the flowers, searching for a few grubs or worms that hadn't burrowed deep in the earth for the winter. The pond had frozen along the edges, so the easy feasting on snails and bugs had ended.

"Well, Jean, what do you think?"

Norah lifted her eyes again to see an old man with fluffy white hair and many wrinkles around his brown eyes standing behind Mrs. Matthews. He wasn't nearly as tall as his wife. For the first time she saw a smile touch Mrs. Matthews's stern face. Hope flared in Norah.

"Are you going to hire this 'little bit of nuthin'?'" the man continued. "Surely she doesn't eat much. There must be something around here she can polish . . ."

"You're supposed to be napping, Robert."

"And miss all the fun, my dear? Certainly not. It's been a long time since we've had a child around. But maybe you're right. She'd probably be too much for you to handle. You're no spring chicken, you know."

There was a moment of utter silence. Tension filled the air.

Norah didn't understand the byplay between the adults, but somehow she knew her life hung on it. She held her breath. She either got work today or the strapping of her life.

Mrs. Matthews took a deep breath. She studied Tommy Kelly long enough to make him squirm, then she nodded. "She can stay—for a month. Come back then and we'll talk about her future."

She held out her hand to Norah. "Welcome to Matthews Farm, Norah. I hope you'll be happy here. Have you had lunch yet? No? I think we have something left. You can call me Mrs. Jean, by the way."

It was a lucky day for Tommy Kelly when he thought of putting Norah out to work, he decided. Now maybe Maggie would shut her yap about there being no food for the other ones. He felt a wave of relief as his daughter went into the house.

"I'll be pickin' up her wages come Saturday evenin'," he called as he set his grimy cap on his head.

The door closed with a bang.

The kitchen was the most marvelous room Norah had ever seen. It was larger by half than the whole cabin her family shared, and it had a huge, warm stove. There was a table with chairs in the center of the room, and the walls were lined with plenty of other furniture.

A row of six windows in the south wall made the room light and airy, and the windowsill was filled with pots of green plants and blooming red geraniums. Norah had seen a geranium once, in Mrs. Welsh's kitchen window, but she'd never seen any plant as lovely as these. Under the windows there was a sink with a water pump. Was there anything so grand as a pump in a house?

Norah's eyes grew huge with wonder. The oak rocking chair next to the cookstove, with an orange cat curled up on a quilted cushion, was the final touch. Excitement filled her tiny body, but she clamped it down immediately. She didn't want to act unseemly. Mrs. Welsh had told her about manners, so she understood such things. She gazed around the room in quiet reverence, admiring the marvelous conveniences and homey atmosphere.

And the food—she hadn't imagined there was so much food in the whole world. It filled the cupboards, stocked the shelves, and hung from the rafters. There was more in the pantry, cellar, smokehouse, and kitchen garden outside. The stove was emitting marvelous smells, sending Norah's belly into a rumbling fit.

She giggled out loud and clapped her tiny hands together with glee, imagining how her four sisters and wee brother at home could eat till they popped. Then she remembered who she was and feared an awful slap—or worse, being turned out even before she started to work.

"Sadie, I believe Norah might like to wash up before she has some lunch."

The pink-cheeked cook shot Mrs. Matthews a startled look before she led Norah to the marble-topped washstand near the pantry and handed her a crock of strong lye soap. "What about clothes? She can't go about in that thing."

Mortified by the reference to the ugly sack she wore, Norah set about washing with grim determination. Mrs. Welsh had taught her to wash the very first day they'd canned string beans, so she did it like an expert.

"We'll think of something. Maybe a dress Bonnie left at home. Undergarments, too. And shoes—her feet are blue. And a coat—poor thing must be chilled to the bone. We'll look this afternoon—the furniture polishing can wait. And Sadie"—Mrs. Matthews nodded toward the little girl—"be careful the food you give her isn't too rich. I doubt if she's ever had a full stomach."

"Hey, Nuthin'! Little Bit o' Nuthin'! Wait for me." Calvin Welsh swung his long legs over the rail fence. "I'll help you tote your load."

Norah didn't slow her pace. She was late leaving the farmhouse because of the spring luncheon gathering, and she knew Mam would be expecting her to bring home some of the leftovers. She only got home once a month now, but she tried her best to help Mam as much as she could since Mrs. Jean informed her that her father squandered most of her wages on gambling and other such evils.

Cal's long legs made short work of the distance between them and he lifted the burlap bag from her shoulders. "This is heavy. What's in your poke, Nuthin'?"

"Clothes. For the wee ones. From the church ladies." Norah kept on walking.

Cal stopped a minute to watch her shift the other bundle she was carrying. She was a funny little thing, all intense and determined. From the top of her wild red hair to the tips of her toes, she was decisive, always going someplace, always in a hurry.

From his advanced age of twenty, he found her quite amusing—a tiny girl with the tenacity of a locomotive. He sort of liked her pluck, though. Who would have imagined any child of Tommy Kelly's having so much backbone?

He'd fallen into the habit of calling her Nuthin' like everybody else—except Mrs. Jean, of course, who was all prim and proper—but he thought of her as Norah. Nowadays her given name fit her. She was scrubbed clean, and she wore real dresses instead of flour sacks. She'd changed tremendously from the dirty little tyke who'd come to help his mother can string beans.

A few puddles from a recent spring rain still dotted the corduroy road. Norah stepped around a large one, not wanting to wet her feet. She wasn't wearing her shoes, and hadn't worn them home since her father had strapped her for putting herself above her kin by showing off shining high-buttoned shoes that had never been worn by anybody else. After that she was careful what she did and said around her family so nobody got his nose out of joint.

"The dogwoods are pretty this year," Cal said.

Norah looked at the tree-covered knoll, realizing that the elegant, white blossoms were indeed beautiful. People like Jean Matthews and the Welsh family spent a lot of time chatting about flowers, weather, and nature. She was coming to understand that folks with full bellies and warm houses saw the world differently from poor people who struggled simply to exist.

"They are lovely flowers," she replied, making up her mind right then that she would always be someone who'd be able to see the beauty in life. "I read about them in a book."

"What? You can read?"

"Are you deaf, Calvin Welsh? Mrs. Jean lets me read every day." Her hazel eyes sparkled with pride.

"Oh, go on!"

"I'm not fibbing. Part of my job is to read one hour every afternoon to Mrs. Jean. And then play checkers with Mr. Robert."

Cal, who was very adept at games, challenged her immediately. "Are you any good at checkers?"

"Not very. I think it's a foolish waste of time, but Mrs. Jean insists." She noticed they were coming to a house near the road, a small cottage with a stone wall. Hastily she crossed to the very far side of the lane.

Cal followed suit. Even now that he was older and basically understood the situation, he still shunned the guilty people, and the house as well.

Norah had no idea what an illegitimate child was, but from the way people talked about the woman who lived at the cottage, she was certain it was something so sinful it was beyond redemption. She marched past, shoulders rigid, eyes straight ahead.

Beyond the house, Norah relaxed and resumed her conversation. "I love to read. Mrs. Jean taught me when I first went to Matthews Farm last fall. I'm going to read everything in her library."

Cal discovered he wasn't especially fond of the topic, so he mentioned seeing pussy willows down by the brook, and then asked about the food served at the luncheon. He even tried to beg a piece of rhubarb pie from Norah, knowing full well she wouldn't give away food meant for her sisters and brother.

"Can you read, Cal?"

"Well, sure. Don't everybody?"

"No. My mother and father can't. I'm trying to teach Mam, but she says she can't see any reason to learn. But Katie, Meg, and Nell have learned, and Rosie knows the whole alphabet. Even Mickey knows some letters. I could teach you, if you want."

He flushed with embarrassment at being caught in a lie. He'd wanted to go to school when he was younger, but his mother didn't hold much with book learning. Farmers didn't have time, she had said. Cal guessed that was right because his Pop could read a bit before his eyes got weak, but he was always too busy to pick up a book.

"I don't know," he said. "What would I read about? I'm just a farmer."

Norah set down her bundle and looked up at him, her hands on her thin hips. "You could read a newspaper. You could read a book about other places." She got a faraway look on her face. "If you could read, you wouldn't have to be a farmer unless you wanted to be."

He picked up the bundle she'd set down. "Why don't you let me have some of that rhubarb pie, Nuthin'?"

"Calvin Welsh, don't you touch that pie!"

He laughed aloud, still carrying both bundles. "All right. You bring a book next month when you come home, and wait for me down by the fence. I'll let you teach me to read."

1

October 1886

The day was dreary as hell. Calvin Welsh stared out the dirty window without seeing the bleak, overcast day. His thin body had long since become accustomed to the rolling movement of the train, just as his senses had accommodated the noise. The only things Cal knew were his own grim thoughts.

Pop's rain-drenched burial the week before played itself over and over in his mind. Thinking of it pained Cal almost as much now as the day it happened. A man's life changed forever when his father died.

Pop had worked hard and died hard. He hadn't been a young man when he took a wife, and he had been forty-six when Cal was born. But they'd been close in spite of the age difference between them. And two years before, when Cal had told Pop he was leaving the family farm to seek adventure in the Arizona Territory, his father had understood, for he, too, had chased a dream. Cal ached now with the knowledge that Pop could no longer share his dreams.

He tried not to think of Norah. Better to let that childhood dream go. He'd been shocked when his mother told him Norah had left for Cincinnati right after Jean Matthews had died, more than a year and a half before. Somehow Cal always thought she'd be in Aberdeen waiting for him when he was ready for a wife. Not that he'd ever mentioned it to her—she'd been too young for talk of marriage at first, and later he didn't have enough to offer a bride. But he'd thought about it for years. He'd always expected it.

"You seem to be troubled, my son. Would you care for some conversation?"

Irritation at the intrusion vanished as soon as he turned toward the old man who was standing in the aisle. "Please sit down," Cal murmured, realizing that conversation was exactly what he needed.

The man lowered his rotund body to the worn velvet seat, and extended his hand. "Dr. Omar Goodfellow, sir. At your service . . . and the Lord's."

Cal took the soft pink hand. "Calvin Welsh, sir."

"Have you traveled far, Mr. Welsh? You look weary."

"From Aberdeen, Indiana. My father died."

"My deepest sympathies, sir. I grieve for your loss."

The old man's obvious sincerity touched Cal's heart as few others with comforting words had. Queer thing, a complete stranger consoling a man. Cal couldn't help thinking that the old fellow resembled an angel, with his halo of white hair, mild blue eyes, and unlined skin . . . an angel sent especially to comfort him.

"Is there other family?" Goodfellow inquired.

"A mother and four brothers." He didn't mention that his brothers were all sturdy farmers with few dreams and little imagination, who'd never go more than fifty miles from home. "My father was a good man. He understood my need to seek new horizons."

"A special man, I dare say. Few people grasp the need to dream. Fewer still have the courage to follow dreams."

Cal relaxed, sensing that Goodfellow was a kindred spirit, and began to talk. About himself, about his father. He talked about the farmland he'd given up in Indiana and his newly acquired property in the Arizona Territory. He even mentioned Norah Kelly.

"When I was little my father and I discovered a squatter family in a little lean-to shack in the bottomland at the far end of our property. This Irishman, his wife, and a whole mess of dirty youngsters. The wife wasn't much more than a child, herself. Winter was comin' on and they didn't have nowhere else to go, so Pop let 'em stay."

"Exceptional man, your father."

Cal nodded. "Folks around had a fit, but Pop said they wasn't hurtin' anything. They're still there, still having babies every year. The oldest daughter turned out real fine, though. Little red-headed Norah." A wistful look crossed his face. "She went to work at a big farmhouse, learned to cook and sew. Got herself educated, an' all."

"I educated myself reading the Good Book." Dr. Goodfellow patted the scuffed satchel he'd stowed by the window. "Now I'm serving the Lord by spreading his word. I sell the book to folks who need uplifting."

Cal, whose Bible reading hadn't got much farther than the "begats," simply nodded. He preferred the derring-dos of adventurers and heroes in novels, but didn't want to offend his newfound friend by saying so.

"And I even give away a few," Goodfellow continued, stroking the worn leather, "to them what can't pay the price."

The conductor made his way down the aisle, announcing that the noonday meal would be served at the upcoming stop. "Best place to eat on the whole trip. If you don't buy another meal till you reach your destination, treat yourself to this repast at Jorgensen's."

Dr. Goodfellow drew a small pigskin pocketbook out of his trousers, and silently counted the coins inside. His tongue flicked worriedly over his bottom lip.

Cal watched as the old man fingered the nickels and pennies in the mended purse. He'd been down on his luck enough to know what that meant. Before Goodfellow could make some excuse about not being hungry, Cal offered to buy his meal. "I don't want to eat alone," he said pleasantly. "Why don't you join me—my treat—so I don't have to sit with strangers. I've been feeling mighty low the past few days, and off my feed. A hot meal might do me good."

Somehow Cal had managed to word the invitation so the old man's pride wasn't offended. He was always that way, never liking to affront anybody.

Goodfellow nodded, accepting the invitation. "A man needs to keep up his strength, especially in times of tribulation. A hot meal would do the trick."

The dreary clouds, which had hung low and threatening for most of the morning, finally parted, and light shone down on the train as it clattered noisily along the flat, barren terrain.

"This squatter's girl. You say she's educated?"

Cal nodded, his straight, sun-bleached hair flopping in his eyes. He pushed it away. "She worked at the big farm, as a maid for the schoolteacher."

"Schoolteachers have maids?" Goodfellow asked, his blue eyes narrowing.

Cal blinked at his tone. "Mrs. Matthews—the former schoolteacher—married real well. He was a widower with four daughters, and a huge, run-down farm. She raised up the daughters and got his farm in shape all at the same time. Pop always said she had the will of a stampeding bull." Cal blushed when he thought how rude that sounded. "She did good by Norah Kelly, though. Taught her to sew real fine. And to read. Norah can read so good she can teach other people." He smiled shyly. "She taught me."

"You don't say?" Goodfellow seemed impressed.

"Yep, I do. That's how I got my place in the Arizona Territory." Cal grinned. "I read about it in a newspaper."

"Somebody was advertising in a back East paper about land for sale in Arizona Territory?"

"Not for sale—for *free!* The town company of Holbrook, Arizona Territory, gave me free land and a free building—just for moving there," he said proudly. No sense in mentioning that the narrow, wooden building was empty. It wouldn't always be. He had plans about someday selling fruit and nuts, candy and tea, maybe even newspapers and books—if he ever got some cash to buy supplies.

"It's a wild town," Cal said, his eyes suddenly glowing. "Right outta one of them dime novels."

"Ya don't say."

"Yessireee, Holbrook is as tough as they come. Outlaws and marauders walk the street just as bold as brass. And the cattle rustlers . . . they're just thick as hairs on a hound's back."

"Really? Isn't there any law in . . . ah?"

"Holbrook," Cal said. He loved telling a story, and Goodfellow looked very interested. "There's a sheriff and a deputy, but the way the cattle companies have been hauling in herds by the boxcar load lately, it's gotten too much for two men to handle. What with the gunfighters hangin' around, an' all."

"You're joshing me."

"No, sir. I wouldn't do that. The very first day I got to town I was in a gun battle."

"I don't believe it," Goodfellow said, utterly amazed.

"I went in the Bucket of Blood Saloon for a glass of beer and this drunken no-good named Kid Keller took exception to my hat. Guess it did look outta place in the real West, but he had no right to knock it off and stomp on it. We mixed it up a bit—I did okay with my fists 'cause Pop taught all of us how to take care of ourselves—and then Kid Keller pulled out a pistol and started blasting."

"Did he hit you?"

Cal pulled himself up straight. "Naw. First couple of shots were at my feet, to scare me, and before he damaged my hide with anything but splinters, Sheriff Treyhan burst through the door with both pistols ablazin' and plugged him in the arm."

Goodfellow breathed a sigh of relief. "Thank God."

"That very day the sheriff saw to it I had a handgun like every other man in town. That's practically the law of the West, you know. I hadn't shot anything but a rifle before, but I practiced every day on tin cans. I'll bet I ate twenty cans of peaches before I got good enough to satisfy Sheriff Morgan Treyhan."

The train whistle announced the upcoming stop.

Goodfellow watched the lanky young man hasten toward the privy, smiling to himself and thinking that what had started out as an ugly

morning was promising to be a most enjoyable
day. And a profitable one. Leaving his satchel
beneath the seat as everyone else was doing,
he followed the other passengers to the dining
hall and found a place for the two of them to
sit.

He was watching the door when he saw Cal
step into the dining room and look around. He
gave the boy a wave. A fine day, indeed. This upcountry rube ambling toward him was such an
easy mark, it was almost shameful to take
advantage of him. But Omar Goodfellow, by
whatever name he happened to call himself, had
been in the cheating-stealing-and-swindling
business so long he simply wasn't able to let an
opportunity pass.

"Sit down, my boy," he said, wiping off a spot
on the bench with a starched napkin. "If this
food is half as good as it smells, you'll be back to
your old self in no time."

"Thank you, Dr. Goodfellow. You're so kind."

The table was laden with heaping platters of
fried chicken and thick pork chops; creamed
peas and snap beans; mashed potatoes, biscuits,
and gallons of gravy; jellies, relishes, and pick-
les. Folks who'd barely moved for days ate like
field hands. Then they topped the meal off with
blackberry cobbler and bread pudding, and
crowded back on the train.

Less than twenty minutes later, lulled by the
gentle sway of the passenger coach as it rolled
along the tracks, and the enormous meal, Cal
dropped off to sleep right in the middle of
extolling the virtues of Norah Kelly.

Goodfellow had listened with mild interest. Only once had the lad mentioned the girl's looks, and he did that almost apologetically, but Goodfellow decided she must be passably attractive—more from the blush coloring Cal's cheeks than from his exact words. Too bad he wouldn't be around to pluck that fair peach, Goodfellow thought, but he'd have to be satisfied with helping himself to the wad of money in Cal's pocket. A man shouldn't get too greedy.

He moved around on the seat, trying to find a comfortable position for his overstuffed body, wishing he could stretch out flat and have a good long snooze. The door of the coach swung open. Goodfellow caught a brief glimpse of the man in the black ulster overcoat who entered the car, but the next moment he was overcome by a gigantic yawn.

So caught up was he in his own gluttonous discomfort, he didn't pay attention to the man walking toward him until the fellow stopped a mere two feet away.

"Hand over all your money, old man."

Goodfellow almost laughed at the squeak in the youth's voice. But then he recognized the metallic gleam of a weapon in the kid's white-knuckled fist. His heart tripped.

The gun barrel looked enormous!

Disbelief surged through him, followed by terror. *He was being robbed!* He leapt off the seat with no other thought than protecting the precious contents of his valise.

"Noooo!!!" he cried as he lunged toward the train robber.

The gun blast caught him right in the chest.

"Oh, shit!" Little Neddie cried. "Why'd you go and make me do that?"

Little Neddie didn't mean to shoot the old fool. It was his very first train robbery, and he was nervous as hell. And the handkerchief disguise kept slipping down his sweaty nose. When the old bastard yelled, it scared him so bad he almost wet his pants. Somehow the gun exploded in his hand.

Cal and the other slumbering passengers in the train car awakened instantly at Dr. Goodfellow's frantic shout and the horrifying report of the pistol. Cal lurched forward to catch Goodfellow and felt another bullet whizz past his ear, splintering the wood veneer behind him.

"Get him before he escapes!"

Pandemonium broke out. Within moments Little Neddie and his cursing cohort in the next car were captured by a throng of angry passengers. The sniveling little coward complained about cruel treatment as he was dragged to the baggage car and tied up. Neddie's partner shut his mouth after he was jabbed in the belly by an old war veteran with a crutch. As soon as both men were secured, the train proceeded to the next stop where they could be turned over to local lawmen.

All the while, Cal held Dr. Goodfellow. He knew the old man was dead. Goodfellow probably had died the moment the bullet tore into his chest. But Cal held him anyway, trying to offer some sort of comfort, and receiving a measure of comfort in return. It was far too close on the heels of his own father's death for him to think rationally about the murder. Tears ran silently down his face as he rocked the man's body back and forth.

An hour later, the train stopped at a place so small it didn't even have a regular depot. The station was simply a freight car that had been stripped of its wheels and set facing the track, with a stovepipe chimney and a signal arm for stopping trains fastened to a sapling pole.

Cal told the authorities what he knew. It wasn't much since he'd been asleep till the gunblast. Other passengers milled around outside the stopped train, inconvenienced by death, waiting to be on their way. Cal explained that Omar Goodfellow was a widower with no family and no home of his own. The blood-caked body was sadly left for the undertaker to bury, and the train chugged on its way again.

This time Cal sat alone, and nobody bothered him. Dark clouds gathered again, and rain began to splash against the smoke-grimed windows. The train ran through the day and into the night. When dawn came, Cal was still sitting by himself.

Finally the conductor announced his stop. "We'll be getting into Holbrook soon, son," he said, looking at his pocket watch. "Only three hours and seventeen minutes behind schedule. That ain't bad for a robbery, and the other delays."

Cal roused himself to go clean up. In the dinky washroom at the back of the car, he splashed cold water on his face and combed his unruly hair. The bloodied shirt he'd been wearing sickened him, so he tossed it out the washroom window.

Moments later as he was gathering his luggage, he noticed Dr. Goodfellow's worn leather valise on the floor by the window. A dark stain spotted the threadbare velvet, and a bullet hole splintered the veneer near the top of the window sash. Those things, and the beat-up bag, were the only reminders of the kindly old gent who'd encouraged Cal to talk about the two people he loved most in the world, Pop and Norah.

Cal almost called the conductor back to report the satchel, but he remembered how steadfast Goodfellow had been about spending his final days serving the Lord by selling Bibles. Cal wasn't much of a churchgoer, but he admired Goodfellow's dedication to goodness.

Maybe if he took the Bibles with him, he could carry on the old man's cause and see that they got into deserving hands. Nobody seemed to notice that he had an extra bag when he stepped off the train at the Holbrook station.

Holbrook was situated on the Arizona Territory's high plateau, between the flat-topped, red-rock mesas and the cottonwood- and willow-lined riverbed of the Little Colorado River. The town was rude and ugly and had little to recommend it. The Atlantic and Pacific Railroad track ran straight down the north side of it like a shiny black snake.

Unpainted wooden buildings clustered together between the track and the river, small and squatty against the expanse of open grassland. In this area of the Arizona Territory, a man could see a hundred miles if the air was right. But today dust devils danced among the clumps of sage, obscuring the view and grating on people's nerves.

"Hey, Calvin," a voice called from the wooden depot. "I'm over here."

"Morgan!" The hollow feeling that had gripped Cal's guts from the moment he heard the bandit's pistol fire and saw Dr. Goodfellow fall began to seep away.

The wind gusted and a tumbleweed bounced along the dirt street, rolled under a passenger car, and continued on its way north to the red mesas of the Navajo reservation.

Since Cal was the only person getting off the train in Holbrook that afternoon, the stop was short. He squinted his eyes against the relentless dust, and walked slowly toward his friend. As he shook Morgan's outstretched hand, the whistle blew, signaling that the train was prepared to get under way.

A riderless horse came galloping toward them, shying wildly at the sudden shrill blast of the whistle, then turning south and racing down the road that led to the Little Colorado River. A Mexican woman, holding a black shawl around her face to protect herself from the blowing sand, was carrying a cloth-covered basket of freshly made tamales to sell. She shouted at the horse to stop, and her two small children laughingly chased after it.

"Boy, am I glad to see you." Morgan Treyhan grabbed two of the suitcases and started down Central Avenue toward Cal's unpainted clapboard building.

Although they were nearly the same age and shared a common ancestry, Cal Welsh and Morgan Treyhan were as different as men could be. Open-faced and friendly, Cal stood more than three inches taller than Morgan and looked more like a gangly youth than a mature man of thirty. While his gait was always languid, he really wasn't a lazy man—he knew how to work as hard as the next fellow—but he was a dreamer who loved to lose himself in adventure novels.

Morgan Treyhan had all the adventure he needed in the life he led. As sheriff of Holbrook, he put his life on the line every day of the week. He was broad in the shoulders and unusually strong and muscular, had tanned, weathered skin, shoulder-length black hair, and Celtic eyes that were neither sapphire nor ebony but somewhere in between.

"Wind's blowin'," Cal commented unnecessarily, as his ill-fitting suit jacket gaped wide and his hair was whipped into his eyes. Nothing seemed to have changed since the day he left.

Morgan didn't answer. He wasn't much for small talk, and chatting wasn't easy on such a day as this. All a man got was a mouthful of grit. He nodded to the newspaper editor, who was trying to keep his hat on and carry a stack of flapping papers at the same time. When they reached their destination Cal unlocked the door to his house, and they went inside.

"Burton Almstead got shot up real bad Saturday night," Morgan said, setting the bags on the wood floor. Cal didn't own any furniture, except a pot-bellied stove he'd bought from a fellow who had given up and left town.

Even though it was only mid-October, Cal shivered and set about making a fire. "Will Burton be okay?"

"Myrtis fixed him up best she could," Morgan answered, looking around for a sturdy box to sit on. Several packing crates filled with smaller boxes had been pushed against the far wall. Morgan brushed off the accumulated dirt that had filtered through the cracks in the walls since the last time Cal had cleaned, and set his find by the stove.

Cal flung himself down on the thin sleeping pallet on the floor. "Where's the new doctor?"

Morgan gave a mirthless laugh. The physician who was temporarily helping out while Doc Robinson was away on a family emergency had turned out to be a sorry excuse for one. "Gone. Again. The town company's looking to get somebody else. And I've got to find another deputy. Even if Almstead survives, he'll be laid up for months."

"Who ya gonna get?"

"Jed Oakes wants the job."

Cal laughed. "I'll just bet he does. And he wants the combination to every safe in town, too. Any other volunteers?"

This time Morgan smiled. His teeth were white and nearly straight. "I was thinking of you."

"Me! I'm not a lawman. I dig wells and read books. And make plans for someday making this store pay off."

"Calvin, I need a man I can trust."

"You can trust me, all right, but I wouldn't do you much good otherwise."

"Do you have any coffee? I haven't had more than four hours sleep a night since the shooting."

Cal went out back and pumped some water, then put the coffeepot on the stove. "I got some crackers, if the mice didn't get into 'em while I was gone."

He rummaged around in a box that served as his pantry, then set out the soda crackers, two chipped cups filled with canned peaches, some broken pieces of jerked venison, and a molasses chew each. Morgan poured the coffee into gray ironware mugs while Cal searched some more.

"Thought I had sugar here someplace."

"It doesn't matter. I drink it black half the time, anyway," Morgan said, biting into a cracker. It wasn't true; he hated black coffee. He just wanted Cal to stick around, so he could get an answer about the deputy job.

They ate mostly in silence. The jerky was rock hard and required a lot of chewing.

"Only good thing about the trip," Cal said as he reached for his piece of candy, "was my mother's cooking."

"Too bad she didn't teach you."

"That's the truth! If it weren't for canned peaches and sympathetic women, I'd starve plumb to death."

"I think the reason you get more supper invitations than I do is because you're so damned skinny." Morgan gnawed away at the candy, wondering if he was ever going to get it unstuck from his teeth.

"That's probably true," Cal agreed, feeling a little better about life now that his belly was full. "One look at a skinny feller, and a woman wants to fatten him up." He paused a second. "What's the reason you get more breakfast invitations than I do?"

Morgan hid his grin behind the coffee cup. "I'm working night and day, trying to keep the peace. Maybe Widow Hawkins wanted to thank me for keeping her safe by filling me up with griddle cakes."

Cal snorted. Camilla Hawkins had finally given up on steering Morgan to the altar and last summer had gone to Albuquerque to marry a rancher. Though she was only twenty-seven and really quite attractive, Cal suspected that her unsavory past prevented Morgan from taking her seriously.

Cal wasn't sure of the details because Morgan wouldn't discuss them. All he said was that he'd discovered some information about the young widow that made him realize she was a liar and a cheat. Whatever infatuation Morgan had initially felt for Camilla, it had ended with that revelation. And Cal was relieved. He'd always suspected that Camilla was a very selfish woman. He wanted someone special for his friend—a woman as wonderful as his sweet Norah.

"So what about the job?" Morgan asked.

"I'm not good about breaking up fights, an' the like."

"Cal, you're a big man who shoots straight—and I trust you. I can't ask for more." That wasn't exactly true, but for the time being, Morgan simply wanted somebody honest. "Except for Saturdays, and the Fridays the train crews change shifts, you'd work days until three. When the rowdies are out, we'll both need to be around."

Cal looked at his unfinished store. If he was ever going to propose to Norah, he knew he'd have to be able to offer her more than a drafty building and some wooden packing boxes. "Would I get paid?"

"Twenty-five dollars a month."

Cal nodded. "Then you got yourself a deputy."

By Friday morning, Cal decided his new job as deputy sheriff wasn't so bad. Of course, he hadn't lived through a rough-and-tumble Saturday night yet. But he liked being out on the street talking to folks. So far his only crisis had been hauling Jed Oakes to the jailhouse for not paying Lily Mae for an hour of pleasure.

Cal wasn't sure there was a law on the books against cheating a whore, but he ran Jed in just the same. The man was nothing but a two-bit thief, no matter whom he dealt with.

Later he ran into Crom Rogers and Henry Copper trying to kick down the wool shed by the depot. Cattlemen and sheepmen were always fighting, but Cal wasn't going to put up with that nonsense.

"Behave yourselves, you damned fools, or I'm going to throw you in jail!"

After a little argument the two drunken cow-boys decided to go back to the Bucket of Blood.

Down the street a bit he was hailed by Morde-cai Smith, who lived in a Mormon settlement southeast of town. Smith had half a dozen of his children in the wagon, but only one of his wives.

"What did you decide about diggin' the well?" Cal asked, catching the smallest child as he tum-bled out of the wagon and handing the tyke back to his sister.

Smith tugged at his grizzled chin whiskers, and Cal had to fight a smile. The Mormon's looks had always amused Cal. Just a few wisps of gray hair wandered at will on his otherwise bald head, but the man had chin whiskers a foot long.

"We'll need the water before next spring," Smith was saying. "Will you have time now to dig a well—with your job as deputy?"

Cal coughed and cleared his throat. "I'm free most late afternoons and evenings. I can start first of next week—work an hour or so every day. Best to get it finished before the ground freezes."

The Mormon nodded and drove on. The youngster who'd fallen out of the wagon was leaning over the tailgate again, waving like mad. Cal grinned and waved back.

Later that afternoon, after Morgan relieved him at the office, when he was just wondering what to do for the rest of the day, Cal bumped into Ferdinand Wattron.

"Come on by the post office, boy," Ferdie said. He was a stocky man with a handsome, florid face and thick dark hair. "I been savin' your mail since you left for Indiana. Come on by and pick it up. Clarabelle made a pie last night. Bet she'd cut you a big piece."

Clarabelle was Ferdie's older sister. The two of them lived behind their store at the end of the street, in a two-storied building that housed the fancy goods and the post office. Nobody but Ferdie could have guessed how well fancy goods would sell in a town like Holbrook. Folks—even the men—seemed starved for the extra touches of civilization that he sold, such as silver match-boxes, silk handkerchiefs, and lavender perfumed soap.

The physician, Dr. Thomas Robinson, who'd been in California for several months with his ailing mother, had an office upstairs over Wattron's store. The fly-by-night doc who had been Robinson's replacement before he took off for greener pastures had a temporary office set up in the hotel.

The first thing Cal saw when Ferdie handed him his mail was Norah Kelly's neat handwriting, but Clarabelle Wattron breezed in at that moment and insisted he sit a spell. He couldn't be rude.

"This is wonderful pie, Miss Clarabelle," he said as he ate his second piece. "Sweet potato is my favorite." He always told her that, no matter what kind she served.

"Why, thank you, Calvin," Clarabelle replied.

He'd once heard his mother refer to a neighbor's appearance as unfortunate, and he thought the term applied to Clarabelle Wattron. She had none of her brother's handsome looks. In fact, her only interesting feature was a nose the shape and color of a crabapple. But she dressed in ruffles and ribbons, wore her fading hair in ringlets, and cooed and flirted like a girl of sixteen.

"I feel so safe knowing that you're helping dear Sheriff Treyhan." She squeezed his arm.

Cal blushed. He didn't know how to answer such foolishness, so he simply stuffed more pie in his mouth.

It was more than an hour later when he let himself into his store so he could read Norah's letter in privacy. It had been over a year since he'd heard from her—which was his fault because he was rather poor about answering letters—and he didn't want to share the pleasure of her words with anybody else.

After pouring himself a cup of the coffee left from breakfast and emptying his pockets of the cookies Clarabelle had sent home with him, Cal carefully slit open the envelope with his knife. His heart filled with joy when he saw that there were several pages inside. It had been so darned long! A man shouldn't be expected to love someone from afar for such a long time.

He took a big bite of the sugar cookie, savoring the crackle of writing paper as he unfolded the letter, and read the first few lines.

Then he read it again.

"No . . ." he whispered.

For a moment the missive hung in his numb fingers as he fought against the searing pain in his heart. Forgetting his coffee and the half-eaten cookie, he forced himself to lift the letter again and read.

The words blurred before his eyes, but they didn't change. He almost wished he'd never learned to read.

My dear friend Calvin:
    I'm asking for your help because I have nowhere else to turn. You see, I am going to have a baby.

2

Sheriff Morgan Treyhan pushed a callused hand against the scarred swinging door of the Bucket of Blood Saloon. So far, it was a quiet night, but nobody knew better than he how quickly trouble could erupt. Especially in this place.

There was nothing for the nonworking man to do in frontier towns like Holbrook except hang around saloons, drink, gamble, and stir up mischief. Boredom alone could drive men to dangerous lengths, and coupled with alcohol, it could turn even the most mild-mannered men into mean bastards.

The weight of the badge rested easily on Morgan Treyhan's chest. He preferred to cope with the hazardous duties of his job by using his wits and powers of persuasion, but if they failed, his huge fists or twin .45s usually did the trick. His reputation as the untouchable Ironman didn't hurt either.

More than one would-be gunfighter had
backed down after staring for an eternal
moment into the black eyes of Treyhan's six-
shooters. Still, he thanked his lucky stars that
most of the fast guns looking for action went
to Tombstone. There might always be the danger
of some snot-nosed kid trying to make a
reputation—every sheriff faced that possibility.
But so far Holbrook hadn't attracted any of the
feral beasts who'd shoot a man just for the hell
of it.

He stood poised in the doorway for a
moment, cautiously surveying the patrons of
the dimly lit tavern. There wasn't much of a
crowd on a Tuesday evening. The Bucket of
Blood, with its unsavory reputation, attracted
mostly cowboys, drifters, and toughs. In the
middle of the week, few cowboys got to town,
and without the extra brawn—and guns—they
contributed, the other thugs stayed relatively
meek.

Morgan's sharp eyes scanned the length of
the narrow adobe building. Nobody had bothered
to clean the oil lamps recently, so he could
barely make out who sat at the last table, the
one at the end of the long mahogany bar near
the rooms at the back. In the low-burning lamplight, Morgan could only see some poor fool
drinking alone.

In spite of himself, his glance moved to the
painting behind the bar. Once there had been a
beveled mirror in an elaborate frame hanging
between twin mahogany cabinets. But the damned
thing had been shot out so many times that the

owner gave up and commissioned a painting from an itinerant artist who had been passing through town. Bar none, the huge nude was the ugliest painting Morgan had ever seen. She was a veritable pink sow with yellow curls, now wearing only a grimace instead of a vapid smile since the cowboys routinely took target practice on her teeth.

He shouldered open the other door and went in.

Eldon Maples listlessly swiped a gray rag inside a glass. If the town didn't have an ordinance against it, Eldon probably would have served drinks in dirty glasses. The bartender was somehow related to the Bucket of Blood's owner, and Morgan was certain that was the only reason he had the job. It didn't take too many wits to pour beer in a glass, but Eldon messed up as often as not.

"Evening, Eldon."

Eldon nodded glumly. "Sheriff."

"How's business tonight?" Morgan's gaze swept over the few patrons playing cards at a nearby table. The middle-aged drummer in the plaid suit had been here three days running. Morgan made a mental note to find out what he was selling. Either business was very good for him to stay so long, or he was making out at the card table.

Eldon grunted something, holding up the glass he was cleaning. He wiped his nose on the bar rag and tried to look innocent. Then, noticing a stubborn dirty spot on the glass in his hand, he spit on it.

Telling himself the whiskey served at the Bucket of Blood would kill anything, Morgan managed not to comment. Eldon was too damned dumb to understand the town ordinance anyway so he'd just be wasting his words.

"Who's that at the end table?" he asked instead, thinking the slouched figure might be a local.

"Yer hired help." Eldon set the now-shining glass on the dusty mahogany shelf beside the painting and reached for another dirty one.

"What?" Morgan strained to see back that far. The place was so dirty, he decided it was a good thing the lighting was poor. The Bucket of Blood Saloon was a far cry from The Cottage, an elegant gentlemen's resort farther down the street.

After taking a step or two closer Morgan recognized Cal's bright red shield-front shirt, the one he'd bought the day he pinned on his deputy's badge. Morgan also noticed the nearly empty bottle of Tennessee white rye on the table. He'd never known Cal to put down more than two beers in an entire evening. Had the deputy's job already proved to be too much?

"Evening, Calvin," he said softly, as he approached the table.

"Morgan, my dear friend!" Cal bellowed when he finally managed to focus his eyes. "Sit down! Sit right down and have a drink!"

Morgan pulled a chair around so his back would be to the wall and lowered himself into it. "You got a problem tonight, Cal?"

Cal shook his head vigorously. "No problem at all. Everythin' is wonnerful."

The sheriff was not convinced. He'd noticed that the cardplayers took a moment to look him over but evidently had decided he and his deputy were of no consequence.

"M'bride's comin'. I'mmmm gettin' mar-reed," Cal mumbled, lifting his glass and draining it. Then he fumbled in his pants pocket and pulled out a wad of paper. "Mar-reed. Here, see fer yerself."

Morgan glanced around the room before uncrumpling the paper. It was a telegram. The message was short: "CAL: AGREE TO IMMEDIATE MARRIAGE. ARRIVING SATURDAY'S TRAIN. NORAH KELLY."

Morgan was stunned! Who the devil was Norah Kelly? He'd been friends with Cal for more than two years and never once did he recall hearing her name mentioned. Cal talked all the time, but he'd *never* said a word about marrying anybody. If Morgan had known anything about such a scheme, he wouldn't have offered his friend the deputy position. After all, too many lawmen out here died with their boots on.

Morgan reached over and removed the bottle from Cal's hand. "You've had enough celebrating for one night. Let me get you home. I'm afraid you're gonna feel like Hector's pup in the morning."

Cal started to sing when they walked out the door. He sang well and loudly, but the bawdy ballad he was howling wasn't the sort of song he'd normally want the whole town to hear.

Morgan was so busy trying to keep him upright, and quiet him down, that he didn't notice the two men standing in the shadows by the hitching post. Cal wasn't a heavy man, but at the moment, he was practically a deadweight.

Several store windows had lights in them because most of the owners lived in back of their shops, but only the saloons and hotels were open for business. Organ music drifted out from behind the fancy goods store at the end of the block. Evidently Clarabelle Wattron was baking. She baked pies on the nights Ferdie visited his current lady friend, and she always played the pump organ while she waited for her pies to bake. Everybody in Holbrook knew where Ferdie was by the sound of the pump organ. Morgan thought it was a shame Clarabelle didn't have a family to fuss over. She so loved to fuss.

The tune Clarabelle was playing confused Cal. He stumbled on the words to his dirty ditty just before he tripped over an old boot in the street and almost fell.

Only Morgan's greater strength kept the two of them from landing in the dirt. Or at least Morgan was not in the dirt. Cal had sort of slithered to his knees.

"Oh, for the love of God!" Morgan muttered, leaning over to edge his shoulder under Cal's limp body.

With his deputy over his shoulder, he trudged the rest of the way to Cal's place. The door wasn't locked. Cal never bothered with the lock unless he was away on a trip. Halfway across the room, Morgan tripped over something heavy and hard. He cursed and staggered before he managed to locate Cal's sleeping pallet, where he dropped him with a thud.

Cal merely sighed, his mind completely closed to the unpleasantness of the world. Grumbling about ingrates, Morgan found a lamp and the matches.

"M'gettin' mar-reed," Cal mumbled just as the match flared.

"That's a damned good reason to get skunked," Morgan said, reaching down to pull off Cal's boots.

A gunshot shattered the night air. Then a second one.

Morgan's pistols were in his hands before Cal's boot hit the floor. He saw the valise in his path just before he stumbled, managed to right himself, and raced out into the darkness, muttering obscenities in every language he knew.

Gunfire sounded yet again.

By the time he burst into the Bucket of Blood, one of the men there was slumped dead on the floor. Eldon, whose hair had been permanently parted by flying lead, held a shotgun trained on the second robber. Blood dripped off Eldon's ear and onto the bar.

The drummer in the plaid suit held a stubby little derringer in his shaky fist as he talked to another cardplayer, a bald gent clutching the bar rag to a bloody sleeve. Morgan noticed the other two cardplayers were nowhere to be seen.

"Who shot him?" Morgan asked, looking down at the dead man on the grimy floor.

"I did," the drummer answered. "After he blasted the barkeep."

Morgan simply nodded. Shootings were so common in this rough little town that he no longer felt the sick horror he once had over quick, violent death. "Where's Norman?"

"Out back pukin'," the drummer said, his meaty fist still clenched around the gun. "Blood makes 'im sick."

"And the other one? The fellow with the fancy black garters on his shirt sleeves?" Morgan noticed the captured man's eyes flick toward the door. That involuntary gesture was enough to make him wonder if the man with the black garters was in on the robbery. But why the devil would anybody risk getting shot over a paltry card game?

"You—hot shot! Up against the bar! Drummer, put your gun away and come over here and check him for other weapons. Eldon, keep your gun pointed at his middle while I go outside and check around."

All he found was Norman leaning against the outhouse door. He gave Morgan no argument when instructed to go home. He'd lost tonight, anyway.

Morgan went back in the Bucket of Blood. "How bad are you hurt, Eldon?"

"My head aches like hell, an' I'm bleedin' all over the place," Eldon complained. He thought real hard about plugging the other bandit but decided against it. Sheriff Treyhan still had his pistols in his hands, and Eldon didn't want them turned on him. The sheriff could shoot the eyes out of a high-flying crow and never disturb a feather.

"Better close up for the night, then."

"We ain't through with our game," the bald cardplayer said, sounding highly affronted.

"Hell, man, you're bleeding on the cards! Don't you think you better call it a night and have somebody look at your arm?"

"But who wins the pot?"

"Split the damned thing! Then get out of here!"

Morgan shoved his right gun into the holster and motioned with the left toward the bandit. "Move toward the door real slow."

The young drifter did exactly as the sheriff ordered.

"Eldon, I'll send the undertaker over for the gent on the floor just as soon as this tough bird is behind bars. You might as well have him look at your head"—he gestured toward the bleeding man at the poker table—"and his arm. No sense in waking Myrtis."

"Sure. Digger is as good as a doc, anyways."

"Then lock up when he leaves." Morgan started through the swinging door, then remembered something. "You, drummer, stop by my office tomorrow afternoon. We need to talk."

The traveling salesman, quite pale now from his unexpected encounter with western violence, readily agreed.

The lamp was burning when Cal woke up. The entire room was spinning and his stomach threatened to rebel against him. He sat up slowly, peering at the bright light, wondering what in the devil had happened to his head.

His temples ached, his ears rang, his nose was stuffy, and his mouth tasted like last month's socks. He'd been kicked by a mule once and had felt nearly the same way. But he couldn't remember meeting up with a mule tonight. Then the call of nature proved to be too strong for him to think of anything else.

When he got back inside his stomach churned and burned so bad, he scrounged around his pantry in search of the baking soda.

"Where'd I put that stuff?" he muttered, wondering desperately if he'd live until morning. Not that he cared a lot—death would be pleasant compared to how awful he felt right now.

How had he gotten in such a fix? He remembered his trip to the Bucket of Blood, and as he pondered his reasons for the unprecedented binge, he thought of the agitated emotions he'd experienced since receiving Norah's letter. Somewhere during the course of the evening, as he tossed down drinks in celebration and sorrow, he vaguely recalled seeing Morgan.

"Where is that damned soda?" Cal flung a box at the wall in sudden fury. The sound of splintering wood cooled his anger, and he turned to search the rest of his house.

Across the room now, fumbling in his coat pocket because he thought he might have bought the soda before the weather change, Cal gazed sadly at his store. This shell of a building wasn't what he'd planned on bringing Norah to when he married her. He was sorry he hadn't worked harder at finishing it when he had had the time, sorry she was coming to marry a poor man.

"Ahhhh," he breathed as his fingers hit pay dirt. He'd left the soda in his coat. Relief was near.

As he started back toward his makeshift pantry for a glass and spoon, he spied Dr. Omar Goodfellow's worn bag in the middle of the room. The very thought of the saintly old man brought tears to Cal's eyes.

His blurry vision presented him with an amazing sight. There, knocked out of the battered valise, were two Bibles, one with its binding torn. And spilling from the split cover was a shining metallic puddle.

Cal's foggy brain interpreted the shiny spot as a biblical sign, some mystical promise from God. He moved toward the golden glow with a smile on his parched lips.

"Jehoshaphat!" he cried.

The floor was covered with gold coins!

Dumbfounded by the sight at his feet, he could only stare. Twenty-dollar gold pieces littered the floor by the valise—hundreds of them. Cal simply looked at them for the longest time, unable to believe what he saw. Finally he leaned over and picked up a coin. "Norah, you're not going to marry a poor man, after all."

*   *   *

Sometime during the night the wind had begun to blow, not as strong as the spring gales but enough to rustle the cottonwoods and the willow trees and ease the autumn heat wave. Nearly everyone who had moved to town had gone to the riverbank to dig up willow and cottonwood saplings and replant them by their own buildings. The little trees weren't much yet, but they showed promise.

The residents of Holbrook appreciated the weather change and bustled about in a sprightly manner, seeing to important business. Others found the mild temperatures just right for going fishing or packing a picnic and riding up to the mesas for a spectacular view of the countryside.

Herrick Nash sauntered into the sheriff's office at twelve minutes after one, feeling much more trepidation than anyone would suspect from his jaunty appearance. Today he looked particularly resplendent in buff stripes and a maple-leaf red brocade vest.

"Good afternoon, Deputy. Your sheriff asked me to meet him here."

Cal turned his bemused expression to the traveling salesman. In spite of a hangover the size of P. T. Barnum's hapless elephant Jumbo, he was overjoyed at his good fortune—a fortune in gold to be precise.

He'd reasoned it all out, of course. The money had been Omar Goodfellow's entire life savings, collected over a lifetime of being saintly. And since Goodfellow had no kin to give the gold to, Cal felt justified in keeping it for being a friend in Goodfellow's final hours. Hadn't he bought Goodfellow his last meal?

He hadn't told anybody about finding the money yet. He wanted to savor the secret knowledge that he was rich a while longer—it was a pleasure unlike any other. And besides, it was only fair that he tell Norah first. He could hardly wait till Saturday.

"Sheriff Treyhan ain't here yet," Cal told the drummer. "He usually stops by right after he has lunch."

Nash nodded. "I'll wait, if that's all right with you."

"It's fine with me. Take a seat."

Nash looked skeptically at the wooden chair. Somebody had wired the rungs together, but the seat was torn and the back was broken. "This office could use some new furniture. Everything is worn out."

"We get a lot of traffic through here. Saturday nights especially. That's rough on furniture."

"I could give you a good price on new chairs."

"Are you a furniture drummer?" Cal asked.

"Household supplies and home furnishings," Nash replied quickly, suddenly feeling more at ease, though he was still a trifle jittery about having killed a man.

"I've been giving some thought to buying a few things," Cal said cautiously. Never before in his life had he possessed two extra gold pieces to rub together, and he was afraid of losing his head and squandering his newly acquired fortune.

Nash recognized an easy customer when he saw one. Putting on his most helpful facade, he scooted the wobbly chair closer to the desk and asked, "Exactly what did you want to purchase?"

When Morgan finally arrived at the office nearly an hour later, Cal still wore the bemused expression. The sheriff assumed the look stemmed from a well-deserved hangover and promptly began to question the salesman.

"Do you need me anymore today?" Cal asked later as Nash got up to leave.

"I don't think so," Morgan answered. "When are you going to be finished with Mordecai Smith's well?"

"Probably Friday—I want to be finished before Norah gets here. I expected Mordecai and a couple of his boys to help me, but they took off down country. Only the women and the youngsters are home."

"I'll see you in the morning then," Morgan said.

Cal caught up with Herrick Nash outside. "I'll stop by your hotel room on my way out of town to pay you." He was as thrilled with his purchases as a kid with an all-day sucker.

"You'll never regret this, Deputy Welsh. A good bed means a good marriage." Nash grinned at Cal's crimson flush. "Your bride will bless you."

"I gotta well to dig," Cal mumbled, mortified at hearing his most intimate relations with Norah discussed on the street where anybody could hear.

"I'll get your order off today," Nash assured him. It was the biggest order Nash had gotten the entire trip, and he was bent on giving Cal his

most attentive service. "And before you know it,
your house will be a home. Your bride is a most
fortunate woman."

"I gotta go."

"Don't work up too many blisters digging that
well. You need to be in top form, boy. You know
Saturday's the most important day of your life."

Norah Kelly had managed to keep her roiling
stomach under control the entire way, through
endless miles of swaying motion and greasy
meals. Now as she approached her final destination she felt like she was about to lose her
belated breakfast.

She hastily slipped into the tiny washroom
and bathed her face in tepid water. Someone had
lowered the window, and dusty, smoke-tinged air
blew in, plus a few cinders. She concentrated on
deep breathing, and eventually the queasy feelings
passed. Again she bathed her pale face, then
removed her hat to straighten her hair.

"I look like the wrath of God," she said to her
reflection.

Somehow that seemed appropriate. She
wasn't sure a person should get away with a big
sin as neatly as she was about to do. Too many
years of Jean Matthews's strict Presbyterian
teachings had left her anticipating some serious
retribution.

Dear Cal. How like him to do something as
foolish as proposing marriage right out of the
blue.

He'd been her friend as long as she could

remember. She'd only approached him with her dilemma because there was no one else, but she hadn't expected his reaction. She'd never imagined he'd ask to marry her.

She couldn't visualize herself married to Cal Welsh—especially the intimate part. Even thinking about it made her uneasy. Cal seemed like a big, overgrown boy. It was impossible to imagine being his lover.

But she didn't have much choice. Unless taking her shame into her father's house was an option, which it wasn't. Tommy Kelly had never been shy about passing his affections around, but he'd beat his daughter senseless for showing up with a babe in her belly and no husband in sight.

Cal was offering her a way out of the fix she was in, so she'd best be grateful for the opportunity he was handing her—a future for her and the baby.

She refused to think about Sonny—about the hot kisses which made her knees weak and her mind weaker, about his handsome face. About his lies, and his cruel betrayal. She took a deep breath and sternly reminded herself she had put everything about the city of Cincinnati behind her when she boarded this train.

A rap on the door brought her around sharply. "Your station, ma'am. Holbrook's coming up."

For one brief moment, Norah was utterly terrified. She felt like an abandoned child.

Norah Kelly, this is unworthy of you.

The words in her head reminded her so much of Jean Matthews that she had to smile. Then her eyes filled with tears. She cursed the heightened emotions that came with her pregnancy.

How she wished Jean Matthews were still alive. She was the only one who ever had believed Norah Kelly could amount to something, despite the taint of the Irish papist who sired her. Everybody else called her Nuthin' and treated her the same way, but Mrs. Jean had expected her to be more than a squatter's whelp, and somewhere along the line Norah began to expect it, too.

Norah knew the possibility of a good life was in her own hands. And the baby growing inside her body would depend on her for a decent outlook, too. She grasped the door handle firmly and went out to face her future.

Standing by the door with the conductor, waiting for the train to stop, Norah was appalled at the sheer ugliness of the town they were approaching. It looked barren, windswept, and dismal.

Although some of the buildings were painted and had trees growing in front of them, for the most part everything was the color of dirt and weathered lumber. Norah thought it was awful. In Aberdeen, even the run-down shacks like the one her parents lived in looked better than the main buildings in this rude town.

There was a sinking feeling in her stomach. She searched the depot platform for Cal, torn between wanting to see him there and hoping he wouldn't be there because this was the wrong destination.

"Are you sure this is Holbrook?" she asked

the conductor, not quite able to keep the wobble out of her voice.

He gave a little chuckle. "Yes, ma'am. It ain't much yet, but it shore is growin'. Is someone meeting you?"

Norah nodded. "My fiancé." Surely he hadn't forgotten she was coming.

Even as she rejected that absurd idea, her gaze fell on a man with curly black hair and a black Stetson, and her stomach gave a lurch. His back was toward her as he talked to a man in an atrocious plaid suit, but she knew instantly that he was not Sonny. The man on the platform was taller than the unscrupulous cad who had seduced her. This man had wider shoulders and longer hair, and unlike Sonny, who wore only the finest-cut suits, this man definitely dressed as a westerner.

The neat gray trousers, unbleached muslin shirt, and black leather vest might have been called shabby compared to Sonny's tailored finery. But as she stared, trying to adjust her body to the final jerky motions of the train, the dark-haired man turned and looked right at her. His face was amazing in its strength, more rugged than handsome with his weathered skin and well-trimmed, black, brush mustache. Her whole body reacted—not because she recognized him, but because of the power and danger that emanated from him.

Where was Cal? Even as the train jerked to a hissing halt, she began to feel a sense of trepidation.

Morgan Treyhan forgot all about the drummer he was talking to. There'd been another saloon incident involving the furniture salesman, and Morgan was relieved that Herrick Nash had decided to head farther west. But the moment he saw the redheaded woman with the conductor, everything else flew from his mind.

Why hadn't Cal told him she was beautiful? The man had talked his ear off for days, but not once had he mentioned how utterly exquisite she was.

For some reason Morgan was expecting a female version of Cal—a wide-eyed farm girl with no expectations other than a good, ordinary life—not this titian-haired vision in a deep green traveling dress. Morgan so doubted that this was she that he actually looked to see if any other woman was disembarking.

What astonished him most was his body's lustful reaction to his best friend's intended. Normally a man of iron self-control, he felt a tightening in his groin that both shocked him and threatened to embarrass him in front of a trainload of travelers. A staggering thud to his back shifted his attention above his trousers.

"Some muscles you got there, boy. Damn near busted my hand."

Herrick Nash was smiling heartily, pounding him on the shoulder like an old friend. Morgan hastily steered the salesman forward.

"So what about your office?"

"I'll talk to the town company," Morgan said evasively, and immediately forgot about the drummer. He started purposefully toward the train, intent on the words he had to say to the woman.

She swayed as she walked down the steps, and Morgan was filled with a desire to protect her. She was smaller than he'd first thought, barely five feet tall, though her figure was full and womanly. He could see weariness written on her pale face, and something else. Fear?

As she descended the steps, Norah still thought the conductor was putting her off in the wrong town. Surely this couldn't be Holbrook. This dreary place was nothing like what Cal had described in the letters he sent to his family. It was merely a barren cluster of clapboard shacks on two or three streets south of the railroad track. How could it even be called a town? Even Aberdeen was bigger than this, and a lot more attractive. Where was the crystal clear river? Where were the stately green trees, the majestic mountains?

"Miss Kelly?"

Norah realized the dark man was striding toward her, and her heart began to pound.

"Are you Norah Kelly?"

"Yes." Behind her, the enormous engine began to hiss and groan, deafening her to the sound of his deep voice.

"I'm Sheriff Morgan Treyhan," he said loudly as he reached down to pick up two of her bags. "Will you come with me, please."

Light flashed before Norah's eyes, and then everything went dim. The commotion of the engine turned into a roar. Her knees buckled. Suddenly, there was a loud thud and then her arms were held in a bruising grip. She gasped at the pain, but her head cleared.

She stood staring at the silver star on Morgan Treyhan's leather vest.

"Are you all right?"

"I'm fine," she replied, although she was anything but. She was alone, scared, four months pregnant, and apparently under arrest for some crime unknown to her. She stepped away from him and glanced down at the bags he'd dropped. Then she saw the guns on his hips. "Is there a problem, Sheriff?"

Morgan could see that she was barely standing upright but still rigidly holding on to her dignity. He couldn't help admiring that. He hoped she had courage to go with it. "There's been an accident, Miss Kelly."

Norah blinked.

"Calvin Welsh fell into a well—"

"Cal?" she interrupted. "Something's happened to Cal?"

"Yes, ma'am. We think he fell backward into a well he was digging for a local farmer. He was working out there by himself, and nobody knew he was down there all night." Morgan still couldn't believe how long it had taken him to realize something was amiss and start searching for his deputy out at the Smith place. By the time he'd gotten Cal out of that damned hole, his friend was sick and delirious.

Since Morgan had gotten him home Cal had asked about Norah every time he'd been conscious. That wasn't very often. Cal was very sick.

Norah was barely taking in what the sheriff said. One moment she'd been annoyed because Cal was late, the next she'd been confronted by the tall, imposing lawman. Now he was telling her Cal was hurt.

"He has pneumonia. He's in bad shape." Morgan didn't mention the town was still without a doctor. He'd telegraphed Winslow, and a doctor had arrived on the next eastbound train, but by then the doctor could only confirm what Myrtis and the undertaker had already told him—Calvin Welsh might die.

Her hazel eyes were enormous with shock and her face parchment white, but Norah Kelly maintained a tight grip on her emotions. "Take me to him," she said.

Morgan grasped her elbow, and they began to walk swiftly to Cal's place.

A boy stuck his head out one of the doors. "Want I should bring the bags, Sheriff?"

"I'd appreciate it, Jimmy."

Norah clutched the hand at her elbow. In doing so, she brought her arm tight across her body, holding herself together, protecting the life within her.

All she could think about was helping Cal. He'd done so much for her already, sending her the ticket west, offering her his name.

"I can help him get better. I know about herbs and potents," she told Morgan. Jean Matthews had taught her well. She was certain she could cure chest congestion.

Morgan knew she didn't notice how towns-folk came out of their stores to take a look at her. It wasn't often that a lone woman came to town, and Morgan didn't think there ever had been one as lovely as Norah. He could understand the town's curiosity. Even Lily Mae roused herself enough to saunter out of the Red Rock Saloon and into the street.

"This is Calvin's building, ma'am." Morgan opened the door for her. "He lives here."

Norah gasped aloud as the front door of the weathered, unpainted dwelling opened into a nearly empty room. Cal told his mother he had a wonderful house, but this was just a shell of a building! There wasn't even a bed inside, only a pallet on the floor. And Cal lay on that crude pad, white-faced and ill, covered with a rough gray woolen blanket.

Beside him, sitting on a box, was a weathered old woman with walnut-brown hair, and a squint-eyed fellow in bib overalls and a denim blouse.

"Is that the doctor?" Norah whispered, pulling her thoughts together.

"No, that's the—" Morgan paused, appalled that he almost said the undertaker. "Digger's a friend. He helped me get Cal out of the well."

He let go of her arm then, and Norah realized how tightly she'd been hanging on to him. "Myrtis, Digger, this is Norah Kelly—Cal's intended."

"A little bit o' nuthin'."

They all looked at Cal as if the dead had spoken. He looked like hell, but he had a ghost of a smile on his thin face, and his eyes gleamed at Norah.

"Heard you fell in a well, Calvin," Norah said, trying for a bit of levity but failing miserably when her voice cracked. She reached for his hand.

"Beware of the unexpected, Nuthin'," Cal said hoarsely. "It'll get ya every time."

A huge tear rolled silently down Norah's cheek.

"This must be Saturday," Cal said after a long pause. "Get the judge, Morgan. This is my wedding day."

3

The lad, Jimmy, came loping into the bare storefront room lugging Norah's valises, one on either side of his thin body. "Where you want I should put 'em?"

"Oh, just down anywhere," Morgan told him. Then he dug a silver dollar out of the pocket of his tailored gray twill pants and handed it to the boy.

Jimmy's eyes bulged. He hadn't expected more than a dime, if that. It was less than a block from the train station to Cal's store building, and the lady's bags hardly weighed anything. But he grasped the coin quickly and buried it deep in his own pocket, lest the sheriff change his mind.

"Jimmy, I need you to run one more errand— an important one," Morgan said as the eleven-year-old turned to go. "Find the judge and bring him here. Look over at the Bucket of Blood first. If he's drunk, tell Eldon I said to pour some coffee down him. We need him sober enough to perform a wedding."

The boy's eyes were so wide it was a wonder he could see out of them as he scampered away. He could hardly wait to spread the word.

By the time Morgan turned his attention back to Cal's pallet, Norah was down on her knees, struggling to help Cal to a more comfortable position. The modish bustle of her traveling dress jutted out at an exaggerated angle from her graceful back, and the trim green velvet hat, with its single robin's-egg blue feather curled along the brim, was more stylish than anything Holbrook had seen.

But being the excellent judge of character a lawman had to be to survive, Morgan knew she'd look graceful and appealing even in a flour-sack dress. What the hell did her clothes have to do with her character? Dammit, his body was behaving as if he were sixteen instead of thirty-two. And the worst part was that she belonged to his best friend.

Norah wrinkled her nose at the smell of Calvin and his bedclothes. No wonder he wasn't getting any better! The odor of soured perspiration was enough to make him sick, even if his chest hadn't been congested. Why, the blankets were damp with sweat. She'd fix that!

As soon as she had Cal propped up against the wall with a rolled-up coat at his back, she got to her feet and beckoned for Morgan to follow her to the front of the building, out of Cal's hearing.

"How in the name of all that's holy is the man supposed to get well under conditions like these?" she demanded.

Morgan was startled by her vehemence.

"I want a decent bed for him in here, immediately, including a feather mattress, real pillows, and bed linens." She looked around the bare room despairingly. "I don't care if you have to steal them! He needs some clean underwear and a shirt, too. I'll heat some water to scrub him from the skin out, then I'll need some rubbing alcohol or witch hazel, and mustard to make a plaster."

She reached up to unbutton the ivory lace jabot from the neckband of her traveling dress, then the lacy cuffs from the bottoms of her sleeves so they could be rolled up out of the way. Lastly she removed the stylish hat from her head and set everything on a wooden box in the corner.

Morgan simply stared at her. She was so incredibly beautiful. And as feisty as a banty hen.

"Come on, man! We haven't got all day. I've tended sick folks before. If we're going to save him, we've got to get him cleaned, doctored up, and in a decent bed off that cold floor. Doesn't the local doctor know anything?"

Morgan touched his fingers to the brim of his hat in a typically western gesture of deference to a lady. Then he started out the door to do her bidding, a slight smile tugging at the corners of his mouth. Yessir! Miss Norah Kelly was about to set Holbrook on its ear, for sure. And it might prove to be the best entertainment the community had seen since the medicine show had gone through town last spring.

He strode purposefully down the street and around the corner to the Holbrook House. Norah was absolutely right about the condition of Cal's building, and of Cal himself. Morgan was ashamed he hadn't noticed before, that Cal's classy bride-to-be from the East had to point out the gross deficiencies to him. And he was angry, too—angry that he wanted so damned much to please her.

The scowl on his face was fearsome as he loped up the front steps of the hotel.

"Angus MacKay, where the hell are you?" he demanded as soon as he was inside.

A gray head popped up from behind the registration desk, and Walter Gates, the new clerk, stared at Morgan in leery fascination. "Uh, Mr. MacKay's in his office, Sheriff. You want me to go get him?"

"No, I know where it is." Then he headed in the proper direction, wondering why he intimidated Walter. The middle-aged man had arrived on the train from St. Louis about a month before, to work for MacKay. From the very beginning he'd acted like he'd never seen a sheriff before, or he'd seen one too often.

Not all easterners were scared of him, Morgan thought. Miss Norah Kelly damned sure wasn't! Then he frowned because he couldn't seem to keep the woman out of his thoughts. He'd better get a grip on himself. A man could get killed in Holbrook if he didn't keep his wits about him, especially if he was a lawman.

As his boot heels echoed on the wooden floor of the hallway, Morgan made up his mind to keep an eye on Walter. Any man that afraid of the law might have a reason to be. He paused long enough to knock once on the door to Angus's office before pushing it open.

"How are ye today, Sheriff?" the thin, dark man with a beaky nose asked as he looked up from his papers.

"I've got a problem, Angus. Cal Welsh has been real sick since we got him out of that well."

"So I've heard." The Scotsman didn't believe in wasting words any more than money.

Morgan hated asking MacKay for a favor, but this one was imperative. "Cal's bride-to-be arrived on the train today, and she's trying to get Cal's place cleaned up. We need a bed for him. Have you got a spare?"

"Nay, mon, only what I've got in m'rooms."

"We'll just have to take one of them." Morgan's flint-eyed stare warned the innkeeper not to push him too far.

"Why should I give up the profit from one of m'rooms for Cal Welsh? The mon's nothing to me."

Morgan's eyes narrowed and his mouth thinned. "Let's just say I've seen a few things about this hotel that stretch the rules of the town company, Angus. And I'm wonderin' if you really want me to investigate them. I'm a very thorough man."

It would have taken a man with considerably

more guts than Angus MacKay possessed to argue with the sheriff at that moment.

"Aye, that ye are," he agreed.

Like everybody else in town, Angus was nosy about the woman who'd come to marry Calvin Welsh. He figured he might get a real gander at her when he delivered the bed. Maybe even get on the good side of her, which might prove interesting if Cal kicked the bucket. Angus fancied the ladies, but alas, there weren't many ladies in Holbrook to fancy.

"Ach, well, I suppose I can make do with one less bed for a bit. The Lord knows it would be a real shame for a new bride not t'have a proper bed for her wedding night."

Morgan was surprised that the wily bastard put up only a token fuss before he started dismantling a bed from a room that had two. Normally Angus pinched a penny until it screamed bloody murder.

But Morgan had too much on his mind to wonder why Angus was suddenly willing to play Good Samaritan, probably for the first time in his stingy life. "Oh, Miss Kelly specifically requested clean linens and blankets, and a decent pillow for Cal. But send a couple more while you're at it. She may need to prop him up if she can't get rid of the congestion."

"Is she a doctor, then?" the Scotsman asked with a smirk.

"No, but I understand she knows about herbs and healing." Morgan turned and strode back down the hallway. Then he yelled over his shoulder for Angus to bring some clean towels along with the sheets and blankets.

He took the shortcut down the alley to Wilson's Mercantile. Having no idea whether Cal owned a change of underwear or a clean shirt, he figured it best just to buy them along with the mustard and witch hazel and some soap.

Miss Norah Kelly struck him as a woman who was definitely well acquainted with soap, so he asked for both carbolic soap and perfumed. Mrs. Wilson gave him a bar of lilac soap. He'd bet his prized Colt .45s Cal didn't own any of *that*.

Then with his purchases under his arm, he headed back to Cal's building. He had to push his way past the crowd from the Red Rock Saloon—some carrying mugs of beer—that had gathered outside Cal's, craning their necks to see through the dirty window.

Two steps inside the door he came to a dead stop, and his jaw dropped in surprise. The place looked like a whirlwind had been through it— one about five feet tall, with copper-colored hair and a tongue as sharp as a skinning knife.

Myrtis was raising a cloud of dust fit to choke a horse as she swept the accumulation of dirt away from the far wall where Norah wanted the bed set up, away from the draft coming in from the front and back doors. Digger was helping Angus pack in the bed and other stuff from the hotel.

And over in the other corner, behind a makeshift screen of two crates and a blanket, Norah had Cal stripped to the waist and was scrubbing him within an inch of his life, head and all.

"Now, Norah, that's enough!" Cal protested weakly, as she reached for the bedclothes covering the lower part of his body. "You've already washed down as far as possible, and . . . I feel better already. Just a little tired."

Norah snorted as she pushed his hands away. Cal was very pale, every effort exhausted him, and he was laboring for every breath. Yet he was trying so hard to appear healthy. If that wasn't just like a man! She felt like shaking him, but instead she tried to lighten the situation.

"And you'll feel much better when we've washed 'possible,' too, and tucked you into that clean bed your friends are setting up for you."

Cal blushed.

"Oh, for heaven's sake, Calvin Welsh! It's not like I didn't have four brothers that I washed from the day they was born. I'll wager you haven't got a thing I haven't seen before." The moment the statement was out of her mouth Norah stopped, appalled. Since she was pregnant, Cal might realize she'd seen a man's privates before, but she hadn't meant to taunt him with it.

"Well, you haven't seen mine!"

Norah gave him a quick cuff on the arm, then grinned at him. "Not yet, laddie. But since you asked me to be your wife, I suppose I'll be seeing a lot of it from now on," she said matter-of-factly. Having grown up in a one-room shack where privacy was unheard of, she had few illusions about the human body and how it was used between men and women.

"Oh, and here's the sheriff. I'll put a mustard plaster on your chest right away. That ought to break up the congestion some."

"You go fix it," Call said thankfully. "Morgan can help me finish washing."

Morgan was struggling to keep a straight face as he approached Cal's pallet. Who would have ever believed that easygoing Cal Welsh would have chosen such a bold, dauntless little spitfire as the love of his life?

Not only was she going to clean up Holbrook single-handedly, but she'd have Cal on the straight and narrow path in no time at all. *If he got better.* The awful thought came unbidden. Morgan hoped Norah might even get Cal well by sheer determination.

He was delighted with Miss Norah Kelly. He liked her spunk, her ability to organize people, and her will to get things done. If anybody could light a fire under Cal, it was she.

Then he sighed as he realized how much harder she was going to make his life. She was going to marry Cal as soon as Judge Harvey was sober enough to perform the wedding ceremony, yet his attraction to her was growing by the minute.

Morgan had never allowed himself to be infatuated with another man's woman, and he didn't relish the idea of starting now, with his best friend's wife. But his heart wasn't listening to his rational mind. It was thudding in his chest as though the smile on Norah's lovely face was truly for him instead of the supplies he had brought her. He might even be willing to change places with Cal—sick as he was—if it meant Norah would be lavishing such care and attention on him.

His heart had damned near stopped when he overheard Cal complaining about Norah's bathing him. The vision of Norah bathing *him,* running her soft hands all over him, had brought his body to rigid attention.

He would give anything to have her caressing *his* body and telling him how much more familiar she was going to become with his masculine equipment. He'd have chased everybody else out and laid back and enjoyed it.

Morgan brought himself back to the present with a jerk when he realized Norah was speaking sternly to him.

"Pardon me, what did you say?"

Norah shook her head in disbelief. "I asked if you were able to get the things I need."

"Yes," Morgan mumbled as a flush started up his dark features. He placed the brown paper parcel in her hands, then hunkered down on the floor beside Cal's pallet.

After helping Cal perform a quick wash under the protection of the blanket, Morgan looked toward the back wall where Angus and Digger had set up the bed. Myrtis had immediately abandoned her sweeping in order to supervise the operation, but neither Angus nor Digger seemed to appreciate her suggestions. From the sounds of their raised voices, he suspected all hell was about to break loose.

Norah suddenly noticed the direction his attention had taken. "I'd appreciate it if you'd see they don't kill each other—at least until after we get Cal settled. His strength is about gone as it is."

Morgan looked away before his mind could make some stupid, lewd suggestions about his own strength. He was an expert at busting up fights. He went straight for Myrtis, having learned long ago that removing the instigator, however he had to do it, was the quickest way to diffuse a hot situation.

Usually a quick, hard right to the jaw was the most satisfactory method. But Morgan wasn't about to hit a woman, even if she had started the trouble. So he just marched over, stopped in front of Myrtis, reached down, and grasped his hands below her ample hips and slung her over his shoulder like a sack of feed.

She was so startled she only made a squeak of protest, and hadn't gotten her breath back by the time he set her down next to Norah.

"Here, Myrtis, you help get Cal dressed. I'll settle Angus and Digger."

"Well, whyn't you just say you wanted me over here?" she demanded. "No cause to go a'scarin' a body half to death!" she said to his retreating back.

A grin twitched the corners of Morgan's mustache as he realized Myrtis hadn't been picked up by a man in twenty years.

Cal was sleeping. His breathing was labored and his fair skin flushed with fever, but at least he was clean and comfortable.

The crowd of curiosity seekers no longer hung

around the front door. Digger and Angus had
gone back to the Holbrook House for a washstand, complete with pitcher and bowl, and a
table to go beside the bed. Angus had insisted,
and Norah couldn't refuse. She didn't want to
get off on the wrong foot with the townspeople
and Cal's friends the first day she arrived.

Ferdinand Wattron had brought a small
gateleg table and two matching chairs. Clarabelle came by later with a teakettle, a tin of tea,
and one of the pies she had baked the night
before. Mrs. Ethel Norris, whose husband sold
boots and a few articles of clothing such as
leather vests and chaps, contributed two
unmatched china cups and saucers, with a sur-
prisingly pretty blue teapot. And Mrs. Beatrice
Wilson from the mercantile had brought a
small oval mirror, insisting that every bride
needed to know she looked her best for her
husband.

Mrs. Flora Harrison, the stationmaster's wife,
had her thirteen-year-old son, Albert, lugging a
heavy rocking chair while she carried a cast-
iron lamp with a hand-painted china shade
carefully wrapped in a quilt. She explained the
things had belonged to her late mother, who
would have been delighted for them to go to
help a young couple set up housekeeping. By
the time Mrs. Harrison left, Norah was close to
tears.

She was so tired she was about to fall over in
her tracks, yet at the same time she felt too
nervous to sit down. Morgan was inserting pegs
in the wall so she could hang up her clothes, and

Myrtis had filled the teakettle and put it on the stove to heat so Norah could freshen up.

She'd brushed the worst of the sandy dirt from her skirts and was just putting the lacy frills back on her green dress when the judge stumbled through the door, his face extremely pale and his hands trembling.

When Judge Harvey arrived, Norah felt relieved that Myrtis and Morgan had stayed. Drunken old reprobate! This was the last straw!

The judge must have really tied one on, Morgan thought as he went to greet him. When Morgan saw the flash of fire in Norah's eyes he hoped she wouldn't make a scene over her wedding being performed by a tipsy judge. He knew Cal wouldn't give a hoot as long as it was legal, but the lady might. Women could be real sentimental about such things.

Judge Harvey squinted his eyes, trying to adjust to the dimness after the bright sunlight outside. He looked around the large single room, his bloodshot eyes shrewdly assessing Norah before they came to rest on Morgan.

"Well, Sheriff, you're a real sly dog," he said, his words slurred. "Had no idea you was fixin' to marry. Happy to accommodate you, though. You and your lovely lady."

Norah looked startled, and Morgan disgusted. "Not me, Judge," he said. "Cal over there is to be the lucky bridegroom, as soon as we wake him up."

The judge swiveled his gaze around until it settled on the bed and the obviously ill man sleeping in it. Surprise, along with the effects of his two-day drinking binge, caused him to sway on his feet. He reached an unsteady hand toward the wall to support himself.

"We could put this off until he's feeling better?" he suggested.

"No, we can't," Morgan said. "Cal insists this is going to be his wedding day, no matter what." Then he looked more closely at the judge's pasty complexion and led him toward a chair at the table. "Here, sit down. I'll get you a cup of coffee."

"Don't need any more dammed coffee! Eldon tried to drown me in the filthy stuff. You wouldn't have a drink on you, would you?"

Morgan started to say no, then remembered the half bottle he'd found in one of Cal's boxes and retrieved it. Ignoring Norah's indignant glare, he added a generous slug to Harvey's coffee. He figured it might be the only thing to keep the judge upright through the whole ceremony.

"You'd best wake up the groom," he told Norah.

Norah sat on the edge of the bed, studying Cal's flushed face and the way his indecently long lashes fanned out on his cheeks. He looked young, and vulnerable. And so very dear. Pushing a damp lock of hair away from his eyes, she realized his fever had come down some. It seemed a shame to disturb him when he was resting so peacefully, but Morgan was right. Cal had insisted they were getting married today, no matter what.

She trailed her fingers down the side of his face and around his jaw, tickling him under the chin. Such a sensitive face he had. So kind, gentle, and—above all—loyal. Norah had loved him for years, as a friend and brother, but she'd never thought about marrying him until his letter came. Now, she was determined to be the best wife he could ever hope for.

He opened his eyes reluctantly, and then a slow smile spread across his thin face. "So it wasn't a dream after all. You really are here. And we're getting married as soon as the judge comes."

Norah smiled, too, a trace of mischief lurking in her deep hazel eyes. "You sure you don't mean nightmare, Calvin? I've been told I'm a very bossy female, and stubborn along with it."

Cal clasped her hand with both of his. "That you are, Bit o' Nuthin', and have been since you were knee high."

"Last chance to change your mind," Norah reminded him softly. "I don't deserve you."

"Balderdash! It's me that doesn't deserve you. But I've always wanted you."

Norah raised a disbelieving eyebrow at him, trying not to notice how weak his grip was.

"It's true—I've always intended to marry you. Even when you were such a wee bit of a thing." Cal shut his eyes but continued to rub his callused fingers over her small soft hand. Then he turned his frank blue eyes to meet hers squarely. "I used to wonder sometimes if I was unnatural, having such . . . possessive feelings about a child."

Norah brought her other hand up to clasp both of his, remembering how Cal had always been there during her childhood when she needed someone to talk to. He had understood dreams about wanting more than she had, and he had never thought she was strange, or trying to act above herself, when she swore her life was *not* going to be like her parents'. That she was going to *do something* besides just survive!

"There's never been anything unnatural about your feelings for me. A little foolish, perhaps." She swallowed and blinked back the tears threatening to spill over onto her pale cheeks. "I hope you never regret this, Calvin Welsh!"

He reached up to brush the tears from her lashes with his thumbs. "That I'll never do, Little Bit. I've waited too long for you to belong to me."

Cal wanted to pull her toward him, to hold her properly and guide her coppery head to rest upon his chest as a lover should, but he couldn't. He was saving what little strength he had so he could at least sit up to be married properly. He could only comfort her with his hands on hers, though he longed to do more. Norah Kelly had had precious little comforting in her life. "Trust me, darlin'. Everything will work out fine."

Norah wasn't sure that was true, but she knew he believed it. And she was very thankful for his warmth and caring. Her heart in her beautiful eyes, she bent her head down to kiss him lightly on the mouth.

Morgan caught the tender byplay between them and gritted his teeth. Before, he had felt heat and desire when he looked at Norah. But now, seeing her in Cal's arms, the way they looked at each other, the way she kissed him, Morgan felt cold. And empty. And old.

Suddenly there was a hollow space in the middle of his chest that he'd never been aware of before and had no idea how to fill. For the first time in his life, the lawman truly felt alone—and he didn't like it one damned bit.

He reached down and hauled Judge Harvey to his unsteady feet and began to propel him toward the bed. Morgan wanted this wedding over so he could get the hell out of here, back to his job, and to the tasks and feelings he understood.

Morgan stepped out onto the wooden sidewalk just as loud shouts filled the air. For a brief second he thought all the hoopla was over Cal's wedding, but pounding hooves from up the street and the whistle blast of an approaching freight train changed his mind. Racing the train had recently become a favorite pastime among the rowdies and cowpokes.

A woman's scream chilled Morgan's blood, and he turned to see Jimmy crossing the street, his mind on the candy stick he'd just purchased. Without another thought, Morgan dashed toward the boy, intent on saving him from the frenzied horses.

They hit the ground and rolled out of the way just as the horses thundered past.

"My candy!" Jimmy cried.

Morgan saw that it was covered with dirt and dung. Fury raged within him, but when he

spoke his voice was calm. "Don't worry, lad.
The winner of that race will buy you more
candy."

The riders saw the steel in his eyes and realized how easily they'd gotten off. Not only did
they replace young Jimmy's horehound stick,
they bought him a sack of marbles.

Cal was dozing. He'd hardly been able to stay
awake through the short ceremony, and his eyes
had slid shut before Morgan and Myrtis left, taking Judge Harvey with them.

Norah was exhausted, too, for her pregnancy
left her tired all the time. And this had been a
trying day. She wanted nothing more than to
crawl into bed and sleep for a week. But it was
not possible. Even if Cal weren't sick and needing
constant care, she would have been busy. First
thing, she had to make curtains for the storefront
window. Morgan had nailed Flora Harrison's
quilt up to afford them some privacy for the
night.

With the lamp on the table turned low and the
stove stoked for the night, Norah was enjoying a
wash before going to bed. She would have loved
a bath, but Cal didn't have a tub. And, truth-
fully, she'd have been too tired to carry and heat
the water for a bath anyway.

With a sigh she slipped her pink flannel gown
over her head, then began to undo the coils of
her long hair. It was only going to get a lick and
a promise tonight—she didn't have the strength
for the usual one hundred strokes she gave it

daily. She stroked the brush through its length a few times, then pulled it to one side to begin the loose soft braid she usually slept in.

"Leave it loose, Norah, please?" Cal's voice was so soft she hardly heard him.

"I thought you were asleep," she said, to cover her embarrassment, as she wondered how much of her bathing he had seen. He was her husband and had a right to see as much of her as he wanted, but it was going to take some getting used to.

"Oh, I had a wee nap. But only a dead man could have slept through a wedding night with you." He held out his hand for her to come to him.

She started to blow out the light.

"Leave it. I want to be able to see you as you sleep in my arms."

Norah swallowed nervously, then walked to the far side of the bed, lifted the covers, and crawled in beside her husband. Cal opened his arms so she could snuggle next to him, her head on his chest.

"Calvin . . ."

"Shuuush," he whispered as he threaded the fingers of one hand through her hair and began loosening the braid she'd begun. He stroked her hair and massaged her scalp with his fingers until she relaxed. Then he began to trail his hands slowly down her body, gently claiming his territory.

"Don't worry, darlin', we're going to have years together—hundreds of nights to be together as man and wife. Tonight I just want to hold you, to revel in the fact that you finally belong to me."

"Oh, Cal." She sighed.

"I know, love. Things aren't just as we might have wished them to be. But we're together, finally. Now and forever. That's the most important thing." He stroked his hand down over the slight mound of her abdomen, then came back to rub it gently.

"Oh, how I wish the baby were yours!" Norah gasped.

"Why, it is, love. From this day forth. I'm a farmer born and bred. I know that who plants the seed isn't nearly as important as the one who nurtures it. And this child is going to be loved and nurtured by both of us. You're my wife, and you're carrying my child. Don't you ever forget that, Norah Welsh!"

She buried her face in his chest to hide her tears, but he lifted her chin with one finger so he could look into her eyes. "There's nothing you can't tell me, darlin'. I'm not going to judge you harshly, I love you too well. So if you ever want to talk about what happened in Cincinnati, I'll be here for you."

Norah hugged him. "Maybe sometime, but not now. Now I just want to lie here, in your arms, and realize how lucky I am to have you."

Cal kissed the top of her head. "Whatever you want is my pleasure." Then his eyes fluttered closed and he slid into a deep, restless sleep.

*　　　*　　　*

It was after two when Sheriff Treyhan made his last rounds. It had been a wild night, as Saturdays often were, and he missed Cal's help. Not that Cal was a particularly good deputy. It just made Morgan feel good to know another man was backing him up.

He saw the light in one of the store windows and realized the building belonged to Cal.

A surge of jealousy stabbed him clear through. No man sleeps through his wedding night, especially not with a woman as lovely as Norah.

He was halfway down the block when he remembered Cal's gray pallor as Judge Harvey finished the ceremony. He wondered if Cal's condition had worsened. With great reluctance, he went to the back door, listened intently for a while, and then silently turned the knob to look inside.

Feeling like a criminal and a pervert, he opened the door enough to see the room. A sigh of relief escaped him when he saw there was no crisis. Cal slept in the bed while Norah sat rocking in the chair beside him. Morgan closed the door quietly and walked to his house across the tracks.

After three days, Norah felt pleased with Cal's sudden progress. He seemed to be getting better little by little. Not only was he improving physically, but their relationship was working out just fine. In many ways it was as if they had slipped back in time to when they were younger. When he was awake, they talked and laughed and teased each other like children.

Each night they went to sleep in each other's arms, though Norah always got up later to spend the night in the chair. She was afraid he might need her and she would be asleep. Sometimes during the day Cal wanted her to just sit by him so he could touch her. Except for the hours he slept, or when someone came to visit him, he watched her. At first it made her nervous, but he explained with his sweet smile that he still couldn't believe his good fortune in finally having her for his wife.

Norah was moved. Never in her life had anyone wanted her that much just for herself. Cal didn't care whether she worked or not. In fact, he preferred that she didn't. He wanted the pleasure of her company, to know that she was there. And he was so delighted with everything she did. He watched her making a home with the few things they now had, then smiled a secret smile and told her things were going to be better.

"I'll be up and around any day now, Norah," he told her. "We can work together to get the store building whipped into shape."

"That's right."

"I have plans for the future."

Norah shook her head, and kissed him as she went by. She didn't put a lot of faith in Cal's words or his dreams, but still her heart filled almost to bursting as she listened to him. She *wanted* to believe him. She *wanted* to trust in the visions he saw of their future together. She *wanted* it all to be true, more than she had ever wanted anything in her life.

But she wasn't sure. Most of the surprises life had dealt her had not been pleasant.

Don't be such a gloomy gus, she admonished herself. It was a lovely day. The sun was shining brightly, though the air had a sharp bite to it.

She saw that Cal was sleeping peacefully, his breath coming more easily, without the horrible rattle that had scared her so.

He was emaciated and weak, though. Keeping him down long enough to truly get well was going to be a major problem, she feared. Already he was making noises about wanting to get up and get on with things. What things, she had no idea. She realized he was like a large child, needing to be entertained.

Suddenly she had an idea. Making sure he was still sleeping soundly, she put her traveling cloak on over her everyday dress, grabbed her drawstring purse, and hurried toward Wilson's Mercantile.

Around the block, she encountered Eldon on his way to work.

"Howdy, Miz Welsh. How's Cal doin' today?"

"Better." Norah beamed. "He's talking about getting up and helping fix up the building."

Eldon smiled in response to Norah's happiness. "I don't have to be to work just yet. Think I'll walk down and check in on Cal."

"You do that. He'll enjoy seeing you. He loves to have people stop by."

She found that the mercantile had a new supply of dime novels, so she bought two for Cal. Those should help keep him occupied for the time being. She thought about stopping by the sheriff's office to ask Morgan if he knew of anything else to keep Cal quiet long enough to convalesce properly, but she vetoed the idea. Morgan hadn't been by for a while, and he had been gruff the last time he was there, muttering something about cattle rustlers. It couldn't be easy keeping a wild frontier town like this quiet, she supposed. In comparison, keeping Cal down should be a snap.

While she was at the mercantile, Norah also purchased four apples, a pound of brown sugar, and a bit of cinnamon. The day after her wedding Morgan had brought her a large cast-iron pot with a bail and a lid. He called it a Dutch oven, showed her how it would fit on the top of the potbellied stove, and told her how she could cook in it and bake, too.

Already she had made biscuits in it. The first couple of tries had not been so great until she'd learned to control the temperature, but Cal had eaten one with butter and a bit of jam someone had brought, and seemed to relish it as much as if it had come from his mother's oven. Alice Welsh was a real expert at baking, and she had taught Norah how to make biscuits when Norah was so small she had to stand on a chair to reach the table.

"Are you going to bake a pie?" Mrs. Wilson asked as she wrapped up Norah's purchases. "I know them books must be for Cal. He shore does love 'em. I'm glad he's feeling good enough to be a'readin'."

Norah smiled at the motherly woman behind the counter. "I don't think I'm brave enough to tackle apple pie in the Dutch oven yet. I'm going to bake the apples, though. Fill their centers with butter, sugar, and cinnamon. Cal's mother says they are his favorite."

"On good terms with yore mother-in-law, are you?"

"Yes, Alice Welsh has been my friend all my life." Norah was anxious to get back to the store building and to Cal, but Mrs. Wilson wanted to visit and Norah didn't want to be rude. All the townspeople had been so good to her and to Cal since she came.

When she finally got away, she was surprised at the chill in the air. She shivered and pulled her cloak tightly around her as she hurried down the boardwalk. The temperature had dropped sharply in the time she'd been gone, and the wind had risen. It whipped around her skirts and rattled the windows of the buildings she passed.

Her head bent against the wind, Norah bumped into Myrtis just as she passed the Red Rock Saloon. "Forgive me, Myrtis! I wasn't looking where I was going."

The older woman nodded. "Ya 'pear to be in a right hurry. Is Cal taken worse?"

"Oh, I hope not. He was sleeping peacefully when I left, but it's gotten so cold all of a sudden. I hope the fire hasn't gone out in the stove. I only meant to be a few minutes. It wouldn't be good for Cal to get chilled at this point."

"No, it wouldn't," Myrtis agreed. "Here, I'll

come along wi' ya. I was a'comin' to check on him, anyways."

The wind flung the door open as she turned the knob, and Norah went flying in with it. She hurried to push it closed and latch it again behind Myrtis.

"Make yourself comfortable," she bade the older woman. "As soon as I put my things down and tell Cal I'm back, I'll pull the front curtains closed. That should help keep out some of the cold."

Norah started toward the back, then stopped and stared. Cal was not in the bed. She looked around the large room hurriedly, but he wasn't anywhere to be seen. "Myrtis, he's not here! Where can he be? He wasn't even able to get out of bed by himself!" Her voice grew more shrill and frightened with each word. Dropping her purchases on the table, she ran out the back door calling his name.

Myrtis followed more slowly, her face set in grim lines. They found him crumpled on the ground about ten feet from the privy, in his nightshirt only, his feet bare. He was unconscious, and cold—so cold.

Norah was terrified. She didn't know where her strength came from, for Cal was a big man, but she and Myrtis managed to drag him inside and get him into the bed. She piled on him every blanket and coat that she could find, while Myrtis built up the fire until the small stove roared.

She forced hot liquids into him, warmed up cloths for his chest and towels to wrap him in, but to no avail. He alternately shivered and burned.

"What else can I do, Myrtis?" she pleaded. "I've done everything I know how."

"He's delirious, child. There's nothin' else you can do now."

"Oh, why did I leave him? He didn't have to have books to read, or baked apples. He was so much better! It's all my fault!"

"No!" Myrtis said sternly. "It's not yore fault. And he wasn't that much better. He jist seemed t'be. He was already out o' his head, or he'd a'not tried goin' to the privy by himself with nuthin' on but his nightshirt. I been expectin' this. That's why I was a'comin' to check on him."

Norah's eyes were brimming with tears as she stared at Myrtis. "You mean you knew he wasn't really getting better? Why didn't you tell me?" Her voice was an anguished whisper.

"I feared it, child. He has pneumonia, and there's not much we can do fer that. But you was so determined he was gonna get better. And he loves ya so much. I thought it jist might work. Miracles do happen. But not this time." She started putting on her coat and heavy scarf.

"Where are you going? I don't believe you! Cal is going to get well. We're going to spend the rest of our lives together!"

"Yore goin' to spend the rest o' his life together. Not yours. I'm goin' to git Digger to come help with him. Then I'll stop by and tell Morgan. He'll want to be here, too. Now pull yoreself together, girl! Calvin Welsh loved you

better than anybody else in his whole life. Don't
you dare let him down now. Buck up. Make
yoreself some tea, and put on a pot o' coffee.
The worst is yet to come."

Norah put the coffee on, and the teakettle,
then she sat on the bed beside Cal, brushing the
hair back from his forehead, memorizing his
beloved features with her eyes and her fingers.
Part of her refused to believe he was dying, but
another part had always known this was all too
good to be true.

When Morgan burst through the door with
Myrtis behind him, Norah was still sitting there,
still stroking Cal's face, silent tears streaming
down her face. Morgan's heart swelled into his
throat. He had charged out of his office to come
to the aid of his friend, but he realized it was
Norah who truly needed their help.

Cal was dying, and they would do all they
could to ease his passage, relieve his suffering.
But he had the easy part in this drama. Norah
was the one who had to deal with the broken
promises and shattered dreams his death would
bring. She was the one who needed Morgan's
strength to get her through this ordeal. She had
traveled almost two thousand miles to make a
life with Cal, a life that was fading away before
her eyes.

They did all they could—Morgan, Myrtis,
Digger, and Norah most of all. The men held
him down when he was delirious and having
wild hallucinations. The women nursed him in

every way they knew how. Finally, two days later, he slipped into a coma.

Cal died in his sleep in the wee hours of Friday morning with Norah holding his hand. She was still sitting there, grasping him in her arms, tears streaming down her face, when Morgan stopped in during one of his rounds checking out the town. She was so exhausted, both physically and emotionally, all she could do was rock Cal's body and cry silently for a wonderful man and a future that would never be.

4

Clarabelle Wattron felt her body grow tense with impatience, and she took a deep breath. She was trying to be gracious to the Widow Welsh as the younger woman dug into a small pigskin pouch to find enough coins to pay the postage on the three letters she was mailing. After all, it was her Christian duty to be kind to widows and orphans. But in her heart, Clarabelle could feel a deep well of resentment forming because of the young widow's fragile beauty.

Norah Welsh was breathtaking, even in stark black mourning clothes. Standing beside the girl, Clarabelle felt like an enormous, clumsy heifer with no grace and little charm. She felt foolish in her ruffles and sausage curls when she looked at the simple, elegant dress Norah wore.

Norah carefully counted the pennies, then accidentally dropped them and had to start again. Writing the letter to Cal's mother about his death was the hardest thing she'd ever done—far worse even than telling Cal about her pregnancy. Cal's people were simple folk who'd never understood the wild and wonderful plans he'd had for his life. Norah hoped she had conveyed the idea that his life hadn't been a failure.

The letter to her own family hadn't been easy either. Knowing the note would be read to the entire family by one of her younger sisters, Norah simply told of her brief marriage and Cal's sudden passing.

She also told them of her decision to stay in Holbrook for the time being. She hadn't mentioned the baby yet, but she knew she couldn't put it off forever. The thought filled her with trepidation. Her family must never know the baby wasn't Cal's. Never!

Clarabelle saw the girl suddenly go pale as chalk and noticed how badly her slender fingers began to shake. Poor little thing! Widowed so soon after the wedding. Alone now, and probably scared silly in this wild town. All of Clarabelle's feelings of jealousy vanished, replaced instantly by motherly concern.

"You look a little peaky, Mrs. Welsh. I'll bet you're not eating right. Perhaps you'd like a good cup of tea and some pie."

Norah started to refuse, but the thought of a hot cup of tea was too tempting to pass up. "Tea would be lovely," she murmured. It wasn't until then that she realized her knees were shaking.

Before she knew it she was seated at a cloth-covered table in a cozy yellow kitchen with blue gingham curtains, enjoying the best piece of custard pie she'd ever eaten. She couldn't remember when she'd last had anything to eat. Was it breakfast the day before?

"I didn't realize I was so hungry," she said, her voice raspy from the volume of tears she had shed.

"I don't imagine Cal had much in the line of grub at his place." Clarabelle sat down and picked up her own daisy-flowered teacup. She had fed a lot of men since she'd moved here, but seldom did she have another woman at her table.

Women were scarce in the Arizona Territory, and decent women were rare indeed. There were several married women in town but they were always busy with husband and family, so Clarabelle had little in common with them. She wondered if she could remember how to make proper conversation with another lady.

The color was beginning to come back into Norah's face, tinting her cheeks a delicate peach. She smiled at Clarabelle's comment about Cal's pantry, and wondered if the woman had seen the inside of Cal's building before the townspeople had donated the furnishings. "He didn't have much in the way of cooking supplies, I'm afraid. I've wondered if he ever ate."

"He ate at the hotel or the café, like most of the men in town. And he got a number of dinner invitations. I don't suppose he had to cook much." Clarabelle refilled both cups.

They talked about Cal for several minutes more, sharing remembrances of him. Norah felt the tightness in her chest ease and realized how rigidly she'd been holding herself. It had been an effort to control her fears and nightmares since he died. "I'm glad he had such good friends here," she said.

"He *was* a good friend," Clarabelle said, her eyes misty. She flicked a crumb off the blue gingham tablecloth. "I'll miss him."

"I've known him as long as I can remember," Norah told her. "Our house was next to his family farm." She sighed and finished the pie.

"It ain't my place to ask, I know, but out here in the West a person has to be practical. This can be a harsh place for a woman alone. Are you going back to your people?"

Norah shook her head. She'd been able to think of little else the past few days. She did not have the extra money to return home to Indiana, even if she'd wished to. Considering her situation, staying in the Arizona Territory was the best thing she could do. At home, her family would guess that the baby was conceived in Cincinnati by someone who had refused to marry her. Poor as they might be, they'd judge her as harshly as everyone else in Aberdeen would. She'd be scorned, perhaps even shunned. No, it was better to stay here, where she had a chance. Maybe Clarabelle would advise her about available work.

"I have no immediate plans to leave town," she said. "I was thinking of making some use of Cal's store, and setting up a business. Of course, the store needs a little work. . . ."

"It needs a *lot* of work," Clarabelle interrupted, concerned that Norah might plan to compete with her own fancy goods business. "It's a drafty barn!"

Norah giggled at the woman's bluntness. She couldn't help it, though her dignity wilted a bit. It was foolish to pretend about Cal's store when the whole town knew the building was merely an unfinished shell.

"I need to make some money so I can put up partitions and finish the rooms. Even if I wanted to sell the building, which I don't, it would need some things done to it before anybody would buy it."

"The first thing you need to do is start preparing for winter, or you'll freeze to death. Newspapers, that's whatcha'll need!"

Norah blinked, completely at a loss.

Clarabelle jumped up and began to slice some bread and cheese and cold beef. She set the slices on the table along with a dish of canned cherries and some chowchow relish. "You can get piles of papers down at the *Critic*. Here, help yourself. You look like you could use a good meal."

Norah was still trying to figure out why she'd want piles of newspapers. If she was to look in the advertising section, surely one paper would do. She accepted a dish and began to eat. How could she possibly still be hungry after the pie?

"Once you get the right thickness of paper on the walls to insulate yourself from the weather— and the danged blowing dust—then you can add wallpaper, if you've a mind to be fancy." Clarabelle smiled widely, pleased to be able to help.

"It's a big building," Norah said lamely. She was astonished that someone would use newspaper for insulation. But the West was remote, and she guessed folks made do with what they had.

"Get young Jimmy to help you. His father's a conductor for the A and P—he's gone a lot. Jimmy's a hard worker, and he appreciates any little extra he can make. You'll have that place airtight in no time at all. Winters get cold here, you know."

Norah knew all about cold winters and drafty buildings, but she didn't tell Clarabelle. She preferred not to think about how gruelingly poor her family had been when she was little, or how many times she and her sisters had gone to bed hungry. And her father too lazy to work! She shook the harsh memories from her thoughts.

After Clarabelle made more tea, Norah brought up the subject of finding work. She'd carried a small amount of money in her corset when she came, but it wouldn't be enough to keep her through the winter. "I worked for Shillitos' Department Store in Cincinnati as a seamstress."

"You want to be a seamstress?" Clarabelle asked. She didn't sew at all well. Her skill was playing the organ.

"It's what I do best."

Once Clarabelle realized her fancy goods business wouldn't be jeopardized, she immediately thought of half a dozen people who might need sewing done. The first being Frank Reed, the newspaper editor. Built like a barrel with short arms and legs, Frank would be a challenge.

"The man is a walking ragbag. It doesn't help that he gets beat up every few weeks. His suit weren't no great shakes to start out with, and being thrown off the hotel balcony into the horse trough didn't help it at all."

"Clarabelle, are you gossiping about poor Frank?"

Morgan Treyhan stood in the doorway with a devilish smile on his weathered face. He tipped his hat to Norah and nodded a greeting.

Passing off the sudden leap of her senses as any normal woman's startled reaction, Norah dipped her head in return and tried to ignore him. It wasn't easy. He had a way of commanding every situation.

She was as astonished that the sheriff had a humorous side as she was to see Clarabelle color up and get all flustered. The big woman was blushing like a Georgia peach, and Morgan appeared to enjoy having her in a fluster.

Norah frowned into her cup. Perhaps the sheriff was some sort of lady's man. The thought made her bristle. Well, he'd better not expect *her* to twitter and coo. She sat up straighter in her chair and finished her tea.

"You're not thinking of reforming Frank, are you, Clarabelle?" Morgan couldn't quite hide his deep chuckle.

Norah realized he and Clarabelle were simply old friends who often teased each other. It surprised her. She hadn't met him under the best of circumstances, and their subsequent encounters had been strained and fraught with pain for both of them, but this side of him stunned her. It was easier to think of him as a hard-bitten gun-man than as a real human being.

"I was not gossiping," Clarabelle said indig-nantly, fluffing her tight curls. "And I certainly wouldn't waste my time trying to reform *that* man! He's beyond hope. I was merely agreeing with Mrs. Welsh that the town could use a good seamstress. Frank Reed, above all."

Morgan didn't answer. With the grace of a wildcat, he moved from the doorway toward the table and pulled out a chair, laying his hat on the chair next to his. "If you've got anymore of that pie, Clarabelle, I'd be obliged. Last night was a rough one."

Norah's eyes strayed to his gun belt. The holster seemed to be as much a part of him as his blue eyes or his wide shoulders. She wasn't accus-tomed to seeing men carrying handguns. Back home she'd seen a few rifles that had been used for hunting, though her own father had been too poor to own one. But she'd *never* even imagined a place where half the citizens of the town would pack enough weapons to start a war.

He felt her gaze on him and his heart leapt. For one brief moment he thought she was gazing at the buttons on his gray twill trousers, and his body reacted instantly, but then he realized it was the .45s that attracted her attention. A wry smile touched his mouth, and he turned to take a plate from Clarabelle.

"Mrs. Welsh intends to remain in Holbrook," Clarabelle told him.

"Oh? There's not much here." Morgan couldn't think why a woman so lovely, and so obviously from the city, would want to stay in this wild western town. She didn't look like she had the stamina to stand up to a hard wind, but he knew from the way she had tried to save Cal that she had grit. He liked that. He just didn't know if he wanted her staying. With all the other problems he had, he sure as hell didn't need woman trouble.

"I'm thinking about opening a business in Cal's store." Norah decided the best way to make certain her vague plans became reality was to announce them to the world. Morgan Treyhan was the top man in this windblown world, and she wanted him to know she was a permanent resident.

"A sewing business," Clarabelle said. "And I was telling her that Frank Reed definitely needed her services. He's such a ragamuffin."

"Frank's a firebrand," Morgan told Norah, in case she didn't know. "Somebody's always mad at him. Mostly the cattlemen, but he doesn't play favorites. He rubs everybody the wrong way sooner or later."

"Didn't *you* mention needing a few clothes?" Clarabelle asked, interrupting whatever else he'd meant to say.

Morgan chuckled at Clarabelle's obvious attempt to drum up business for Norah. "I guess I did say something about it. My trousers are worn and I haven't had a new shirt since I came to town almost three years ago." The demon in him made him add, "Perhaps Mrs. Welsh isn't accustomed to making men's trousers."

"I was well taught, Sheriff," she said coolly.

The one thing Norah had complete confidence in was her sewing skills. "And I've had years of experience. Give me a little time to get my place arranged, and you can come over for a fitting."

Simon Mendel, the tailor who had made the clothes Morgan now wore, was an old man. Morgan thought suddenly that he wasn't sure he could cope with Norah's hands on him the way Simon's had been. It wouldn't be the same impersonal action. A woman's hands, especially a beautiful woman's soft white hands, moving the measure over his hips, around his waist, and up his inseam, would be more than any lonely man could bear.

Norah saw the frown on the sheriff's face and wondered why he often looked so hard and unapproachable. He certainly wasn't trying to win her over! Immediately she chastised herself. Morgan had helped her tremendously with Cal, and even more after his death. She would be forever grateful.

"If you'd like, I could begin by turning the cuffs on your shirt. They're a bit frayed. I can do that in the evening by lamplight. I owe you something for finding a bed for Cal, and for the chair."

"You don't owe me anything. But I'd appreciate it if you could mend a few things for me. My ma taught me to sew on a button, but that's about it. Besides, my evenings are darned busy."

"What happened last night?" Clarabelle asked.

"A couple of gents were discussing the fracas down in the Pleasant Valley. A new fellow in town—called Bad Bunky Lindstrom by lawmen in several states—is a mean know-it-all. And the discussion got a little heated."

Clarabelle sniffed. She knew the altercation between cattlemen and sheepherders in the Pleasant Valley area was escalating into an all-out war. Folks all over the Arizona Territory were taking sides. She hoped a long, cold winter would cool down the situation. "Are you going to get another deputy?"

Morgan glanced at Norah, wondering if the subject would upset her. "Not right away. I don't know anybody trustworthy enough who can do the job. One of the boys from the Hashknife outfit wanted it." He turned to Norah to explain. "'Hashknife' is the nickname for the Aztec Cattle Company."

"I see."

"I think he's a good man. But with the Aztec Cattle Company having their headquarters here in town at the Brunswick Hotel, I thought that might tilt the balance toward the cowboys, so I said no. I'd like to keep this town neutral." He pushed his chair away from the table, picking up his hat as he rose.

"I'll bring several shirts by your place tonight after supper, Mrs. Welsh. Every one I own needs attention. But I insist you take pay for your work. Clarabelle, as always, thank you."

"Look over there!"

Norah had paused on the wooden sidewalk to allow Jimmy to make a very important marble shot in what appeared to be a life and death battle

with Albert Harrison, the stationmaster's son.
She glanced up and gasped.

Indians!

A large band of mounted Indians approached
from the north side of the railroad tracks and
began to cross onto Central Avenue. They were
the first ones Norah had ever seen.

"Navajos," Albert told her, as if that somehow
explained their presence.

With her heart beating madly, Norah looked up
and down the street, waiting for somebody to give
the signal that an attack was under way. Nobody
seemed in the least bit afraid. She swallowed hard
and forced herself to be calm. The boys, like most
everyone else on the street, watched with avid
curiosity but no more anxiety than they would
show for a horse race or a fistfight.

Morgan walked up the street and approached
the mounted leader. They spoke gravely for several moments.

"Sheriff! Sheriff! Are we being attacked?"
Frank Reed yelled.

Norah felt her cheeks burn with embarrassment as some of the men near the saloon began
to laugh and hoot. She'd almost yelled the
same thing herself. But after seeing how Morgan had the entire situation under control, she
was mortified to watch Frank make a fool of
himself. The only one in town who noticed
Frank was a hen who went into a feathery flutter
when he disturbed her chicks.

"Sheriff, are we in danger?"

"Don't be a jackass, Frank. These men are just
passing through."

The editor looked faintly disappointed that a massacre wasn't imminent. But he squared his beefy shoulders and made the best of a bad situation—he plunged into the group of riders with the eagerness of a politician. The Indians ignored him, concentrating instead on quieting their horses.

Suddenly their leader nodded to the sheriff and urged his mount forward at a trot toward the river road. The others followed quickly.

Frank, unfortunately, had not been prepared for the horses to move. In their midst as he was, he was shoved by flanks and shoulders, nudged by noses, and swatted by tails. His notebook and pencil fell to the ground. Trying to catch the precious tools of his trade unbalanced him, and he pitched forward. An unshod hoof came solidly down on his shirt sleeve, ripping it off.

"The mighty white man," said a passing Navajo.

His companion simply grunted in disgust.

Moments later Morgan stopped to speak to Norah. She hadn't moved an inch from where she'd stopped to watch the boys shoot marbles.

"A band of horses was stolen from those men," Morgan said. "I told them the horses didn't come through town, but a large number of animals crossed about a mile up the river sometime during the night."

Norah nodded, then stepped past Frank, who had crawled to the sidewalk and was scribbling on his dusty notepad. Norah didn't notice Frank's filthy, flapping sleeve. She was too intent on going home to lie down.

*   *   *

The wind had picked up by nightfall and Norah shivered as it seeped through the hundreds of cracks in the wall. First thing tomorrow she was going to march down to the newspaper office. If some layered newspapers and a little flour paste would keep out the cold air, she didn't care what it looked like. Comfort came before beauty.

And she would also wash the grimy front window. What with blowing dust, the smoke from the trains passing through, and the soot from her own stove, the window was so dirty nobody could read the SEWING sign she'd put up.

She was making business plans in her head as she ate a small meal of tomato gravy over a slice of the bread she'd gotten at the bakery. Cal's little potbellied stove and Morgan's Dutch oven were inadequate for fancy baking, so Norah was patronizing Schriener's Bakery. She didn't mind because the fat loaf of bread was tasty and reasonably priced, and the Schrieners were friendly.

A knock on the door set her heart to pounding. It was already dark outside, and the tinny piano music from the Red Rock Saloon floated out on the night air, mingling with coyote cries. Men could be heard talking on the street, calling to one another or arguing, and a woman's shrill laughter burst out a time or two. Most of the merchants had retired to their living quarters, leaving the rowdies and drifters the run of the streets. She knew they would have torn the place to pieces—racing up and down the streets, yelling and brandishing their sixguns, and shooting out any lights they saw—except for the iron will of Sheriff Treyhan. Some of the older residents had told her how things were before Morgan had come to town.

"Who is it?" she called. Norah had been in the city long enough to know not to open a door to a stranger.

"Treyhan."

Instead of calming her down, the sound of his gravelly voice made her heart continue to thump. She'd never known any other man who possessed the power to make her feel threatened and protected all in the same instant. She didn't understand it, didn't want to understand it. She merely wanted the feelings to stop.

"Come in, Sheriff."

As he stepped inside, Morgan Treyhan couldn't believe what she'd done to Cal's place in the short time she'd lived there. With the aid of a few meager sticks of worn furniture donated by stingy old MacKay at the hotel, and odds and ends by other folks, Norah had created a cozy little niche for herself. Some ingenuity with boxes and crates protected her from the prying eyes of passersby.

"I brought the shirts," he said. Being alone with her made him as nervous as a caged lion. The attraction he'd felt from the first moment he'd seen her grew stronger each time he was nearby, and today in Clarabelle's kitchen he'd nearly gone crazy. Considering the situation—Norah being his best friend's bride and widow all in the space of a week—his lustful thoughts disgusted him.

His sudden scowl caused her to jerk her hands away at the same time he passed the shirts to her. Seeing them falling, they both made a dive for them, and somehow ended on the floor together.

There was dead silence.

Then Norah began to chuckle. And Morgan's deep laugh followed in its wake.

"I'm sorry," they both said at the same time, and their foolish laughter only increased.

"Let me help you up," he offered as he climbed to his knees, his hands closing over hers.

The laughter died out of her hazel eyes as he gazed into them. Tension sang through the air, thick and compelling. Morgan's body tightened violently with a sudden, powerful need.

"Norah," he said hoarsely, his hands gripping hers more tightly.

Whatever he had planned to say next was drowned out by a long, spine-chilling scream.

Norah nearly fainted on the spot. She'd never heard anything so horrifying in her life.

"Oh, hell," Morgan muttered. "Beg pardon, ma'am." He stood up slowly and pulled her to her feet. Bowing his head a minute, he collected his wits. Then he reached down to pick up the shirts and his hat.

Another scream, equally as loud but in a different key, rent the air.

"What is that?" Norah whispered. Was the town so lawless that women were being murdered in their beds?

"Girls over at the Red Rock Saloon. Fighting."

He handed her the shirts. "These are pretty well worn, as you can see, but I haven't had time to get new ones made. I'd best go break up that brawl. I don't want those floozies in my jail. I've got enough trouble without that!"

It wasn't until she'd closed the door and locked it against the madness of western life that Norah looked at the shirts. They were of a fine-quality unbleached muslin, expertly made but threadbare. All of them had been mended at least once, and one had a bad three-corner tear with a crude patch that was coming off. Morgan Treyhan didn't need the cuffs turned; he needed new shirts.

Tossing them on her bed, Norah put water on to heat for tea and began to search in the trunk of sewing supplies she'd brought with her. She knew she had some muslin nearly as fine as that of the sheriff's shirts. Before the kettle was boiling, she had the fabric spread out on the gateleg table. Using the shirt in the worst state of disrepair as a pattern, she began to cut. She planned to have two new shirts made for him and the others mended by the time he returned tomorrow.

He was her first customer and she wanted him well satisfied. When he found she'd stitched the garments so quickly, he'd spread the word about her. She knew a happy customer meant better business.

She sewed as fast as her nimble fingers could work, only allowing herself one brief pang because she'd sold her treadle sewing machine before she came west. Norah wasn't one to lament what she couldn't change. She'd simply make do without a machine.

Beyond the thin walls of her building, the dusty sage-scented air grew cold with the promise of winter. The wind blew steadily for a while, then settled down, only to gust up again.

Norah worked well into the night, ignoring the nightlife outside, cutting and sewing until she was too tired to worry about rowdy drunks and fistfights that might turn into gunfights. Finally, she realized she was seeing double and it was growing cold because the fire had died down to mere coals. She yawned and went behind the privacy screen to change into her nightgown.

Life would be hard out here, she thought as her hand searched in the dark for the armhole. But she could make it on her own. She'd work hard to get the building liveable before the baby arrived, trading sewing for services whenever she could. This building was better than what she'd grown up in at that, and she was thankful her friend Cal had been so kind and generous. And she was so very sorry about his death.

Wiping away a tired tear, she climbed into bed. With the absolute knowledge that she could take care of herself and her baby, she sank into a deep, peaceful sleep.

Late the next morning, as she was finishing a neat row of buttonholes, there was a sharp knock at the back door. And then another.

Automatically, Norah moved the simmering

kettle over the fire so tea water would be ready if she wanted to offer her guest some refreshment. It was sunny outside, and far warmer than it had been in days. She'd already gotten a stack of papers and talked to young Jimmy about helping her tomorrow.

This afternoon she planned to enjoy herself a bit. She needed some time to relax. She thought she'd take a walk down to see the river south of town. The walk would do her good, and she wanted to know why folks laughed when she mentioned the river.

She opened the back door and gaped.

A painted lady stood outside!

The woman couldn't have been more than twenty, if that. She wore a ruffled aqua wrapper with torn lace on the bertha collar, and scuffed green satin shoes. Norah couldn't stop staring. The woman was a sight—black hair that hadn't seen a brush that morning, and the face of a china doll, though blurred because last night's paint hadn't been washed off yet.

"Yes?" Norah asked cautiously. She'd never had a strumpet come calling before. Back East, that type kept to themselves, but perhaps things were different out here.

The woman was looking her over with as much rude curiosity as she herself was displaying. Norah lifted her chin and stood a little taller. "May I help you?"

"They said you was a looker."

"I beg your pardon."

"The men. At the Red Rock. That's where I work," she said, just in case Norah didn't know who she was, though she found that difficult to believe. She had quite a following for miles around. "They's all talkin' about ya. Says you's fine lookin'. I 'spects they'll be callin' on ya, soon-like."

"Oh," Norah said, thinking perhaps she should close the door now.

"Morgan said ya took in sewin'. Said to come talk to ya. I need yer help makin' sompthin'."

For a brief moment Norah had the impulse to strangle the sheriff with his own muslin shirt-sleeves. The very idea, recommending her services to a woman of questionable virtue! But she quickly recalled that her own virtue couldn't stand too much close scrutiny.

She, who had received strict moral guidance from Mrs. Jean, had still managed to stray mightily from the path of righteousness—and was carrying the proof in her belly. The heat of shame stained her fair skin. She had no right whatsoever to condemn this girl. She took a deep breath and allowed herself to see her as an equal.

"I'll pay real good," the girl continued, naming a figure that made Norah's brows rise. "And I won't tell nobody you done it. In case the old biddies want to get nasty about yer helpin' me."

Norah wondered what Jean Matthews would have done in a situation like this, then she realized Mrs. Jean would *never* have been in a situation like this. She had lived responsibly and respectably her entire life. In one traitorous, enlightening flash, Norah realized how boring Mrs. Jean's life had been.

"What sort of sewing do you require?" she asked, interested in spite of her better judgment.

"A dancing costume."

"You're a dancer?" Norah asked, a little surprised.

The woman laughed wickedly. "No, ma'am, I ain't. I'm a first-class whore. I just thought it would be fun to wiggle somethin' different fer a change. My name's Mazie, by the way."

Norah had no idea how to respond to such naughtiness. "Mazie, I do not make indecent garments," she said stiffly. She didn't say more because she couldn't think of anything else. And besides, the absurdity of the entire situation was beginning to amuse her.

"Oh, it comes way down to here." Mazie lifted her wrapper nearly up to her knees. "And the neckline ain't bad, neither."

Norah was thankful Mazie didn't bare her *entire* bosom. In case she'd ever wondered, she now knew that Mazie wore undergarments, skimpy though they were.

"It's all done, 'cept I can't get it to stay together. Those blasted straps broke last night, and the feathers fell off. Lily Mae thought I lost the top on purpose to get more business, but it was an accident."

"I see." Norah hesitated. "Oh, I guess I could secure the straps." She could not believe these words were coming out of her mouth. Being in the West was making her as bold as brass. Was she really going to work for a confessed lady-of-the-night?—she couldn't even bring herself to think the word *whore*. "And tack down the feathers."

Mazie squealed like someone who'd won a horse race. "Morgan said you would. He said you was spunky."

Suddenly disconcerted by her own audacity, Norah glanced down the alley to see if any of her neighbors were about. A sleek gray cat bounced by, taking home a prize mouse. Otherwise, the alley was empty. "I'll thank the sheriff later," she said.

"Ain't he a peach!" Mazie sighed. "I been hankering after him since I come to town. But he don't spend no time with Lily Mae 'er me. An' I even offered to do him for nothin'. Guess he ain't got time. But he sure does got the equipment! Makes me pant just thinkin' about it."

Norah blushed clear down to her high-topped shoes. A lady wasn't supposed to know what Mazie was talking about, but she did, and it gave her a thrill of excitement. She told herself it wasn't her place to be pleased that Morgan didn't frequent the local brothel. What the sheriff did wasn't her business, but the shaft of pleasure didn't go away.

"I'll have some time this afternoon to work on your dancing dress," she said. "If it's clean. I never work on soiled garments." She felt ashamed about her rudeness when she saw Mazie color up beneath the paint. Whatever had possessed her to say such a mean thing?

But for Cal's kindness, her own sewing skill, and the grace of God, she could be in Mazie's position. She knew many women were forced to seek Mazie's type of employment to keep body and soul together. She softened her voice, vowing

to be more understanding in the future. "You
wouldn't believe how many rich women I did
sewing for back East who weren't as clean as
they should have been."

"Rich folks is hard to unnerstan," Mazie
said, as if she were well acquainted with the
whims of the wealthy.

Sonny's handsome face flashed into Norah's
mind with only a twinge of pain. He'd been so
charming, mannerly, and educated, yet he'd used
her for his own desires and then tossed her and
their child aside like so much trash. She couldn't
fathom that sort of cruelty. "Yes, indeed they
are."

5

A bullet shattered the front window, embedding itself in the soft newspaper insulation on the wall and destroying the night's blanketing peace.

Norah awoke with a cry in her throat and fear clutching her heart. A second bullet, which sheared off the doorknob, splintering wood from the door, told her it was not a dream. Her house was under attack.

"I'm comin' in, woman!" a drunken voice called. "Jist lay back and git ready fer a man."

She bolted from the bed, trying to find some sort of weapon in the dark.

Outside, lantern light flickered in the darkness. The sound of boots running up the hard-packed street coincided with fingers pawing at the door, trying to get it to open. There was a loud call, a cry of pain, and a few more shouts, then the sound of men pounding one another in a vicious fight. Grunts and curse words penetrated Norah's fearful brain as the sickening thud of punches landed hard on solid flesh. And finally there was the sound of a body flopping to the ground.

"You okay, Sheriff?" someone called.

Some of her fear ebbed when she knew Morgan Treyhan was out there. She hoped he was all right. Anxiously, she strained to hear his answer.

"I'm fine. Haul this bastard over to the jail and wait for me. You better wake Myrtis. I think I broke his jaw."

Norah stood huddled against the far side of the privacy screen, breathing hard and listening to the men in the street. Apparently the attack was over.

With shaking hands she found a match and lit the lamp, carefully replacing the glass chimney. After setting it back on the table, she hurried to the front to examine the damage.

The door opened with a bang just as she reached it, and startled, she stepped sideways away from it. Then she gave a cry of pain.

"What happened?" Morgan demanded, shouldering the door closed against the night air.

He had a gun in his hand, she noticed, even though her attention was on her right foot and the piercing shard of glass she'd stepped on.

"Are you hit?" Morgan holstered the .45 and grabbed her arms. "There's blood on the floor!"

"My foot." She gasped as his fingers dug into her flesh. "I stepped on some glass."

Before she knew what he was about, she felt herself being lifted in the air, and for a brief second she thought she was fainting. Then she crashed into the hard muscles of his chest, and his rigid arms held her tight against him.

Instinctively, her hands caught at his shirt-front and her arms wound tightly around his neck. Dizzy and terrified, she laid her head on his shoulder, her warm breath sighing in his ear.

"Oh, God," he muttered, trying to control the foolish things he was feeling. He'd dreamed about holding her this way, her nightgown hitched up, her red hair loose and flowing, her lips brushing his neck. In the dream, naturally, she'd been welcoming him as her lover.

Reality was very different. She was frightened and hurt, and had little notion of his lascivious thoughts. She had no idea how often he thought about having her in his arms, no idea how badly he wanted to turn his head right now and find her lips.

With more energy than necessary, he plucked her arms from his neck and plopped her down on the bed, inadvertently catching the hem of her flannel nightgown on his gun belt and exposing the whole of her thigh. And even more, if the truth be told.

With a startled cry, she grabbed the night-gown and pulled it down, her cheeks flaming with embarrassment. Mortified at what had happened, and more than a bit aroused by her nakedness, Morgan simply stared at her. Then he saw blood seeping onto the sheet, drop by crimson drop.

Cursing, he found a bowl and the teakettle, and poured in some of the tepid water, taking his own handkerchief to clean the wound. In one part of his mind, it registered that Norah wore nothing whatsoever beneath the soft flannel that outlined slender thighs and full, ripe breasts. It would be so easy to strip the garment off.

Almost as if her body responded to his innermost thoughts, her nipples hardened against the fabric. Morgan quickly knelt beside her to tend the cut, sloshing water over her foot and onto the sheet.

"Sorry," he mumbled, lifting her foot higher to see if all the glass was out.

Norah was trying modestly to keep her knees together and her legs covered. "If you wash that much more, I won't have any skin left."

He glanced up at the waspish tone of her voice and chuckled. Only a hammer and nails could hold the nightgown down tighter. Her hair was in a tangle, her cheeks flushed, and her eyes just daring him to step out of line. She was gorgeous! The wave of desire that hit him nearly knocked him senseless.

The door banged open again. Norah gave a frightened cry, and Morgan jumped to his feet, gun in hand.

"What's going on in here?" a voice demanded.

"Is my prisoner all right, Myrtis?" Morgan asked, surprised that he was still able to speak sensibly. He'd been on the verge of pushing Norah down on the bed and loving her till morning's light.

"He's still unconscious. Ya pack a mean punch, Ironman. What happened t'her?"

"Mrs. Welsh stepped on some broken glass. I think the wound is clean, but you better take a look at it while I see about boarding up the window. It's getting cold in here." Morgan was anything but cold. However, he realized that anybody who cared to look inside could have an unobstructed view of the building.

"You jist rest, honey," Myrtis said pleasantly. "I'll get you fixed up real quick. That cut looks bad but it ain't deep. No, sir, it ain't. It'll be a nuisance 'cause it'll hurt like a son-of-a-gun to walk on. Morgan, fer chrissakes, sweep up that glass! That crunching is gittin' on my nerves."

A tiny smile touched Norah's lips. Morgan mumbled something she didn't hear but was certain was very rude. Myrtis meant well, but she was as rough as a cob.

"When are you gonna think about gittin' yourself another man?" she asked Norah.

"Myrtis!" Morgan was outraged. Broken glass clattered off the dustpan into an empty crate used for rubbish. "Let it be."

Myrtis, however, had no intention of letting the subject drop. "Eastern ways don't work out here. This girl needs a man t'protect her against such toughs as Denning. He was comin' in here tonight to have his way with her."

Morgan gritted his teeth at the thought. He remembered the rage that had overcome him at the thought of Darby Denning breaking into Norah's house and hurting her. He'd hit the man far harder than necessary to subdue him, that was certain. The thought of another man touching her nearly drove him crazy.

"A woman needs a man," Myrtis insisted.

"How come you don't have one?" Norah asked innocently.

Morgan began to laugh, and the old woman cackled at the joke.

"Girl, I've buried three husbands, and that's enough! Not one of 'em was worth the powder to blow 'em to hell, if ya wanta know the truth. But I loved 'em, and grieved over 'em when they kicked off. I don't want another. 'Course nobody's breaking down my door lustin' after my body, neither." She pushed her walnut-brown hair out of her eyes and sighed. "I guess there ain't much left for me t' do here. You keep it clean and don't wear shoes unless you go out."

Norah knew how to take care of herself as well as Myrtis, but she minded her manners and didn't say so. She knew the older woman meant well, no matter how cantankerous she sounded.

"If you'll wait a minute, Myrt, I'll walk you home."

"I don't need no escort."

"Don't argue so much," he said, hammering the last nail into the board on the window. "There. That should keep out the wind till you get the glass replaced."

Norah stood up, wincing a bit as her foot touched the wood floor. "Thank you, Sheriff. I appreciate all your help."

"Don't mention it," he said.

For a moment they stood gazing at each other.

"Well, what are we waitin' fer?" Myrtis asked.

"Nothing," Morgan snapped. "Good night, Mrs. Welsh."

"Sheriff."

At the door he hesitated. It was apparent from the condition of the doorknob that the door couldn't be locked. "Myrtis, you wait outside. I'll push that trunk against the door and go out the back way."

"That really isn't necessary, Sheriff," Norah protested. "It's only a few hours till dawn."

"It *is* necessary," he told her as he shut the door on Myrtis's back and walked over to the trunk, hefting it with ease. "She's right, you know. Out here a young single woman attracts all kinds of attention, because women are so scarce."

"I do nothing to attract attention," she insisted, believing what she said.

He was smiling as he walked toward her and stopped, taking her firm little chin in his hand. "Oh, yes, you do," he said softly, his eyes alight with danger. "You're beautiful, and you're alone." He leaned forward and brushed the tip of her nose with his lips. "That drives men crazy."

She gasped at the utter impudence of his action and his remark.

Morgan didn't appear to notice. He turned and strode to the back door, his footsteps loud against the wood of the floor.

"It's been a month since Cal died," he said as he opened the door. "That's time enough for folks out here. It won't be long before men come courting."

She was shocked—because of what he said, and because of the emotion she saw blazing in his eyes. Sheriff Treyhan desired her, and he was telling her in every way but words. If she'd had any doubt before, his burning look dispelled it. She had no idea what to say or how to respond.

"You'll need to lock the door behind me," he said, walking out and shutting it with a bang.

"That's nonsense," she muttered as she turned the key in the lock. "East or West, proper behavior doesn't change."

Nevertheless, it was more than an hour, and two cups of tea later, that she drifted off into a fitful sleep. At first she blamed it on the freight trains that thundered through town, shaking the building and contributing to her restlessness. But that wasn't the cause of her insomnia. The words Myrtis had said, and which Morgan confirmed afterward, kept playing themselves over in her mind. *Men will come courting.*

"Well, not for long," she grumbled. "Not when they see the shape I'm in."

The men came at seven in the morning.

Norah never relished being at a disadvantage, and opening the front door to a crowd of men while she stood in her nightrobe and slippers definitely put her off her stride. Her head ached, her foot throbbed, and she was a bit testy—certainly not at her best.

"We're here to fix the window," Conrad Putney told her. A lean, leathery man with silver hair, although he wasn't yet thirty, Putney had been hired only days before as Treyhan's new deputy, replacing Cal.

He looked Norah over with insolent eyes, and she took an immediate dislike to him.

"It's very early," she said. "I wasn't expecting anyone so soon."

Putney stepped into the doorway, brushing against Norah's breasts, and instantly she moved backward. His smile was positively nasty.

"Now that you're here, you might as well do the job," she said with ill grace. More than anything she wanted to take the broom to Deputy Putney's backside.

The men ambled into the house, apparently enjoying her disheveled appearance and the unkept bed.

"Sheriff Treyhan sent us over. To make sure you're safe from any further harm."

The words should have been comforting, but something in Deputy Putney's flat gray eyes made her skin crawl. Norah fought the impulse to pull her robe tighter around her. He meant to frighten her, she knew with absolute certainty. Her mouth went dry with sudden fear, but instinct told her not to let him see it. He'd be more dangerous if he knew she was afraid of him.

She fixed him with a cool gaze. "Thank you, Deputy. It was kind of the sheriff to send you."

By the time the broken glass was removed from the windowsill, Norah had managed to get out to the backhouse and slip a dress over her nightgown. She absolutely refused to be leered at any longer. It only emphasized the warning she'd had last night.

Feeling the need to get away for a spell, she

strolled down the alley to the Holbrook House to look at the supply of samples brought in by Mr. Pierce, the clothing man from St. Joe, Missouri.

The trip was a mistake. Not only were the clothes made of sleazy material and several seasons out of style, Mr. Pierce was a leering, groping menace.

"Behave yourself!" Norah snapped, after the third time she evaded his hands. "Or I'll scream for the sheriff."

Mr. Pierce looked downright petulant, but he did back off. Something in her eyes told him she meant exactly what she said. He figured no bit of lace was worth a run-in with the law.

Mrs. Wilson walked in at that moment, and Mr. Pierce gave her his best smile and began to extol his goods.

Norah took the opportunity to make her escape. She wasn't even out into the lobby when she heard Mrs. Wilson gasp.

"Willie," Norah said to Mrs. Wilson's son so that everybody in the lobby could hear. "I think your mother needs you. Mr. Pierce is having some difficulty keeping his hands to himself."

Willie looked bewildered, but the desk clerk and several hotel guests immediately rushed to the door of the parlor where the clothing was displayed.

Feeling fortunate to have avoided Mr. Pierce's sweaty paws, and in truth, more cheerful than she'd felt since she arrived, Norah took the long way home. She stopped at the bakery to purchase a loaf of bread, exchanging small talk with Bruna Schriener, the baker's round-faced wife.

"Der's been more rustling," Bruna told her. "Da sheriff yust picked up some sammiches—he likes da corned beef." She beamed at Norah. "I put it down myself."

Norah saw Morgan ride out from the livery stable, heading toward the river at a gallop. She hoped Deputy Putney and his men were finished with her window. She didn't want them in her house when Morgan was out of town.

After the bakery she stopped to browse at Wilson's Mercantile, just in case Putney was lingering at her shop. She treated herself to some lemon drops, a sweet she adored but seldom indulged in. As she was paying her pennies, she noticed a parcel of shiny blue satin that Mr. Wilson had started to wrap.

Only one woman in Holbrook would wear such a bold shade—Mazie. Norah imagined there'd be a tapping on her back door in a day or two. A smile touched her mouth as she turned to leave. She and Mazie had reached an understanding of sorts. Mazie needed her skills, and she needed the extra income the saloon girl provided. They kept their business discreet. As Mazie said, the busybodies didn't need to know.

Norah was washing her new window when Mordecai Smith stopped his wagon in front of her store. The Mormon, his three oldest sons, a smaller Indian boy, and a huge, mousy-haired woman of about thirty-five all got out and came to her door. Norah realized nothing she had planned to do would be accomplished that morning, so she gave up with good grace. She opened the door to Smith's knock.

"My sons and I will build your partition," Smith said without preamble. "I promised Calvin."

Norah didn't know what he meant but moved aside as the blond rawboned youths and the young Indian began to unload lumber off the wagon and carry it into the building.

"I'm Dolly," the woman said shyly.

Never had a name been so unlikely. There was nothing whatsoever pretty or delicate about Dolly. She was as ugly as a mud fence, poor soul—one of the creatures God forgot to finish. She stood well over six feet tall, with a burly body and coarse, mannish features. Her hair was thin and wispy, her skin blotchy, her eyes small and red-rimmed.

"Pleased to meet you, Dolly. I'm Norah Welsh. I was about to make some mint tea. It's been a difficult morning, and I thought I needed a moment to collect myself. Would you care for some?"

Dolly blushed and nodded, seeming surprised at the offer.

Norah ushered her to the table. Dolly sat with her hands clenched tightly while the fragrant mint leaves steeped. She was silent, but her sharp eyes touched everything in the room.

"It's not much of a place, is it?"

Dolly glanced at Norah's face. She gulped and then spoke cautiously. "It could do with a bit of work." Then she blushed fiery red.

Norah busily poured the pale green liquid. "It needs more than a bit. But I think if I keep at it, it will be a comfortable place to live."

"I sew."

The words were so softly spoken that Norah could barely make them out. "That's nice," she replied, not knowing what else was expected. "Sewing has always brought me pleasure."

Dolly nodded fervently.

They sat quietly, each with her own thoughts, drinking their tea while the boys hammered in the background.

Finally, Mordecai told his sons he was going to the mercantile and gave them instructions about what to do while he was out. "Isaac, you do Joseph's share. He's coming with me." He motioned the Indian lad to come down off the ladder and accompany him.

"Do you need help?" Dolly asked, as soon as the front door closed. She still clenched and unclenched her large, workworn hands, but her face suddenly became animated.

"What sort of help?" Norah asked, curious about the sudden change in the woman.

"Sewing."

Norah didn't know much about Mormons, although she'd heard a thing or two since she came to town. She did not believe Mordecai Smith would encourage any of his wives to work out of the home.

Dolly glanced at the boys, who had slackened their pace since their father left and were joking quietly among themselves. "Cephus, when will you be done?"

"Won't be long," the tallest boy answered. He brushed a hank of blond hair out of his eyes, and gave his younger brother a little push. "If Heber does his share."

Heber, who was feeling a bit cocky, pushed back.

The partition was a floor-to-ceiling wall, finished on one side, in the center of the large room to separate the shop front from the living quarters. Each end had been left open as a walkway. Cephus and Heber were shoving each other through the right doorway.

"Don't tease, you two," Dolly admonished, then turned back to Norah, her eyes filled with hope.

"I'm sorry. I don't have extra work." Norah saw the sudden tears before Dolly had a chance to lower her eyes, and wondered what could be happening in Dolly's life that made working out of the home so important to her. "But I have been thinking about fixing a changing area for customers over in that corner. I could use help putting up curtains and painting boxes. I'd pay for the help, of course."

"I could do that!"

"Will your husband let you?"

"I'll tell him you asked me. He owes Cal the price of a well, and he don't want to let go of the cash money, now that Cal is gone. He's a tight one, he is. I think I'll remind him of the debt. He wouldn't want to cheat a widow."

Astonished as she was at the information, Norah had no intention of being part of an untruth—one was enough for a lifetime—so she asked, "Dolly, would you be so kind as to help me fix up my store to better accommodate customers?"

"I'd love to." Dolly's smile lit up her whole face.

"I say the old bastard skipped out on us." Harcourt Barr looked morosely out onto the street, unhappy to watch yet another afternoon slip by without any word.

"He wouldn't do that," Dowie Johnston protested. "He's the one what figured out the plan to rob that old house."

Harcourt made a rude noise. "And he's the one what's got the gold, asshole! And we're stuck in Philadelphia."

Dowie looked affronted. He was a small, nervous man who bobbed around like a bird, picking at things. "Omar wouldn't skip out on us. He's a good man. I trust him."

"You're an idiot."

Fat Tony Roscoe didn't enter into the discussion, which had been going on for more than three weeks, ever since Omar Goodfellow failed to show up at the Philadelphia Museum of Art for their Friday morning appointment. The argument had escalated when the white-haired old rascal didn't appear at the backup meeting the following Tuesday afternoon at Fairmount Park.

Fat Tony moved softly around the tiny kitchen, preparing their afternoon meal. It was late and he was getting hungry. The kitchen left a lot to be desired, but Fat Tony was a genius with food.

Antone "Fat Tony" Roscoe was rare among thieves because he was indeed portly, bumbling, and good-natured. To outsiders, he appeared slow-moving and slow-witted, far more interested in food than money. But this ploy, together with his appearance, made him an excellent crook. Being underestimated kept him in business.

The three men had gathered in an unremarkable brick row house that resembled so many other dwellings in Philadelphia. It had been Omar's idea for them to split up after robbing the Hudson River estate and meet far away from the sharp eyes of the New York police.

Fat Tony didn't see anything unusual about the plan. He'd teamed up with Omar on a number of heists and confidence games; Omar was brilliant, and his plans had always kept Fat Tony in money and out of jail.

Transportation being what it was and crooks having a tendency to get into jams, Omar always devised plans that took the unexpected into consideration. So when Omar didn't show at the museum the first time, Fat Tony wasn't worried. He'd merely shrugged, rented the row house, and repeated the instructions. But now, he, too, was beginning to worry. Had something happened to Omar?

"One more week," he told the feuding pair, slicing a loaf of bread filled with sausage, onions, and peppers. "If he don't show by then, we'll head west. I know all his hangouts. We'll find him."

"I don't give a bat's bunghole about the old man," Harcourt snapped, grabbing up his plate and going back to the window. "I just want the gold."

The train was on time for a change, and Mordecai Smith had gone to the depot to check on a shipment he was expecting. Norah had talked him into coming back the following week to build a counter for her shop and had mentioned needing a woman to do a few things. Mordecai had immediately volunteered Dolly's help.

Norah was annoyed because he'd done so without asking his wife, so she took perverse pleasure in knowing she and Dolly had fooled him. At times Mordecai Smith reminded her a great deal of her father.

The Smiths were just loading up their wagon to go back home when Jimmy came running down the wooden sidewalk, calling to Norah.

"There's a crate for you at the depot," he told her, "and it's *this* big." He stretched his skinny arms as far as they could go and wiggled his fingers.

"My sons will bring it here for you, Mrs. Welsh," Mordecai said gallantly. "We're always glad to help a lady."

Norah broke into a fit of coughing when she saw the same stunned look cross the face of every member of his family. Yes, indeed, the man was very much like Tommy Kelly.

"Do what your father says," Dolly instructed the boys.

Fifteen minutes later, when the train had puffed away and the townsfolk had nothing more interesting to do than peer in her door and window, there was quite an interesting sight to see. Norah stood scarlet-faced in the middle of her shop, gaping at an enormous brass bed.

Morgan saw the cluster of people milling around Norah's place and hastened his steps, fearing that something terrible had happened to her. The first thing he saw, as he shouldered his way to the door, was Mordecai Smith looking at Norah like a lovesick bull.

Then he saw the bed, gleaming in the light. It was the biggest bed he'd ever seen, and so shiny it almost put his eyes out. Evidently the Smith boys had assembled it right where they uncrated it.

"Oh, my God," he muttered. What he'd told Norah last night about men coming to call on her hadn't been an exaggeration. He hadn't imagined it would begin immediately, though. But if word got out she had a bed big enough for one hell of a romp, men would be lining up to help her fill it.

"Well, it finally came," he said loudly, stepping into the room. "It's a beauty, isn't it? And roomy enough for a big ox like me."

In unison, everyone turned to stare at him. He simply went on talking, hoping he could change things, give Norah a little more time before she had to deal with Mordecai and the others.

"Looks like that drummer got the orders mixed up, though. He's such a windbag, I thought he might. Cal ordered a little surprise for Norah. And I ordered the bed for myself."

Mordecai looked positively deflated.

"Smith, do your boys have time to haul this thing across the tracks to my place? They can leave it on the porch."

Mordecai tugged on his beard, weighing the time spent against the goodwill gained, and finally nodded.

The boys laughingly loaded the gleaming bed frame on top of their supplies and climbed into the wagon. Dolly didn't wait for anybody's help getting in, and nobody offered.

"I'll be back," Morgan said quietly as he walked out the door. "I'll help you clean up the mess."

Norah was about to close the door when Frank Reed came bustling up.

"Mrs. Welsh, I heard you got a new bed in on the train, today."

"No," she answered, thinking she dearly needed to lie down for a few minutes. "Sheriff Treyhan got a new one."

"Oh." Frank was obviously disappointed. His jacket pockets had been ripped, as if someone had given them a yank in a moment of anger, and they were flapping in the wind. "Well, I heard someone shot out your window recently and tried to break in. What happened?"

"Someone shot out my window and tried to break in. If you hurry, you can catch up with the sheriff and get the details." She closed the door before he could say anything else.

*   *   *

She was lying with her feet up and a cold cloth over her eyes when Morgan opened the back door and stepped in.

"Are you asleep?"

"No. I'm lying here quietly having a tizzy fit! Did you find your cattle rustlers?"

"No sign of them. Are you mad at me?"

She didn't pretend to misunderstand him. "For taking the bed?" She removed the cloth so she could look at him. "Absolutely not. I don't want the entire town speculating on why I need a bed that big. Or if I might be interested in sharing it."

"A furniture salesman came to town right after Cal got your wire saying you were coming. I imagine Calvin was in the right mood to buy, and the fellow took advantage. I wonder what else he ordered?"

"There's no telling. Calvin Welsh didn't have a lick of sense when he got to dreaming. I only hope whatever else he bought was practical."

Morgan thought about telling her exactly how practical a good, wide bed could be, but then changed his mind. She didn't look like she could stand many more shocks in one day. He figured he'd retain her goodwill by keeping his fantasies to himself.

"How's your foot?"

"Better. Thank you for asking."

He smiled at her. He'd already heard about her and the clothing man, and he'd convinced the gent to move on. She was one hell of a woman, there was no question about that. "I'll look in the crate for the packing receipt, and pay you for the bed."

"You don't have to do that."

"Of course I do. That way it will be an honest deal. I'll be happy to sleep in a bed long enough so my feet don't hang over the end, and you'll get some extra money."

A pounding on the door interrupted any protest she planned to make.

Cephus Smith stood in the doorway. "Sheriff Treyhan, is Mrs. Welsh here?"

Norah came around the partition to the door.

Cephus nodded to her. "Ma'am. We picked up another packing crate at the depot that was meant for you. Dolly noticed it a bit outta town and made Pa bring it back."

The boys lugged a very heavy box into the shop and then hurried out, anxious to be on their way home.

Morgan locked the door and pulled the curtains against any nosy passersby.

"I'm afraid to look," Norah told him.

"Could it be worse than a brass bed, with the whole town watching?"

She began to laugh, thinking how horrified she'd been when she first saw that bed. "No. No, not ever."

His muscles strained against the fabric of his shirt. Nails shrieked and wood cracked. After that, he had the crate open within a matter of moments.

"Oh my!" she gasped, unable to think of anything else when its contents were finally exposed. She covered her mouth with her hands, then burst into tears.

Standing in the middle of her sewing shop was a brand new Singer sewing machine. A final gift from Cal.

6

Bunky Lindstrom had few of the softer emotions known to mankind. Sharp-faced, hard-eyed, and lean to the point of emaciation, he was savage in both appearance and temperament. A man of seething hatreds and violent mood swings, he had no friends and few acquaintances who were willing to tolerate him. But the one person he came close to loving was his aunt, Winnie Ralston.

Aunt Winnie had rescued Bunky from a brutal stepfather who had beaten his mother to death. She'd taken him into her home and treated him better than anybody ever had in his eight years of life. Unfortunately by then he'd been tortured, abused, and molested; so he trusted no one, male or female.

Aunt Winnie fed him, comforted him, and poured out all the affection and devotion a scrawny spinster could possess. In return he had come to care for her as much as he was capable of caring for anyone. Like a beaten dog, he wasn't capable of much besides seething rage. Yet he felt a degree of fondness for Aunt Winnie. In fact, since he was a teenager and was forced to leave their Kansas home or be hanged for assaulting a young girl, he had managed to visit her every two or three years for no other reason than because he missed her.

So he'd been damned surprised when he'd slipped into town a month ago to discover she'd married a widower and moved west to the Arizona Territory. After all, she must have been fifty. And she'd never even been passably pretty.

Certain that the widower had somehow tricked his unsuspecting aunt into marriage for her money—not that she had much—Bunky had decided to go to Arizona and rescue her.

Nathan Ralston had come as a shock. Only in the mirror had Bunky ever seen such cold eyes. Over a bottle of rye, Bunky learned enough about Ralston's past following the War Between the States to understand that the older man had been a border raider back then. Another name for a cold-blooded killer.

When he saw how happy Aunt Winnie was in her neat little house on the north side of Holbrook's train tracks, however, Bunky revised his plan to throttle Ralston. He'd bide his time. The house and Winnie's clothes—Bunky observed with some confusion that his aunt looked better than he'd ever seen her—gave him the idea Ralston had a bundle of money stashed away.

Bunky wasn't fool enough to let an opportunity for easy money pass.

"Morris," Aunt Winnie said, calling him by the name nobody else dared to use. "Nathan has to make a trip down south. Some business in the Pleasant Valley. I hear there's some trouble down there between cattlemen and sheepherders."

Bunky ate the food she put before him even though food had little appeal for him. He always ate what she fixed, though, because he knew it made her happy to feed him. "When's he going?"

"Right after Christmas, if the snow holds off. Folks say this has been a dry year."

"Oh."

"Mighten you go with him? Make certain he don't come to no harm? I worry so."

Bunky looked at her soft brown eyes. She would never be a pretty woman, but the lavender wool dress she wore was well made and flattered her. She looked so sweet and trusting. He didn't have the heart to disappoint her.

"Guess I don't have nothing else to do. If it don't snow. I ain't going over the Mogollon Rim in the snow."

"Good. That would be downright dangerous. I won't let Nathan go either, if it's snowing."

A light flickered in Bunky's hard eyes. It was the closest he ever came to amusement. The idea of Aunt Winnie controlling a killer like Nathan Ralston was enough to make a man roll on the floor laughing. Only Bunky didn't laugh. He didn't seem to know how.

"After Christmas," Bunky said. "I'll stay here till then."

"I'll tell Nathan," Aunt Winnie said. "He'll be right glad for the company."

Morgan pulled his coat closer around him as he waited for the clattering freight train to pass. Patience was one thing he'd learned since moving to Holbrook—he waited for at least one train every day.

There seemed to be more trains going through all the time, and more trains stopping. Holbrook had become the fastest-growing freight station along the A & P Railroad.

He'd even heard rumors that the big cattle conglomerates like Aztec planned to expand. The thought made him frown. The stockyard was constantly full, and the beeves were breaking the fences and running wild. And then there was the rustling. Morgan shook his head.

Not only was his job getting tougher every time some petty thief stole a cow, but he could already see how the huge herds were affecting the grassland. And the river, which had been crystal clear when he first arrived, was often full of mud. He wondered if the fish would survive till he had a free day to go fishing.

Annoyed at the length of the train, he began to pace. "Why hell, there could be a major crime going on right now, and here I am, waiting for the damned end of the train."

It wasn't much of a joke. The increased freight business meant more traffic congestion and accidents, fistfights, and a noticeable rise in tension between cattle and sheep men.

There was also a meaner breed of desperado coming to town. Bad Bunky was one of several young toughs just itching for trouble. What worried Morgan most was that his deputy, Conrad Putney, seemed more than a little friendly with the wild bunch. Morgan was afraid of losing control of the town. If things went sour, he'd need to have Putney on his side.

The caboose rumbled past, and Morgan stepped across the tracks. Frank Reed was coming toward him. The editor's hat had been smashed almost flat.

"Morning, Frank," Morgan said as he strode past. He didn't ask what had happened to the hat. He truly didn't want to know.

The morning passed quickly, and it was nearly eleven before Morgan gave any thought to leaving the warmth of the stove in his office and making the rounds in town. He'd gotten to the office late and had spent more than an hour catching up on some paperwork. At least he'd attempted to do paperwork. Mostly he'd thought about Norah.

"And I'm driving myself crazy!"

The words echoed off the wall. He was damned glad the jail was empty for once. Even with the partition between his desk and the cells, any occupant could have heard him. The news that he was talking to himself would have spread through the town like wildfire.

But the words were nothing less than the truth. He was going mad thinking about her. Last night he'd dreamed about her, a dream so real he could still taste the flavor of her kiss. He could still feel the satin of her skin. He couldn't remember ever wanting any woman as much as he wanted Norah. Certainly not Camilla.

He was surprised how long it had been since he'd thought about her. It had been close to a year since Camilla had left town. Morgan had been so disillusioned with her lies that all but a few of his feelings had ended right then. Only the anger remained, and the wariness.

Before she'd come to town, before she'd welcomed him into her bed, Camilla had worked in San Francisco, fleecing rich old men of their money and pride. Morgan had only heard the tale by chance when another law enforcement officer, an old friend of his from Monterey, had come through on the train and had recognized Camilla at the hotel. Naturally he informed Morgan about her and told of an incident where the pigeon had killed himself after his pretty young lover stole all his money. After a violent argument with Morgan, Camilla had taken the next eastbound train to Albuquerque and immediately found a husband. Morgan pitied the poor sap, knowing how close he'd come to being in the man's shoes.

Morgan had been with only one other woman since Camilla left—a singer who was traveling across the country, entertaining in small towns, bringing a brief spate of "culture" to the Wild West.

He kept telling himself that was why he wanted Norah so badly, because it had been so long since he'd been with a woman. But he knew that wasn't the truth.

*   *   *

Norah noticed even the most hardened of folk became curiously sentimental as Christmas approached. The roughest adventurers grew friendly. The most brazen women turned demure. The whole town changed as the days ticked by. Everybody waited in growing anticipation.

She was no exception. She'd wept into her pillow more than once lately, wishing she was back in the big Indiana farmhouse with Jean Matthews and Mr. Robert, helping prepare the enormous amounts of food and decorations they traditionally fixed to share with friends, as well as the baskets for the needy.

In a moment of extreme weakness she even admitted to missing her father. Although she had little use for his lazy Irish ways, she had to concede he was a charming rogue when he set his mind to be. She missed her family terribly, especially the small children. And it would have been a comfort to have her mother near her right now. A woman who'd borne thirteen children and showed no signs of stopping would know what the process was all about. Norah wished she had that knowledge.

But it wasn't to be, so there was no sense tormenting herself. Instead, she threw herself into a fury of gift making. The townspeople had been so kind to her the past two months, and she intended to give every one of them a token of her thanks.

As she sat at the cloth-covered table near the little black stove compiling a Christmas list, she thought of how many friends she'd made in Holbrook. Clarabelle, Myrtis, and Dolly had become especially close. And Morgan. He might make her uncomfortable with his sharp tongue and his hot glances, but she counted him as a true friend.

A flush of heat touched her cheekbones as she thought of him. Not a day had gone by since Cal's death when Morgan hadn't stopped to check on her. And sometimes late at night, when she was fighting the demons of fear and loneliness and lit the lamp to soothe her troubled mind, he came to the back door when his shift was over and asked for a cup of hot tea. He'd chat a bit, telling her funny stories about his life or the town, until she relaxed.

Then he'd leave the way he'd entered, so nobody would gossip. Norah appreciated his concern, and the fact that he'd never been the least bit forward. On a few occasions, when his guard was down, she'd seen the longing in his dark eyes, so she knew beyond a doubt he had feelings for her, but his behavior on those long dark nights was above reproach.

She tried not to think of how important his visits had become to her. Or how she, too, in a few moments of weakness, longed for something more than tea and tenderness.

"Now, isn't that ridiculous in my condition!" She forced her mind away from wayward thoughts of hot kisses and back to the list she was making.

It was quite long. Not only did the gifts represent her gratitude, they kept her hands and mind busy during the long evenings. Coming up with ideas and supplies for gifts in a place as remote as Holbrook was a challenge.

Fortunately, she had skill and imagination, as well as a trunk full of fabric and frills. She'd just discovered a dozen plain silk handkerchiefs in the trunk, a forgotten gift from Sonny. When he'd first given them to her, she'd treasured them above gold, thinking them too precious to remove from the wrapping paper, and later she couldn't bear the pain associated with the delicate silk so she'd hidden them away. Now she was thankful to have the exquisite squares to edge and embroider with her fine needlework. They'd make lovely gifts.

For Clarabelle, she made a simple lace collar and cuffs, so very different from the flounces and ruffles the older woman normally wore. Norah thought the quietly elegant design would be very flattering and hoped Clarabelle would wear them. For Myrtis she made a red calico apron, and a blue one for Dolly. She knitted woolen scarves for Ferdie Wattron, who went out at night, and Frank Reed, who always looked chilled now that winter had arrived, and a cap and gloves for Digger.

But she didn't know what to give Morgan. She knew he'd also be sharing the Christmas meal with Clarabelle and Ferdie, so her gift needed to be something she could take to the holiday table. She longed to make him a fine linen shirt, imagining the fabric stretching over his wide shoulders, but she decided it would be far too personal a gift.

Instead she monogrammed his initials on a linen handkerchief and wrapped it around the last novel she'd read to Cal. In her heart, she knew that the sheriff would treasure the silly, melodramatic book as much as she did, because Cal had been such a dear friend.

Deciding she might try to make some taffy on her little stove, she threw on her cloak and headed over to Wilson's Mercantile to buy sugar.

"Did you see the paper?" Willie Wilson asked.

He was a plain fellow a few years older than Norah, but she often suspected he was a bit simple, since his parents told him everything to do and he obeyed without question.

"No," she answered, wondering what Frank had done now. "I haven't seen today's edition."

"There's a reward," Willie told her, his pale brown eyes round with delight. "For a sea serpent."

Norah blinked. "What?"

Willie chuckled at her astonishment and grabbed the newspaper from the counter. "P. T. Barnum offers twenty thousand dollars for skin of a sea serpent," he read. Then he laid the paper back down. "Ain't that the beatenest thing?"

"Yes," Norah answered.

"Twenty thousand dollars! That's the biggest reward I ever heard of."

"Willie, you dust those tins of Dr. Pierce's Favorite Prescription and make room on the shelf for the Golden Medical Discovery," a voice called from the back.

"Yes, Mama."

Beatrice Wilson bustled in from the living quarters behind the store and shoved the feather duster into Willie's hand. She shook her head at Norah. "That dratted Frank Reed. Imagine putting such a story on the first page! The whole town's agaggle over the reward. What fools! We're hundreds of miles from the ocean, but everybody's goin' on, arguing how to spend the money. Darn Frank's ornery hide! Do you need something, honey?"

"A pound of sugar," Norah replied. She didn't understand why Mrs. Wilson was in such a tizzy.

Frank had a right to print what he wished. The story about Barnum's reward was silly, but that was no reason to keep it out of the paper. Besides, people had to make their own entertainment in such an isolated spot. She suspected Frank understood that.

"I can't bake much on my stove, but I thought I could try some Christmas candy."

"I love homemade candy," Beatrice said wistfully. "My mother made such wonderful things for Christmas when I was little. That was the happiest time of my life. She died when I was eight, and I was sent to live with relatives."

"How lucky you are to have good memories," Norah said, remembering her own bleak childhood.

Morgan left the Holbrook House after consuming a particularly greasy lunch of some undefinable meat and gravy.

"Howdy, Sheriff."

"Digger. You're not going in there to eat, are you?"

The undertaker gave him a questioning look. "Must be bad today."

"Try the café."

Digger shook his head. "That's where I ate yesterday."

A wagon loaded with game pulled up to the front of the hotel and three dirty, blood-splattered hunters crawled down.

Angus MacKay came out the wide door as two of the hunters started to unload a huge elk carcass. "Nae here, ye fools! Take it back to the shed by the kitchen, nae through the lobby!"

"Kinda turns yer stomach, don't it?" Digger said as the wagon pulled away.

Morgan, whose stomach had been queasy since his lunch, hastened to agree. They started up the street.

"Are you going to Clarabelle's for Christmas?" Digger asked.

Morgan grinned. "Course I am. She puts on the biggest feed."

"'Cepting for Angus." Digger frowned at the idea of spending a holiday with the penny-pinching Scot. "Eatin' at the hotel with a bunch of drifters and drummers ain't the same as havin' a family meal."

They sidestepped a Hashknife rider who appeared to be in a hurry to get to the Brunswick Hotel.

"Maybe Bruna Schriener will make me a sandwich," Digger said.

They started up the back way to the bakery,

only to see the hunters again. Angus MacKay and the town butcher, Charlie Cook, stood in the middle of the alley embroiled in a loud argument about who was buying the game in the wagon. The hunters watched, passing a jug back and forth between them.

"Look at those dumb bastards," Digger said. "I'll just bet they contracted with both the hotel and the butcher shop for the game they brought in."

"Too much of Eldon's rot-gut probably pickled their brains," Morgan said. "But as long as they're not selling stolen cattle, it isn't any of my business."

"I ain't hungry. I'll spend the next month wondering if the meat I'm eating is as dirty as the vermin what shot it. Let's take this here obituary over to Frank."

They cut through the alley between Cook's Meat Shop and The Cottage, where they came upon the manager from the Aztec Cattle Company in conversation with two eastern gents.

"This is the one saloon in town where a gentleman can get a good glass of whiskey," the Aztec manager was saying.

"My God, how do you stand this place, Martin?" The easterner who spoke looked horrified.

"It's going to make me a rich man in a short time, Theo." Martin nudged a chicken off the top step with his boot. "That's worth a little inconvenience."

The other two did not look convinced.

"They're bloodsuckers," Digger muttered. "Ruining the land because of their greed."

He and Morgan stepped out onto the sidewalk

just in time to see Mrs. Wilson buttonhole Frank Reed.

Morgan groaned as he watched her whack the editor with a rolled-up paper.

"Are you going to save him?" Digger asked.

"I save him at least three times a week. He can handle Beatrice Wilson."

Then a man's scream ripped through the air.

Thundering down Central Avenue toward them came a wild-eyed team of four horses hitched to a careening wagon. Runaways! A frantic man ran after the wagon, yelling at the top of his lungs. If anything, he only incited the horses to further mania.

Morgan dashed out into the street, dodging a rider on a black gelding who seemed oblivious to the commotion. At that moment the tongue of the wagon dropped to the ground and was driven into the dirt with a terrible force. The sharp crack of breaking wood could be heard above the voices of the people who'd turned to watch the drama. Morgan's stomach lurched when he saw the two wheelhorses thrown to the ground.

Already crazed with fear, the two lead horses continued to pull, attempting to drag along their fallen harness-mates. They only succeeded in drawing the wagon up on top of the flailing beasts. Morgan reached them at that moment, with Digger only seconds behind.

"Dear God, there's a child on that wagon seat!" Digger cried.

Morgan turned his head in time to see the fellow who'd been chasing the seat pluck a little girl from the seat and fall weeping to his knees. The child, who couldn't have been more than three, seemed completely unruffled.

"You men! Come over here and help," Morgan ordered. "Let's get this team unhitched before another train comes along." All he could think about was how glad he'd be when the snow came and people stayed home to tend their fires.

The sky was dark and overcast, and the wind was blowing cold and hard when Norah left her house to walk the short distance to Clarabelle's, carrying her basket of food and gifts. Christmas dinner was to be served at three, but she wanted to arrive a few minutes early in case Clarabelle needed any help.

She'd dressed with care in a black wool dress she'd made especially for the festive occasion. None of her other good clothes would fit over her ever-increasing figure, even the things she'd let out at the seams. Though fitted and bustled in the back, the new dress was loose at the waist, and she wore it with an apron that matched the heavy ivory lace on the jabot and cuffs.

Norah had spent hours agonizing over whether or not she should wear the apron. It concealed her pregnancy almost as much as the work aprons she wore. She knew it was dishonest to keep the baby's existence hidden, but she didn't want the holiday spoiled by the reaction she feared her friends might have. What if they shunned her? She didn't think she could stand their rejection on top of the pain of Cal's death.

So in the end, she had tied on the apron, grasping this one extra day of happiness before the truth about her condition was known.

She saw Morgan coming toward her across the street and waved.

"Merry Christmas, Sheriff Treyhan."

"And a Merry Christmas to you, Mrs. Welsh. Allow me to take your basket."

"Thank you." She tried not to notice how handsome he looked in his good black suit. Nor did she acknowledge that he'd recently bathed with fine lavender soap. A lady wasn't supposed to think such things. She simply held out the basket.

At that very moment the wind gusted violently. Norah's heavy winter cloak blew open, and she grabbed the flapping fabric, swiftly closing it around her before she got chilled.

But not swiftly enough. Not before Morgan saw her garments flattened tight against her body. Not before his shock when he saw her swollen breasts and belly outlined in bold stark truth.

She's pregnant, he thought, as a cold knife of bitterness tore at his gut.

In the first instant of discovery he thought the child was Cal's, but a second later he thrust that idea aside. Even if Calvin Welsh had been capable of consummating his marriage to Norah at the end of October—which Morgan sincerely doubted—this child still couldn't possibly have been his. Norah seemed too far gone for the baby even to have been conceived on Cal's earlier trip back East. From the brief look he'd had at her rounded body, Morgan imagined the baby was created in the summer, or earlier.

She was smiling at him and saying something. He murmured some noncommittal words and made a bit of a production of securing his hat against the blustering wind, numbly taking her arm to escort her the rest of the way. His heart had turned to ice.

The Wattron house was full, warm and fragrant with food when they arrived. Myrtis, Frank, and Digger were there ahead of them, sharing a Christmas toddy with Ferdie. And to Morgan's astonishment, Dolly Smith was also there. He couldn't imagine Mordecai allowing one of his wives out of his sight, but he had no time to ponder the matter. Another fellow walked into the room right behind them. Despite his neat gray suit and bowler, Morgan instantly pegged him as a drummer.

"I'm Quinton Rose," the man said pleasantly when Morgan introduced himself. "Miss Wattron was kind enough to invite me down to dinner."

Morgan raised an eyebrow. *Down?* Was it possible that this little man with the pink nose and big ears had rented a room upstairs? Morgan knew there was another suite of rooms down the hall from Doc Robinson's office, but the Wattrons had never attempted to rent them. Was he wrong about Rose's occupation?

"What line of work are you in?" he asked.

"Mousetraps," Quinton Rose answered. "I sell Little Nippers. The finest mousetraps in the country."

"I see," Morgan said. "I must have missed it when you came in on the train."

"No, I didn't come by rail. I rode up over the Mogollon Rim with some of the Aztec riders. Quite an exciting adventure, I must say. Breathtaking scenery, Sheriff."

Morgan nodded, helping himself to a piece of taffy Norah had just set on the sideboard. It promptly stuck to his teeth, keeping him occupied for a couple of minutes. He glared at Norah, but she didn't notice.

"Just passing through?" he asked when he was able.

"I've decided to stay a bit, set up headquarters here. Everybody needs mousetraps. Miss Wattron has let me a room."

"Wouldn't Flagstaff be more convenient? Or Albuquerque?"

The drummer's nose colored up more pink than before. He glanced at Clarabelle as she set a ham on the laden sideboard beside the roast beef and wild turkey. He shook his head. "I think I'll be comfortable right here."

Morgan met his eyes with a steely gaze. "There are some fine folks in this town."

A lesser man might have been intimidated, but Rose returned his look with equal determination, although the sheriff was at least six inches taller. "No one knows that better than I, Sheriff. I didn't expect to find a jewel in such a windblown place. But now that I have, I plan to stay."

Morgan merely nodded. The salesman had a fine way with words, but he intended to keep a wary eye on him. He wondered what Ferdie thought of the situation. Probably nothing. Ferdie was too busy passing the time with the A & P Railroad engineer's wife to notice what was going on with his own sister.

Norah caught his eye as she put a bowl of mashed potatoes between bowls of glazed carrots and buttered turnips, and gave him a quick smile. He smiled back, but there was a hollow place in his heart where trust had been.

She looked beautiful, her red hair shining in the lamplight and a happy flush on her cheeks. The elaborate apron she wore covered any sign of her pregnancy. Morgan was certain it had been designed to do just that very thing. He realized she was having a good time.

Well, what the hell do you expect her to do, he asked himself grimly. *Do you expect her to go around long-faced and dejected just because you found out she's pregnant?* He wondered if Cal had known. At this point it didn't make any difference. Cal was dead, so Norah's possible deception of him was unimportant.

Except to me. For the first time, there amid most of his friends, he admitted how important Norah was to him—far beyond a toss in the sheets that he lusted for. He scowled fiercely at the thought and damned her cheating heart.

"You're looking mighty fierce, Sheriff," Ferdie commented. "Something on the groaning board you don't much like?"

Morgan hauled his angry thoughts back to the holiday fare. "Everything looks grand. Ah, I'm just hungry."

"I'll bet you skipped breakfast," Norah teased as she set down a basket of hot rolls. She gestured for him to pick a place at the table.

"Yeah," he admitted. "And I think I missed supper last night, too. I'm famished."

Out of sheer perversity he offered her the chair beside his. It would be utter hell to brush elbows with her all afternoon, to smell the sweetness of her cologne each time she moved and listen to her voice for the next few hours, but he wanted her close. He needed her close. Things between them were about to change. He knew it and relished it, as much as he feared it. When he walked her back to her place, he planned to confront her about the child. But for this brief spell, he was going to enjoy having her near.

"When is your baby due?" Morgan asked when the sewing shop door closed behind them later that night, his voice deceptively soft.

Norah's spine stiffened. It was the first time she'd heard the words spoken aloud. *Your baby.* In a nervous gesture she ran the tip of her tongue over her bottom lip.

Morgan saw her hand go protectively to her stomach even before she opened her mouth to answer. His voice hardened against the desire he felt to protect her. "Cal didn't know, did he? You tricked him into marrying you."

Her chin raised instantly. "What an absurd thing to say! Of course, I told Calvin. He was my friend. That's why he made me an offer of marriage."

Looking down at her in the dim light from the

lamp she'd left burning, seeing the combination of anger and vulnerability, he believed her. The rage he'd felt all afternoon suddenly dissipated. "I'm sorry," he muttered.

"Cal saved my letter, and I have his. You can read them if you wish. Then perhaps you'll believe me." She was not about to let him off easily, though she didn't quite understand why she felt so brutally wounded.

"I believe you, Norah." He moved close and took her cold hands. "I guess I'm just a little wary of beautiful women with mysterious pasts. But that's my own problem, not yours."

Strength emanated from him like a warm cloud. More than anything, she wanted to be enfolded in his arms, to rest and be comforted. She held herself rigidly, though, making certain she didn't weaken. She would not depend on him or any other man.

"When is the baby due?" he asked again.

"March. Around the first, I think."

"You'll be needing help. I hope Doc Robinson is back by then, but if not we'll ask one of the Mormon women to come to town. I don't think we've had a baby born here yet. We'll get you the best nursing we can find."

Unbidden tears filled her eyes at his unexpected kindness. She'd been anticipating more questions, perhaps even a condemnation of her indecent behavior. Morgan was a difficult man to understand.

Without thinking, he gathered her to him. "I told Cal I'd take care of you. You have my word that you and your baby will be safe."

She tried to pull away, but he was too strong and his arms were too comforting. "Thank you," she whispered, at last slipping her arms around his waist. For the first time since she left Cincinnati, she relaxed and let go of her fear of the future.

7

Norah had just sat down at the sewing machine when there was a rap on the back door. She knew who it was before she answered. Three days had passed since Christmas, and she'd found little packages of hair pins, ribbons, and fancy soap by her doorstep each morning. Only one person left gifts at her back door.

"Come in, Mazie," she said.

"Are you sure?" Mazie asked, carefully searching the alley for anybody who might be watching.

"It's cold out here. Come in and sit by the stove."

"Curly Yates asked me to marry him," Mazie said when she'd taken a chair.

Norah immediately noticed Mazie's plain blue dress, so very different from the garments she normally wore, and her thick hair held back in a simple braid. Her face was washed clean of the usual paint, and the only perfume she had on came from the scent in rose soap. Mazie looked young, vulnerable, and terribly afraid.

"Is he good to you?"

Mazie nodded. "He's polite to other folks, too, and soft-spoken. He's been to school some and says he'll teach me better if I want to learn. He don't fight none, and he ain't a boozer. And he's real gentle when he touches me."

Norah wondered what this Curly thought about Mazie's profession. The girl apparently read her mind.

"Curly don't mind about me workin' at the Red Rock, but he wants me to quit and go to California with him. His sister has a place near Hollister, and now that her husband is dead, she wants Curly to buy it so she can move to San Francisco."

"What did Mr. Yates do here?"

"He's worked for Aztec Cattle Company for a spell, but he quit yesterday. He says there's a lot of trouble comin'. He wants us to leave on today's train. What do you think I should do?" Her wide eyes beseeched Norah. "I'm scared."

"Do you like him—*really* like him?"

Norah had decided months ago she didn't believe in love. What she'd felt for Sonny had been a foolish illusion born out of loneliness. She did, however, understand respect and affection. That's what she'd felt for Cal. "If you like him enough to tolerate him for the rest of your life, perhaps you should take the chance."

"What if his sister finds out about me? About what I been doin'? She might turn him against me."

Norah didn't answer immediately. "There aren't many guarantees in life. That might be a problem, or maybe not. I think if you become a friend to her, she'll like you and stick by you no matter what."

"Maybe you're right." She gave Norah a weak smile. "I really do want to go with Curly. I've been sweet on him since the first time we—"

Norah smiled at Mazie's fiery blush.

"Guess I better get to packin'. Lily Mae's gonna be mad as hell."

"That's because she'll miss you. So will I, for that matter. But I wish you well. Be happy, Mazie." Norah was a bit disconcerted when Mazie hugged her fiercely, unable to contain her emotions or her tears.

Two hours later, Nathan Ralston rode out with his nephew-by-marriage, Bunky Lindstrom, heading south across the Little Colorado River toward the Mogollon Rim. Winnie stood on the porch of the neat white house, waving and weeping.

Ralston's face was stony. He loathed Lindstrom. The younger man was a killer to the core, and Ralston wondered if both of them would get back alive. He'd been so concerned, in fact, that he'd visited the town lawyer to make out a will and left an envelope detailing every crime he knew of that Bunky had committed.

Not that Ralston was lily white by any stretch of the imagination. He'd killed his share of men, but mostly during the war, and afterward when things in Missouri and Kansas had been crazy. He hadn't killed anybody who hadn't deserved to die, although his conscience bothered him about each one.

Bunky Lindstrom was a different breed. He was cruel, and he enjoyed causing pain. Ralston knew he had to watch his back if he wanted to survive.

Winnie, of course, had suggested that Bunky accompany him. Ralston couldn't be angry with her. He loved her, and he had from the moment he'd seen her in the bank in her hometown. She'd dropped her handbag on the floor, and he'd stopped to help—he had a weakness for fragile women. He'd married her five days later, never once mentioning he'd stopped at that particular bank to rob it. She still didn't know.

Winnie Ralston stepped into Norah's store shortly after her loved ones rode off. She was feeling mighty blue and decided to indulge herself for once.

"May I help you, Mrs. Ralston?"

Norah had set up the Singer sewing machine near the window where the light was good most of the day. She continued sewing up the center seam of a sheet she was making for Sheriff Treyhan.

"I hope you can, Mrs. Welsh. I'd like a dressing

gown made." Winnie untied the string on a parcel. "My husband brought me these dress goods when he came back from a trip. I thought it would make a pretty gown."

Norah stood up and walked to the worktable, laying out the pink linen. It was some of the finest she'd ever seen, as soft and sheer as pure silk.

"I have this old lace my mother made," Winnie told her. "Maybe you could use it, too."

"That's exquisite!"

"My mother's family were lacemakers," Winnie said proudly. "I only wish some of them had lived to teach me. Can you use the lace on the gown?"

"Of course. It would be beautiful on a wide collar, don't you think?"

The front door opened and Sheriff Treyhan stepped in, followed by Tod Willis, the coffin maker.

"Good morning, Mrs. Ralston. Mrs. Welsh."

"Good morning, Sheriff. How can I help you?"

Morgan saw her glance toward the large section of white muslin at the sewing machine. His sheets—the ones he'd dreamed about so often, and had only now found the courage to order. It was damned hard to look at those sheets and not remember his fantasies of who he wanted in them. He hoped nobody in the room saw the color that heated his face. "Tod is here to make you a chest."

"I thought all you made was coffins," Winnie said, her eyes bright with curiosity.

Tod removed his cap. "No, ma'am. I'm a full-fledged carpenter. Only I get lotsa work makin' coffins around this danged place 'cause so many people get themselves plugged. Holbrook's almost as bad as Tombstone fer killin's."

"So I've heard," Winnie said.

Morgan shifted a bit as the two discussed how the world was going straight to hell, and leaned a shoulder against the wall so he could watch Norah without appearing to do so. She was wearing a big green apron that completely covered her dress. He'd noticed as soon as she started her business that she always wore cover-all aprons when she worked. Since Christmas Eve there wasn't much about her he didn't know.

"Tod's got some good-looking cedar that would make a fine chest," he told Norah after Winnie and Tod concluded their conversation. "And he's got some pine boards that might work as shelves for the shop. I got to thinking about all that cloth you brought with you. You'll sell more if your customers could see what you have."

"The trunks are all right for storage," Norah protested.

"With shelves, everything will be on display." Morgan turned to Winnie. "Mrs. Welsh's trunks are filled with the latest things from Cincinnati."

"Oh, I'd like to see! Just as soon as you get the shelves up."

Morgan avoided Norah's scowl. He intended for her to have as much business as she could handle.

The front door opened yet again and a tall, skinny fellow in a rumpled striped suit walked in. He smelled strongly of beer and wasn't quite steady on his feet. Norah stepped back from the odious stench, her stomach suddenly a'flutter.

"What do you want?" Morgan demanded of the stranger.

"I want the woman," the drunk said. "I heard there was a single woman in town, and I wanna marry her." He peered at Winnie and Norah, trying to focus on his prey.

Morgan took him by the arm, whirled him around, and shoved him out the door. "There are three single women in Holbrook, and none of them wants to marry *you*."

The drunk straightened his jacket, which didn't help the wrinkles one bit, and looked very affronted. "Well, hell, well just hell."

Morgan slammed the door and glared at Norah, his look reminding her that he'd warned her about men coming courting.

"Some people are just so forward these days," Winnie said. "Why he didn't even wait for an introduction!" She looked startled when Morgan laughed.

Harcourt Barr had been a petty thief since he was nine, but he'd never been especially adept at it. The woman he was attempting to rob at that moment was hanging on to her purse with the strength of a python, bashing him with her umbrella, and screeching her fool head off.

Fat Tony Roscoe was watching disgustedly from the corner. "Go save the old battle-ax," he finally told Dowie Johnston. "Before we all end up in jail."

Dowie scampered down the block, chased Harcourt away, and helped the woman collect her wits. She gave him a dime for his trouble.

"I thought sure Omar would be here in Steubenville," Dowie said mournfully when the three of them had regrouped at a nearby café to sample some of the good Dutch food Ohio was famous for. "It ain't a big place, but he and I hid out here once when we was on the run."

"One of his wives lived here," Fat Tony mentioned as he shoveled Dutch apple pie into his mouth.

"Well, why don't she help us?" Harcourt asked.

"She's dead."

"That's damned inconsiderate of her!"

"I'll tell Omar you said so, Harcourt. When we find him."

"If we find him, Antone. *If* we find him. I think he skipped out on us. With the gold, of course."

"We're leaving tomorrow," Fat Tony said. "We'll keep going west till we get the gold."

"We gotta do somethin' to get a little ready cash. I'm tired of freezin' my ass off in boxcars."

"I'm tired of walkin'," Dowie put in.

"Fine, Harcourt," Fat Tony huffed. "Just make sure it's smarter than your last trick. Any snot-nosed kid coulda done a better job of grabbin' that woman's pocketbook."

*   *   *

Winnie had finally left Norah's and gone to the post office, hoping to share a piece of pie with Clarabelle. She didn't often leave her cozy home and her adoring husband, but like everyone else in town she knew about Clarabelle's organ music. She didn't think it was quite right for Ferdie Wattron to be bedding the engineer's wife, but men would be men.

Tod was laboriously explaining his qualifications for building things besides coffins. Norah had put on the teakettle while he talked.

She looked tired, Morgan thought. He was certain she hadn't slept well the night before. He'd seen her light on before he'd gone home to bed after making his rounds. He'd almost knocked at her door, but the disturbing fact of her pregnancy stood between them.

He was already battling Cal's ghost. Now he realized that yet another man stood between them, some unknown son of a bitch who'd pleasured himself on her body the way Morgan longed to do. Someone who'd hurt her badly. There was no doubt in his mind that Norah—a lonely, naïve country girl trying to make her way in the big city—had loved the bastard, because she wasn't the sort to bed a man for any other reason. *Seduced* and *abandoned*—the words echoed in his head, making his gut churn with rage.

How the hell could anybody who knew her not want Norah forever? Cal Welsh had jumped at the chance to have her. *I would, too.*

He cleared his throat. "There's somebody I need to talk to out in the street. Can you handle things in here, Tod?"

The carpenter looked faintly disconcerted. "Sure, Sheriff."

"I don't think all this carpentry work needs to be done right now." Concerned about her budget, Norah worried that Morgan's plans for the sewing shop were far more extensive than her own.

"It's necessary," Morgan said. "Tod needs the job." He slammed the door before she could say another word.

The following day Norah walked up to the post office to mail a letter to her family. In it she told them about her life in the western town and informed them she was going to have a baby. She was curious when she noticed the mouse-trap salesman behind the fancy goods counter happily changing Clarabelle's display. Ferdie was nowhere to be seen.

It was raw outside, the wind was blowing a gale, and the taste of snow was in the air. So far the weather had often been cold and windy, but there'd been no snow.

"Would you like a cup of tea before you go back home?" Clarabelle asked.

"Gladly." She removed her gloves and sat down at the table while Clarabelle poured water from the sizzling kettle into a fancy pot.

"I don't have any pie today," Clarabelle told her as she handed Norah a cup. "Would you like some bread and jam?"

That was interesting, Norah thought. She knew she'd heard music the night before.

On her way out, she got a good look at Quinton Rose. He wasn't a handsome man by any means, but if a person overlooked the pink nose and big ears he could be termed nice looking. It didn't take a genius to see that Clarabelle was smitten. Norah considered telling her a thing or two about well-dressed men with charm and manners but dropped the idea immediately. Just because she'd been such an idiot didn't mean that Clarabelle would be.

"She's a brave woman," Quinton said after the door had closed behind Norah.

"What?" Clarabelle asked.

"To have a baby out here, so far away from civilization, or even a doctor."

To her credit, Clarabelle managed to close her gaping mouth and utter something, though later she couldn't quite remember what.

"I guess babies get born everyplace," he said, arranging a display of pearl-handled pens with a silk hankie and a pink rose off an old hat. He looked pleased at how nice the pens showed up beneath the glass countertop.

"Yes," she said. She was shocked to her shoe buttons but managed to contain it. Why hadn't she noticed?

And why hadn't Norah told her?

Quinton moved closer to the doorway of the living quarters. "Will your brother be home tonight?" he asked in an undertone.

Just then one of the young Mormon settlers who lived south of town came in to get his mail.

"It's gonna snow." He shivered as Clarabelle handed him several envelopes. "Hope I get home before it starts."

The door banged open with the force of the wind when the man opened it to leave. A tumbleweed bounced up the wooden sidewalk.

A flush tinged Clarabelle's face as she fussed behind the postmaster's cage. A tense silence filled the room.

"I'm going upstairs," Quinton finally said.

"Will you be down for supper?"

He shook his head. "I'll get something at the hotel. Maybe have a drink or two afterwards."

She was alarmed. It would be the first time since he'd moved into the rooms upstairs that he wouldn't be joining her for the evening meal. Ferdie had been gone almost every night lately, so it was just the two of them, talking and laughing like people who belonged together. And last night . . . what happened last night was beyond anything she'd ever imagined.

"I'll listen for the music." His voice was so soft she could barely hear him.

"What?"

"The organ music you play when Ferdie is with that woman. After you play a few songs, I'll come back. You can either spend the rest of the night baking pies, or spend it with me."

"Quinton, I'm not sure about this."

"Clarabelle, I'm not staying in Holbrook because I like the scenery. Or because it's a great place to sell mousetraps. I'm here because of you. I loved you the first minute I saw you!"

She moved swiftly to where he stood and laid her plump hand on his arm. "I love you, Quinton Rose. But this is happening so quickly, I can't think."

He pulled her into the living quarters, behind the heavy curtain, and into his arms, kissing her until her eyes were dazed with longing.

"I can't think, either," he whispered. "All I can do is feel."

It was nearly nightfall on a dark and dreary winter evening when the front door of the sewing shop opened and Dolly came in, carrying a small cloth sack.

"Can I stay here for the night?" she asked, setting the sack down and peeling off her coat and numerous scarves.

"Of course," Norah answered. "I'll be glad for the company. I didn't realize you were in town."

Dolly was busy putting wood in the stove. "I just rode in. I put the horse up at the livery stable." She peeked at the corn chowder that was simmering on the stove. "I've left Mordecai Smith. I'm not going back."

One of the things Norah was learning from other westerners was when to mind her own business. She knew Dolly hadn't made the decision lightly, just as she knew she'd find out about it when Dolly was ready to tell her.

"You could probably use a cup of tea."

Dolly's chuckle was unexpected. "I do believe that tea is your solution for all of life's problems."

Norah smiled. "I think you're right."

Later, when they were replete with biscuits, chowder, and canned peaches, Norah asked Dolly if she was seeking a full-time job.

"I can't pay you much until the building is finished, but I can manage a small salary, and naturally you can stay here. I'm getting more work than I originally expected."

"I'd like that," Dolly said. "And I've delivered a lot of babies, so if the doctor isn't back before your time comes, you'll have somebody you can trust."

Norah set down her teacup. "How did you know?"

Dolly laughed softly. "Your eyes, your skin, the way you stand, the way you touch your belly—a hundred ways. I knew the first day I met you. I'm figuring sometime in March."

Norah knew there wasn't any sense in pretending anymore—not with Dolly. "About the first week, I think."

"Did you see a doctor before you left the Midwest?"

Norah shook her head. "I expected to find a doctor here. Cal thought Doc Robinson would be back long before this."

"If he isn't, you've got me. And Myrtis, though I figure she's better at gunshot wounds than babies."

"That's a comfort to me, Dolly. My mam delivered all her kids at home—thirteen so far, and she's expecting again—but I wasn't there much after I was old enough to understand the process. I guess I never thought about me doing *that*." She blushed at Dolly's whoop of hearty laughter.

"Does anybody know but me? It isn't a secret you can keep much longer."

Norah pursed her lips. "Sheriff Treyhan knows. He figured it out, too."

A flicker of speculation lit Dolly's eyes, vanishing as rapidly as it had come. "The sheriff's a good man."

"Yes, I suppose he is."

Dolly cocked her head at Norah's decidedly cool tone. From what she'd observed, Morgan Treyhan considered Norah more than his best friend's widow. She wondered what he'd said to Norah. It was a good guess that he was jealous that somebody besides himself had fathered the baby.

"The high-minded sheriff wasn't exactly joyous about my condition."

"Because he knows the baby isn't Cal's? Anybody who can count will figure that out."

Dolly was nothing if not forthright, Norah decided. "I had hoped people wouldn't realize it."

Dolly insisted on being practical. "Folks might buzz for a few days. Then something else will happen. It always does. There'll be a shooting or a robbery—or even a hanging. It won't be long before everybody forgets that the babe got here early—especially when they look at a brand new life."

The town company held the annual New Year's Eve supper at the Holbrook House. Angus

MacKay was unusually cordial about opening his establishment to the whole town for the evening. That was probably because the town company paid for the use of the dining room and parlor as well as the huge hunks of beef that were served. The rest of the food was donated by the ladies of the town. But since business was slow in the winter and Angus sold all the liquid refreshments, he was pleased with the bargain.

Dolly had no intention of going to the festivities—she had said so right from the beginning—and Norah had no intention of letting Dolly stay home alone. Myrtis got into the discussion, and so did Winnie Ralston, who had nothing better to do since her husband was out of town.

Norah immediately began sorting through the yards of dress goods she had in her trunks and found a soft rose wool she'd originally intended for her seven-year-old twin sisters. She'd gotten involved with Sonny a short time afterward and hadn't gotten to use the fabric. She decided it would be perfect for Dolly.

"Oh, no," Dolly said immediately. "My brown dress will do."

Norah didn't believe the thin, faded cotton would do to feed pigs in, but she kept the thought to herself. "Not for a party. I want to make this for you."

"It's too pretty for me. Make it up for Myrtis."

"Myrtis already has a dress of garnet satin."

"Well, maybe for Winnie."

"Winnie's dress is indigo silk broadcloth.

Nathan had it made for her in St. Louis right after they were married. I'm making this up for you, so don't argue."

"You're a hard-headed woman, Norah."

Norah chuckled, but she fashioned Dolly's dress exactly as she wanted.

And when Dolly donned the woolen gown on New Year's Eve, she was stunned at her own appearance. Norah had heated the curling iron over the lamp and created soft curls around Dolly's face, piling the rest high on top.

"Oh, no," Dolly protested. "I'll be too tall!"

"You won't be any shorter with your hair peeled back like an onion. But this way you'll be pretty."

Dolly was so astonished at anyone calling her pretty that she shut her mouth and let Norah do anything she wanted. She was still dazed when Norah gave her a cloak to wear and opened the front door.

The hotel was crowded when they arrived. Nearly everybody in town came for the supper. The rowdies would naturally leave early for a livelier brand of entertainment, but before they did they intended to partake of the food and inspect the women.

Norah wore the black dress she'd made for Christmas, this time without the apron. There were a few raised eyebrows when people saw her full figure, but mostly people were out on the town to have a good time and didn't give her a second thought.

"I am so full I feel like a tick," Myrtis complained. "I hope the fiddlers are good tonight. I feel like dancing."

"Clarabelle is going to play something on the piano," Norah said. "I think she said Ferdie is going to sing with her."

"I'm surprised he has the strength," Winnie commented. "He's busy night and day."

Clarabelle played three songs. She and Ferdie sang exceptionally well together. The Harrison family also performed, and Willie Wilson recited a poem as his mother looked on proudly.

The fiddlers were just warming up when Morgan came into the lobby with Lily Mae in tow. She did not look happy—her feathers drooped and her purple dress was torn. Not one damned thing had gone right for her since Mazie had eloped with the cowboy, she kept saying when she wasn't cussing her head off.

"Angus, Lily Mae needs a room for the night," Morgan said.

"Is she setting up business here?" Winnie was watching the lobby with great interest.

"Looks to me like she's under arrest," Myrtis said. She couldn't decide whether the show in the lobby was more exciting than the lanky cowboy with a red beard who'd just asked her to dance.

"Wait here," she told the bearded wrangler. "I'll be right back."

Myrtis bustled out to talk to Morgan.

"What's he saying?" Winnie asked Dolly, who was tall enough to see over the crowd.

"I think he's asking about Norah," Dolly said. "Myrtis is pointing in her direction."

"I want to know about Lily Mae."

Myrtis filled them in before she danced off

with the cowboy. "Lily Mae shot one of the men over at the Red Rock. He said there were no good whores left in the world, and she filled him with lead. I gotta go clean him up, but I'm gonna do a little dancin' first. I might not get another chance."

Lily Mae had plugged the guy in the shoulder. She'd been aiming at a target a little lower, but a brawl had started behind her and her shot went wild. Angus MacKay was quite disgruntled that Morgan wouldn't let her set up business at the hotel, with him getting a share of the profits, of course.

Before Morgan left the hotel he talked to Norah. She wasn't dancing in spite of the many offers she had. She allowed people to think it was because of mourning for Cal, but actually, she didn't know how to dance. And this certainly wasn't the time to learn.

"I want to walk you home."

"Thank you, Sheriff, but you don't have to bother. I know you're needed elsewhere. It's not far. And besides, Dolly is with me."

His hand touched her elbow, and he bent down so she could hear him above the fiddle music. "I'm walking you home. It's snowing and the boardwalks are slippery. Don't argue. And don't leave till I get back."

"All right," she said, feeling better than she had in days. "Happy New Year."

New Year's Eve was a hell-raiser, the wildest night the little town had ever known. The year of

1887 swept in on the wings of a storm, wrapped in ice and sprinkled with blood. Morgan wondered what the rest of the year would bring after such a turbulent beginning. Fortunately, the law-abiding citizens sought the warmth of their beds shortly after midnight.

Morgan and his deputy were up until daybreak, in spite of the bitter cold, strong wind, and drifting and blowing snow. By the time the first fingers of dawn reached the high plateau, the jail was full of the most violent men, and Digger had carted off two bodies. Myrtis had patched up Lily Mae's victim before returning to the dance. The female in question spent the most restful evening of her career.

"I don't know why I keep this job," Morgan muttered as he crossed the tracks, careful not to step on the icy steel rails. "I could be a farmer, raise a few pigs, and a whole herd of youngsters."

He stopped suddenly, realizing it was the first time he'd ever thought of being anything but a lawman. Of course he didn't know a single thing about farming and didn't plan to learn, but that wasn't the point. What he'd really been thinking was that he was tired of a thankless job where half the people wanted to kill him and the other half wanted some favor.

The idea of a wife and a family held a lot more appeal now than it had in the past. He turned and looked back toward Central Avenue, toward Norah's building. He wondered what it would be like to enjoy a dance instead of patrolling it. Or, better, what it would be like to spend one New Year's Eve making love to a beautiful woman instead of tramping in and out of saloons, breaking up fights, scuffling with drunks, and watching bodies hauled away because of some stupid disagreement.

He thought of spending the night in his big bed with Norah. Even as exhausted as he was, the idea heated his blood. *Now that's the way I'd like to earn the nickname Ironman!*

8

The potbellied stove was completely cold when Norah woke up that morning. Not a single live ember remained from the fire she'd had the night before, and she thought she'd banked it well, too. The truth was that the stove was not big enough to heat the whole area.

After putting her bare feet down on the wooden floor, she jerked them back under the covers. That floor was like ice! She needed kindling to start the fire, but first she searched under her pillow for her flannel dressing gown and the two pairs of Cal's woolen socks she'd put there the night before. Her feet were so swollen she couldn't fit them into her shoes anymore. And if she could have gotten her feet into the shoes, she wouldn't have been able to bend over to button them. Her stomach was so big she couldn't even see her feet when she was standing up.

Norah found the whole situation depressing, but Dolly kept telling her it was all very normal for her stage of pregnancy. Norah was very tired of being pregnant, tired of being so large and ungainly, and tired of being tired.

She didn't sleep well anymore because there was no way she could lie and be comfortable. So instead of sleeping through the night, she slept in short snatches, waking up stiff and uncomfortable, then having to shift into a different position. That was why she was awake now, before daylight even.

She'd woken up cold, with a painful throbbing in her lower back, and not able to find any position to ease the discomfort. She felt cranky as a bear and figured she might as well get up and build a fire so she could have a cup of tea and toast a slice of the bakery bread.

After that she'd get her sewing basket and work on some of the baby things she still hadn't finished.

She fumbled with the chimney of the lamp on the table beside her bed but finally got it off and the lamp lighted. Then she eased the chimney back on after she'd turned the wick down so the lamp wouldn't smoke.

Now that she could see where she was going, she eased herself out of the bed and went to the woodbox by the back door for kindling and some newspaper to start the fire in the stove. Dolly usually built the morning fire, but she was still sleeping and Norah didn't want to wake her. And even though Dolly had been good company, there were times when Norah liked to be by herself.

After the fire was burning brightly, Norah
took the teakettle to the water bucket to fill it.
But the water had a thick layer of ice on it. As
she lifted the bucket to the stove to melt the ice,
she was thankful it was less than half full.

Even so, the motion put a strain on her
already aching back. Norah put her hand on her
back and tried to arch her swollen body to ease
the pain. When it refused to go away, she
decided to forgo a cup of her precious Earl Grey
tea in favor of some made from willow bark.
The imported Earl Grey blend, which had been
a birthday gift last spring from Sonny, was
almost gone. Norah hoarded it like gold because
she doubted she would ever be able to afford it
again.

Now she bent over the box she kept her herbs
in, searching for the cloth drawstring bag of
dried willow bark. Young Jimmy had stripped
the bark from the branches of his mother's
weeping willow tree when Cal had been so ill.
Willow bark tea brought down fevers, and it
also eased pain.

Clutching the bag, Norah was again struck
by grief over Cal's death. She missed his gentle-
ness, his laughter, and his devotion to her and
the child he was so determined would be
theirs. How she wished she had him to talk to!
She could share both her joys and her fears
about the baby. She had decided on names:
Christopher if it was a boy, because that was
Cal's middle name, and Colleen if it was a girl.

Cal's family was Catholic, as Norah's was,
though it was a rare occasion when any of the

Kellys saw the inside of a church. Norah had attended the Presbyterian church with Jean Matthews. Cal had asked that the baby be baptized Catholic. He'd even talked about going forty-five miles to the nearest Catholic church, in Concho, for its christening. Norah intended to honor Cal's wish, whenever a priest came to town.

Then the baby kicked—hard.

"Very well, Christopher Mark or Colleen Mary. Let me make my tea and have a bit of toasted bread with it to stave off the heartburn, and we will rock by the fire while I finish embroidering your gowns." Norah often talked to the baby, telling it what she was doing and why.

Myrtis said that was because she was lonely, and she needed to marry again as soon as possible. Dolly had often mentioned Norah's being lonely, but she had never suggested remarriage. It was hard to tell what Dolly thought. Norah would have loved to talk to the Mormon woman about what it was like to be a multiple wife, but she didn't know how to broach the subject without offending her. It must have been humiliating for Dolly when her husband chose other wives. In any event, something had been the final straw, driving her away from her husband forever.

Norah was just thankful her pregnancy had stilled the town's controversy about her finding another man, at least for a while. She had accepted Cal's proposal because they'd been friends for so long. But she wasn't sure she'd ever be able to trust another man that much again. And she wasn't about to place her life, and the life of her child, into the hands of a man she couldn't trust.

With the store building and the wonderful sewing machine Cal had bought for her, Norah could provide a home for herself and the baby. She didn't have to marry to get a roof over their heads and food on the table, and she didn't intend to do so.

Steam was rising from the water bucket.

Norah stopped her musing, lifted the water off the stove, and set the tea to brewing. Then she filled the teakettle and put it on a corner of the stove to keep it hot. That way Dolly could have some when she got up, too.

At the foot of her bed stood the cedar chest Morgan had given her—as a peace offering, and an awkward apology for thinking she'd deceived Cal. Norah hadn't really wanted to accept it, but she needed something to keep baby things in. And it smelled wonderful.

Norah smiled as she lifted the lid and removed the tiny gowns she wanted to work on. Then, wrapping herself in a quilt from her bed, she settled into the rocking chair and proceeded to monogram the gowns with the initials CMW in gold, surrounded by blue forget-me-nots.

She rocked gently and embroidered, finishing two of the three white flannel gowns with hoods and drawstring bottoms. But as she was threading her needle with gold floss to begin the third, a sharp pain sliced through her back, and her abdomen knotted.

Norah gasped, then breathed again. When it

passed, she put both hands to her abdomen, feeling for the position of the baby. "Ah, child, don't be so fierce! I understand your wanting to turn over, but do you have to take all my inner parts with you?" She continued to rock gently and smooth her hands over her rounded belly.

"I know it must be confining for you in there, love. And you'd like to be free so you can kick and stretch to your heart's content. It won't be long now. I've not done this before, you understand, so we'll have to work through it together and learn as we go. But Dolly tells me the time is almost here.

"Then, I'll be able to hold you in my arms as I rock you. And you'll sleep in that lovely old cradle Myrtis brought me, right alongside my bed, wrapped in the soft quilts we've been making.

"My mam's had thirteen babes, and only the last one had a cradle. I bought it at Shillito's, fixed it all up, and took it home to Mam. She was so happy she cried. The other babes had been lucky to have a dresser drawer to sleep in.

"But, don't you worry. Mothers and babies have been doing this since the beginning of time." Norah felt a trembling in her abdomen and continued to stroke the child.

"It's all right to be afraid, my darling. I am, too. But let's think of it as an adventure, shall we? One more journey into the unknown. We've already made one. We came out here from Cincinnati by ourselves. That was scary, too. But we made it. And Cal was so glad we'd come."

Tears welled up in Norah's hazel eyes. "Unfortunately, he had an appointment with his Maker.

But he would have loved you, and been so proud of you. Cal may have been feckless in a lot of ways, but he was good. He knew how to love, and how to show it. I felt more precious and adored during the week I was his wife than I ever have in my life. I wish I could have given you that, too."

Norah continued to rock and hold her child with both hands and cry silently for the gentle husband and father who was lost to them until she fell into an exhausted sleep.

Dolly found her slumped sideways in the rocking chair. The fire had almost burned out in the stove again.

The large homely woman built up the fire without disturbing Norah. She knew how difficult the last few weeks of pregnancy were, and how scary. She remembered her own turbulent emotions, the lonely tears she'd cried, the sorrow when her first two babies had been stillborn—and how devastated she'd been when the third, a tiny, delicate girl named Sarah after her own mother, had died before she was two.

And then Mordecai had taken his second wife.

Dolly had always known her husband didn't love her. She and her little sister had been taken in by the wagon train of Latter Day St.s after their parents died and left them alone on the farm in Kansas. Polly was pretty, delicate like their mother, while Dolly had inherited their father's rough-hewn features and large build.

Mordecai Smith, an aging bachelor, had fallen hard for Polly, who was far too young to marry. So he'd offered to marry Dolly, with the understanding Polly would become his second wife as soon as she was sixteen. The sisters weren't Mormon and didn't understand plural marriages, but they were young and alone, and they wanted to stay together.

Like many homely women, Dolly had a deep well of passion and love to give. Mordecai Smith was delighted to return the passion, but not the love she showered upon him. He accepted it as his due but found it embarrassing.

He'd have been elated to receive such tender emotions from Polly, but he thought a woman as homely as Dolly had no right to such romantic feelings, or the expectation that he would return them. Surely she understood no man could look upon her mannish build and heavy features with tenderness or joy. He had often told her she was one of the unfortunate creatures God had over-looked in his magnificent design.

Dolly was a good woman, though, loyal and hard-working. She even had an unexpected wry sense of humor. So Mordecai was a dutiful hus-band and gave her a respectable station in life, but that was all. He held his more tender feelings in reserve for Polly.

Then Polly had caught pneumonia and died about a month before Dolly's second baby was due. Both husband and wife mourned, but they couldn't grieve together or help each other through the tragedy. Then when Dolly's second baby boy was born dead, with the umbilical cord wrapped around his neck, she had to grieve alone again.

And this grief was worse than any of the rest.

Dolly knew her husband mourned, but not for whom. She couldn't fault him for that, because she wasn't sure how much of her own sorrow was for the lost child she had desired so deeply and how much was for her sister who had shared all the previous tragedies of her life with her.

She expected Mordecai to turn to her for affection since Polly was gone, but it didn't happen. When she wanted to cuddle with him in bed after a long, hard day's work, or when she needed the warmth of an embrace, he didn't want to be touched. She excused his behavior in a hundred different ways, until the evening she caught him in a sheltered spot by the river with Peggy Foster. They were laughing and teasing each other.

Mordecai had no reservations about stroking Peggy's face and running his fingers through her hair. And while Dolly watched with her heart in her mouth, her husband trailed a line of gentle kisses from Peggy's ear, down her throat, following his busy fingers as they unbuttoned her dress. When his greedy mouth closed upon Peggy's perfect breast, Dolly unconsciously emitted a painful wail.

The lovers were startled. Peggy blushed beet red, and Mordecai pulled her dress over her bared breast, but neither made any apology to Dolly.

A month later Mordecai and Peggy were

married. That was fifteen years ago. But the memories were as vivid in Dolly's mind as if it had happened yesterday. The open wound to her heart had long since healed, but the pain and anger remained. It didn't lessen when he took Edna as his third wife.

And she had mourned anew this morning, lying on her cot earlier and listening to Norah telling her unborn child how loved and cared for Cal had made her feel during the week she had been married to him. Dolly would have given anything for that one week of love and belonging to a man who actually wanted her. Wanted *her*— not just a woman to do for him, a female body to slake his lust.

So while Dolly felt sorry for Norah, she didn't pity her. Norah was a widow about to bear a fatherless child, but she had a home and a way to make a decent, honest living. And she was pretty. As soon as her child was born, men would be drawn to her again. She wouldn't have to raise her child alone if she didn't want to.

With a sigh, Dolly pulled on her heavy boots, threw a coat on over her night clothes, and took the water bucket. She opened the back door and peered at the angry black storm clouds overhead. The temperature had risen in the last hour before dawn, and Dolly knew that meant snow was coming, again. Perhaps the worst storm of the winter, which would be followed by a spell of bitter cold. Once cold and fog settled into the Little Colorado River valley, they stayed, while surrounding areas enjoyed much warmer temperatures.

Dolly took Norah's washtub down from its hook on the wall and began filling it with water she had retrieved from the well. With a wicked storm on its way and a baby due at any time, a good supply of water and wood inside were absolute necessities. Then she checked the supplies of food and coal oil for the lamps. From the looks of the sky, she figured she had until about nine o'clock to make her preparations.

Harcourt Barr, Fat Tony Roscoe, and Dowie Johnston were huddled together in a boxcar with about thirty ewes as the train chugged into the station at Indianapolis. It had been a frigid trip from Columbus, Ohio, and the three men would have frozen but for the warmth of the wooly creatures.

"I ain't goin' another mile without a ticket!" Harcourt declared as they tumbled out of the car before it totally stopped.

"Remember," Fat Tony said, "we're supposed to be Omar's kinfolk, worried 'cause we ain't heard from him since last fall. I'll do the talkin'. You two just try to act halfway smart."

"What if nobody remembers him?" Harcourt whined. "My feet's wet, and pert near frostbit."

Fat Tony looked thoroughly disgusted. "If Omar came through here, somebody will surely remember him. That angel face of his sticks in people's minds."

Fat Tony was right. Both a ticket seller and a porter working in the train station positively identified the kindly old gentleman they had assisted on his travels in the fall. And they had been so impressed by him they even remembered his destination: St. Louis.

Morgan stamped his feet on the wooden platform and shoved his hands deeper into his coat pockets. If he wasn't so damned stubborn, he'd go inside the depot to wait for the east-bound train this morning. But he didn't like Harrison, the stationmaster, and he'd rather stand outside in a blizzard than share a stove with such a bastard.

Delbert Harrison was supplying cattle thieves with shipping schedules. Morgan had no proof of this other than his gut instinct, which hadn't failed him yet. He knew a number of other men were also involved, but the operation was too smooth for them not to have inside information. One of them was bound to slip up, and then he'd have them all.

A blast of wind caught his hat and lifted it. He grabbed it just before it could sail away. Damn, it was cold! Snow couldn't be far off.

That scared the hell out of him. What if Doc Robinson wasn't on the incoming train? What if tomorrow's train was delayed by the snow?

Norah's baby was due any day now and Morgan was worried. He told himself babies were born every day, but nobody he knew had had one recently, so his fear grew with the rising wind.

He saw Flora Harrison come to the window and look out. Morgan wondered if she knew about her husband's dirty dealings with the rustlers. Flora was such a gentle woman, kind and thoughtful to folks, ready to help a stranded traveler. Could a woman live with a man and not know all his secrets?

It was hard to understand how any man with a nice family could get mixed up with thieves. Yet Morgan knew from some questions he'd asked of a lawman up in Colorado that Delbert Harrison had left his last post under a cloud of suspicion.

"Damned cold out here, Sheriff." The editor was wrapped in so many clothes he looked twice his normal size.

"It sure is, Frank." Morgan hunched against the wind.

"Waiting for somebody?" His news nose said there had to be a story in the making if the sheriff was up before breakfast to meet the train.

"I thought Doc Robinson might get in a day or two early."

"It's a shame about his sister."

Doc Robinson's recent letter that told of his mother's passing also said his sister had collapsed of heart failure several weeks before their mother died. She'd only been forty-nine and had left a husband and five children.

"Yes," Morgan agreed. "Doc's had his share of tribulation."

"I sure hope he's back before Mrs. Welsh's time comes. The whole town is worried."

Morgan nodded. "I'm glad Dolly's here with her."

"Ain't that something? It sure was a sight when old Mordecai came after her and ordered her back home—and she refused. He turned so red in the face I thought he was gonna keel over. Hey, that's the train whistle."

Morgan noted that Frank didn't suggest that they wait inside the station house, either. Could it be that he, too, suspected Harrison of aiding the rustlers? For all his firebrand reporting, Frank was a smart editor.

The train chugged into sight, and a few brave souls came out in the cold to meet it. Quinton Rose, the mousetrap man, slipped out of the passenger coach and waved to Morgan.

"Sheriff, I've got something for you."

He strode across the wooden planks and handed Morgan an envelope. "The conductor gave it to me. It's from your doctor friend."

Morgan felt his stomach sink.

"What does it say?" Frank asked, his reporter's curiosity bursting at the seams.

Morgan quickly glanced at the note. "Doc's in Flagstaff. There was a big fire last night, and he got off the train this morning to help with the injured."

Quinton Rose watched him carefully. "Dolly's with her," he said.

Morgan looked up from the note, his face awash with worry. He sighed. "Women have babies all the time."

Frank, prudent for once, refrained from mentioning how many women didn't make it through the ordeal. "Maybe she'll wait till the doc gets back here," he said.

"Maybe."

Harrison came out of the depot and exchanged

words with the conductor. The conductor reached
into the car behind him and pulled out a gilded
bird cage, handing it to Harrison. Then Delbert
went back inside the station, not bothering to
speak to the three men standing outside.

"Nice bird cage," Morgan said.

"Mrs. Harrison has lots of lovely things in her
home," Rose told him.

Morgan raised a questioning brow.

"She had mice."

"Oh."

"She doesn't have an honest husband," Frank
said loudly, not caring who heard him. "I see
him out in the alley a couple times a week, meeting with thugs, slinking around like a snake.
Unless he's checking out folks' outhouses, he's
up to no good!"

The first snowflakes started floating down at
eight thirty that morning. Dolly sighed with certain knowledge that Doc Robinson wouldn't be
arriving anytime soon. She would have to
deliver Norah's baby, with Myrtis's help.

All the foodstuffs and supplies had been
inventoried and Dolly was wrapping herself in
her coat and scarf. First she was going to Wilson's
Mercantile to order what they needed to be
delivered. Then she'd get Myrtis.

Norah was in the early stages of labor. This was
a first baby, so it might be a long time yet. But
Dolly would rather have Myrtis there, waiting
with them, than go for her after the baby started
coming.

She had delivered a number of babies by herself, but she knew Myrtis wanted to be present, and the company of another woman who knew what to do was always welcome if anything went wrong.

"Let's stop at the newspaper office," Dolly said.

"Why?" Myrtis asked. "I already read last week's edition."

"They're to paste, not to read. It's still cold in that building—and I intend to remedy that."

Norah was pacing the floor in front of the stove. She was worried. If Dolly was right about the bad weather that was coming, would they be able to keep this barn of a building warm enough for a baby? Why hadn't she insisted on finishing the insulation work last week?

There was a terrible banging at the front door, but it took her quite a while to get there to open it.

"Howdy, Miz Welsh!" Jed Wilson from the mercantile doffed his hat. "I brought the things Mrs. Smith ordered. Figgered she was right about the storm that's comin'. Oh, and there's a couple of crates of stuff from the train station, too. Where do you want me to put 'em?"

Norah hardly knew what to say. She hadn't ordered anything, but perhaps Cal had. And she could hardly keep the man standing out in the cold while she thought about the possibilities.

"Can you put them right here in the front, Mr. Wilson? Then we can sort them out later."

"Sure 'nough, ma'am. If you'll jist hold this here door for me, I'll get 'em right inside." He proceeded to do so in handy fashion. "Would ya like fer me to open them crates fer ya? I jist happen to have a crowbar in the wagon."

Norah nodded. She knew he was dying of curiosity about what was in the crates, but then so was she.

He came blustering back in, brushing snow off his coat, and pried the top off the first crate.

"Dress goods," he said with disappointment.

The crate was full of bolts of cloth—fine white linen, lace, and broadcloth, and three bolts of velvet in jewel tones. Norah stood open-mouthed. She had not seen such fine fabrics since she'd left Shillitos.

Then Jed Wilson started on the second crate. It, too, held bolts of cloth, but they were all unbleached muslin, soft and delicate enough for the finest pillowcases and sheets—or shirts and blouses and dresses.

"Well, I'll be dogged!" Jed Wilson pushed back his hat with his gloved thumb. "Was Cal plannin' on opening up a dry goods store, Miz Welsh?"

Norah heard the antagonism in Jed Wilson's voice, but she was having a hard enough time dealing with her own emotions without worrying about his. She dashed the tears from her eyes with the back of her hand.

"No. They're for me. To sew. He knew I always wanted a dressmaker's shop."

"Well, I wish you luck, ma'am."

"Thank you, Mr. Wilson. Will you be able to

order other fabrics and findings for me as I need them?"

"You bet. You jist let me know. We can get things from San Francisco in a week if we telegraph 'em and tell 'em to hurry."

Finally the talkative storekeeper went on his way and left Norah to her treasures. Dolly had told her to be very careful and not do anything until she got back, but Norah couldn't resist the bolts of velvet. She tugged the emerald one from the crate, then almost doubled over from the pain in her abdomen and lower back. She dropped the green velvet back on the top of the crate and started toward her bed.

Maybe Dolly was right. Maybe she should lie down until the other women returned. Just as she reached the rocking chair, however, she felt warm fluid gushing from between her legs, so she eased herself into the chair instead.

After a few moments she lifted the skirt of her duster to see if it was blood. No, thank God, it was a clear fluid. Evidently her water had broken. The baby was coming. But what was she supposed to do now? And where was Dolly?

9

Colleen Mary Welsh made her appearance in the middle of one of the worst snowstorms to hit Holbrook since its official founding. She arrived at approximately four o'clock in the morning. Both Dolly and Myrtis were very relieved it was over. It had been a long ordeal, because Norah was such a small woman and narrow in the hips. But she was a picture of ecstasy as she held her perfect daughter in her arms.

Morgan had checked in three times that day—first at about noon, then at six in the evening, and finally after midnight—each time to be told things were progressing normally. Uneasy, but unable to do anything to help, he went home to bed.

He came by the next morning at ten o'clock on his way to breakfast at the hotel. Wisps of smoke were coming from the chimney, but everything was quiet. Alarmed, he unlocked the front door with his key, stepped in, and then tripped on the crates of fabric that had been delivered the day before. Muttering a curse, he shoved them out of the way and strode past the partition to the back.

He couldn't believe it. They were all asleep, piled under many blankets, and the fire was almost out in the stove.

"What the hell's going on?" he muttered.

Then he heard a tiny mewling sound and followed it to the cradle beside Norah's bed. Squatting down on his heels, he pulled the quilts aside with one finger to expose a tiny face dominated by huge dark eyes and wisps of raven hair.

"Well, I'll be damned," he said quietly.

"You most certainly will!" Myrtis hissed from the back of Norah's bed. "Why did you wake the baby? What are you doing here, anyway?"

"Checking on you. It was quiet in here. That worried me." He looked back down at the baby in the cradle and smiled as she yawned and then closed her eyes again. "Everything went all right?"

"Yes. We told you it would."

"It's colder'n hell in here, Myrtis. How are you going to keep that baby warm?"

"Well, make yourself useful! Build up the fire and put the coffeepot on." She climbed out from under the covers and put her coat on over the plain flannel nightgown Dolly had loaned her. She hadn't thought to bring one of her own because she figured she'd just go home. But the storm had been so bad that neither Norah nor Dolly would hear of it.

Myrtis sat down at the table and pulled on her woolen socks, then slipped her feet into her boots. "So what's the weather like?"

"It's stopped snowing, but the wind has piled up drifts six and eight feet high in places. I had to shovel snow to get here."

"Well, that ought to keep the rowdies out of trouble for an hour or two. Maybe all day. Think you could stand two quiet nights in a row?"

Morgan poured scalding coffee into two cups and handed Myrtis one. "I could stand a whole bunch of them, but I'm not planning on having them."

Myrtis glanced to see if the other two women were still sleeping. "Anybody in particular got you worried?"

Morgan stirred sugar into his coffee and watched the black liquid swirl in the cup. "That nephew of Winnie Ralston's is as mean as a rattlesnake. And besides that, he's a walking powder keg. I've seen his kind before. They have an itch to kill. William Bonney was like that."

Myrtis nodded. She'd seen men like that before, too. "That husband o' hers ain't no prize, neither. And she looks like such a nice little woman, too."

"She probably is. Maybe she's like you Myrt," Morgan teased, "and thinks every woman needs a man, no matter what."

"Usually that's true, and you know it." She dropped her voice lower. "Course I ain't in the habit o' includin' killers and Mormons in my eligibles, neither." She cast a glance toward where Dolly was sleeping. "Now she's a right fine woman, and knows a lot about birthin' babies, too."

"Maybe she's had a lot of experience. They have a whole passel of kids out at the Smith place. At least a dozen."

Myrtis shook her gray head. "Fifteen, but none of 'em are hers. She told me her three died. She helps raise all the others though, including those two Indian kids they picked up somewhere. Why do you suppose they came here, anyway?"

Morgan shrugged. "The Mormons are starting a lot of settlements hereabouts."

"I heard they all think Utah is the promised land. So whyn't they stay there?"

"A lot of the Mormon men are being sent to the territorial prison in Utah for having more than one wife."

Myrtis looked astonished. "I thought the Mormons ran everything up in Utah. Why're they sending themselves to jail? Not that I don't think they deserve it! But men ain't in the habit o' givin' themselves what they deserve."

Morgan grinned as he brought the coffeepot over and refilled their cups. "It's a federal law, Myrt, and the federal marshals have really begun cracking down on it."

"If it's agin' the law to have more'n one wife, then whyn't you arrest Mordecai Smith?"

"Because I'm not a federal marshal. I got better things to do besides watching to see what woman has a baby by what man. And besides, I figure if a man's dumb enough to have more than one wife at a time he deserves whatever he gets!"

Myrtis made a swipe at his handsome head. "I still say it's like turning women into slaves. And that's what the War Between the States was about. My first husband was killed at Manassas. He was the best of the three. I'd hate to think he died fer nuthin'."

Morgan got up to add wood to the stove, and the baby began to fuss again. In two steps he was at the foot of the cradle. He bent over, slid his large callused hands down inside, and lifted out the whole bundle of baby and blankets. He shifted the bundle expertly into the crook of his arm and returned to his chair. Once there, he rested one booted foot across the other knee and propped the baby up in the space provided, peeling away enough of her blankets to determine if she was wet.

"Well, ain't you a surprise!" Myrtis marveled.

Morgan grinned. "I was one of ten, Myrt. Though three of my brothers were killed in the mines. I couldn't stand it. Figured I'd rather die of lead poisoning than be buried alive down in the bowels of the earth. Missed the kids, though, and my ma. But she wanted me to get out, too, while I still could. All she asked was that I learn to read and write and send her a letter now and then, and she'd get the priest to read it to her."

"That why you got all them books at your house?"

"Hummph. How long since this little lady's been fed, Myrt? Is she about due to be needing her mama?"

"Yeah, but I'll take some soft cloth and make

her up a sugar tit. Her mama needs to sleep a while longer if'n she can."

Morgan frowned. "I thought you said everything went all right."

"It did. It was jist real hard, bein' the first. And she bled right smart, so she needs to rest and git her strength back. Me'n Dolly are gonna stay awhile. See if'n we can't finish gettin' that paper pasted at the top of these walls, and fix the places that got wet when the roof leaked."

Morgan looked up. "Hell, yes! No wonder it's so damned cold in here. You sure you can do that? I could send Conrad Putney over to lend a hand today."

"Please don't do that, Morgan." Norah spoke up in a soft voice. "I don't like that man . . . the way he looks at me. And with me being in bed . . ."

She didn't need to finish the statement. Morgan could imagine it all. Hell, he didn't like the way any man looked at her, not even old Grandpa Taylor who was eighty-two. And he didn't want any other man seeing her in bed, either.

"We've got to get some more heat in here, Norah," he said sternly. "Don't want this little girl to freeze solid."

Norah smiled. "I see you've met my daughter."

"Yeah. She hasn't had much to say, though. Didn't tell me what her name is."

"Colleen Mary Welsh."

"She's a beautiful little girl. Cal would be very proud."

Norah bit her lip. "Yes, he would."

Then Colleen began to squirm and fuss again.

"Would you bring her to me, Morgan? She probably needs to be fed."

Morgan was frozen to his chair. The thought of tucking the baby in next to her mother and seeing that tiny rosebud mouth close over Norah's breast paralyzed him for a moment. "Uh, sure, just a minute."

Norah found his embarrassment endearing, and when he lifted the bedclothes to slide the baby in next to her, his large callused hands so gentle, she couldn't help teasing him a little.

"You were supposed to leave the outer blankets in the cradle, Morgan."

"Too damn cold in here," he muttered as he watched her offer her breast to the baby and the tiny mouth greedily close over her engorged nipple. But the expression in his dark eyes was hot. As Norah glanced up at him, she felt seared by it, fused to him somehow.

He backed away from the bed. "Uh, I'll be back later. I gotta see about finding another stove."

Then there was a pounding at the front door, and a voice calling, "Sheriff! Sheriff Treyhan, you in there?"

Morgan lurched toward the front. "What the hell has happened now?"

He unlocked the door to find young Jimmy on the step, bundled up in all the clothes he owned, with only his eyes visible.

"Get in here out of the cold!" Morgan ordered, slamming and locking the door behind the boy. "Now what's happened?"

Jimmy shook his head and began unwrapping

the scarf that covered his mouth. "We saw you comin' this way earlier. And another big crate came for Miz Welsh on the midnight train. Albert's pa says it's a stove, and the Widow Welsh might be a'needin' it in this weather. So I come t'find ya."

"The train's able to get through all right? What about the snowdrifts?"

"There ain't much 'atween here an' Albuquerque for the snow to drift against, I guess. Anyway, the engineer said the tracks was clear enough when he came through. Might'a' changed by now. Have to wait and see if the next train makes it on time, I reckon."

Morgan nodded. "Come in here by the stove and thaw out a minute while I get my stuff on, then we'll go see about that stove. Cal had the right idea, but it's a hell of a time for it to arrive!"

"Ain't it!" Jimmy agreed cheerfully, his nose red from the cold. "Sure has been fun seeing all the stuff Mr. Welsh ordered for Miz Welsh, though."

Yeah, for the whole town, Morgan thought as he shrugged back into his fleece-lined coat and gloves.

"Hello, Jimmy," Norah greeted the boy. "Want to come meet my baby?"

"Oh!" Jimmy's eyes widened. "You got a baby! When did you get her?"

"About four o'clock this morning—while you were still in bed asleep."

"Where'd it come from?" Jimmy asked. "There weren't no train come at that time."

"Come along, boy," Morgan said.

Norah looked at him quizzically.

"He says a stove came for you on the train last night. Seems Cal was being practical, after all."

"Lordy, d'ya suppose it's a cookstove? Now that would be a fine thing indeed!" Myrtis's excitement was contagious.

"We'll find out when we get there." He looked over at Norah. "You might be thinking about where you want it. But I'd suggest that wall over there by the door." Then he collared Jimmy, who was staring at Norah and the baby with a rapt expression on his young face, and the two headed out.

Dolly waited until they had left, then she got out of bed, too. "Did I hear something about a cookstove?"

"Maybe. Don't know yet. All the boy said was that a stove came on the train last night. But we can sure *hope* it's a cookstove."

Dolly nodded as she looked around the back room area, mentally rearranging things to accommodate a cookstove.

About two hours later the women heard a commotion outside. A flatbed wagon with one huge crate and three smaller ones in it had been backed in front of the privy. Two men who were too bundled up to be identified were unloading heavy planks and leaning them slantwise against the bed of the wagon as Morgan came bounding in the door.

"Norah, you and the baby get bundled up in that bed. Cover up your heads if necessary because we're going to have to have this door open while we bring the stove in. Myrtis, you might want to build up the fire in the other stove, and put on a pot of coffee. And Mrs. Smith, do you suppose you could put together a bite to eat? I don't know whether my men have eaten yet today or not, but I haven't."

Dolly nodded. "Maybe we could move Norah's bed closer to the stove, with the headboard facing the door. It's high enough to break the wind."

"Good idea," Morgan said. "Let me call the men in."

"Oh, I think you and I can move it, Sheriff."

Morgan looked nonplussed for a moment, then silently agreed that the Mormon woman was certainly big and strong enough to do the job. It didn't set well with him, though.

"Is it a cookstove?" Myrtis demanded.

"Yes," Morgan answered crossly, "and a damn big one at that. It took three of us to push the thing down a ramp onto the wagon. There's no way we could lift it. Cal must have bought the biggest and heaviest one they had! Everybody bundle up now, we're gonna have to open the door."

The heavy planks were levered between the back of the wagon and the doorway. All three men got into the back of the wagon and heaved until the largest crate was sitting on the planks at the top of the makeshift ramp. Then they pushed it down the ramp and into the store building.

Once it was inside, they quickly slid the

smaller crates down the planks and came inside, stamping their feet and blowing on their hands.

Myrtis had hot coffee ready, and Dolly had made some cheese sandwiches. Morgan and his two helpers, Herb and Jack, shucked their outer garments and settled down on top of the stove crate for a sandwich or two and some coffee.

Now that the door was closed, Norah pushed the covers back so she could see what was going on.

"Are you sure it's all right for you to be spending all this time doing this, Morgan?"

"Putney knows where to find me. But anybody with a lick of sense is going to be inside where it's warm today, not out starting trouble."

Myrtis laughed. "Maybe you ought to apply for a sheriff's job at the North Pole, Morgan."

"No, thanks, this is more than cold enough to suit me."

After they rested a few minutes, the men started taking the huge crate apart and laying the black cast-iron pieces of the stove in specific places on the floor.

About that time Digger and Tod stopped in to see what was happening.

"I thought ya was a'buryin' that tinhorn who got hisself shot at the Bucket o' Blood night 'afore last," Myrtis said to Digger as she poured coffee for them.

"Not in this weather, I ain't! He ain't a'goin' nowhere. Tod nailed him up real tight in that coffin, and we put him in the back room. Cold as it is, he won't even stink." Then Digger looked surprised as Myrtis kicked him and tilted her head in Norah's direction. "Oh, pardon me, Miz Welsh, but it's the God's truth!"

"I'm sure it is, Digger," Norah said wryly.

Meanwhile, the other three men were arguing about how tall the stove was going to be and where the stovepipe fit. Finally, the man called Herb got the long ladder from the front part of the building, put it up against the wall, and began cutting a hole to put the pipe through.

"I don't think they sent enough pipe, Sheriff. This is a tall building, and if the pipe doesn't go at least two feet above the crest of the roof, the stove will always smoke."

"Well, go see if Wilson's got any. Jack and I can handle this part. We might even put Digger and Tod to work."

Before dusk the new cookstove was in operation. The water reservoir was filled, and Dolly had a savory stew simmering in the Dutch oven and bread dough rising to put into the oven. She had promised the men a substantial hot meal for their labors.

Since the building was finally warm, the men removed the quilt draped around Norah's bed and pushed the bed back in place.

Myrtis had contributed an apple pie to the meal, and the smell of baking apples and cinnamon, along with another pot of coffee, had whetted all their appetites. They didn't even mind that the table wasn't big enough for all of them to sit down.

"Don't worry about that none, ma'am," Herb assured Norah. "We can set here on the floor jist fine. With grub that smells that good to fill yore belly, a man don't rightly care where his behind is."

Holbrook finally dug out from the blizzard a week later, and things were back to normal. The trains were on schedule again. A lot of snow was still left, especially in the mounds where it had been shoveled. In many of the neighboring areas it was down to just traces, but a cold, foggy miasma continued to hang in the valley of the Little Colorado River.

The weather didn't prevent half the town from stopping by for a look at Colleen Mary and Norah's wonderful new cookstove.

Clarabelle Wattron stopped by with a dried-apricot pie. "I figured you wouldn't be getting out anytime soon, and I couldn't wait to see the baby." She blushed until her entire face was the color of her nose. "And I don't make as many pies as I used to."

Myrtis shot Dolly a knowing look, but Norah studiously ignored the both of them. Everyone had been talking, of course, about how Clarabelle didn't play the organ and bake on the nights when Ferdie was visiting the railroad engineer's wife anymore. Not since the Little Nipper man came to town.

"Would you like to hold Colleen?" Norah asked her.

Clarabelle's pale eyes lit up. "Oh, could I?"

"Of course."

"But I haven't held a baby since Ferdie was little."

Norah chuckled. "Believe me, it's not something you forget how to do. Although sometimes you're amazed by how *small* they are."

"You have younger brothers and sisters?" Clarabelle asked with interest. It had never occurred to her that the elegant Mrs. Welsh had spent any time raising children.

"An even dozen, to date," Norah said. "My mam just had another."

"Oh, my!" Clarabelle scooped Colleen from Norah's arms and began to walk around the room with her, cooing and playing with her baby fingers.

"Well, now that Clarabelle's here yore not likely t'be a'jumpin' up doin' something foolish," Myrtis declared. "Me and Dolly are gonna do some more work on these walls."

"The two of you have done too much already!" Norah protested. "Why, you've rearranged everything in the shop, moved the small stove in there, and tried to wait on me hand and foot besides."

"Gotta have somethin' t'do to keep busy. I never was one fer settin' around much."

"But—"

"It's either us or some yahoos Morgan will send over here," Myrtis said.

"The work must be done," Dolly said. "So just let us do it."

Norah sighed in defeat. The store building was much warmer now.

"My, this is a fine cookstove!" Clarabelle cooed as she stood in front of it. "Even mine is not so grand."

Norah agreed that it was indeed wonderful, then sat down in the rocking chair. She really felt like lying down on her bed, but she couldn't do that with Clarabelle present.

Clarabelle was still talking baby talk to Colleen while Norah rocked gently back and forth with her eyes closed, trying to draw her strength, when someone banged on the back door. Clarabelle glanced toward Norah, then went to answer it herself.

It was Jimmy. "Howdy, Miz Wattron, I need to see Miz Welsh."

"Come in, then. And be quick about it. We can't heat the entire outdoors!"

Jimmy scooted in and came to a stop in front of Norah's chair as Clarabelle slammed the back door. "You've got more stuff!" His eyes danced with excitement. "Three crates at the station. They came this morning!"

"Three more?" Norah echoed. "What on earth now?"

"Dunno. They're marked F–R–A–G–some-thing. I couldn't read all the letters."

"If they're marked *fragile*, I'll bet they're dishes," Clarabelle chimed in. "Run and see if Mr. Harrison's sending them over with some-one!"

"Sending over what?" Myrtis demanded as she and Dolly came in from the front.

"We're not sure. Dishes, maybe."

The crates were duly delivered and turned out to be full of dishes, glassware, flatware, and pots and pans of every variety. But Norah had no place to put them. The other three women decided Norah must have some cupboards.

"I can't afford to have anything else done now!" Norah protested, but no one paid attention to her. They were too busy unpacking and admiring all the things Cal Welsh had ordered for his bride.

"One thing about Cal," Clarabelle mused, "he never did things by halves. Now I really have to go and start dinner."

Declaring she needed a breath of fresh air, Myrtis left with Clarabelle and went in search of Tod Willis, the coffin maker Morgan had hired to build the cedar chest for Colleen's things.

"Looks like snow agin, Tod," Myrtis announced when she found him. "What would you say to a nice warm inside job?"

It snowed for two days, then during the night high winds whipped the snow into monstrous drifts. And before people could get dug out from that, the ice storm hit. The trains couldn't get through. Cattle and sheep out on the range were dying from exposure.

Farmers and ranchers had flocked to the Little Colorado River valley during the past ten years because it was covered with high grass. Wild hay grew for miles in every direction. The Aztec Cattle Company, owned by a group of eastern businessmen, had claimed every other section along the railroad tracks and brought tens of thousands of cattle into the country. Now, during the ice storm, thousands of those animals were dying.

Old-time cattlemen who came to the area

from Texas and New Mexico understood the amount of grassland it took to support cattle in this country. They feared that Aztec and similar big outfits would overgraze and ruin the land for everybody.

Morgan was weary after three days of sleeping only an hour or two at a time. Times of distress brought out the best in some people and the absolute worst in others. Morgan knew his vigilance could not lag. Conrad Putney had taken a prisoner to the county jail in St. Johns before the storm hit and had been unable to return. So Morgan had to defend the town alone.

He hadn't seen Norah and Colleen since the storm began, and he found he needed that more than he needed sleep. If he weren't so exhausted he'd tell himself how stupid he was being, but he was too tired to be rational so he followed his feelings.

He wanted to be in the same room with Norah, to talk to her and see her smile. No, that was a lie. What he *really* wanted was to feel her snuggled closely to his body in bed. He was too exhausted to do anything more than that just now, but he would give all that he owned to go to sleep with her in his arms. Instead, he would have to settle for an hour in her company before he went to collapse in his lonely bed.

When he arrived at Norah's back door, Tod Willis answered it.

"Howdy, Sheriff, come in, won't ya?"

Morgan didn't trust himself to say anything so he just nodded and stepped through the door, leaving it for Tod to close.

Norah looked up from the table where she was bathing Colleen in one of the largest kettles Cal had bought, and smiled. "Morgan! How good to see you. Come sit down. As soon as I get this young lady out of her bath, I'll get you a cup of coffee."

"No hurry," he said quietly as he hung his sheepskin coat on the back of the chair he was going to sit on. He could have gotten his own coffee, but he liked the idea of Norah waiting on him. Especially with Tod present. So he propped his left ankle over his right knee and leaned back in the chair, watching the bathing process.

When Norah lifted the baby out of the water with one hand and wrapped her in a towel with the other, Morgan reached forward. "Let me have her."

Norah watched as his large hands clasped her daughter so gently. It amazed her how good he was with the baby. Her father had never been. She smiled as he plopped Colleen in his lap and began rubbing her with the soft huckaback towel.

She poured him a cup of coffee and took out one of the cinnamon rolls she'd baked the day before to go with it. He looked exhausted. She wondered when he'd slept last.

"Would you like some breakfast? I could fix ham and eggs."

"No thanks, Norah. I couldn't do justice to it now. Maybe later."

"You should be home in bed!" Norah said, then blushed when she saw the glitter in his dark eyes.

"I'm headed that way."

"Miz Welsh," Tod interrupted, "would you come and show me jist how high ya can reach comfortably so I'll know how tall to make this dish cabinet?"

"Certainly."

Morgan scowled. That was a ploy to get Norah away from him, and Morgan recognized it. Tod Willis had certainly built enough cabinets to know how tall to make them without Norah's help. "Say, why do ya need dish cabinets, anyway?" he asked.

"Oh, haven't you heard?" Norah frowned. "No, I guess we haven't seen you since then."

"Since when?"

"The arrival of the three crates of dishes and glasses and pots and pans that Cal ordered. I had nowhere to put them. So Myrtis got Tod to come build cabinets."

Morgan reminded himself to have a talk with Myrtis. And where in the hell had Cal gotten the money to pay for all the things he bought? Had his father left him money? Surely Cal would have mentioned that.

"And really, Miz Welsh, while we're at it we oughta build ya a dry sink and a pie safe. Ya need someplace ta keep those wonderful baked goods ya been makin'."

And how the hell did Tod know what wonderful baked goods Norah made? Morgan wondered as he took a bite of the cinnamon roll she'd placed next to his coffee.

"Maybe later, Tod. I'll have to make you a whole new wardrobe to pay for these cabinets."

Morgan choked on his coffee. The mental image of Norah running her hands down Tod's legs while she fitted trousers to him made him feel ill. He wished to hell he'd never hired Tod to build the cedar chest for Colleen's things.

To keep his mind off the idea, he began to dress the baby in the clothes Norah had laid out.

"You do that really well," Norah said as she watched him expertly diaper her daughter.

"Nothin' to it, really. We had a lot of kids around our house. Seems like one of 'em always needed its pants changed."

Norah picked up the baby and finished dressing her, giving Morgan a chance to drink his coffee.

"This is really good," he said when he'd swallowed the last bite of the cinnamon roll. "I didn't know you were a baker, too."

Norah started to tell him that in her family a person had to do it all, but she was interrupted by a knock on the front door.

"Good grief, who can that be!" She handed the baby back to Morgan and went to see.

Mordecai Smith and two of his sons stood outside, bundled up in many layers of clothes.

"Why, Mr. Smith, what brings you out in such terrible weather?" Norah asked, praying that he had not come after Dolly and that he would not make a scene.

"A very important matter I need to speak with you about, Miz Welsh."

"Oh, well, come in out of the cold—all of you." She led the way to the back. Norah didn't like the way Mordecai Smith looked at her. She'd much rather deal with whatever he wanted in front of Morgan and Tod.

Smith, on the other hand, was not at all pleased to find Tod Willis building cabinets for the Widow Welsh and Sheriff Treyhan bouncing her daughter on his knee. He had not expected other men to be courting her quite so soon—or so blatantly. That baby couldn't be much more than a week old.

"I'd like to offer you something hot to drink," Norah said, "but all I have is coffee."

"That's all right," Smith assured her. "The heat from the stove will be fine." He proceeded to go and stand in front of it, preventing a great deal of the heat from getting to the others.

"What may I help you with, Mr. Smith?"

Mordecai fidgeted a bit, pulled his ear, then raked the fingers of one hand through his chest-length beard. Finally he cleared his throat. "My sons here have a very special occasion having to do with the church coming up, and they don't have the proper clothes for it. Each of them needs a suit and two shirts. Can you make them?"

Norah was stunned, then realized that Dolly had probably done the sewing in the Smith family.

"Yes, I can. I have some fine worsted, both in black and gray, and white broadcloth for shirts. Would you like to see it?"

"No, that won't be necessary. I will trust your judgment. Can you have them finished in three weeks' time?"

"If that's when you need them. Just let me take the boys' measurements."

Morgan watched Norah easing her measuring tape around the bodies of the Smith boys, then he watched Tod and Mordecai watch her. It was bad enough to see Tod looking at Norah like a lovesick bull, but for a man who already had three wives to be salivating over her was enough to make Morgan fighting mad.

Too tired to act on his anger, he started to get up and leave, then caught Norah's beseeching look and the slight shake of her head. He eased himself back onto his chair, telling himself what a damned fool he was. He had better things to do than referee Norah's love life. He had a town to keep civilized. The combination of the bad weather, the financial losses, and the lack of mobility was causing even normally shy men to turn into fractious rowdies.

But he wasn't budging from Norah's kitchen just yet no matter how tired he was. He had the best position in the house, and he meant to keep it. Neither Tod nor Mordecai would challenge him.

Kid Keller and Joe Baldwin were playing blackjack for matchsticks in Walter Gates's room at the Holbrook House. Walter was still on duty downstairs at the desk, and would be for at least another hour. Delbert Harrison was scheduled to meet them there at ten o'clock to talk about when Aztec was due to bring in more cattle.

"Do you reckon Putney will make it t'night?" Joe Baldwin asked around the matchstick he was chewing on. "Nobody's seen him since he left for St. Johns last week."

"He's probably havin' the time of his life playin' big shot. He likes workin' both sides of the law."

"It's handy for us, too."

"Yeah, long as it lasts. Everybody knows he's a piss poor deputy. And when Lindstrom comes back, Putney'll be back down on the same level with the rest of us."

"I wouldn't try t'buck Lindstrom," Joe said.

"Nobody who's fond of livin' would," Kid Keller agreed as he turned up an ace to go with his queen. "Twenty-one. Pay me."

A little over two weeks later, Mordecai Smith came back to town to pick up his sons' new clothing, alone and all spruced up and in his best clothes. He'd even trimmed his beard. He left his wagon right in front of the shop.

Norah saw him from the window and frowned. She had a slight headache and was in no mood for nonsense.

She was in the shop alone because Dolly had gone to help Myrtis nurse Flora Harrison. They were doing everything they knew to keep a bad chest cold from going into pneumonia.

"You didn't bring the boys so I could try these on them?" Norah asked when he walked inside.

"Not necessary," he said, tracking the dung and mud from the street on the braided rug by the door. "You measured them *very* carefully."

Norah blinked at his tone. He sounded as

though he were suggesting something improper on her part. "I always do, Mr. Smith," she said briskly. "You can't tailor clothing without proper measurements." She wrapped the suits individually in brown paper, tying the parcels with binder twine. "Each of your sons has a suit and two shirts, and there are a dozen linen collars for them to share. That will be twelve dollars and eighty-four cents, please."

When she looked up he was standing practically on top of her. "No money needs to pass between us, my dear."

Norah moved back two steps. "Whatever do you mean?"

"A man doesn't pay his wife to do what needs to be done."

"Wife?" Norah felt as though she'd been poleaxed.

"I can see you're surprised, my dear, but that can't be helped. I meant to speak for you the last time I was in town, but your house was cluttered up with the sheriff and that coffin maker!"

"Have you lost your mind, you old fool? I never heard of anything so ridiculous in my life! Besides, Dolly is my friend!"

Mordecai shrugged. "All my wives are friends."

Norah's eyes blazed fire, and her Irish temper got the best of her. "Give me my money, then take these packages and leave!"

"No sense getting het up. You need a husband. I need a strong young wife. It's perfect."

Norah grabbed the broom and began pushing the Mormon back toward the door. "Understand this, old man. I'm not sure I'll marry again at all.

But if I do, you can bet I won't be any man's fourth wife!"

Just then Morgan opened the shop door, and Norah shoved Mordecai outside and threw the packages after him. They bounced off the side of his wagon and landed on the muddy boardwalk.

"That'll be twelve dollars and eighty-four cents, Mr. Smith. Send your sons back with it. I don't want you in my shop again!"

Then she slammed the door shut and whirled on Morgan. "And don't you say a word. Not . . . one . . . single . . . word!"

Morgan raised his hands silently in mock surrender, but he couldn't keep the twinkle out of his eyes.

Norah stomped off toward the back, muttering vile curses about all men.

Morgan lowered his hands, grinned, then sauntered into the kitchen after her.

10

Despite more than a week of clear spring weather, snow still lay deep in the shady patches beneath the ponderosa pines. The muddy, rutted trail up the rocky side of the Mogollon Rim had frozen solid during the cold night, forcing the early morning travelers to exercise more caution than normal. Nathan Ralston rode in tense silence, his breathing harsh in the high mountain elevation as his horse picked a path over the icy mud and broken stones.

He was anxious to get home to Winnie. It amazed him how terribly much he'd missed her. Age was apparently making him soft in the head, he thought, at least where his wife was concerned. He'd begun thinking about retiring, getting a little place in some quiet wholesome town, and living the rest of his life in peace. A man deserved a little peace and quiet before he met his Maker, even a man like him.

Nathan also wanted to get away from the forced and loathsome companionship of Bunky Lindstrom. In the nearly three months he'd spent in the Pleasant Valley with Lindstrom, he'd come to reevaluate his original low opinion of Winnie's gun-toting nephew. He'd been too damned kind! Bunky was worse than barnyard filth. He was a human monstrosity—bent, twisted, and damned.

Even five minutes in the younger man's company set Nathan's wary nerves on edge. He didn't trust Bunky. He knew as surely as he knew which way was up that Bunky wanted to kill him. Good instincts had kept him alive in other times and in other company, where men didn't make old bones. His instincts were screaming at him right now, and had been since he woke up from a nightmare last night.

He was frightened.

A movement caught his eye, and he turned in the saddle in time to see a winter-thin fox leap out at a rabbit and catch it in its sharp teeth. Scarlet droplets stained a pristine puff of snow, and Nathan turned his head away from the savage attack. Ahead of him Bunky rode in sullen silence.

Nathan had often wondered what went on in Bunky's mind, but no longer. He didn't care. All he thought about now was getting Winnie out of Holbrook and away from her nephew's evil influence. He urged his horse around a fallen tree in the path and allowed himself to lag a few more paces behind. With any luck Bunky would grow tired of his slower pace and ride on without him.

Half an hour later they entered a meadow where nearly a dozen deer stood in the patchy snow placidly eating the tiny green shoots of grass that heralded the coming of spring. On a naked branch of a white-barked aspen perched a red-tailed hawk, relaxed but watchful. Nathan felt like the hawk, ready to attack or retreat, whichever the circumstances required.

They rode a ways further, slowing as the trail sloped downward into a boulder-filled gully. A recent heavy storm had eroded the course, deteriorating the once hard-packed earth and leaving only a narrow, treacherous passage.

Bunky's horse stumbled, and he swore. He slipped off the horse and moved the animal off the trail to allow Nathan to pass.

"I think he loosened a shoe," Bunky muttered, sounding more disgusted and angry than he usually did. "You go on ahead. I'll catch up."

"I'll stop in Show Low to get something to eat," Nathan said. "I can wait if you want."

"Don't bother. I think I'll ride over to St. Johns. Tell Aunt Winnie not to expect me till she sees me."

A sense of relief seeped into Nathan's tight shoulders. He sighed to himself, feeling years younger, and urged his horse across the gully.

The bullet hit him in the back just as he reached the other side of the gully. A second one struck slightly below the first. And the third, apparently an afterthought, knocked off his hat, grazing his skull in one long, even line.

Spooked by the gun blast, the horse flung Nathan out of the saddle and plunged into the deep woods. Nathan fell with the force of a toppled pine tree, pitching facedown in the mud beside a lichen-covered boulder. He lay there, unmoving.

Bunky walked slowly up to the crumpled form of the man his aunt had married and poked at him with the shabby toe of his high-heeled boot. He felt nothing, neither glee nor remorse.

"That was too easy, old man. I wanted to see you suffer some."

He hunkered down and felt Nathan's neck for a pulse. It was there, faint and erratic. He curled his lips a bit. "So ya ain't dead yet, huh? Good." He pointed his pistol toward the incline and began firing. Rocks and debris rolled downward, partially covering the bleeding body.

"If you don't bleed to death first, some animal'll get ya. Or you'll freeze to death tonight. No matter what, Winnie's a widow."

After giving Nathan's uncovered leg a vicious kick, he swung up on his horse and calmly resumed his ride.

Rock chips cut sharply into Nathan's cheek as he listened to Bunky ride away. The dirt and debris piled on top of his body prevented him from taking a deep breath, but breathing hurt. He cursed himself for being stupid enough to turn his back on Bunky. Even one minute had been too long.

A sense of sadness filled him. He'd never see Winnie again. Sweet, wonderful Winnie. He closed his eyes and let the smell of moist, cold earth permeate his being. This was what it felt like to die.

The muscles at the back of Morgan's neck bunched into a tight knot, and his jaw clenched in an effort to remain silent. The mayor and two of his cronies stood in front of Morgan's desk like a trio of black-clad magpies bobbing and squawking.

"Why wasn't I told about the town company meeting?" Morgan asked when Mayor Whitehall paused for air.

"Oh, well, you were busy and we didn't want to bother you with such an unimportant matter."

Whitehall might own The Cottage—the most genteel drinking establishment within a hundred miles—and he might consider himself a cut above other businessmen in town, but like the rest, he was scared of a confrontation with Treyhan. He fluffed his bushy black mutton-chop whiskers and tried to look dignified.

"Unimportant, my ass!" Morgan slammed his hand on the desk, causing all three men to flinch. "Withdrawing the funds to pay a deputy's salary is not a trivial matter."

"See here, Sheriff Treyhan," Whitehall said, "you are employed by the town company, and you answer to us." He blanched at the sheriff's glare and looked to the butcher for help.

Charlie Cook was too smart to try to threaten Morgan. He'd only agreed with Whitehall's decision because he had ambitions to become town mayor. "The town can't afford a deputy. Twenty-five dollars a month is far too much for the town company to pay a man to walk the streets at night looking in store windows at the women, wiggling doorknobs, and drinking free beer at the Bucket of Blood."

Morgan flushed at the lacerating description of Conrad Putney's performance. It was close enough to the truth to wound him, but that wasn't the point. The mayor and his friends had made the decision without warning and behind his back. It was a betrayal of trust.

Morgan was furious—at Putney for being such a lousy lawman and at the company for being so goddamn sneaky. He needed a deputy. He needed a few hours a day to call his own, to relax. He hadn't had a whole day to get on his horse and ride away from Holbrook since last July—unless he was escorting a prisoner to another jail, and that was no vacation. Nine months was too long for a man to go without a day off.

"You can afford a New Year's Eve party. You can afford pyrotechnics for the Fourth of July. You can afford to give eastern merchants free buildings to lure them west. Why can't you afford to protect them once they get here?"

"You protect them! That's why we hired you." Snuffy Abbott ended every conversation with a snuffle, and wiped his nose with the back of his hand.

Morgan sighed and rubbed his neck. He already knew the argument was futile. The town company had made its decision. At the moment his only option was to quit, but he didn't want to do that. This nonsense wouldn't last long, though. Something would happen to change the company's decision.

"I can't work twenty-four hours a day, gentlemen." Morgan told them. "I need to sleep sometime."

"We know that, Sheriff. We're not asking you to. The members of the town company plan to become unpaid volunteer deputies. With our help, and that of other men in Holbrook, you don't need a deputy."

Morgan burst out laughing. He couldn't help himself. The idea of these soft shopkeepers running around with pistols chasing the territory's worst desperados seemed ludicrous.

The small portion of the mayor's chunky jowls that wasn't covered with hair flushed. "We've formed a vigilance committee," he said.

"Vigilantes! What in the hell are you thinking about, arming ordinary men and sending them out on the streets with a license to kill? That's not justice—that's an invitation for disaster!"

Whitehall puffed himself up like a balloon. "You exaggerate, Sheriff Treyhan."

"And *you* are an idiot!"

Charlie Cook and Snuffy Abbott both started to laugh.

Whitehall was furious. "Nevertheless, Sheriff," he said as he tried to collect his shattered dignity, "you *will* get rid of Putney. And you will accept the help of the men of this community."

"Oh, that's just dandy!" Morgan rose from his chair, towering over the mayor by several inches. "The storekeepers will take on the desperados. Well, which one of you vigilant citizens is going to take on Bunky Lindstrom? I've received word he's over in St. Johns. I figure in a week or two he'll be back our way, just looking for trouble. You all remember Bunky, don't you? He's a killer. Now, if you'll excuse me, I have rounds to make. Then I'll tell Putney you fired him."

Morgan had just lit the lamp when Conrad Putney arrived for work. He was more than an hour late.

"I had business with Lily Mae." Putney smirked. "Couldn't tear myself away."

Morgan realized he was not going to be sorry to see the last of his deputy. He'd never much liked the man, and he didn't trust him. He'd heard more than one rumor that the women in town found Putney's overtly sexual glances and remarks annoying and offensive. If it hadn't been for his own inconvenience of being left without help, Morgan would have bid him good riddance.

But his instincts told him that Holbrook's law enforcement problems were on the rise. Spring was here and all the varmints were coming out of hibernation. Being left alone with only a handful of bumbling do-gooders was not going to solve anything for Morgan. This move by the town company was sending criminals a gold-plated invitation. When the word got out, Holbrook would damn well have more than twenty-five dollars worth of trouble.

"Sit down, Conrad. I've got some bad news."

Putney lowered himself lazily into a chair and took out the makings of a cigarette.

"The mayor came to see me today. The company has decided to terminate you."

Putney had just closed the sack of tobacco with his teeth and was in the process of licking the end of his cigarette paper. He paused, glanced up at Morgan, then finished sealing the cigarette. "Why?" he asked. He struck a match on his thumbnail and lifted the flame, squinting against the curling smoke.

"Mayor Whitehall says Holbrook can't afford a deputy."

"Bullshit! You put 'em up to it."

"What?" Morgan stared at the other man, surprised at his cynical response.

"You had me fired, Treyhan. Maybe lard-butt Whitehall made the decision, but you put the bug in his ear." Putney had neither raised his voice nor changed his lazy slouch in the chair. He took a puff of tobacco. "Because of the woman—old skinny Cal's hot little redheaded widow. I seen how you look at her. You don't want no competition. Especially me."

"You're crazy. The mayor and two company board members told me this morning." Morgan reached in the desk drawer for an envelope and then slid some money across the table. "Here's the rest of your pay. I want your badge now. You're through."

Putney stood up swiftly and flung the silver star on the floor. "I coulda had her any time I'd wanted to, Sheriff. *Any time.* But I prefer an honest whore like Lily Mae. I get my dollar's worth from her, and she don't expect nothing more. She don't expect a man to turn a blind eye towards that bastard she's packing 'round town."

Morgan had never exercised as much self-control as he did at that moment. He wanted to break Putney's neck with his bare hands. He wanted to gouge his eyes out and shove his teeth down his throat. He wanted to beat the son of a bitch to a bloody pulp. And Putney saw it in his eyes. He turned and practically ran out the door, his bravado all used up.

Even after the thundering slam of the door faded away, Morgan remained stark still, clutching the edge of the desk, knowing that if he moved a muscle he'd go after Putney and kill him for the filth he'd said about Norah. He took a deep breath and finally sat back in his chair. He had paperwork to do, so he'd better get started.

Later that night, Morgan knocked at Norah's front door. She answered almost immediately.

"Are you working tonight?" he asked as he stepped inside.

"Mrs. Harrison ordered new sheets to go with a bed coverlet her sister sent from New York City. They're to celebrate how much better she's feeling. I wanted to finish them for delivery first thing in the morning." She went back to the sewing machine and stitched a last seam.

Morgan leaned up against the counter to watch her. "Does she buy a lot from you?"

Norah nodded, tying the end threads and getting up. "Here, hold these two corners. You can help me fold."

Her hands brushed his as she folded ends together. Morgan wanted to grab her into his arms but instead stepped back while she took the sheet from him and laid it on the counter, smoothing her hands over it.

"Where's Dolly?" he asked.

"Down the street visiting with Winnie. Colleen's asleep. It's nice to be alone."

"Do you want me to leave?"

Norah flushed at her unintentional rudeness. "I didn't mean that." She put her hand on his arm. "Please don't go."

It was all he could do to stand still. He wanted so badly to touch her, to hold her close and smell her scent, to feel her lips beneath his.

"I like talking to you," she said shyly.

Morgan chuckled. "Good," he said, and flung his arm around her shoulders in a most brotherly fashion. "I've had a terrible day. Why don't you make me some of your famous tea? Then I'll tell you my troubles."

She giggled and put her arm around his waist— for balance, she told herself. They bumped through the door, laughing like children, then shushed themselves as they went into the living quarters.

Only a dim light burned, and Norah made no move to turn it up. Morgan was certain she had no idea what a lovely picture she made in the faint lamplight. He thought she was prettier than when he first saw her. Confident, healthy, and gorgeous. Even her figure was better—fuller, more womanly.

"I fired Putney today."

Norah looked up from her tea brewing. "What did he do?"

"Nothing that I caught him at. But I'm sure there were several things I missed. Mayor Whitehall and some of the other great thinkers in town have decided they can't afford two lawmen. They're going to be volunteer peace officers." Morgan sat down in the rocking chair and leaned back.

Norah finished pouring the tea and handed him his cup. "You're teasing me, aren't you?"

She was standing in front of him. He wondered what she'd do if he pulled her onto his lap.

"Nope. I'm dead serious." He sipped the hot tea. "When I told Putney, he threw his badge on the floor and stomped out. He's been drinking at the Bucket of Blood ever since."

She settled in the other chair. "I don't like him."

"Putney? Not many women do. For that matter, neither do I."

"He made me uncomfortable. The way he looked at me, I mean."

"All men look at you, Norah."

Annoyed and embarrassed, she waved his words aside. "Not the way he did. Not . . . nasty."

Morgan told himself Putney would never offend Norah again. "I don't figure he'll stay in town. He'll probably drift down toward Tombstone. That's more his style."

"What will you do about a deputy?" She was genuinely concerned. After Cal's death, when she had had so much trouble sleeping, she'd discovered what long hours Morgan worked. Having a deputy gave him some free time.

"Mayor Whitehall and his friends have volunteered to serve the people of Holbrook at no cost."

"Oh, bosh!" she said. "One of those fools will shoot himself in the foot."

He chuckled aloud. "Or the backside. I'm glad Doc Robinson is back."

"Are you going to *allow* those store clerks to arm themselves?"

"It's their right. And until they get in my way, I'll let them play at being deputies. That's what they're doing right now—playing lawmen. I'm on my dinner break."

She stood up quickly. "Then let me get you something to eat."

"No. I didn't come here for you to feed me. I'll get something at the café."

But she didn't listen to his protest. Instead, she rushed around the kitchen fixing him a plate. It was a relief to break the spell of their conversation. Those few moments were too close to what she'd once imagined having with Cal, which had never come to pass. Feeling guilty, she was glad to have something to occupy her hands and her mind.

Morgan sighed as the momentary closeness

between them dissipated. He felt cheated, angry for some reason he didn't truly understand, and frustrated as hell. He rose and followed her to the stove. Even though he kept telling himself to give her more time, he couldn't seem to hold back any longer.

"Norah." He reached out and took the plate from her, putting it half-filled on the top of the stove. "Come back and sit with me. I need to talk to you."

She looked up, saw the turmoil in his eyes, and put her hand out.

Morgan never knew if she meant to reach for him or ward him off. Dolly opened the front door at that moment and bustled back into the living quarters. Norah picked up a spoon and finished filling his plate.

"Oh, hello, Sheriff. What are you doing here? Did you know there's a fight down at the Bucket of Blood?"

"Good," Morgan said. "Mayor Whitehall will handle it. I've come here to let Norah fix my dinner."

"Morris! You startled me," Winnie Ralston said to her nephew as he walked unannounced into her kitchen. It was late, but she'd just taken a black walnut cake from the oven. "Where's Nathan?"

"Aren't you glad I'm back, Aunt Winnie?" Bunky asked petulantly. Never in his life had his aunt failed to make a fuss over him when he arrived at her house, no matter the time or his condition. It annoyed the hell out of him that she asked about Nathan before fawning over him.

"Of course I am, darling. Would you like something to eat?"

Bunky allowed himself to be cajoled into eating. Winnie fried a big beefsteak with onions and made gravy for the boiled potatoes. He ate with more enthusiasm than usual. He'd felt positively chipper lately, ever since he'd put the slugs in Nathan's back. He sopped up the gravy with a piece of bread, then held out his cup for more coffee.

"Why isn't Nathan with you?" Winnie asked at last. She'd been waiting for Bunky to mention something about her husband, aware that her nephew was playing some sort of game with her. But her patience was growing thin. She wanted her husband.

"I'm not his keeper!" Bunky snapped.

"Morris!" Winnie snapped back. "Where is Nathan?"

Bunky couldn't have been more surprised if his aunt had slapped him full in the face. *Never* in all the time he'd lived with her had she spoken to him with a raised voice. He shoved the chair back and knocked it over as he rose to his feet. "Goddammit!" he yelled. "Don't you get ugly with me!"

A tremor of fear tightened Winnie's midsection, but she pushed it aside. She was not intimidated by him. Why, she'd practically raised him. "Where is he?"

Bunky glared at her. Damn her. She'd spoiled

his homecoming. "Tombstone," he lied. "He went the hell to Tombstone!"

The crash of the door still vibrated in the air as Winnie picked up the overturned chair and lowered herself into it. Her hands shook so much she had to clasp them together. She didn't believe Bunky. Not this time, not about Nathan. Nathan wouldn't go off without telling her.

A fear greater than anything she'd ever known seized her. She'd always known her nephew was a troubled boy. She'd loved him unconditionally, but she was not blind, nor was she stupid. She was certain something terrible had befallen her husband.

Nathan would not leave her, and he would not leave the cash box he had hidden so carefully behind the loose board in the chicken coop. Slowly she rose and picked up her shawl. As hard as it was for her, she knew she had to talk to the sheriff, to tell him Nathan was missing.

Jewel had only been working at the Bucket of Blood a week and already she'd doubled the saloon's rowdy clientele. She loved her work. A swarthy woman with black hair and heavy breasts, Jewel was only passably good looking. Yet few men complained—or even noticed. She was incredible in bed.

Unlike many prostitutes who got into the profession either by bad luck or worse circumstances, Jewel had chosen to be a whore. She'd discovered she had a talent for pleasuring a

number of men a few years back when she and a
bunch of miners up north had spent the winter
snowed in at a mining camp.

Her ne'er-do-well husband had somehow
managed to freeze to death in a snowbank that
winter, but Jewel hadn't wasted any time mourning. After all, there had been lots of men eager to
console her—with affection and money. By
spring, she'd collected most of the gold in camp
and decided to find a bigger town with some
fresh, new faces.

After that, Jewel had moved from one western city to the next until the previous winter
when she'd gotten sick and almost died. Consumption, the doctors had said. And they had
recommended the Arizona Territory.

When she'd gotten off the train in Holbrook
the week before, Jewel had stopped the stationmaster and inquired about the most dangerous
saloon. She had walked to the Bucket of Blood
even before going to the Holbrook House to rent
a room.

Eldon, the barkeep at the Bucket, wasn't sure
he was pleased at the increase in business.
Sure, Jewel was keeping his pipes cleaned out,
but he'd worked so hard because of the extra
customers that he barely had the stamina to visit
her himself after work.

Eldon swiped a dirty rag over a puddle of
spilled beer and glanced at the men sitting at the
back tables. He felt a puff of superiority knowing
he didn't have to wait in line. Jewel always stuck
around when he closed the saloon, avid for his
kisses. Just thinking about it made him tense up,

and once when he took her back to the hotel, she'd invited him upstairs.

He frowned when he saw Conrad Putney come from the back room, buttoning his trousers. Putney visited Jewel at least twice a day. Eldon found that very annoying.

Bunky Lindstrom swaggered through the swinging doors at that moment, taking Eldon's mind off of Jewel's long line of customers. Bunky always caused trouble.

"Evenin'," Eldon said sociably, though he wished Bunky would do his damage at the Red Rock Saloon instead of the Bucket of Blood.

Bunky slapped his hand on the bar but didn't reply.

Eldon cautiously poured him a beer, and then watched him walk off when he spotted some acquaintances. Joe Baldwin, Kid Keller, and Conrad Putney had spent the evening playing cards in the back, during which time each had visited Jewel and each had ordered a round of drinks.

There was a moment of silence when Bunky approached the table, but Putney quickly pulled out a chair for him and Bunky sat down. They talked a few moments, the cards forgotten, and then Bunky stood up.

Striding back to the bar, Bad Bunky slapped down two silver dollars. "That's for the woman," he said.

Jewel demanded twice the amount most prostitutes got for her services, but few men objected. Those that did were shown the way to the Red Rock Saloon.

"Thank you," Eldon said, putting the money

in a special box. He felt proud that he never cheated Jewel out of a dime of her earnings. "You can wait in line behind those gents back there."

"Like hell I will," Bunky snarled. "I don't wait on no whore."

The saloon got real quiet as Bad Bunky marched past all the men who were waiting and down the dimly lit hall to the back room. Nobody had the guts to protest. Not even Mayor Whitehall, who was taking his turn as volunteer deputy.

Willie Wilson, who'd waited for the past three days to get up the courage to sneak away from his vigilant mother, had just shed his virginity in Jewel's fleshy body. He lay on top of her, panting in exhausted pleasure when Bunky slapped him on the backside. Willie screamed in terror, thinking his mother had discovered him.

"Get out, you dummy. Or I'll tell your mama where you were."

Willie jumped off the bed, grabbed his long johns, and hopped out into the hall. Bucky pelted him in the back with the rest of his clothes as he struggled to dress himself. Mortified at getting caught buck naked with a wicked woman, he ran barefoot out the back door.

"Should I be flattered?" Jewel asked.

"Shut up, slut," Bunky said, pulling her to her feet and slapping her hard in the face.

Outside the little room, the men sat in stunned silence as Bunky and Jewel fought. And Jewel did indeed fight. She grabbed the umbrella from the umbrella stand by the bed and slashed

Bunky's face with the metal tip. And she cursed, shouting to the world about Bunky's limp, useless stick.

"Do something!" Eldon yelled at the mayor, who was sitting at a table.

Whitehall had turned the color of bread dough. He stood up slowly and pulled out his pistol just as Jewel let out a chilling scream. Whitehall took one step, turned a bilious green, and rushed for the front door.

"Let's get out of here," Conrad Putney said to his friends. "I ain't getting paid to break up fights anymore."

"It's a woman," Joe Baldwin protested.

"She's a damned good whore," Kid Keller reminded him.

"Either of you willing to face down Bad Bunky over some two-dollar slut?"

All three of them stood up and walked out of the saloon. The mayor was washing his face in the horse trough.

Jewel screamed again.

"Get Sheriff Treyhan," Whitehall ordered as he leaned against the hitching post.

Putney laughed aloud. "Get him yourself, you big coward. You fired me, remember?"

Seconds later, Morgan came crashing through the back door of the Bucket of Blood. When Eldon saw him, he grabbed his own shotgun and moved to where he could watch the men in the bar. At least Bunky wouldn't get any help from them.

"Lindstrom! Let her go."

Bunky had Jewel down on the floor, and he

was choking her. He didn't even hear the sheriff enter the room.

Morgan blasted a shot into the floor by Bunky's left knee, and a second over his head at the wall. Bunky rolled sideways, his hand dropping toward his gun. The pistol flew from his hand as it barely left the holster. Morgan's shot caught him square in the arm, taking all the fight from him. He shrieked, rolled, and cursed, but he was through.

Jewel sidled away, clutching her throat and gasping for breath through blue lips. Morgan only glanced at her, seeing if she was badly hurt, but he got an eyeful of dark skin and black hair. She must have had hidden talents, he decided, because she wasn't much to look at.

"Get on your feet," he told Bunky.

"You shot me," Bunky said incredulously. "It hurts."

"It's about time you learned that, tough boy." Morgan shoved him out into the hall.

Jewel followed them into the bar, as naked as the day she was born.

"I need a drink, Eldon." She didn't seem to notice that every man in the room was staring in rapt attention.

"Do you want I should walk you home, Miss Jewel?" Eldon asked, genuinely concerned.

Jewel downed her second whiskey. "Hell, no! I like life fast and nasty." She gave a little cough and grinned at Eldon. Then she turned to the crowd. "So, who's next?"

*   *   *

Morgan opened Bunky's cell early the next morning and hauled him out. Jewel had refused to press charges, saying she'd had the best night of her career. Every man paid extra and wanted seconds.

Morgan was disgusted, but he had no choice except to let Bunky go. It gave him some satisfaction to know the prisoner had spent a miserable night after Doc Robinson dug out the bullet.

"I want you out of Holbrook in fifteen minutes. Don't come back again."

Even with his face pale, his arm in a sling, and his holster empty, Bunky remained defiant. "Go to hell, Treyhan! Nobody throws *me* out of any town. I go where I please, when I please."

"Not in my town, Lindstrom."

"Anywhere!" Bunky screamed.

The screech went several notes higher when Morgan lifted him by the shirtfront and tossed him out the door into the muddy street.

"You're a dead man," Bunky screamed as he crawled to his feet. "I'm coming back to kill you!"

"Like you did Nathan Ralston? Your aunt was here last night to tell me that he's missing. She didn't say so, but I suspect she thinks you murdered him. If he's found dead, I'll bring a posse after you. Count on it."

Bunky's eyes bulged in disbelief. "Aunt Winnie? She told you?" He turned and staggered toward the alley, a shortcut to the livery stable, where his horse was waiting.

*   *   *

Morgan thought he had the makings of a full-size headache when Quinton Rose stopped by to deliver his mail. Mail service to the sheriff's office was one of the services Rose had started after he'd begun hanging around Clarabelle's shop. Morgan had to admit he liked the mouse-trap salesman, and he'd found nothing questionable in his past except a fondness for the good things in life.

"I thought this might be important," Rose said, handing him an envelope from the Atlantic and Pacific Railroad Company.

"Thanks." He slit it open and glanced at the missive. "The A and P is offering rewards for train robberies."

"I hear that's downright popular these days."

"So far we haven't had any. That's about the only thing we haven't had." Morgan looked at another envelope. It was addressed to him by name, in almost illegible handwriting.

"Clarabelle wants to know if you have plans for dinner."

Morgan wished that he could say he was spending the evening with Norah, sitting close to the stove, eating her good cooking, and playing with Colleen, but he shook his head. "No plans at all."

"Good," Rose said, thankful to have some respite in his own rocky romance. "Come over at six."

When the door closed, Morgan opened the letter. The writing was shaky and faint, as if penned by somebody old, illiterate, or very ill.

"Oh, my God," Morgan whispered. "Nathan's alive."

11

Norah was sitting in front of the large storefront window of her sewing shop enjoying the morning sunshine streaming in. Colleen's cradle was by her side, and she was finishing up the last of three shirts she'd made for Morgan. His wardrobe was now quite respectable.

The terrible cold spell had broken, but there was a lot of sickness in the Little Colorado River valley. Both Myrtis and Dolly had been running day and night to help tend the ill, even though Doc Robinson was back.

Norah was sure the relentless wind was the cause of the sickness. Myrtis had scoffed at that idea, and maybe she was right. Maybe the wind couldn't carry sickness. But it whipped and moaned and whistled until it wore a person's nerves to a frazzle. It sapped energy and strength and made folks downright crabby.

Maybe that was what was wrong with her.

And then again, maybe it was because today was her twenty-first birthday, and no one in Holbrook knew—or cared, probably. This was the first time in her life she had been totally alone on her birthday. May Day 1887 was very lonely. A tear slipped down her cheek.

Norah brushed it aside angrily and went into the kitchen to fill the teakettle. She had never had much use for people who sat around feeling sorry for themselves instead of doing something to change the situation. And she had little sympathy for herself, either.

She reminded herself of all the good things she had—a beautiful daughter, a home and a business that met their needs, and a number of wonderful friends. So what if they didn't know about her birthday? It wasn't the end of the world. The sun would still set tonight and rise again tomorrow morning. Life would go on. And so would she.

The teakettle whistled. Norah meticulously warmed the teapot before she put the tea to steep, as Jean Matthews had taught her so many years before. Then she inserted the pot into the quilted tea cozy and placed it in the middle of the table. Exact routines brought a certain amount of comfort to life when everything else seemed out of your control.

Jean had taught her that, too. Mr. Robert Matthews had confided to Norah, "When the world is going to hell in a hand basket, Jean always has her tea ritual to fall back on. You might remember that, Little Bit. Troubles come and troubles go, but tea goes on forever!" The twinkle in his eyes had made Norah uncertain as to whether he was serious or not. But the older she got, the more she figured he was both teasing and serious.

With everything in place, she felt better already, and went in to the sewing room for Colleen's cradle.

She had barely reached for the cradle when the cowbell on the front door clanged. One of Norah's hopeful suitors had fastened it there to let her know she had a customer in the shop when she was in the back. At first she'd been afraid it would scare the baby, but Colleen had adapted to it quite well, just as she had to the customers who came in and out of the shop daily.

Only this was no customer. It was Myrtis, Dolly, Morgan, and Clarabelle, all with their arms full. "Happy Birthday!" Clarabelle crowed. "See, we did surprise her! Oh, isn't this fun!"

Norah was speechless.

Morgan took Colleen from her and guided her into the kitchen, where the women had already proceeded with the goodies.

"How did you know?" Norah whispered.

"Cal told me you were born on May Day."

"Why would he have told you that?"

Morgan chuckled. "You wouldn't believe all the things Cal told me about the wonderful Miss Norah Kelly." His full brush of a mustache twitched. "I sure as hell didn't!"

Later that afternoon Winnie Ralston quickly closed the shop door behind her before the wind could yank it out of her hand. Then she leaned against it for a moment to catch her breath.

"What can I do for you today, Mrs. Ralston?" Norah asked.

"Oh, I don't rightly know," Winnie said as she walked beside the shelves stacked with fabric. "I needed something to take my mind off my worries. This awful wind makes me so nervous I could jump right out of my skin even if I wasn't so concerned about Nathan. So I thought I'd come look at your pretties."

Norah had already heard the rumors when Nathan Ralston hadn't come home. Some said he'd gone to Tombstone; some said he was dead. Some wondered what Bunky had to do with his disappearance. She could understand why Winnie was worried.

"Were you thinking about a new dress?"

"Not really." She fidgeted and blushed. "You'll probably think it's uncommonly foolish for a woman my age, but I like for Nathan to help me pick out the styles of my dresses."

"Not at all," Norah assured her. "If both of you enjoy it, that's all that matters."

Winnie beamed. "Oh, we do! And Nathan is so good at it! He knows a lot more about styles than I do. I can't imagine where he learned."

Norah could. While she was the head seamstress and designer for Shillitos' Department Store in Cincinnati, she had encountered quite a few men of means who liked to help their women pick out the clothes they wore. But the women those men were dressing were their mistresses—not their wives.

"So what did you have in mind?" she asked the older woman.

"Don't know exactly. Hear it's your birthday."

Norah nodded, not sure what to say.

"How old are ya?" Winnie persisted.

"Twenty-one."

The older woman looked pensive. "I'm old enough to be your ma. Never had any kids o' my own. Raised my nephew, Morris, but never figgered t'marry till Nathan came along. Never expected any man t'be wantin' t'marry me, if ya tell the truth."

"Life is sometimes full of surprises," Norah agreed.

"Now ain't that the truth!" Winnie was fingering the fine batiste curtains Norah had made for the store window. "These shore are purty. I ain't never seen none like 'em before."

Norah smiled as she looked at the very full, billowing curtains with their ruffled edges and tiebacks. They were her one true extravagance since she'd come to Holbrook. "This style was very popular in Cincinnati."

"Whaddya call that bit on top?" Winnie sketched out the rounded shape with her hands.

"A swag."

"My, that sure is fancy. Could ya make curtains like that for my house?"

"The whole house?"

"Yes, I want them all alike. It will make the house so light. And Nathan will like 'em. He likes fancy, stylish things."

Norah looked at her bolts of fabric. "I don't have enough batiste for curtains for the whole house. But I can make up what I have while Mr. Wilson orders another bolt from San Francisco."

"How long will that take?"

"Ten days, I believe he said. If it's in stock."

"Oh, that's not so bad, is it? When can you start?"

"As soon as the baby wakes up, I'll come measure your windows."

Perhaps Winnie should have worried more about her nephew. In St. Johns, about fifty miles from Holbrook, Conrad Putney, Kid Keller, and Joe Baldwin were playing a round of three-handed poker at the Trail Rider's Inn.

"What would you have done if any of those Hashknife riders had recognized you?" Conrad Putney demanded. "Maybe you've got a hankering to end up swinging from a rope, but I don't."

Kid Keller flushed. "If'n you was so damned smart, Treyhan wouldn'ta fired you!"

"And if any of ya had the sense of a rabbit, ya wouldn't be holed up in here!" rasped the voice of Bunky Lindstrom behind them.

Their heads swiveled around.

Putney was halfway out of his chair to do battle before he remembered who was doing the insulting. Bad Bunky was a mean son of a bitch.

"I dunno what ya mean b'that," Joe Baldwin complained.

"If ya had a lick o' sense ya'd be shippin' those beeves out by train by the hundreds instead o' sellin' 'em here and there to hotel kitchens and dirt farmers, two and three at a time."

"Yeah, sure," Putney drawled. "Drive 'em all the way to the railhead in Albuquerque. Or maybe you think we ought to ship them from Holbrook?"

"Of course not, asshole! Just git yer buddy Harrison ta bribe one train crew. Then the train would stop along some empty space, and ya could load up a whole car of beeves and ship 'em wherever ya want. Ya jist tell the train crew if they don't do what ya say, ya'll kill 'em."

As he made his nine-o'clock rounds Morgan noticed a faint light through Norah's store window. He went around and knocked on the back door.

"Who is it?" Norah asked cautiously before she unlatched the door.

"Treyhan."

She shot the bolt Morgan had hired Tod Willis to install after Colleen was born, then pushed the door open. "Would you like some coffee?"

"Yeah, I need something to wake me up." He hung his hat on a wall peg.

"Are things that quiet tonight?"

"So far. But it's early yet. Things'll get rowdy in a couple of hours. They always do on Friday night. It's not as bad as Saturday. But with the train crews changing on Friday, it's always a lively night on the town."

Norah set about making a pot of strong coffee. Morgan eyed the filmy white fabric she had spread out on the table.

"I stopped by Wednesday afternoon, but you weren't here."

"That must have been while I was measuring Winnie Ralston's windows. She wants new curtains for the whole house."

"Hummmn." Morgan didn't understand about women and their need for new fripperies.

"What she really wants is something to keep her mind occupied until Nathan comes home. She's worried sick about him."

Morgan still didn't say anything. Part of him felt guilty for not telling Winnie that her husband was alive, that he'd managed to survive Bunky's back shooting because a Mexican family had come along and rescued him. But another part didn't trust Winnie. Bunky Lindstrom was her nephew. Morgan couldn't be sure where her loyalty lay.

Nathan Ralston had figured Bunky was out to get him. Otherwise he wouldn't have left a letter with the lawyer, marked "To be opened in case of my death."

Morgan was in a quandary. He never would have known about the letter if he hadn't bumped into Lawrence Hunt at The Cottage last Friday night. The lawyer had asked Morgan if he knew the truth about what happened to Nathan Ralston. Rumors had been running rife for two weeks, and Hunt was concerned because Ralston had given him a sealed envelope to keep in his safe.

"I tell you, Sheriff, it was real spooky. I'm not used to doing business with gunslingers. But he was real polite. He told me, 'If I come back from this trip all right, I'll pick it up. But if anything happens to me, I want it to go to Sheriff Treyhan.

It'll tell him who done me in.' Then he walked out and climbed on his horse."

Morgan had eyed the lawyer silently, knowing there was more to the story.

"Now we all figure something happened to Ralston," Hunt explained quietly.

"So are you going to give me the envelope?"

"I don't think I can, legally, Sheriff. You see, he wrote on it, 'To be opened in case of my death' just before he gave it to me."

Morgan was very curious about the contents of the letter, but he shook his head. "Sorry, Larry, I don't have any evidence that he's dead. I guess you'll just have to keep the thing a while longer."

The lawyer had staggered out of The Cottage, and Morgan had continued on his rounds. According to the letter he had received that very day from Ralston, he was in bad shape and wasn't sure he was going to make it. But he'd had the presence of mind to tell Treyhan that Bunky had shot him in the back, even if his writing was almost too shaky to read.

If the letter had come a little sooner Morgan could have kept Bunky in jail for attempted murder. Now he'd have to go get him. If he had a decent deputy to leave in charge in Holbrook, he would have already ridden to St. Johns after him. But he couldn't leave his town unprotected. He'd just have to wait for Bunky to make good on his threat of coming back to Holbrook to get him. Damn Mayor Whitehall and his penny-pinching town company!

"Does that ferocious scowl mean I burned the coffee?" Norah asked him.

"What? Oh, no. I was just thinking how I'd like to let our illustrious mayor really be responsible for the town for a while. He'd decide we need *two* good deputies, damn quick!"

"I thought he'd already come to that conclusion—last week at the Bucket of Blood. Myrtis said it was all over town about the mayor having to throw up while that woman was practically being killed, and you had to save the day for everyone."

At first Morgan looked startled that Norah would have heard about Jewel. Then he realized that in a town the size of Holbrook everybody heard everything. "I'll bet Myrtis carried the word faster than the wind herself," he grumbled.

"Maybe she did, with good cause. She's very fond of you, Morgan Treyhan. If anything happened to you, she'd be like an avenging angel."

He looked startled again, and then he grimaced. It was a hell of a thing about women like Myrtis and Norah. A man didn't know whether to admire them or strangle them. But it was damned sure they never failed to surprise him, no matter how long he knew them.

"Have you ever thought about being anything besides a lawman?"

Morgan grinned at her. "Besides every Saturday night, you mean?" Then he pushed his hair back from his forehead. "Yeah, I'd like to have a small spread of my own—run a few head of cattle and raise some horses. But it takes a long time to save that kind of money on a lawman's pay."

Norah nodded. "That may be, but it's important to have the dream—a goal to work toward."

Morgan got to his feet and reached for his hat. "That may be, but my goal right now is a relatively quiet town. So I'd best be out seeing to it."

Norah reached out to touch his arm. "Thank you so much for the surprise birthday party. I was feeling a bit glum and alone."

Something turned over inside Morgan's heart as he looked deep into her eyes. He wanted to clasp her to him and assure her that she'd never be alone, or lonely, again. But all he did was touch his forefinger to the brim of his hat in a western salute. "My pleasure, ma'am."

Finally, all the talking and playacting the three of them had been doing along the train route paid off. Fat Tony, Harcourt, and Dowie took the advice the conductor had given the paying passengers and sat down to a meal at Jorgensen's. And during the meal Fat Tony began regaling the assembly with the fiction of their dear brother whom they had lost track of. There wasn't an uninterested person at the table, including the hasher who was serving the meal.

She stopped with a bowl of mashed potatoes in one hand and a gravy boat in the other. "Last fall, ya say?"

Fat Tony nodded. His mouth was too stuffed with pork chops to speak.

"Sounds like the sweet old man what was here eatin' with the tall lanky young feller we pert near couldn't fill up. Your brother?" she asked skeptically.

"Different mothers," Harcourt volunteered.

Fat Tony chewed his mouthful carefully and swallowed. "Did you happen to hear where he was headed?"

The plump woman shook her blond head as she placed the potatoes and gravy on the table and removed the empty dishes. "No."

Fat Tony couldn't help showing his disappointment. "Do you suppose anyone else might have heard Omar say where he was going?"

The woman shook her head again. "Don't matter none where he was a'goin', though. 'Cause the old man is dead. Conductor told us all about it on the next trip through." Obviously delighted to be the center of attention for once, she continued to tell her story. "Seems the train was held up about twenty miles down the track, and the kid bandit killed the old man. Real sad story. The lanky young feller what bought the old man's dinner here held his bleeding body all the way to the next train stop."

Everyone at the table stopped eating to listen, though one of the women passengers turned pale at the mention of blood.

"Wouldn't hardly let go of it even then, he was so broke up. But o' course they had to bury him." Then she remembered she was speaking to a relative, and flushed. "Right sorry about your kin."

Fat Tony looked properly broken up himself, as did Harcourt and Dowie. They hadn't really thought about Omar being dead. The old confidence man had always had more lives than a dozen cats. Dead! They were truly stunned.

That evening they stood at the foot of Omar's grave behind a tiny church. The part-time preacher told them the railroad had paid for the old man's burial and the simple marker. Some young feller on the train had given the railroad people the old man's name.

Harcourt kicked at a clod of hard dirt as soon as the preacher left. "So what happened to the gold?"

"Yeah, Tony, where's our money?" Dowie demanded.

"The tall, skinny feller must have it. We'll just have to find him."

"How?" Dowie asked.

"We'll stop at every hick town and watering hole along the railroad till we do."

Dolly was helping Norah finish the rolled hems on Winnie Ralston's curtains for her kitchen, dining room, and back bedroom. Finally she stood up and stretched the kinks out of her back.

"Think I'll walk over to Wilson's Mercantile and see if those bolts of batiste you ordered have come yet. I do wish you'd take my advice to make her pay you in advance for all this work."

Norah looked up in surprise. "You don't think Winnie's honest?"

"Winnie never thought past that husband of hers. It's worse now than ever. Maybe you haven't heard, but there's talk that he's a bad sort. Not as bad as her nephew, I'm not sure anybody is." Dolly shook her head. "My point is that if Nathan Ralston shows up and wants to leave in the middle of the night, Winnie would go with him and forget all about this sewing you're doing—and how much she owes you. You can't afford that. There's not many other folks here who can afford curtains like that. You might never be able to sell them."

Norah was a bit defensive. "I did ask her to pay for the fabric I specially ordered."

"Good. Now just make sure she pays you for these when you deliver them. You have a very good and honest heart, Norah. But not everybody else does."

Norah had been hearing variations of the same lecture from both Myrtis and Morgan lately. And not just about Winnie. She sighed. Dolly was right. If she was to be a success in business, she had to know where her money was coming from. These curtains were very expensive to make, in both fabric and time. She shouldn't be angry at Dolly for mentioning it.

"Thank you for caring," she said. "I appreciate it. Would you check at the mercantile to see what colors of buttonhole twist Mr. Wilson has? I'm out of white, and I need some orchid for that dress of mine, and buttons. If he doesn't have any to match, just do the best you can. I can conceal them under a pleat."

"You can do wonders with a needle, and that's a fact. Let me take a scrap of that material along."

When Dolly returned she was very pale and

tight-lipped. "The curtain fabric hasn't come yet, but I was able to get some thread just a shade darker than your dress. And these mother-of-pearl buttons will be lovely, I think." She grasped the edge of the table for support and carefully lowered herself into a chair.

"Dolly, what's wrong?"

"Mordecai and some of the children are in town. Here's the money for Isaac and Heber's suits. They turned out beautiful, and the boys look so handsome in them." Dolly's voice broke.

Norah reached out to clasp Dolly's work-worn hand. "Do you miss them so very much?"

Dolly sniffed. "Yes. I helped raise them all. I feel like they are partly mine. I used to tell them I claimed a third of them—the part I could hug."

Norah didn't know how to say what she was thinking except just to say it. "Then perhaps you should go back."

"No!" Dolly choked out, and Norah saw that the older woman's eyes were awash with tears. "I'm never going back to Mordecai! I'm going to get a divorce. Will you help me write a letter to Brigham Young?"

"Yes, but what has happened?"

Dolly shook her head mutely.

"What did he do that you can't be with children you love and miss so desperately?"

Dolly gripped the edge of the table so hard her knuckles turned white. She swallowed painfully a time or two. "He—he took Mary for his fourth wife!"

"Who is Mary?"

"Mary Yazzie. You met her brother Joseph when they were building the partition."

"The Indian boy?"

Dolly nodded. "Mary was seven and Joseph was four when they came to us eight years ago. Mordecai put them with me because I had no children. She's only fifteen and never had a chance to find a young man to love her. Now Mordecai has taken her to bed and made her his wife. He's old enough to be her grandfather. I can't stand it! I won't be a part of it anymore!"

Nathan Ralston shifted in the hard chair next to Morgan's desk. He was still pale and hollow-eyed, obviously a man who had been seriously ill and was a long way from full recovery.

"So, are you willing to swear out a warrant against Bunky?" Morgan asked him.

"Yes," Ralston rasped. "I want him dead for what he did to me! But it'll take more than a warrant to bring him in. He's a vicious killer."

"Then why did you go down into Pleasant Valley with him?"

"Winnie didn't want me to go alone. She asked her nephew to accompany me."

"You'd have been better off holing up with a rattlesnake."

Ralston nodded. "I know. But Winnie doesn't understand about Bunky. She still sees him as the little boy she raised." Then the older man's eyes widened. "That's why you didn't tell Winnie you'd heard from me! You thought she was in on it. Oh, my God, my poor dear Winnie! She must be beside herself."

Morgan didn't know what to say, but he was saved from having to think about it because the door to his office burst open and Willie Wilson rushed in.

"Sheriff, Sheriff, you gotta come quick! Mr. Harrison's been shot dead, and Albert's shot, too. He's bleeding real bad!"

"Where?" Morgan leapt to his feet and reached for his double-barreled shotgun. Willie was shaking so much, Morgan wondered if he could answer.

"Over by the Bucket of Blood." Willie turned as pale as chalk dust. "Bunky Lindstrom shot Mr. Harrison, and Conrad Putney shot Albert!"

Ralston groaned and swore.

"Okay, Willie. Are you able to run and get Doc Robinson? Good. He might be able to help Albert."

Nathan Ralston stood slowly, then bent over to tie his guns down.

"What the hell do you think you're doing?" Morgan demanded.

"Protecting your back. I'll give you odds that's where Harrison was shot."

Morgan swore and swung out of his office, heading down Central Avenue at a trot. Ralston walked behind, moving as fast as his wounds would allow, his gunman's eyes not missing a movement anywhere.

A crowd had gathered around Albert Harrison as he lay at the edge of the street near the Bucket of Blood. His father's body lay facedown in the alley about fifty feet away.

Morgan shouldered his way through the crowd and dropped to one knee in front of the boy. "Albert, it's Sheriff Treyhan. Can you tell me what happened, son?"

The boy opened pain-filled eyes that had begun to glaze over. "Pa was havin' a drink in the Bucket o' Blood while I was shifting boxes in the train warehouse. When I got done I come to find him. He was comin' from the alley there, and he was mad when he saw me. Yelled at me to git on home. Then there was a shot, and . . . and Pa fell down.

"I tried . . . he's dead! Shot in the back. Bad Bunky Lindstrom came out o' the alley, still holdin' his gun. I grabbed Pa's pistol. I was gonna shoot Bunky like he did Pa." Albert's voice faded. "Deputy Putney shot me! I hurt awful bad. Am I gonna die?"

Morgan's mouth was a thin, grim line. "I don't know, son. Here comes Doc Robinson. He'll do all he can for you. Where did Putney and Lindstrom go?"

"Acrost the tracks," one of the onlookers answered.

Flora Harrison came running up the dusty street, her fashionable garnet skirts held up so she could move faster. She took one solemn look at her husband's body then stumbled toward her son, too shocked to utter a sound. She gathered her son's bleeding body into her arms, trying to rock and soothe him, but Doc Robinson made her put him back down so he could attend to the wound.

Nathan Ralston was standing behind Morgan.

"If that bastard's frightened Winnie I'll kill him myself."

Morgan grabbed the older man's arm and held on. "Albert, were Lindstrom and Putney alone?"

The boy's head was now cradled in his mother's lap, and she was finger-combing his hair back from his face as the doctor tried to pack bandages into the hole in his stomach.

"No, there were four of them." Blood bubbled out of his mouth, and Morgan turned away. It was bad enough for adults to be shot down in the streets, but a kid! He couldn't erase from his mind the sight of the always elegant Flora Harrison cradling her dying son in the lap of her blood-stained dress.

A few moments later, Morgan set out purposefully for Winnie's house, with Nathan Ralston two steps behind him.

Farther back, they were trailed by curiosity seekers who didn't want to miss anything but didn't want to get close enough to be shot, either.

Norah approached Winnie's back door with the brown paper parcel of curtains under her arm. She knocked three times, then waited for an answer. When none was forthcoming, she knocked again. Surely Winnie hadn't forgotten she was coming? She was just about to knock a third time when the woman appeared from around the side of the house with a pan in her hands.

"Oh, there ya are, dear! Just let me put this down. I've been feeding my chickens."

"I didn't know you had chickens."

"Oh, yes! Nathan loves fresh eggs for his breakfast. And then ya always have a chicken fer the pot when ya need it. Besides, I like having chickens."

"Is Nathan back?" Norah asked as tactfully as possible.

Winnie's face fell. "No, and I still haven't heard a word. I'm going t'have t'speak to him about that when he gets home. I been so worried."

"It must be lonely for you."

Winnie sighed. "Well, I'm not alone now. My nephew, Morris, is back. He brought some friends with him this time."

"Does that concern you?"

Winnie wrung her hands in her coverall apron. "Probably not, dear. But I don't feel comfortable with these friends of Morris's. I don't think they're good companions for him. And t'tell the truth, I'm afraid they'll lead him inta trouble."

Norah's mouth fell open. All the tales she'd heard about Bad Bunky Lindstrom had no connection to a timid Morris who might be led astray by unsuitable companions. Was Winnie actually that blind to her nephew's true nature?

Winnie blushed at the sight of Norah's expression. "I know it's silly of me. He's a grown man now, but I suppose he'll always be a small boy t'me."

A shot sounded from the direction of the Bucket of Blood. "Goodness, I do wish those young men would find something else t'do besides fire off their guns. It makes me so nervous! And I can't see the fun in it, neither. Too many people get hurt, or killed. But I suppose they have t'do something to amuse themselves."

A second shot followed the first. "This really is too much! I wonder what Sheriff Treyhan is doin'. He ought t'be puttin' a stop to such shenanigans."

Norah could hardly wait to get the curtains delivered and get back to her own home and a modicum of sanity. She hoped she never got used to people shooting guns in the streets for fun and acting like hooligans.

She and Winnie had barely spread the curtains out on the dining room table when the front door slammed, followed by angry voices in the front part of the house. Norah looked up in consternation.

Winnie laid her hand on Norah's arm. "No, dear, it's better t'just let 'em be. They'll settle it amongst themselves, whatever it is. Will ya help me hang these? I'm so anxious t'see them up. And I ain't sure I know how t'do it proper."

Norah nodded and dragged a chair up to the nearest window, trying to ignore the rumble of angry male voices coming from the front. She was just stretching up to hang the first new curtain after removing the old ones when she heard the kitchen door open quietly. Nathan Ralston slipped inside silently with a sawed-off, double-barreled shotgun in his right hand.

"Oh!" she exclaimed as Ralston snaked his left arm around his wife from behind and clasped her mouth shut before she even knew he was there.

"Quiet! Not a word," he warned, as he eased around to where he could see into the front portion of the house. "Get under the table, both of you," he growled. "And keep quiet." He pushed a stunned Winnie down, then assisted Norah.

Without another word Ralston slipped back to where he could watch the front, then stood silently with his back to the wall. He was pale and breathing harshly, but both hands were on the shotgun as he held it vertically against his body. He was tensed, ready to whirl into the next room and put the shotgun to use at the slightest notice.

Norah remembered one night when Morgan was carrying a shotgun on his nightly patrol of the town. When he noticed her eyeing it warily he said, "All guns are deadly, but a shotgun with a sawed-off barrel can do as much damage to a body as a cannon. And one man can carry it and fire it at close range. It's meant to put the fear of God into men who won't listen to anything else."

Now her heart was in her mouth, pounding with such ferocity that she couldn't have spoken if she'd wanted to. It was Morgan's gun Nathan Ralston was wielding with such deadly competence. Norah recognized the carved stock. Winnie just looked stunned, staring at her husband in silence.

Norah felt stunned, too, trying to comprehend what was happening. Was Morgan outside somewhere, waiting for Ralston to get into position, or had Ralston killed Morgan and taken his gun?

Then the front door banged open. "Hold it right there, all of you! The first man who moves is dead!"

Norah almost fainted with relief as she recognized Morgan's voice.

"Goddamn you, Treyhan!" Bunky snarled.

"Go ahead and draw, Bunky," Ralston taunted from his ready-to-kill position in the doorway.

"You're dead!" Bunky screamed, as he whirled toward Ralston, drawing his gun as he moved.

"No, but you are." Ralston dropped into a crouch, and fired one barrel of the shotgun. Then he swung to his right about thirty degrees and fired the other one with hardly a pause.

The shotgun blasts hurt Norah's ears and almost masked the sound of a window exploding and a piece of furniture cracking as a man fell against it. Everything was happening so fast it was hard to distinguish the sounds.

Bunky's bullet slammed into the table above Norah's head, showering her with wood splinters. She screamed just seconds before two .45s spoke in the other room.

One body hit the floor with a thud. A man cursed, followed by the sharp retort of another handgun. Glass shattered. Someone screamed piteously. There was a scuffle of feet as if someone was trying to run. Then Morgan's guns spoke again.

"Don't do it, Putney," Morgan warned with steel in his voice. "At this range, my guns will tear your guts open like you did to that thirteen-year-old kid."

Bleeding badly, Putney let the gun drop to the floor. "I didn't know it was a kid when I fired," he said in a whining voice. "I just saw somebody going for a gun. Anybody woulda done the same thing." He slumped forward onto the carpet.

"Like hell!" Morgan shouted. He didn't care if his former deputy was unconscious or even dead. Morgan intended to have his say. "There are witnesses who'll swear differently. You deliberately shot that kid before he could even get his pa's gun out of his holster. You're going to swing for this, Putney. Plan on it."

12

For Morgan, attacking Winnie's house was like a slow-moving nightmare. He'd waited out by the scraggly rosebush until he knew Nathan was inside. Bunky and his cohorts were squabbling like nasty schoolboys. They wouldn't have noticed an approaching freight train.

With the stealth of a big mountain cat, Morgan crossed to the corner of the house, then ran crouching for the steps. He knew he had to get inside quickly or one of the people gathered to watch by the depot would give away his position, or be hurt.

With his heart beating madly, Morgan raced up the steps and kicked in the wooden door.

A gun blazed and the shotgun went off like a cannon. And Norah screamed.

How the hell he knew it was she, Morgan never could say. He simply knew. And the thought electrified him like a bolt of lightning. A thousand versions of fear flashed through his brain in a single second. He had to rescue her! He had to live long enough to get her out of there.

Using the doorjamb as protection from flying lead, he shot off round after round at the men who were firing back. The shotgun blasted again. A man shrieked in pain. Another gasped in surprise.

It was over as quickly as it had begun. Morgan stood in what was left of the parlor, guns ready, looking wildly around for Norah. The room was deathly quiet. Gunsmoke mingled with the sunbeams reflecting off broken glass.

Bunky was dead.

His gun hung limply from his crooked trigger finger. His mangled body was slumped back on the yellow brocade serpentine-backed sofa. Conrad Putney lay bleeding onto the pale green needlepoint rug in front of him. Joe Baldwin's cheek rested against the front windowsill. The bullet that shattered the window had been the only one he'd fired. Kid Keller slumped dead in the corner, his rifle still resting on his knees.

"Norah!"

"She's okay. They both are." It was Nathan's voice.

That was the only thing that kept him from charging into the kitchen to check on her. Putting a lid on the cauldron of his emotions, he did the job he'd been hired to do. He stuffed his handkerchief against Putney's badly bleeding wound. He wanted Putney to live. The rest of them only needed Digger's attention.

As he hunkered down to talk to Putney while he waited for the doctor, his mind kept turning to Norah. He pushed the *what ifs* from his mind. She was all right, and so was he. That was all that mattered. But another part of his brain wanted to shout and scream and shake the daylights out of her for putting herself in jeopardy.

After he realized Putney had passed out, he looked toward the kitchen. He was surprised to see Nathan walking toward the front door.

Doc Robinson rushed into the house and knelt beside Putney. After a cursory examination, he glanced up. "He'll live. That's a real bleeder, but I'll try to keep him healthy."

"Good." Morgan straightened up. "I want him to go to trial. What about Albert?"

The doctor shook his head, his expression grim. "He didn't make it. Flora's taking it real hard."

"I'm sure." Morgan felt sick. He wanted to throttle the already dead Harrison for endangering his own son's life. And that pompous ass Whitehall for his petty economic trimming that left the town vulnerable to ruffians. A wave of rage toward Putney hit Morgan so hard he had to fight to keep from raising his pistol and saving the town the cost of a hanging. He hated a crooked lawman with all his heart. He forced himself to move away.

He could see Norah in the kitchen, standing beside Winnie, offering her a measure of comfort. He ignored his own feelings. He was too raw right now to deal with them.

"Why did Nathan leave?" he asked.

"Winnie told him to," Norah answered.

"He killed Morris!" Winnie wailed.

"Bunky shot Nathan in the back last month and left him to die out on the Mogollon Rim," Morgan told her. "Hell, Nathan's barely out of bed. Bunky also shot Delbert Harrison—just minutes ago near the Bucket of Blood."

"Oh, God, we heard shots," Norah said, realizing how commonplace gunfire had become in her life. She and Winnie had complained about rowdies.

"Harrison is dead. So is young Albert—Putney hit him when the boy tried to help his father."

"Oh, no." Winnie began to weep.

"Winnie, if you want to see Nathan, he's walking toward the front gate," Morgan said, his voice so harsh it hurt his throat. "I think he's leaving."

She gave a sharp cry and lunged forward, but at the door to the parlor, when she saw her nephew's bloody corpse, she burst into fresh tears. "Oh, Morris. Why did you have to go and do this?"

Morgan couldn't help her. Bunky was bad to the core. Maybe he'd been born that way. But there was still Nathan. "Do you want Nathan, Winnie? He needs you right now. He's still in bad shape. He needs you."

She nodded, making an effort to control herself. "He's my husband," she said, sobbing. "I belong with him." Without another glance at Bunky, she made her way across the shattered glass and broken furniture that littered her once-lovely rug and went outside.

Morgan turned to Norah. "Are you all right?"

"Of course." Her speech was as crisp and starchy as the summer-green dress she wore.

When her chin began to wobble, she clenched her jaw tight and dug her nails into her palms. He looked wonderful to her. So strong—so alive. *She* was falling apart at the seams. When the gunfight had started she'd been absolutely terrified he'd be killed. She barely recalled screaming. All she remembered was the gunfire that seemed to go on forever.

She was shaking inside so badly she thought she would scream again and never stop. She looked him square in the eye and dared him to offer her sympathy.

Morgan's lips tightened to a hard line. Damn her! She was as white as the pristine curtains that lay on the kitchen table. The only color to her was her red hair and green eyes. The house was shot to hell. Bodies were strewn about like debris after a flood. And Norah appeared more controlled and regal than bloody Queen Victoria!

Fury burned through Morgan like prairie fire, because she'd been so scared and wouldn't admit it, because she'd scared him so goddamn bad. "Why the hell did you get in the middle of this?" he yelled, his restraint ripping apart.

"To annoy you!" she yelled back, the color seeping back into her cheeks. "That's my only purpose in life!"

The injustice of his attack washed away all weakness. Anger unequal to anything she'd ever known surged through her. Before she could snatch up the rolling pin lying on the dry sink and attack him with it she turned on her heel and stormed out the back door.

In the yard, one of Winnie's chickens cackled with joy after laying an egg. Norah felt her blood churning through her veins and she wondered if she'd ever feel normal again. She broke into a fit of weeping that reached her battered soul. Afterward, she leaned against the chicken coop and stared at the mesa for quite some time, trying to adjust her mind to the horror she'd just witnessed. Giving her head a little shake, she realized it was impossible. Sudden, violent death didn't fit into her world.

It was time to go home.

She was walking back to her shop when she met Dolly running up Central Avenue. Dolly had Colleen in her arms.

Without a word, Norah reached out and pulled the baby tight in her arms. Life was so very precious. Again she cried, but this time the tears were gentle.

Dolly allowed her to cry without a word, but she did take her arm and pull her over by the wool warehouse so she could have a hint of privacy. Winnie's yard was filling with people who'd come to help or simply to gawk. That was the nature of folks.

"Are you going to be okay?" Dolly finally asked when she saw Digger driving his dead wagon up the street.

Norah nodded. "Three of those men are dead and Putney is wounded. Bullets were flying around like bumblebees, but Winnie and I weren't even scratched. It's hard to understand why." She saw Beatrice Wilson heading toward them. "Will you watch Colleen a little longer? I don't think I can talk to anybody right now. I need time alone."

"Don't worry about a thing. Why don't you go down by the river? Nobody will bother you there."

Morgan found her by the Little Colorado more than an hour later, standing by a huge cottonwood tree, watching the water go by. From where he stood, he could see that she'd relaxed some of her rigid control. She looked young and sad, and extremely vulnerable. For some reason that disturbed him even more than her restraint.

Recently the cottonwoods on the riverbank had leafed out, providing a shiny green canopy of shade from the sun. The smell of young tender willow growth gave the air a rich smell. Morgan walked slowly toward her.

"I've been looking for you. Dolly told me you were here."

"I came down here to be alone."

His anger flared again, threatening his already limited control. It was the first time in his years as a lawman that he'd tasted true terror. In all the harrowing situations he'd been in before this, he'd only had his own hide to consider, or that of another peace officer. Never a woman, never somebody he cared so damned much about.

Knowing what little power he'd had over the gun battle—and Norah's safety—had left him shaky and sarcastic. "Are you looking for trouble, or are you just plain stupid?"

She whirled around, shocked at the insulting question. "I was delivering Winnie's curtains! I didn't realize I needed to check with you first to see if you planned to blast her house to smithereens."

He stepped closer, looming over her. "This isn't the big city where you can wiggle your butt down the sidewalk and not expect more than an occasional offensive remark. This place is wild—"

"I don't *wiggle* anything!"

"You can't be trusted for a damned minute. Every place you go, men swarm around you . . ."

"You big oaf! Those men weren't *swarming* around me—they were criminals hiding out from the law." She took a swing at him. "I accidentally stumbled into their midst just before you came in shooting—"

Morgan quickly countered her attempt by grabbing her wrist. If he hadn't been so furious, he would have laughed at her. She was nearly a foot shorter than he, but that didn't stop her.

"The only way I'm going to be able to keep you out of trouble is to marry you!"

"What!" She'd been wrestling with him, trying to escape his manaclelike hold on her. At his words she stopped and nearly fell over.

There was dead silence. A baby jackrabbit with enormous ears hopped down to the wide river, nibbled at a young green sprout on the sandy bank, then took a long slow drink.

Morgan looked down at his boots. "I said, marry me."

"You're crazy." Her stomach was all a'flutter and she could barely breathe.

"No, I'm not. You need a husband to make sure you're safe, and I—" His voice dropped to where it was hoarse with emotion. "I want you. In my house. In my bed. In my life. I want to take care of you, and the baby. I'll be good to you."

Her blood was beating in her temples and her mouth was dry as dust. She told herself it was the surprise of the unexpected proposal. But that wasn't the whole truth. The thought of being in Morgan's bed appealed to her with alarming intensity. She felt a flush heat her whole body.

"Yes."

The word was so soft he nearly missed it. He took her hands in his. "Being a lawman's wife won't be easy, but I'll treat you real good."

She lowered her eyes from the blazing blueness of his. She didn't understand any of the sensations that were bombarding her; she merely knew she was terrified. And bewitched. What was she doing?

Morgan's voice brought her back to reality. "Judge Harvey will be busy this afternoon with Conrad Putney. Do you think you could be ready first thing in the morning? That way we can do it before the judge leaves town. It will be weeks before he gets back."

Tomorrow morning. Could she possibly be ready to marry Morgan by then? Norah's common sense, which had been hibernating until that moment, came out and took over. "What time tomorrow?"

"Nine thirty. Before court convenes. I'll tell the judge to expect us first thing. If that's all right with you." For the first time he allowed her to see just how unsure he was.

She smiled faintly and returned the strong clasp of his hand. "Nine thirty is fine. Dolly will look after Colleen until I get back."

"I can get some of your things tonight."

She gave him a blank stare.

"To move into my house," he explained.

"Oh," she said, realizing he expected her to move in with him right away. "Yes. I guess that's what you should do. I'll have my things packed by dark."

He smiled a bit wryly. "You are planning to live in my house, aren't you? That's what people do when they marry."

"I haven't had time to make any plans whatsoever, Sheriff Treyhan. Your proposal surprised me."

"It surprised me, too, Mrs. Welsh, but now that we've agreed it's the only sensible thing to do, it's time to get on with the plans." He dropped her hands and walked around the cottonwood, absently looking over the water. He felt a bit dazed.

"Norah, I want you to spend tomorrow night with me, and the rest of our tomorrows."

She couldn't think of a reply. Everything she'd experienced today had left her at a loss for words. Yet she felt she was being sensible by marrying him. So why, more than anything, did she want him to put his arms around her and smother her with passionate kisses?

"This is the one you should have married in the first place," Judge Harvey told her sharply. He was never at his best first thing in the morning. "A woman like you needs a damned strong man, else you'll roll over him like a freight train."

Norah's color rose at the circuit judge's blunt words.

"Get on with the ceremony," Morgan grumbled. He reached over and took Norah's hands. In spite of the warm weather, they were icy. He gave her a tiny squeeze of reassurance.

"Do you, Norah Kelly Welsh, take this man, Morgan Arthur Treyhan, for your lawful husband?"

The vows were over in a matter of minutes. For better or for worse, they were married.

"Thank you, Your Honor," Morgan said, reaching into his pocket for a gold coin.

"Aren't you going to kiss her?" the judge asked. "Hell, man, that's the best part of the ceremony. A woman expects it."

Embarrassed to his boots, Morgan leaned down and touched his mouth to Norah's soft lips, then pulled away. He didn't want a drunken old lecher like Harvey witnessing any part of his lovemaking.

Her eyes were round with astonishment, and her cheeks were scarlet. In spite of the brevity of the kiss, she'd felt a jolt of pure attraction toward Morgan.

"You better go home and practice, boy," the judge said. "Even I can do better than that."

"Don't even try." Morgan's eyes were dark with menace. With that he took Norah's arm and steered her out the door.

"We'd best go to my house and change," he said when they stepped out onto the boardwalk. The business day had barely begun, but the street was filling up with people. "I don't suppose you want the entire town carrying on about our wedding day." *Or our wedding night.*

"Yes, I should change." She walked the distance across the tracks and north toward his house as if she was lost in a foggy dream.

They climbed the porch steps in silence. A hummingbird hovered around the tall pink hollyhocks that grew at the front of the house. Morgan opened the door for her and followed her in.

When the door closed behind him, he felt a moment of pure panic. What the hell was he supposed to do next? He'd given very little thought to marriage. Erotic thoughts didn't count, he realized. Now here he was, with a wife in tow, and he had no earthly idea what to do with her.

"Your clothes are in there." He pointed toward the bedroom, then turned on his heels to go. "I left mine out on the back screened porch."

Norah moved like a wind-up doll into the large bedroom, absently noting the big, wide windows before she laid her handbag on the bureau. With jerky, mechanical movements, she removed her hat and shawl, setting them carefully beside her bag. She unfastened the orchid watered-silk dress she'd finished only the previous week and hung it in the pine wardrobe. She'd been too nervous earlier that morning to notice that Morgan had made no comment on her wedding dress. Now she touched the sleek lavender material, wondering what he'd thought of it. And of her.

"Chasing after a compliment!" she muttered disgustedly and set herself to the task of changing. She took off her good shoes, untied the small bustle, removed three lace-trimmed petticoats, and rolled down the ivory silk hose.

Still bemused at her impetuous marriage, she stood holding the soft hosiery in her hands, drawing comfort from their silky texture. What had she done?

Marrying Cal had been a difficult decision because she decided to do so when her heart, however foolish, still longed for Sonny Shillitos. But she'd known Cal forever, and she'd trusted him completely. Besides, considering the circumstances, she had had no choice.

Life was so different now. *She* was so different. Sometime during the course of the long, cold winter the last remnants of her infatuation for Sonny had blown away, perhaps on a gust of chilly wind. He'd been a selfish weakling who'd used her yearning for affection to have his way with her, and then he'd betrayed her. She'd known the instant Colleen was placed in her arms that any man who'd abandon such an exquisite child wasn't worth an ounce of her love.

But that wasn't the only thing that was different. *She* had changed. She owned a thriving business. She was self-sufficient and independent. She didn't *need* a man, not even for protection. No matter what Myrtis and the rest of the town said, she knew that if she'd wanted to she could live forever without another husband. The men who kept approaching her were as annoying as ants at a picnic, but she hadn't married Morgan just to keep the men away.

The only reason she'd stood up in front of Judge Harvey this morning was because she wanted Morgan Treyhan.

Suddenly she understood what she hadn't known before. His strength appealed to her as no man's had ever done before. He was so strong a man he wouldn't feel threatened by her.

She put the stockings aside to wash and began to look in the wardrobe for an everyday dress to wear back to the shop. Morgan had unpacked everything she'd sent over and had neatly put things away.

"I forgot my—"

Norah's hand jerked away from the dress she'd been reaching for.

Morgan stood barefoot in the doorway, with his shirt undone and his trousers half buttoned, staring at the lovely figure his bride made in her fine white underwear. "Norah!"

She turned and faced him, her eyes catching his and holding.

Without another word, he strode into the room and pulled her to him, his wide mouth crushing her soft, startled lips in an impassioned kiss.

Somewhere in his fevered brain was a voice admonishing him to slow down, but he ignored it. He'd waited forever.

Hairpins fell to the floor like raindrops. The silky red twist came apart in his hand, covering her back and his arm with its thickness. A cry escaped her.

Whatever he'd expected from her, it wasn't this fervor. She was in his arms, returning kiss for passionate kiss. Her small, rounded body fit against his as if she'd been made for him only. It was hard to believe that he'd never touched her before today. Groaning, he pulled her closer, trapping her hand between them.

Again, the voice in his head warned him to get hold of his self-control, and this time he made a valiant attempt. He loosened his hold on her, kissing her cheek and her ear and her long white neck.

Her hands caught at his shirtfronts and hastily pushed them out of her way. Morgan shrugged the shirt off his shoulders, then took his hands from her to let it drop. The shirt fluttered to the floor, forgotten.

His skin was hot to the palms of her hands. She gasped softly at the feeling of velvet chest hair. She'd never felt anything so wonderful. Her hands moved reverently. She loved stroking him. From the passion she saw in his eyes, she knew he loved it, too.

Morgan's skillful fingers had her corset off before she was aware of his intent. The little voice of caution was drowned out by the pounding of his heart. He had one goal right now, and that was getting his wife onto his bed. The cambric pantalets went next. He whisked her chemise over her head at the same time his trousers hit the floor. Only the knit of his underdrawers were between them as they stood lost in a fevered embrace. And then there was nothing.

Briefly she was aware of the coolness of the muslin sheets beneath her, but the lure of his white-hot kisses and the thrill of his hands caressing every wondrous secret drove all else from her mind. On and on he kissed her, stroking and teasing, until she thought she'd die from the pleasure of it. And still he continued until everything else ceased to be real except his magical touch.

"Morgan," she cried. "Oh please, Morgan . . ."

"You are so beautiful." His mouth moved from a ripe coral-tipped breast back to her lips. "Norah!"

It was as if a tremendous force of nature, far greater than either of them, swirled about, catching them in its whirling mists, careening them upward, farther upward until nothing else existed. There was no concept of time or place, only the two of them, and exquisite, astonishing pleasure.

Norah awoke to a world of light. Golden streams of sunlight mingled brightly with a whiteness as bright as snow. Her eyes closed again as she sank into a warm, sensual world. Sleep beckoned to her. Her body had never felt so wonderful, so alive, so . . . naked.

No, it can't be.

A hard, warm hand swept from her hip to her breast, dispelling all possibility that this was a dream.

"Are you awake?" a deep voice asked.

"No." She clenched her eyes shut.

"Yes, you are. You're blushing." His leg sprawled over hers and he tugged her close.

"A gentleman wouldn't mention that." She tried to block out the pleasure she felt from his gently stroking hands. Nothing in her life had ever felt so marvelous.

"I'm not a gentleman. I'm your husband—in all senses of the word." He whipped the warm covers off, leaving them both exposed. "Open your eyes and look at me."

She did so shyly, at first not meeting his deep blue eyes, but after encountering the growing evidence of his desire she was too embarrassed to look anyplace else.

"Hello, wife." Morgan was amazed at the turbulent emotions those two simple words aroused.

She gasped in astonishment. "The windows are open!"

Deep laughter rumbled through him. "All four of them."

"It's the middle of the morning!"

He caught her to him, ravaging her mouth the same way he intended to soon plunder her body again. "We're married, Norah. We have a right to be in this bed together, whether it's morning or night." He kissed her again. "I didn't plan for this to happen until tonight, but my good intentions got lost someplace along the line. And I'm not sorry! No man could ever regret *that*."

"Somebody might see us." Her protest was merely a token. His hands were working such magic she could barely think.

"Nobody comes up this far from town. That's why I built the house here, for the privacy." Again he kissed her, deeply and with awe.

Within minutes Norah forgot about the open windows and the time of day. She forgot everything but the fact that Morgan Treyhan was her husband, and nothing in the world had ever felt so right as loving him.

"Where the hell have you been?"

"Not so loud. Where's my sister?"

"Over at the mercantile. . . . My God, what happened to you?"

Ferdie Wattron stumbled from the darkened hallway into the kitchen and painfully pumped water into the sink. With one hand he splashed water over his bruised, swollen face.

"I'll get Doc Robinson," Quinton Rose said.

"No! I'm all right. When is Clarabelle coming home?"

"Not long, unless she stopped to talk to somebody. What happened?"

"Inga's husband, and two of his friends."

"You should have expected it," Rose told him. "The whole town knew."

"How? I didn't tell anybody." Ferdie looked both embarrassed and belligerent.

"I heard it up at the Bucket of Blood the first

day I arrived. Bartender told me whenever Clarabelle played church music all evening long, you was off poking the train driver's wife."

Ferdie flushed, his face looking mottled. "Clarabelle knows?"

"She's not stupid! You run off, day or night, leaving her all by herself with cutthroats and rowdies shootin' up the streets. Something mighty powerful must be keeping you away at night."

Ferdie felt his blackened eye and groaned. "Have you touched my sister?"

"Shut up, you asshole! I'm gonna marry Clarabelle when I convince her to say yes."

"Oh." He limped back toward the pantry. "All right then. I need you to look after her for a week or two while I go upcountry and heal up. I don't want her to see me like this." He began to gather some food and tied it in a sack. "Tell her I've gone fishing."

"Sure," Rose replied. "And when you get back from your fishing trip, Ferdie, I want to talk to you about buying you out."

"What do you mean?"

"I'm beginning to like this town. Clarabelle has a lot of good friends. I think I'm ready to settle down and this is as good a place as any. Little Nippers have made me a nice income the past few years, but I don't want to spend the rest of my life hopping trains and sleeping in lonely hotel rooms. I want to marry Clarabelle. I want to buy your fancy goods store. I want to have a home and a family."

"I ain't planning to sell."

"Take a little advice from a man who's been caught in one or two beds by angry husbands. Your little dalliance is over. Let it go—she's his wife. He mighta yelled a lot and even slapped her around a little, but I'd be willing to bet the two of them are dancing on the feather bed right now."

Dolly didn't say a word when Norah and Morgan finally stumbled into the shop a little after noon. She'd never before seen Norah with her face beautifully flushed and her hair not quite caught into place. Even if Norah hadn't been wearing such a happy expression, Dolly would have guessed she'd been in Morgan's bed by the way he acted.

He displayed that same possessive stamp of ownership and protection she'd seen so often before in other men who'd just staked a claim to a woman.

"Have you eaten?" Dolly asked. "I made lunch." She didn't quite hide her smile when they both flushed with guilt and admitted they were hungry.

Colleen chose that moment to announce she was starving, and Norah immediately pulled herself together and picked up her daughter.

"I'm going to see Judge Harvey this afternoon," Dolly told them. "I want to make certain my bill of divorcement from Utah is valid here in Arizona. I want all ties to Mordecai Smith broken forever."

*　　　*　　　*

Sometime after four, Dolly returned from seeing the judge. She said little about her visit but threw herself into a frenzy of cleaning. "What should I do with this box of books?" she asked as she hefted a crate in her arms.

Norah ran her hand across her face, catching a piece of hair that kept coming out of its pins. "I keep thinking I'll get rid of them." She hesitated a minute. "They belonged to Cal, and I know it's selfish but I can't make myself give them away."

"That's all right, Norah. It's not important." Dolly moved the crate behind the back door where it was out of the way.

"Sure it is. This is your home now and you don't want it cluttered up with my things."

Dolly laughed. "You gave me the courage to make a life for myself. And you gave me a place to stay. Don't worry about that crate of books."

"I'll have Morgan take them over to the house."

"No, leave them here. I might get the yen to read Wild West adventures." She washed the dirt off her hands and walked over to her chair, picking up a shirt before she sat down.

"There's an old valise at the bottom of the box with the Welsh family Bible in it," Norah said. "Cal brought it with him when he came back from his father's funeral. I couldn't even make myself look at it, let alone record his death in it. But I should send that back to Indiana to his mother."

Dolly understood Norah's reluctance. "You don't need to do it today. Clarabelle has invited half a dozen ladies over for lemonade and pound cake—in honor of your wedding. It's supposed to be a surprise. We'll take care of the books some other day."

Norah stood up and gave her a hug. "Thank you so much for telling me. I'd hate to eat wedding pound cake with dust on my face and cobwebs in my hair."

"Go on home now and change, but don't get too dressed up. The baby's sleeping, so leave her here. We're expected at three fifteen, so you'd better hustle. And act surprised when we get there."

"Yes, Mother," Norah teased, but she was delighted at how happy Dolly seemed these days. It was hard to imagine her as the plain, shy woman Norah had first met. She'd already changed the room to suit her taste, having helped Norah cart the last of her things to Morgan's house.

Norah stopped at the front door. "Do you think Clarabelle is sweet on the mousetrap salesman?"

Dolly just smiled as she folded a shirt for Tod Willis she'd just finished hemming. She was fairly certain the Little Nipper man was sharing Clarabelle's bed, since she'd recently seen them in a most interesting clench. Yet she wasn't one to gossip. She'd wait and see, as would the rest of the town. "I think she might be."

"Then I hope he's smitten, too. Every woman deserves that at least once in her life."

Dolly watched her through the front window. She'd never seen Norah look so alive or happy.

And what woman wouldn't be with a man like Morgan Treyhan for a husband? Dolly suspected he was a powerful lover. Women didn't talk about such things, of course, but they weren't indifferent.

From the first time she'd seen Norah and Morgan together, she had sensed the tension between them. She'd seen Norah's hands tremble when he was in the room. She'd watched him shift his body to hide his arousal from view. It was obvious that neither welcomed the attraction, but it was equally plain that the attraction didn't go away. Although she couldn't help feeling a twinge of envy about their exciting new love, Dolly was thrilled for them. She wondered if they were aware they loved each other.

Fat Tony Roscoe hauled his rotund body into the creeping boxcar and landed with a grunt. Damn Harcourt to hell for suggesting they sit in on a card game, he thought. Within an hour all three of them had lost their collective ill-gotten gains.

Harcourt and Dowie followed him and pushed the door nearly closed, then started toward the back wall.

"Don't come any closer."

Fat Tony saw the gleam of a knife blade first. "Who's back there?" he asked.

"Me and my knife."

"Look, mister," Fat Tony said, "we don't want any trouble. We just want to ride in peace."

"Go up to the other end."

"I will not," Harcourt said. He flopped himself down against the side of the car.

Dowie sat down beside him and fumbled in his pockets for the candle stubs he'd carried on their last boxcar adventure.

Only Fat Tony Roscoe stood weaving in the middle of the car, waiting.

"Whatcha waitin' for?" the voice in the dark asked.

"I'd like to know your name, sir."

"Why?" The voice was belligerent.

The guy was also young, scared, and evidently broke, Harcourt thought, or he'd be riding in a coach car. Maybe life wasn't so bad after all. If the kid wasn't too dirty or too ugly, he might make a perfect shill for their next prank.

"I want to know because I'm a gentleman," Fat Tony said reasonably. "And it's polite to ask."

"Oh." There was a pause. "It's Mickey."

"Thank you, Mickey."

Harcourt couldn't believe his luck. The boy was good-looking and fairly well dressed. He wasn't as young as Harcourt would have liked, about fourteen, though he swore he was almost twenty. But he was quick and clever, and Harcourt was certain he'd be a great decoy. If they could just convince him to play their little game.

"I didn't expect you to wait up."

Norah looked up at her husband, and her heart began to pound. She clutched the simple summer dress she was making for Clarabelle, trying to still her shaking hands. "I think I must have dozed off. What time is it?"

"Nearly two."

"So late? What happened tonight?"

"Nothing out of the ordinary. Except Walter Gates surrendered to me this evening when I went over to the hotel to talk to MacKay. Walter thought I'd come for him and confessed to being part of the rustling gang. I was a bit taken aback, but I arrested him anyway."

"He is an odd man."

"Norah, I don't want to talk about drunks or fistfights or even cattle rustlers." He flung himself down in a chair across from her and looked directly at her.

She set her sewing aside and waited for him to continue. Her tongue nervously touched her bottom lip.

"I haven't been able to get what happened this morning out of my mind."

Unable to sit still, she rose and walked to the door, opening it to look out into the darkness. In the distance she could hear the mournful sound of a train whistle. His hand suddenly touched her shoulder.

He felt her grow tense and bit back a curse. Why the devil hadn't he given her more time, instead of jumping on her this morning like a starved wolf? "I've given myself hell all day for rushing you into bed. But all the while I couldn't stop remembering how wonderful it was."

"Morgan," she whispered, turning to face him. She felt the night wind at her back, but even that didn't cool her. Fire ran through her veins. She reached toward him, placing her hand against his chest, stroking it over the silver badge, and up into his thick hair. "I couldn't stop thinking of it, either."

The blood began to drum in his head as her words became clear. His hand moved softly to the back of her neck.

"I don't know if a woman is supposed to tell a man she likes to be touched, Morgan. Nobody ever talked to me about such things. Except Mazie, and I don't think that counts."

He chuckled and eased his arm around her shoulder. "Do you like my hands on you, Norah?"

"Yes," she said, moving a bit closer.

He swallowed. "Do you like my mouth on yours?"

"Yes."

"Do you like me touching your breasts?"

"Yes."

He leaned forward and blew gently at the tendrils curling down her neck. She closed her eyes tightly, her body limp with the pleasure of it. He tugged her against him, laying tiny kisses on her ear and brow and nose. Her arms wound around his neck as she pushed herself against him.

"Yes!"

"Yes, what?" he asked, quietly going crazy as she pressed her hips into his hardness.

"Yes, I like all of it." She'd never felt so reckless or so bold. "Yes, I want you to kiss me. And take me to your bed. Does that make me wicked?"

Morgan slammed the door against the night and lifted her up into his arms. "My God," he said as he strode toward the bedroom, "that makes you wonderful."

13

"*Now you know the plan?*" Harcourt asked.

"A'course I do," the boy answered. "Whatcha think I am, a dummy?"

Harcourt raised his hand to give the little idiot the beating he'd been asking for, but Dowie grabbed his arm.

"We need him," Dowie insisted, and held on until Harcourt shrugged him off. "He's part of the plan."

"Sure. Fine. Just as long as he does what he's told."

The kid looked Harcourt straight in the eye and smirked.

Fat Tony finished the last of the apples and cheese the boy had swiped from a passing farm wagon and topped it off with a swig of well water. The apples were a bit shriveled, but as good as could be expected in the middle of May.

It wasn't much of a breakfast from Fat Tony's standpoint, but it was better than nothing. They were lucky Mickey had spotted the apple barrel when he climbed up after the cheese, and even luckier the farmer and his broad-bottomed wife didn't spot Mickey.

The little fool had good hands, but he took terrible risks. Few crooks lasted long that way. Fat Tony had given some thought to having the boy join them after this heist, but he dismissed the thought. He was too damned fond of his own hide to chance it.

"Let's go over the plan again," Fat Tony said, all the while thinking of the meal he intended to have after the robbery. The beef in this part of the country was superb, and his mouth watered at the thought.

Mickey sighed loudly. If this was a life of crime, he thought he'd pass on it. It was so danged boring. "You give me cash money for a ticket to the next stop."

"Right," said Dowie.

Mickey rolled his eyes. His baby brother Paddy had more on the ball than this blockhead. "I go to the station, look the place over, ask about the schedule, and buy my ticket to the next stop. I'm to keep my eyes open for lawmen or railroad detectives. Then I come back, tell you, and stand watch at the station while you do the job."

Harcourt wanted to smack the little bastard for the nasty tone he used, but Dowie was right; they needed him right now. Their plan required a guard, and it would be worth the annoyance, and the few coins they managed to scrape together for the ticket, to know they'd be safe from unexpected interruptions. He'd get his revenge later.

"Fine," Fat Tony said. "Here's the money. Be back in fifteen minutes."

"Okay, okay," Mickey said. He sauntered away with coins jingling in his pocket.

"Little son of a bitch," Harcourt muttered.

"Leave him be for now," Fat Tony said. "If things get ugly later on, we'll drop him as a little gift for the local constabulary."

Morgan woke up to an empty bed. He lay there a moment, adjusting himself to a new day, to a new life.

"Norah," he called, wanting her to come back to bed. Wanting her.

When she didn't answer, he roused himself, washed his face in the porcelain basin, and reached for his trousers. In spite of their intimacy, he was a bit shy about wandering through the house without his pants. Maybe when she got accustomed to him . . .

The lighted lamp told him Norah had been in the kitchen. The cookstove was hot, coffee was made, potatoes were boiling, and the table had been set for breakfast. Colleen lay in her basket quietly gurgling to herself.

"Hello, little girl," Morgan said as he smiled down at her.

The baby cooed at him and raised her hands in frantic, jerky movements. Morgan could see that she'd been bathed and dressed for the day. She smelled clean and fresh.

"Where's your mama?" Morgan asked, pouring himself a cup of coffee. "I miss her."

Colleen answered him with enthusiasm and determined gestures. Morgan grinned. She was cute as a button, with black curls, dark eyes, and a mouth the miniature of Norah's.

"She couldn't have gone far," he told the baby, "or she wouldn't have left you."

A movement outside caught his eye. He looked out the window and saw Norah on the front porch, pouring water on the hollyhocks. She was dressed simply in a tan blouse with a darker tan skirt, but Morgan thought she was the most beautiful creature on earth.

"I think you got horse-kicked in the head, Treyhan," he mumbled, embarrassed at the tender emotions boiling up in him. "Two or three times."

Norah bustled in the door and stopped.

"You're awake." She mentally chided herself for saying something so stupid, but the sight of him standing there bare chested knocked all sense from her head.

She'd always known he had tremendous shoulders. After all, she'd made shirts for the man! But looking at him now made her breathless. She clenched her hands to keep herself from reaching out to touch him. The need to stroke his skin astonished her.

Morgan wondered if she knew what she was doing to him. The turmoil and desire he saw in her eyes thrust all his good intentions aside. He had to touch her! He barreled across the room in three long strides and gathered her against him.

"I'm awake," he whispered against her mouth, and then forgot everything else. The white-hot fire of her kisses sent him reeling. Was a man supposed to be so crazy when he got married? Morgan didn't know the answer. He only knew he was crazy for Norah. "Come back to bed with me, darling. Right now."

The ticket master talked quite a spell to the mahogany-haired youth with the chipped front tooth and wide green eyes. He'd seldom met a nicer young man, and he was flattered to be asked about schedules and the like, so he gave the lad a few pointers. He also mentioned there'd been a number of robberies along the line and how the railroad was adding guards. Mickey thanked him profusely.

"So whatcha got?" Harcourt asked when Mickey finally wandered over to the meeting place.

I got me a ticket, Mickey thought, but for once he said nothing.

"What took you so long?" Fat Tony asked.

"That old ticket vendor was a gasser— damned near talked my leg off," Mickey said. "There's a half-hour layover. I think we should wait till the very last minute to get there when people are in a rush—"

"Come on let's go," Harcourt interrupted. "The train's already there." He gave Mickey a shove, nearly toppling him over.

Mickey's eyes narrowed. Resentment rushed through his thin body. At that very moment, he made up his mind to look out for himself. Hell, he didn't believe their story about the damn gold, anyway! He had a ticket out of town, and he planned to use it.

Fat Tony saw at once that the station was a thief's nightmare. He realized the kid had tried to warn them when he'd suggested waiting until there was lots of confusion so they'd be obscured by the crowd. They should have listened.

He stopped and looked carefully around, trying to revise his plan for the robbery.

"You lookin' fer something?"

Fat Tony gazed around at the grizzled face of the guard. There was a double-barreled shotgun caught in the crook of the man's arm.

"My boy," he said. "He seems to have wandered off."

"Privy's that way," the guard said. "He's probably back there."

Around the corner, Mickey inched closer and closer to the train.

"Can I help you, son?"

Mickey pulled off his hat at the sound of a friendly voice, and looked up at the man beside him. It was the conductor, not the guard. "I'm afraid I missed my train," he explained, showing the conductor his crumpled ticket. "I'm traveling alone to see my grandmother in Peach Springs. Am I late, or is this the right train?"

"You're just on time, boy. Better get aboard right now. Wouldn't want ya t'miss your grandma." He took Mickey's elbow and helped him along.

Mickey had barely passed the first seat, feeling a sense of relief and well being, when he spotted Harcourt down on the loading platform, and Dowie right behind him. Mickey swung around and dashed away from the window, plowing right into the soft belly of a midwestern matron.

"Oh, I'm so sorry," he said, diving onto the floor after her hatbox at a fortuitous moment, for a second later Harcourt looked directly in the train window.

The whistle blew.

The matron wasn't the least bit hurt, but it had been many years since anybody cared enough to worry about her. She invited Mickey to share a bite to eat. Naturally, he accepted.

"I'm going to Peach Springs," she said. "I own several houses there which were damaged in the recent storm. I'll need to hire a handy man."

The train began to move.

Mickey realized suddenly that Harcourt Barr was looking right at him, shouting his head off.

"Young man, whatever is the matter?"

"Those men out there." He pointed at the furious trio. "I heard 'em planning to rob the station, and I guess they saw me listening."

"Conductor!" screamed the woman. "We're being robbed!"

Paradise. Morgan had spent the most sensual ten days of his life with his brand new wife, and he couldn't think of any other way to describe it except paradise. During the day he walked around in a daze, the aftereffect of their early morning lovemaking. He was barely aware of the mayhem going on around him. Cattle rustling and shootouts seemed of no importance. At night, when he finally saw the town safely sleeping, Norah was waiting for him, intense and ready. Marriage, he'd discovered, was thrilling. He wanted it to go on this way forever.

He was looking forward to years of contentment. He still hadn't gotten used to well-cooked meals or immaculate sheets or the baby lying in his lap. He wondered how he'd lived all these many years without such pleasures.

"We'll be at the shop today," Norah said. She took his empty plate and refilled his coffee cup. He didn't seem to be in any hurry to leave the house. When he reached out and touched her waist she felt a thrill for the small gesture of affection. "We'll expect you for lunch."

"I probably won't get there until late. I want to meet the afternoon train. There's a marshal coming in to see about Walter Gates. This officer thinks Walter might be a fellow wanted back in Texas—for the same type of cattle thefts."

"Did he confess to that, too?" It amused her how the desk clerk had told Morgan about every crime he ever thought about committing, when Morgan had simply gone to the hotel to question Angus MacKay.

"As a matter of fact, he did. I think he wants to go back home."

"I'll be busy at the shop all day. We've had several special dress orders."

Morgan decided he was becoming an expert on the whims of women's fashions. He grinned. "What's going on that requires special dresses?"

"The Fourth of July picnic," she said and then started to laugh when he pulled her down on his lap.

She was breathless when she finally pulled away. "You better scat or you'll be late."

"Let them fire me." He kissed her again, thinking he could never get enough of her.

Colleen broke up their fevered embrace. She was hungry and wasn't in any mood to wait for attention. Norah kissed him quickly, then picked up the baby and began to unbutton her dress.

"Take care," she said softly when he strapped on his holster. As she watched Morgan leave the house, she considered calling him back. It was foolish and she knew it, but she wanted a whole day with him. Never in all the time she'd known him had they managed one uninterrupted day together. She wanted to talk to him—about important things and about nothing. She realized she wanted a real marriage.

"Now that's foolish," she said aloud as the baby began to nurse. "We stood up before the judge. We're married."

Norah leaned down and kissed Colleen, pondering her new life. Did all new brides have such foolish thoughts? Did all women want something different from what they had? She couldn't imagine Jean Matthews mooning about such things. Or even her mother.

She should count her blessings. She and Morgan were lovers. She smiled at the thought of his ardent kisses. Her experience was slim, but she suspected their lovemaking was far beyond ordinary. At least it was compared to Sonny's fast and feeble groping. It might not be nice to compare one man to another, but she couldn't help but notice the difference.

"We need to go help Dolly," Norah told her daughter, determined to value what good things she had. "All the ladies want to be lovely for the festivities. We've got lots of work to do."

The boy stepped onto the wooden platform and looked around the squat, faded, wooden buildings with disgust. This was worse than he ever imagined. "What a shithole."

A tumbleweed rolled past. Beside him, the train creaked and rumbled as the last passenger got off. The fellow was weathered and lanky and smelled like a lawman. The boy sidestepped to let the tall man pass. He was still a bit nervous about the police, even after helping the widow in Peach Springs with her houses.

"Marshal Irving, I'm Morgan Treyhan. I'm glad you could come."

Mickey stood where he was and watched the officers shake hands. Although the one from the train had white hair and was much older, there was a resemblance. He wasn't old enough to understand why, except that they were both hard-looking men.

"I got a room for you over at the Holbrook House."

"Good. I'd like to wash up before I talk to your prisoner. It's been a long trip. But if he's who he says he is, we'll be outta here on tomorrow's train."

The whistle blew and the train began to move. Mickey watched it go with something close to reluctance. Maybe he shouldn't have gotten off. Maybe he should have ridden to the end of the line. This dump didn't look too promising.

Well, at least the cops weren't after him. He'd managed to escape being connected with those birds in the boxcar when their robbery went sour, thanks to the widow. He grinned at the thought of her yelling. What a voice!

"You waiting for somebody, boy?"

The deep voice gave him a start. He glanced around to see that both men were watching him.

"Me?"

The lawmen exchanged glances.

Realizing that his little-boy charm wasn't going to work with these guys, Mickey straightened his shoulders and pulled himself up to his full five foot six.

"I'm looking for Norah Kelly," he said, meeting the local sheriff's deep blue eyes. "She lives here."

The little hooligan had Morgan's full attention right there and then. He took in the dark red hair, wide eyes, and small stature, as well as the little bundle wrapped in a table napkin. His stomach began to sink. "Who are you?"

"Mickey Kelly."

"A relative?"

Mickey was getting irritated at the inquisition. If the lawman hadn't been so big and intimidating, Mickey would have told him to diddle himself. "I'm her brother." He glanced at a pile of dung out in the dirt street. "She's expecting me."

Morgan felt as if a serpent had just crawled into his own little paradise. The kid was lying, of course. Norah had no idea that anybody was coming to visit. From the few things she'd told him about her family, he was certain none of them could afford the trip west. So how the hell had the boy gotten the ticket? Could it be that he was in trouble? Morgan knew the answer immediately—if he wasn't now, he would be soon.

"Her sewing shop is just down the street. See the Red Rock Saloon?" Morgan pointed to the bar on the corner.

"Yeah." Mickey thought that even the saloon was a dump.

"Norah's shop is two doors down from that. Do you have any other luggage?"

"No. Well, thanks for the directions." He shuffled off in the direction Morgan had indicated.

"Runaway, huh?" Marshal Irving said as they walked toward the Holbrook House.

"Worse than that," Morgan told him. "Lots worse. He's my new brother-in-law. And it looks like he's here to stay awhile."

"Ah, hell."

*   *   *

Norah gasped when she saw her brother step inside the sewing shop. "Mickey?"

Dolly stuck her head in from the back room to see a teenage boy who looked a lot like Norah.

"What are you doing here?" Norah slowly took her foot off the treadle and pushed back her chair.

"Aren't you glad to see me, Nuthin'?"

Norah frowned at the childhood name. "What are you doing here, Mick?"

He looked down at his scuffed shoes. "I ran away."

"When? Does Mam know where you are?"

He tossed his sack down on the floor, angry and disappointed. "I thought you'd understand."

Norah tried to pull herself together. "Are you hungry? I'll fix you something to eat."

"Sure I'm hungry."

"This is Dolly, Mick. She works here at the shop. And she lives back here. Dolly, is it all right if I fix my brother some food?"

Dolly smiled at her employer. "Of course. It's nice to make your acquaintance, Mickey. Welcome to Holbrook."

"Thanks. Nice to meetcha, too." He followed Norah into the back room.

She had a meal on the table in minutes. She'd been expecting Morgan, so the food was all ready. "Tell me what happened, Mickey."

"The old man wanted to hire me on with a harvesting gang. I refused. We had a fight . . . and I left."

"I see." Even though she imagined that this

wasn't the whole story, her brother clearly was neither big nor strong enough to do the intense physical labor involved in harvesting. And he was too young. Mickey was as smart as a whip, but their father absolutely refused to allow him to finish school.

"You got any milk?"

Norah took a pitcher of milk from the small cooler.

In her bed by the stove, Colleen began to whimper. Norah went over and picked up her baby and sat down in the rocker. She heard the front door open and Dolly speak to a customer.

"What the hell are you doing?" Mickey asked, when he saw his sister start to nurse the baby. He dropped his fork on the plate with a clatter and stared.

"I'm feeding her."

"Jesus! Is that your kid? I thought it belonged to that other woman."

Norah looked at him with utter astonishment. "Of course she's mine. This is Colleen Welsh."

"Oh, wait just a minute. When did this little surprise happen? And who does it belong to? Some Eye-talian, by the looks of all that black hair. Not poor ole Cal Welsh, that's for damned sure. No wonder you're hiding out in this hell-hole, keeping the kid hidden!"

"Mickey! I wrote Mam and Dad about Colleen right after she was born."

"Like hell—"

A roar interrupted them as Morgan strode into the room, grabbed Mickey with one hand, and lifted him up until they were on eye level with each other. "Don't you ever talk to her that way again."

"She's my sister," Mickey squeaked.

"She's *my* wife. And that's *my* baby. The particulars are none of your goddamn business! Understand?"

"Yes," Mickey gasped, which was all he could do at that point.

Colleen was crying by then. She wasn't accustomed to so much noise at lunchtime, and she definitely didn't seem to like it one bit.

"Morgan, put him down," Norah said.

The rage he'd felt when he heard the boy berate Norah began to fade. Morgan saw her trying to shush the howling baby, her face pale and sad. Slowly he lowered Mickey to the floor.

Dolly was standing in the doorway watching them. "Do you want me to leave?" she asked. "Or should I make some tea?"

Morgan removed his hands from the boy and took a deep breath. Then he reached in his pocket for some money. "Dolly, would you be good enough to go over to the bakery and buy a cake so we can celebrate my wife's brother Mickey coming to visit? Then we'll all have cake and tea together."

Dolly smiled with great understanding. "I'll take my time."

When the door shut, Morgan took Colleen from her mother and talked to her a moment. The baby immediately settled down and was ready to finish her lunch.

"We got off to a bad start," Morgan told

Mickey. "It's my fault. I should have introduced myself at the depot and brought you by."

Mickey sat down and said nothing. He wasn't accustomed to apologies after an outburst of temper. The old man had never apologized in his life. It was a new experience for Mickey.

"I'm Morgan Treyhan. I'm the sheriff of Holbrook. Norah and I were married some time ago, and we live in a house across the railroad track. She owns this sewing shop, and Dolly works for her."

The boy took his measure carefully. "I'm Mickey Kelly, but I think I like the name Michael better. Maybe I'll change it. And I better tell ya I ain't just visiting. I came out here to live with Norah."

"You ran away?" Morgan asked.

"Yes. I won't let him whup me anymore, and I won't let him take my wages, and I *won't* work on a damned harvesting gang. I'll be a desperado first."

Morgan glanced at his wife. She hadn't spoken a word or even looked at either of them. Apparently there were still many things she hadn't mentioned about her life. His conscience gave him a nudge. When did they have time to talk? He worked all day and half the night. When he did get home, all he could think about was making love to her.

That was going to change, he realized with a sense of frustration. Mickey's arrival had already changed everything.

"Can I hold the baby, Nuthin'?"

"She likes the name Norah, just as you like Michael."

The boy nodded. He took Colleen and expertly burped her. This was not the welcome he'd expected, but it wasn't bad. He watched his sister go to the stove to fix another plate. To his amazement, the big sheriff put his arms around her and held her. By damn, the West was a strange place.

He thought about the letter Norah said she'd sent to their parents. It was only a guess, but he suspected the old man probably picked up the letter in town and tossed it away when he found no money inside. That way he could taunt the rest of them for being selfish beggars.

Morgan wanted to make love with his wife. He sat in his office with his hands lying flat on the clean desktop and wondered when he'd get that opportunity again. Last night Mickey was playing solitaire in the parlor when he got home. This morning the kid was sitting in *his* chair when Morgan came out for breakfast. This was not the marriage Morgan had in mind.

Digger opened the door and sauntered in. "You look mean, boy."

"Shut up, you old coot." He started to chuckle. "Damn you—I feel mean."

"Whyn't you go on home fer supper?"

"The volunteer deputy won't get here for another hour."

"Well, hell, can't I play lawman fer an

hour?" Digger scratched his chest. "It ain't that hard, is it?"

"You're right, Digger. It ain't hard."

So he took Digger up on his offer. It felt good to sit down to eat with the family like a normal man did. The meal was excellent. Norah had bought fresh fish from one of the Smith boys who'd stopped by to see Dolly and just happened to have a mess of trout in the wagon.

"How's your day been going?" Norah asked her husband as she passed him the bowl of fresh green beans, also a special treat from the Smith boys.

"Just the normal bunch of rowdies and desperados," Morgan answered as he bit into a biscuit. Norah baked the lightest biscuits he'd ever tasted.

"I met some desperados," Mickey said suddenly. "On the train." He was stuffing mashed potatoes into his mouth as if he thought he might never eat again.

"Where?" Morgan asked.

"In a boxcar."

Norah's fork clattered onto her plate. "What were you doing in a boxcar?"

"I thought you had a ticket to Holbrook," Morgan said.

"Oh, I did." Mickey's face was the picture of innocence. "I just didn't have a ticket *from* Indiana."

Morgan ground his teeth.

"One night a couple weeks ago or so, these three thugs climbed in with me." He stuffed some fish in his mouth. "I never met such fools and liars, especially the guy called Fat Tony. He actually told me that they were hunting for their dead brother Omar's stolen fortune. If those geezers were brothers, I'm a monkey. They was out and out crooks!"

He glanced at Morgan's wooden face. "Can I have a biscuit?" He smiled when Morgan handed him the plate. "Ain't my sister a wonderful cook?"

Morgan grunted.

"You should have heard the whoppers those fools told me. How there was a train stickup, and this here Omar was shot. The robbers was caught and hung right away, but some skinny feller on the train made off with a satchel stuffed full of gold coins. *Thousands* of dollars in gold!"

Morgan blinked as a memory tickled his mind.

But at that moment there was a banging at the kitchen door. Norah got up to answer it.

"Sheriff, you better go over to the jail right away," Digger said when he walked into the kitchen. "Two of your volunteers came in early and they's havin' a fistfight."

"Damn," Morgan muttered, grabbing his hat.

"My, don't that trout look good," Digger said hopefully. "I can't remember when I last et fresh fish."

Norah laughed at the blatant hint. "Sit down, Digger. I'll get you a plate. We have plenty."

Morgan waited impatiently for the frieght train to pass. The train seemed endless. The afternoon sun beat down on Morgan's black hat. His head began to throb.

He was in a lousy mood. He'd somehow burned the lunch of leftover trout and toasted biscuits he'd put together for himself. That infuriated him, because he was acting childish in the first place by eating at the house instead of at the sewing shop. After all, Norah had been expecting him. But he was angry with her.

Or maybe he was angry with himself for being an idiot. When he'd gone home last night at the end of his shift, he'd sharply criticized Mickey for staying up so late again. Norah had stuck up for her brother and the two of them had had words after the boy slammed off to bed. But that wasn't the worst of it.

When he pounced on her in bed—and there was no other word for his behavior—Norah had turned away from him, saying Mickey would hear them. Morgan had gotten furious. More than that, he'd been hurt, embarrassed, and a little ashamed of himself.

Hell, he was still mad! He glared at a lumbering boxcar. Would this goddamn train never end?

You're acting like a lovesick boy.

The thought hit him like a two-by-four across the back of the head. He couldn't possibly be in love with Norah. Could he?

The ground moved beneath his boots. Now that was a laugh—he didn't believe in such nonsense. That was the kind of things poets prattled on about, and he was no poet. What did he know about love, anyway?

The train swayed before his eyes. For a second

he didn't believe what he was seeing, and then he wondered if he'd poisoned himself.

At that moment he heard screams. The ground lurched and bucked. The boxcar directly in front of him rose up in the air and fell again as if riding an ocean wave.

Earthquake!

Before Morgan's astonished mind grasped the terrifying word, ugly, ripping sounds drowned out the yells and shrieks he heard on the other side of the train. He took one step backward and started to run just as the boxcar fell toward him.

Slowly it came, a brown box of heavy wood, a rectangular coffin. Falling, falling. And he moved so slowly. *Run,* his mind shouted. Why couldn't he speed up? The door on the boxcar stood open slightly, a yawning mouth that threatened to devour him.

Norah!

Then he felt pain. And blackness.

"Well, Ironman," Myrtis said cheerfully as she poked at his shoulder. "Looks like the only thing tough enough t'git you down is a runaway boxcar."

Morgan kept his eyes clenched tightly, hoping she'd go away. He supposed he wasn't dead. Surely the Almighty didn't have such a perverse sense of humor as to send him an angel that sounded like Myrtis.

"Ouch!"

"I knew you was awake." She whipped the sheet down before he could grab it and began to poke at his hip.

He swore quite eloquently and yanked the covers back over him. "Don't you have any decency, woman? I'm stripped bare!"

"I ain't blind," she retorted. "You got the right number a' parts."

Morgan closed his eyes again. "Where's Doc Robinson, you old hag?"

"You ain't t'onliest one in town 'twas hurt, ya know. That was quite a shakin' we got. The doc and Dolly are at the hotel looking out for other folks."

"Where's Norah?" Morgan tried to sit up. He knew his wife very well. She'd either be with him, or helping somebody else—unless she'd been hurt herself.

"Oh, lay back down and git a grip on yourself, you overgrown oaf." Myrtis gave an exaggerated sigh. "She's in the other room feedin' the baby."

At that moment Mayor Whitehall burst into the bedroom. "Sheriff, I'm so glad you're alive."

"I share the sentiment, Mayor."

Whitehall looked at him sharply, tugging at his black muttonchop whiskers. "Well . . . yes. You take the next few days off. *I've* got everything under control."

"Where's my prisoner?" Morgan asked.

"Right where he oughta be—just waitin' to hang." Whitehall ambled to the door. "I'm sorry about your wife."

"Myrtis!"

"Oh, simmer down. You'll wake the baby."

"What happened to her?"

"She's just got a few scrapes and bruises.

Seems she climbed over the wrecked train trying t'git t'ya."

He leaned back against the pillows. "Is that all?"

"Well, not quite." Myrtis gave him a look of speculation. "She tried t'lift the boxcar off you—didn't realize you'd slipped through the open door. She fainted from the strain. Said she hadn't eaten any food all day."

14

The Fourth of July dawned hot and still. For more than a week, the weather had been unbearable. Not a hint of a breeze touched the scorched little town. Yet not even hundred-degree temperatures could parch the enthusiasm of Holbrook's residents about the holiday celebration.

Every business in town had prepared for the influx of people from the outlying areas. The hotels were full and every other available room had a waiting list. Tents had been set up on vacant lots. Merchants shipped in extra stock, and the saloons stayed open twenty-four hours a day. Excitement touched them all.

Wagons and buggies from miles around began to gather on both sides of the river all day Friday as folks settled in for the weekend, and a festive atmosphere pervaded the entire Little Colorado River valley. And now on Monday, the morning of the Fourth, tensions had risen to a fever pitch.

Holbrook's streets began to fill with holiday revelers not long after daybreak. Everybody wanted to participate in the Independence Day Parade. People dressed in their finest clothes and came prepared to celebrate the whole day with gay abandon.

"Hey, Norah! Look at this!" Mickey flung open the screen door and dashed into the house. The door closed with a bang. "Ain't this one hell of a town?"

"Stop swearing," his sister said automatically as she leaned over to take a pan of biscuits out of the oven. It was really too hot to bake, but Morgan was home this morning and she wanted breakfast to be truly a family meal.

"Just look at this damned thing . . . you'll cuss, too." He waved a newspaper at her. "It's a special edition."

She set the biscuits on the top of the stove and wiped her hands. "What has that man done now?" Then she gasped. "Morgan!"

Morgan moved slowly around the bedroom. He'd recovered almost completely from his run-in with the boxcar. He'd been damned lucky that he wasn't killed. Now all he had to worry about was a sore shoulder and stiffness in the hips and legs when he got up in the morning. These days he felt as if he were only fifty instead of one hundred.

But to tell the truth, he was enjoying all the time he'd spent at home. He was still only working part of the day, with Mayor Whitehall's volunteers keeping the peace the rest of the time. Since Bunky Lindstrom and the others had been killed, Putney incarcerated, and Gates transported back to Texas, Holbrook had been rather quiet. Morgan didn't expect it to go on forever, but the lull was nice while it lasted.

He pulled on a clean shirt and hobbled out the door.

"Look at this!" Norah shoved a newspaper at him.

"What now?" he grumbled, ready to laugh at Frank's latest exploits. Since Mickey now spent nights at Tod Willis's cabinet shop where he was working, Morgan had a downright cheerful attitude toward the world. It was amazing what a night alone with a warm-hearted woman could do for a man's disposition. "Oh, hell!"

"See, I told you so," Mickey said to his sister.

The headline was the biggest Morgan had ever seen.

"INVITATION TO A HANGING" was splashed across the page.

"I can't believe he did this."

"The town is crawling with people," Mickey said brightly. "I guess they're all planning to stay over and watch Putney swing in the morning."

"How horrible," Norah said sharply.

"I'm hungry. Are you gonna serve those biscuits or frame 'em?"

Morgan let that pass. He was beginning to learn that Norah could put her brother firmly in his place when she was of a mind to do so, and it seemed he got on better with both of them when he didn't interfere. That was a good thing, since the kid would probably be with them for years.

He picked up the coffeepot and poured some for himself, then refilled Norah's cup. They all sat down to eat.

"Can't you do anything about that?" she asked, pointing to the paper as soon as she'd finished saying grace. "It's disgraceful."

"Yeah it is, but I don't think it's against the law. What are you fixing for the picnic?" He settled himself down to enjoy the food, not giving another thought to Frank's wild words.

"Morgan, this is important! It makes the whole town look bad."

"Why?" Mickey asked as he spooned gravy over a plateful of biscuits. "Jimmy told me he'd never seen so many people in town. A hanging's great for business."

Morgan snorted. "I agree that business this weekend has been very good, but it isn't because of the hanging, Mickey, no matter what Jimmy tells you. It's because of Dr. Rehfeld Smedley, the world-famous pyrotechnical artist. Folks have been waiting for weeks to see fireworks. It's all they can talk about."

"Now they have something else," Norah snapped.

"I had no idea Frank planned to bring out a special edition about Putney's hanging." Sometimes Morgan believed that Frank Reed thrived on danger. He took a second helping of ham and gravy. It wasn't long ago he'd eaten every meal in a restaurant, and he still relished Norah's cooking.

"It's dreadful," Norah went on. She wasn't one to give up on an argument until she made her point. "Imagine trying to turn an execution into a public spectacle. Even a reprobate like Conrad Putney deserves to die with dignity."

"But folks'll stay to watch," Mickey told her. "It'll be fun." He yanked an imaginary rope around his neck, stuck his tongue out to the side and made choking sounds.

"Stop that!" Norah said. "That's awful!"

"Then why are you laughing?"

"Because it's awful, you dreadful child." She tried without much success to still her giggles. "Do something useful while I pick up the dishes. Go change the baby."

"Why do I have to do that? Why can't her daddy do that?"

Morgan glanced at Norah. It made him feel foolishly pleased to be called daddy. "Because I'm wearing two pistols," he said gruffly. "That makes grown men shake in their boots."

Mickey looked to see if he was joking and decided he wasn't. "Oh."

In spite of the beastly heat, the parade was an overwhelming success. The band, which had just formed over the weekend, proved to be enthusiastic, if not extremely talented. They led the parade, providing a riotous sound. Nearly two hundred people followed behind, some in wagons decorated with wildflowers, paper streamers, and ribbons. Only three women fainted, which was somewhat of a record, considering how tightly most women laced their corsets. And the crowd along the streets, while loud and boisterous, never once got out of hand.

Afterward everyone from town as well as the visitors moved down under the huge cotton-woods by the river to eat. There was not a woman who didn't contribute enough food and drink for her family and half a dozen guests. Drifters, rowdies, and drummers were all invited to sit a spell and eat. Even the prostitutes dressed themselves in decent clothes in order to attend the picnic.

Pits lined with stones had been prepared the night before and filled with beef to be slow cooked for hours till the meat fell from the bones. Angus MacKay magnanimously provided the beef. Morgan had some thoughts about where the wily Scot had purchased it, but he let the matter pass. One man just couldn't do every-thing.

As evening fell and people were sated with food and drink, the noise level died down. With the setting sun, the temperature dropped quickly, cooling the river valley. A band began to play, and there was some dancing. Finally it was dark. Dr. Rehfeld Smedley, the renown pyro-technical artist, went to work.

The first rocket blasted into the sky and burst into a thousand brilliant stars. The crowd *ahhhed* appreciatively, murmuring to one another.

"Where the hell's the gunfire?" The voice came from deep within the jail.

Willie Wilson tiptoed to the back room and peered suspiciously through the bars at Conrad Putney. He felt very important being the deputy sheriff for the night. He'd found a badge in Sheriff Treyhan's desk and pinned it to his shirt. Of course, the sheriff didn't know he was there. That was a family secret.

Willie's father had drawn the duty tonight, but he was back at the mercantile. His mother didn't want to lose any of the money they might make from customers who wanted last-minute purchases. His parents had discussed the subject in great detail, trying to decide whether to close when Jed Wilson took over his jail watch or to stay open an hour or so after the fireworks ended.

Willie's father, being a conscientious man, took his civic duty very seriously, but he was no match for his wife's strong will. He did not, however, want the other residents to know he shirked his responsibility for a few extra dollars. So, he had gone to the sheriff's office at eight o'clock to begin his shift and spent several minutes joking with Charlie Cook, whom he replaced, before Charlie left to watch the pyrotechnical display.

Willie was quite pouty about having to miss the fireworks. Even the promise of an extra piece of chocolate cake before bed did little to dispel his disappointment. So when the first rocket blast shook the building, he went to the front door and looked out.

His prisoner's voice brought him back inside. The cells were back in another room behind the office. Willie opened the door to the jail and looked inside. The jail scared him. So did Conrad Putney. The former deputy's silvery hair had grown long and shaggy since he'd taken to the outlaw trail and he now had a beard. Putney terrified Willie even more since he shot Albert Harrison.

"What's going on out there?" Putney demanded.

"Fireworks," Willie answered.

Conrad Putney was silent a moment.

Another tremendous blast filled the air and the people down by the river cheered. Willie sighed.

"Where's the fireworks?" Putney asked.

"In the sky."

Putney smiled. He couldn't believe his luck. "Willie-boy, is that you?"

"Yes." Willie backed away from the bars.

Putney began to chuckle. What a twist of fate, he thought, to be fired from the only job he'd ever halfway liked, only to be replaced by the village idiot.

"What are you laughing at?" Willie asked. He hated it when people laughed and he didn't understand the joke.

"You and me are the only ones who ain't watching the pyrotechnics."

"That ain't funny."

"No, it ain't," Putney agreed. "So why don't you let me out and we both can have fun?"

"Go to hell." Willie walked back into the office, shutting the door with a bang.

He sat for the next fifteen minutes in the sheriff's chair, feeling sorry for himself and daydreaming about being a hero who performed daring feats the whole town admired.

"Help!"

There was a crash and a blood-chilling shriek. Willie leapt out of the chair and ran through the door into the jail. Conrad Putney was writhing on the floor of his cell in obvious agony.

"Help me, help me—I'm dying!"

His moan made Willie's hair stand on end.

Quick as a flash, Willie ran back to the office and fumbled through the desk drawer for the keys to the cell. It took several minutes for him to find them, since they were hanging on a wall hook. All the while Putney moaned in anguish.

At the door to the cell, Willie tried the wrong key three times and dropped the entire bunch on the floor with a crash. He was so excited about saving Putney he was practically tripping over himself.

"I'll save ya, Deputy," he said as he knelt down, forgetting that he was the one now wearing the badge.

Before Willie realized what was happening, Conrad had grabbed the keys from his outstretched hand and punched him hard in the side of the head. Willie went down like a rock.

Conrad jumped up, grabbed his jacket, and dashed out of the cell. He tried to lock it but couldn't find the right key. Dropping them, he ran into the office and out the front door. Just as he stepped out into the dark street, an enormous fireworks display went off.

Conrad yelled and threw himself down on the street, certain he'd been fired upon. Red and yellow stars floated through the heavens and the crowd applauded.

"God Almighty," he swore, picking himself off the dusty street. He would head toward the alley, he decided, just in case anybody was wandering around town. Then he'd pick up a horse at the livery and ride out of town.

Back inside the cell, Willie sat up and felt the side of his head. The keys had scratched him, and he sucked in his breath when he discovered blood.

Then he realized his prisoner had escaped.

"Oh, no," he said. "He's not s'posed ta do that."

He moved to the cell door and stopped. On the floor beyond the door he saw the keys. He got down on his knees and reached for them, but he couldn't quite get to them. After wiggling around a bit, he stretched again, his whole body weight leaning against the door. Slowly the door opened, but Willie didn't notice at first. He kept reaching until his fingers finally touched the keys.

"Ah, hell. The door ain't even locked."

Dispirited, he walked into the office and slowly removed the badge. As he opened the desk drawer he saw something he hadn't noticed before—a pistol.

"Oh, golly!" His eyes began to glow. He could still be a hero. He could catch Conrad Putney before Sheriff Treyhan knew he was gone. "Yeah. That's what I'll do."

He shoved the badge back on his shirt and grabbed the gun, standing up so quickly he knocked over the chair.

Willie never knew exactly what happened next. One moment he was thrilled at being a hero. The next moment there was a tremendous noise and he was writhing around on the floor in pain. His foot hurt like fiery hell, and he was cold, scared, and sick to his stomach. All thoughts of daring deeds ended in that instant. When he was able to move, he pulled himself up and limped up the street to his mother.

Something was wrong. Morgan could feel it in his gut. He looked around the crowd. It was hard to see in the darkness, but he was certain that all eyes were on the sky. He leaned over to his wife and whispered, "I'm going to walk over to the jail."

"Right now?"

"Yes."

"Is something wrong?"

"I'm not sure. Maybe. I'd better check."

"All right. Be careful."

Morgan found Mickey with several other boys. "You look after your sister. If I'm not back when this is over, you take her home." He shouldered his way through the crowd and took off for his office at a trot.

"Oh, no," he said when he saw the front door standing wide open.

A quick search told him that not only had his prisoner vanished, the volunteer deputy was also gone. He shook his head at the puddle of blood on the floor. Putney was as dangerous as a cornered rat.

Running up the middle of the street, he noticed all the lights on at Wilson's Mercantile. Hadn't Jed Wilson been one of the volunteers scheduled to work tonight? Morgan ran up onto the sidewalk and into the store. He heard the sound of weeping in the back.

"Jed? Mrs. Wilson?" He pushed open the curtain.

Beatrice Wilson bent over Willie tending his wounded foot.

"It hurts, Ma!" Willie was bawling his head off.

"Jed? What happened? Where's Putney . . . ?" Morgan stopped when he saw the silver star on Willie's heaving chest. "Oh, good God! You damned fool. How could you have let *him* stay alone with Putney?"

"Now wait a minute, Sheriff," Beatrice interrupted.

"Mrs. Wilson, I'm talking to Jed. He was my man on duty."

Jed simply hung his head. "I'm sorry, Morgan."

"Goddammit, a killer's on the loose!"

"There's no reason to swear," Beatrice said huffily.

Morgan's temper snapped. "Lady, you're damned lucky Putney didn't kill Willie. Do you think the few pennies you'll make tonight will be worth *that?*"

Beatrice gasped, shocked that anyone would speak back to her.

"The posse leaves at daybreak," Morgan said to Jed. "You be there!"

He slammed the door behind him, shaking all the windows in the building.

"You're not going, Jed Wilson," his wife said.

"You shut up, Bea," Jed snarled, thoroughly ashamed of his whole family. "For once in your fool life, just shut your mouth!"

They found Putney at dawn Thursday morning, holed up in a pine thicket in the White Mountains near the old Spanish trail. He was still tucked snugly in his bed.

The end was swift and violent. Knowing that he was going back to Holbrook to be strung up, Putney chose to fight them all. He grabbed his gun and started running toward them. But he was dead before he got ten feet.

"We'll stop back in Alpine to rest and eat," Morgan told the posse as they loaded Putney's body on a packhorse. "The town company will pay for everything. Isn't that right, Mayor?"

Whitehall reluctantly agreed.

"After that, we'll ride as far as we can. I want to be back in Holbrook by tomorrow afternoon."

Fat Tony Roscoe stepped onto the wooden platform at the Holbrook station and wrinkled his nose in disgust. An afternoon breeze had begun to blow from the east as storm clouds gathered. The strong odor from the stockyards mingled with dust, stale beer and grease to form a particularly unpleasant smell.

"Are we in the right place?" Dowie asked.

"It's where that conductor said." Harcourt looked around. He'd been in a lot of one-horse towns since they started searching for Omar, but this was the worst. "The skinny guy named Cal got off here."

"No valise was left behind, so skinny Cal must've took it."

Fat Tony had lost fifteen pounds in the last jail they visited—the one they'd broken out of. He'd also lost his even disposition. In his disillusionment with old Omar running out on them, he'd begun to look at life quite differently. This whole goddamn trip had been a nightmare, from beginning to end. Fat Tony meant to have that gold, and he meant to have it today. He'd even kill to get it!

Although it was set in the most barren spot in the country, this little burg hummed with activity. Riders on horseback filled the street. Two boys played catch over and between the rolling wagons. Women bustled about. Saloon music boiled out of one of the buildings.

"I need a beer," Fat Tony said.

"Are you buyin'?" Harcourt asked. Fat Tony's glare kept him from saying more. Harcourt was beginning to worry about the fat man. In the past *he'd* always been the grouchy one, but Fat Tony had turned so mean and surly lately, Harcourt felt uneasy. He'd be glad when this caper ended. Maybe he'd take a break from crime.

They meandered across the street to the Bucket of Blood, dodging wagons clustered around Wilson's Mercantile and cowboys making a beeline for the saloon.

A dirty pink sow lay on her side in the cool

seepage near the horse trough, suckling her rambunctious babies.

"Ain't that appetizing?" Fat Tony grumbled.

None of the cowboys seemed to mind. They pushed into the Bucket of Blood and lined up at the bar. In the back room Jewel was doing a thriving business, and her customers played cards at the back tables while they waited for her services.

Fat Tony, Harcourt, and Dowie were lucky to get a wobbly table near the front door.

"How come you got such a big crowd so early in the day?" Dowie asked the bartender when he went over to get their drinks.

"Jewel," Eldon answered. "She's great for business."

Fat Tony helped himself to the free lunch after swishing the flies off the boiled eggs with his hand. The spread was pathetic, but he filled his plate just the same. As soon as he had the gold in his hands he planned to head back East, going first class all the way.

"I gotta go out back," Dowie said.

"Don't take too long," Fat Tony told him. "I want to locate this Cal feller and get out of this dust pile."

Dowie made his way to the back of the saloon while Harcourt went over to the bar to have a chat with the bartender.

"Damn, that's an ugly picture you got on the wall."

Eldon grunted. "Yep, but we're getting another one soon. We hired us a new picture painter. He's doing something real purty." It was a lie, but Eldon told that to all newcomers. Truth was, he was quite fond of the awful painting.

"I'm looking for a friend of mine named Cal. Tall, skinny bird. Came back from a trip east sometime last fall. I'm told he owns a place here."

"Cal Welsh?" Eldon looked at the man carefully. He didn't look like a lawman. Not that Eldon cared one way or another, but he prided himself on being able to spot one.

"You know where he is?"

"Yep."

"Where?"

"Up on the hill—towards the mesa. The red rocks north of here."

Harcourt didn't recall much being on the other side of the tracks, and there seemed to be virtually nothing up by the red rocks.

Eldon saw his confusion, then enlightened him. "He's in the cemetery." He was feeling magnanimous today. He'd stopped at the Holbrook House this morning to pick up Jewel before opening, and she'd treated him especially fine.

"Cal Welsh is dead," he told the stranger. "Not long after he got back from his trip. He fell in a well."

Harcourt was stunned. This journey had been terrible. One corpse after another. First Omar's old woman, then Omar himself, and now this Cal feller. Who was next? He went back to the table and blurted the news to Fat Tony.

"Somebody has the gold," Fat Tony said, cutting to the bones of the situation. The boiled eggs made him belch. "Go find out who!"

"Do I ask him if there was any extra gold laying around?" Harcourt asked.

"Oh, for God's sake!" Fat Tony lurched out of the chair and buttonholed Eldon.

He waited a moment while Eldon served up two whiskeys for a drifter in dirty blue overalls. "I understand my friend Cal Welsh died. That's such a shame. I was looking forward to seeing him again."

"You from Indiana?"

"A little east of there. What happened to Cal?"

Eldon knew the whole town's business. He proceeded to tell the fat guy about Cal's trip home to his father's funeral, his accident, the beautiful bride who had come in on the train, and Cal's tragic death.

"How 'bout a beer here?" one of the gamblers demanded.

Eldon broke off his story and poured the beer, then waited on two more customers.

Dowie came back from the outhouse just as a bowlegged cowboy still buttoning his fly slouched out of Jewel's cubby hole. The curtain was open and Dowie looked in, just curious.

"Don't be shy, stranger. Come here and sit for a spell."

Dowie glanced around, saw nobody else, then gestured toward himself questioningly.

"You're the only one here, sugar. Why don't you come in and let Jewel show you her treasures."

Dowie marched in the door with a smile on

his face but he hadn't yet gotten his suspenders off when a pistol shot rang out. Splinters rained down on Dowie's head.

"It's my turn, you little twirp!"

Dowie was tossed out into the hall before he could even reply, and his hat sailed out behind him. Jewel's laughter echoed in his ears. Completely deflated, he tugged on his hat and returned to the table by the front door.

"Well, that took you long enough," Fat Tony said grumpily.

"Your cheek is bleeding," Harcourt told him. "What happened?"

"Slivers on the outhouse door," Dowie said. "Let's get outta this dump."

Tod Willis was one of the many men who'd joined the posse searching for Conrad Putney, so Mickey was at loose ends. And he was bored to death. He thought for sure the men would be back by today.

He swept out Tod's workshop and stopped by Dolly's to visit. Then he decided to go to the house and see if Norah wanted him to entertain Colleen.

He was just walking up the front path when he heard Norah scream. He stopped dead still.

She screamed again. Mickey took off running up the stairs, thinking there must be a snake in the house.

He came to a skidding halt when he looked though the screen door.

Dowie held Norah with her arms behind her

back. Harcourt stood in front of her, but she paid no attention to him. She was looking at Fat Tony—he was holding Colleen.

"Where's the gold?" Harcourt asked.

"I told you—I don't know about any gold."

Harcourt hit her with the palm of his hand. "Wrong answer."

Fat Tony flipped the baby upside down, holding her by her ankles. Colleen wailed at such treatment.

"Don't hurt her!" shrieked Norah.

"Tell me where the gold is, bitch," Fat Tony said. "Or in one minute this kid's brains will be splashed all over the wall." He began to swing Colleen back and forth.

"Nooooo!" Mickey yelled as he flung open the door.

For an instant the men were stunned. Then they recognized the little son of a bitch who had been responsible for their last arrest, and they all began to shout. Fat Tony tossed the baby into the crib and started for Mickey. Harcourt followed suit.

Seeing her chance, Norah stomped hard on Dowie's instep. He dropped her arms and howled.

"Run, Mickey!" she screamed. Then she spotted the broom and began to swing it wildly. All the while she yelled at the top of her lungs, hoping somebody from town would hear her.

Mickey was also hollering. He ran and dodged, rolling under the table, thrusting a chair at Fat Tony's legs. With any luck he could reach the back porch and get the shotgun Morgan had out there and blast these bastards all over Norah's kitchen.

At about that time Morgan rode into town. Filthy and tired to the bone, he didn't bother to stop at his office. Putney needed Digger's services, not his. All Morgan wanted was a hot bath, a good meal and his bed. He turned his horse toward home. For once he crossed a clear track, not having to wait for a damned train.

He heard the hollering and yelling, but at first he thought it was just another battle between the floozies at one of the saloons, so he kept riding.

Then he heard Norah's voice. "Mickey, look out!"

There was a crash and then a scream.

Oh God, Norah!

Morgan spurred the horse, leapt off at a dead run, and raced up the porch steps, a pistol in hand. He yanked the screen door so hard it came off the hinges.

Mickey was on top of the stove, swinging the Dutch oven. Morgan's unexpected entrance distracted Fat Tony, who had a tiny derringer pointed at the boy. Mickey beaned him good and proper. The fat man fell like a toppled oak.

Morgan put a bullet in Harcourt's thigh at the same time Norah thrust the broom handle into Dowie's belly button. Both men collapsed to the floor, moaning and groaning.

"What the hell is going on?"

"They're the one's I told you about—the ones on the train. The desperados."

"She's got our gold," Harcourt said, trying to

stop the blood oozing from his upper leg with a grimy monogrammed handkerchief.

"I told you I don't!" Norah still held the broom, ready to attack if she was provoked any further. "Morgan, you know I don't have any gold."

"Your husband had the satchel," Dowie said. "With the Bibles."

"Oh, no!"

Morgan glanced at Norah. "What's the matter?"

She slumped into a chair. "Oh, dear God, no."

"Norah!" Mickey hopped off his perch. "What's wrong?"

She looked up, wetting her parched lips with her tongue.

"There's an old leather satchel at the shop. It's Cal's. I put it with some of his books because there's a Bible in it."

"Holy shit!" Mickey exclaimed, utterly thrilled. "We're rich!"

"I seriously doubt it," Morgan said. "I'll bet my next paycheck that the gold is stolen. Right, gentlemen?"

"I don't have to say nothin'," Harcourt told him nastily.

"I don't have to get you a doctor, either. Mickey, get some rope. We'll just tie these guys to the porch rail till they're feeling chatty. Norah, could you heat up some water? I'm willing to kill for a hot bath."

Morgan locked the gold in his safe.

He'd gone to the sewing shop right after the

three thugs had finished confessing. The gold was there all right, safely hidden, as it had been for months, in a crate of adventure novels.

He wondered why Cal hadn't said anything to him about the gold. Did he know it had been stolen? Morgan finally decided that while Cal had few secrets, the ones he had were amazing.

Morgan knew it was time to go home.

He was more nervous than he had been the day they were married—maybe because he'd almost lost her, maybe because he'd finally admitted what he had.

It was damned strange for a man to live a bachelor's life for almost thirty-three years, and then to marry, anticipating little more than companionship from his wife. And less than two months later to discover himself deeply in love. More in love with his own beautiful wife than he had ever imagined possible.

He lingered at the jail longer than he had to. His prisoners had talked like parrots before he'd even shaved that afternoon. By the time he was cleaned up, he'd sent a telegram to the authorities in New York, telling of their capture. Now they were in their cells for the night.

They'd complained bitterly about the accommodations until Clarabelle had come in with the dinner trays. Normally the food came from the Holbrook House, but there had been a chimney fire in that kitchen during dinner preparations. Clarabelle had agreed to feed Morgan's charges for a day or two. With Ferdie gone looking for new business property, she'd said she had time on her hands, so she'd cooked for a few days. By that time Morgan figured he would hear back about what to do with the thugs.

He locked the front door and looked up at the night sky. To the north there was a thunderstorm. It was too far away for Holbrook to get any rain, but the lightning flashes across the sky were beautiful. A cool breeze gusted around him. He squared his shoulders and headed home.

The kitchen light was on. Morgan guessed that Mickey was there playing solitaire, and he couldn't help being disappointed. He'd hoped to have the night alone with Norah.

He trudged up the front steps. Stopping on the porch, he thought that someday he'd like to get a porch swing. He could imagine sitting in the dark with Norah on a swing.

When do I ever get an evening off? he wondered.

Suddenly Morgan knew things were going to have to change. This town needed him more than he needed it. He had a wife and a child to think about. Tomorrow he'd meet with Mayor Whitehall and get a few things straight. He was going to have a full-time deputy, and he was going to have specific times off.

"Morgan, is that you?" Norah called.

"It's the law, ma'am," he teased as he walked toward the kitchen. "I've come to check out your complaint—"

He stopped dead in his tracks.

Norah was alone in the kitchen, resting comfortably in a high-backed plunge bath beside the cookstove. Her red hair was piled loosely on top of her head with tendrils curling softly about her face and neck. A soft ivory cloth with elaborately crocheted edges hung over the sides of the old tin tub, protecting her delicate skin from any discomfort.

Morgan just stared.

"Come in," she said sweetly. "I have hot water for tea."

The last thing on Morgan's mind was tea, but he dutifully approached the stove and poured hot water into the teapot. He carried the pot to the table and set it down beside two china cups and a bowl of pink hollyhocks. Then he turned to watch his wife.

Quite nonchalantly Norah immersed a fat sponge into the clear fragrant water, and bending sideways, slowly squeezed the lavender scented liquid over her shoulder and breasts.

Morgan's chest tightened. He could hardly breathe. This water nymph seductively washing herself in front of him was so unlike his hardworking, practical wife that he thought she'd been bewitched. Or else he had.

Suddenly he had to touch her. Dropping to his knees on the folded quilt beside the tub, he took the sponge out of her hand and brushed it across the tips of her breasts. Then he bent to trace the path of the sponge with his tongue.

"Your hat," she warned, grabbing the black Stetson before it fell into the tub.

"Ah, hell." He stood up, ridding himself of hat, boots, and gun belt before she could even blink. He was on the floor again, swooping her into his arms.

Norah had known she loved Morgan since the day of the earthquake, and she had marveled at the fact she hadn't known it long before that. How could a woman who prided herself on honesty and self-discipline not realize she'd never have married Morgan Treyhan if she hadn't been in love? Why hadn't the nights she'd spent in his arms made that clear to her?

She guessed she hadn't wanted to admit how she felt. Her love affair with Sonny had ended painfully, and so had her marriage to Cal. After so much heartache, she felt guilty about being happy with Morgan.

"You're getting wet," she murmured.

He let her go only long enough to unbutton his shirt and toss it aside.

Norah laughed, indulging herself in touching his warm, hard chest.

"I think I'm still covered with trail dirt."

"What?"

"I need to be in there with you."

"Oh, no—the tub's too small."

"I don't think so. I'm sure we'll both fit."

"Morgan."

His pants landed on the table beside the bowl of hollyhocks. Norah shrieked as he climbed into the plunge bath. It wasn't a large tub, and it certainly hadn't been designed for two occupants. Water splashed over the sides in gigantic waves, soaking the quilt on the floor.

But Morgan was a very inventive man. He found a way for them both to fit.

"Ohhhh," she whispered, her wet mouth touching his. "I love you."

He pulled away from her and looked deep into her eyes. "Good," he said at last. "I'm glad." He kissed her deeply.

And later, when they were buried deep within the snow-white sheets on the big brass bed, sleepy and sated, he pulled her tightly into his arms.

"Norah," he said close to her ear, "I love you. I think I've loved you always."

15

Morgan would be glad to finally get home. He was tired of big cities, strange food, and swaying railroad coaches. The trip to deliver Fat Tony Roscoe, Harcourt Barr, and Dowie Johnston to the New York State authorities had been exhausting. He'd take rustlers any day over an August day in New York.

God, how he missed Norah! He never wanted to be away from her another day of his life. Or the baby—or even that smart-mouthed twirp Mickey. He couldn't wait to get home to his own bed and his own family.

"My wife will be delighted you decided to make a detour to Holbrook," Morgan said as the train passed some interesting New Mexico land formations. "She's been waiting quite some time for a priest."

"It's my pleasure, Morgan. As I told you before, I don't officially have to be in Santa Fe until mid-September. If I can baptize the baby and say a few prayers for the dead, the diversion will be well worth it. Besides, you've added some excitement to a long, dull trip."

Morgan smiled at that. He was certain a scholarly man such as Father Riordan seldom encountered *his* kind. He looked out the window, watching hills slope into canyons and rise again to flat-topped mesas as the train moved swiftly across the wild, wondrous land.

"Francis," he said, "there is one other thing I'm curious about. . . . I'm not even sure how it's done. But I'd like to marry Norah again." He paused, trying to collect his thoughts. "You see, her first husband died last fall. After the baby was born, I thought she needed a man in her life. So I proposed."

Father Riordan leaned forward, his blue eyes alive with interest. He was eternally fascinated with people. A scholar all his life, he'd discovered the most intriguing subject of all was human nature.

Morgan glanced out the window, trying to explain his impetuous proposal and Norah's equally impulsive acceptance. "She was alone with a new baby in a dangerous town. And I . . . uh, I wanted . . ." A flush tinged his bronze cheekbones.

"I understand, Morgan," the priest assured him with a smile. "Truly I do."

Morgan cleared his throat. "We were married the next morning by the circuit judge—who was sober for a change—and then we both went back to work."

The conductor approached them, stopping to chat for a moment, mentioning President Cleveland's fishing trip and lamenting the fact he seldom had time to fish.

"I think I'll become president," the conductor told them. "That oughta be the easiest job any man could have. Why hell, ya could go fishin' every day if ya wanted, and *nobody* could tell ya no."

When he went on about his business, Morgan and the priest resumed their conversation.

"I bought a wedding ring for Norah when I was in New York."

Morgan patted his coat pocket, remembering how much pleasure buying that simple gold ring had brought him. "I hadn't even thought about it before. And that got me to thinking how all I've done since we were married is eat the meals she fixed, set out my clothes to be washed, and share her bed. Women have different dreams from men, different expectations. Like a gold ring. Till now, I haven't given her wishes much thought or consideration."

"Has she complained?" the priest asked.

"Not at all. And I think we're happy—I have been, at least. I just want her to be glad she married me."

"Does she know you love her?"

"I didn't know till those robbers were threatening her. I told her so that night."

"Why don't you ask her about another wedding? Leave the decision up to her."

"I may just do that," Morgan said, looking out the window.

*   *   *

As the train pulled into Holbrook a summer storm was brewing, dark and threatening, and the wind was blowing a gale. Thunder growled angrily above them. In a minute or so, it would pour.

"Hang on to your hat," Morgan told the priest as they stepped off the train. "We'll head across the street to Norah's dress shop."

Riordan placed one hand on his wide-brimmed hat and dashed along behind Morgan, the hem of his black cassock flapping as he ran.

Norah gasped when she saw Morgan. "You're three days early!"

Although Dolly, Clarabelle, and Mrs. Norris from the boots and leather-goods store were all in the shop, Morgan swept his wife in his arms and kissed her soundly. She was breathless when he let her go, and she appeared a bit dazed. Then she saw the priest.

"Morgan, where are your manners?" She was blushing like a schoolgirl.

Morgan grinned. He'd never been so glad to see anybody in his life. Lordy, lordy, he was crazy about this woman!

"It's all right," Father Riordan told her. "Your husband sorely missed you."

At that moment there was a thunderous clap outside and a jag of lightning, and the rain came down like a waterfall.

"Oh, dear," Mrs. Norris said. "It's raining too hard for me to go out. I guess I'll have to stay till this is over."

Morgan noted that she didn't seem the least bit unhappy. And why should she? The priest's visit was an event. It should provide her with several afternoons' worth of friendly gossip.

After the introductions, Dolly suggested they all adjourn to the back room for tea. Clarabelle had brought a plate of cookies when she arrived, and Norah had some fresh-baked bread.

"Father Riordan came out of his way to baptize Colleen." Morgan held the little girl in his lap and let her grab hold of his mustache, then he tickled her tummy until she laughed out loud. "And to perform any wedding that might be upcoming."

Clarabelle blushed the color of a beet and set her cup down with a clatter. She cleared her throat. "Quinton and I are going to get married. He's decided to leave the mousetrap business and give up traveling. He's buying out my brother's part of the business."

The other women all tried to act surprised, but it wasn't easy. Clarabelle was a changed woman since the mousetrap man came to town.

"What about Ferdie?" Mrs. Norris asked.

"He decided not to stay in Needles. Do you know the thermometer reached 135 degrees there last month? Ferdie's last letter said he was going to look over Prescott. The climate's better and it's more centrally located."

"He'll do fine, Clarabelle," Morgan assured her.

She nodded. "I just wish he was able to be here for my wedding."

When the rains let up, Morgan escorted

Father Riordan to the Holbrook House. Once there, Morgan suggested that the priest make the hotel his headquarters.

"Angus," he said when the proprietor came out to greet them, "why don't you show Father the best room in the house?"

"Aye, I will indeed," MacKay said. "And I'd take it as a special favor if you'd be my guest. Food and lodging and whatever else you'll be needing."

The priest accepted with sincere thanks and allowed MacKay to lead him upstairs.

Morgan smiled as he watched them go. He had known that MacKay would make the offer. Though Morgan had never been able actually to connect him with Gates, Putney, and the cattle rustling, he was certain that the Scot was somehow involved. It was a tiny slice of justice that MacKay's guilty conscience prodded him to pay for the priest's visit.

Ten minutes later, Morgan found Mickey at the sheriff's office. The boy was mopping the floor.

"You don't have to do that," Morgan said.

"The mayor hired me. It's been raining every day, and people have been trackin' in street muck. It was gettin' thick in here. I think lard-butt Whitehall was afraid you'd gun him down if you saw it."

Morgan chuckled. The kid was incorrigible. A Kelly all the way to the bone! "I'm not supposed to be in till Saturday. Why are you mopping today?"

"I didn't figure you'd stay away from Norah

that long," Mickey told him. "Besides, your new deputy from Durango arrived yesterday."

"Oh?" Morgan braced himself for the worst.

"Name's Burt Adams. He's a true-blue peace officer."

Morgan couldn't decide if that was a compliment or an insult. "What's that supposed to mean?"

"It's just information."

"Anything else?"

"He ain't the kind of son of a bitch that shoots down kids in the street."

Morgan nodded. He walked carefully across the clean floor and sat down in his chair. "Have a seat. I have some information for you."

Mickey looked wary but seated himself without comment. The worst thing that he could imagine right then was that Morgan was sending him back to his family. Then he'd have to hire out on a harvesting team and send all his money home to the old man. Hell, he'd run away first!

"There was a reward for returning the gold," Morgan told him. "It's enough to pay for you to go to Santa Fe to school."

Mickey shook his head, not believing what he'd just heard. "I don't want the reward. It's yours . . . and Norah's."

"We have all the stuff Cal bought. The reward is over and above the amount Cal spent. Mick, you saved Norah's life. If you hadn't beaned Fat Tony with the Dutch oven, he could have shot both of you."

The boy studied his feet.

"There's a priest who rode in with me. He is going to teach in Santa Fe. He'll get you admitted to the school. You'll get a far better education there than you ever could here. You've got a good mind. This is a chance to really make something of yourself."

"Does Norah know?"

"I wanted to talk to you about it first. It's your decision. If you don't want to leave here, you don't have to. We could put away the reward until you're of age. No matter what, it belongs to you. I just want you to give the idea of school a fair shake."

"I'll think about it," Mickey said. "Will you wait to tell Norah until tomorrow?"

"I could do that. There are some things she and I need to discuss. I might forget the reward money until morning."

"I'm sure you will if I sleep over at Tod's tonight."

It stormed off and on all evening. As soon as Colleen was fed and put in her cradle for the night, Morgan picked Norah up in his arms and carried her to bed.

"God, I have missed you!" He buried his face in the red cloud of her hair.

"I didn't think you'd ever get back." She kissed him with a fervor that stunned him. "My sweet love."

Later that night, in their big brass bed, Morgan proposed marriage—again. She lay close against him, stroking his chest and nuzzling his neck.

"We already did that." Norah giggled. She pulled his head down and kissed him.

"I'm serious." He was having a hard time concentrating, so he moved away from her and propped himself up on one elbow. "Norah, listen to me. I rushed you before the judge. Now I realize how unfair that was to you."

"I married you because I wanted to, Morgan." She reached out and touched one finger to his cheek.

"You deserved a party and a wedding cake." He wanted to take her in his arms again, but he knew he had to have his say.

"Marriage isn't a party. It's two people making a life together. We're doing that. I wish you could spend more time at home, but I understood your job when I agreed to be your wife. I love being your wife."

"This time I want to marry you for the right reasons—because I love you. I want us to make our promises before a priest and witnesses. And I want you to wear my ring." He reached under the lamp and produced the plain gold ring.

"Oh, Morgan, I want that, too!" She flew into his arms. "Yes, yes," she said, her throat so tight she could barely speak.

It was the end of August when Father Riordan was ready to leave for Santa Fe. During his stay in Holbrook he performed one christening, three weddings, and two funerals.

The prostitute Jewel was found dead in her hotel room when Eldon went to pick her up one morning. Doc Robinson said she had accidentally taken an overdose of the opiate she used for consumption. And some drifter turned his gun on himself—nobody knew him or the reason.

"Sorry I can't stay for the Grand Ball," the priest said to Norah as they walked toward the depot. "It sounds like a delightful gathering."

"The band is coming from Albuquerque," Dolly said. She'd been making fancy dresses for the town ladies for the past two weeks and was caught up in the excitement of the upcoming gala.

"I'll be back when school is out next summer," Father Riordan said. "And I promise to inquire about a priest coming here to stay. That's a nice piece of land the Church bought, but it needs a building and a pastor."

Flora Harrison joined them just before the train arrived. She'd stayed with the Norris family since her tragedy but decided she needed a change of scenery. Before Albert was born she worked as a teacher, and Father Riordan thought she might get a position at a girl's school in Santa Fe.

They stood at the depot and watched the eastbound train roll into the station. Norah took a deep breath.

"I'll miss you," she said softly to her brother, giving his hand a tight squeeze.

"Sure," Mickey answered. He hoped she wasn't going to get all mushy. He was feeling a bit peculiar himself, so he didn't want to have to put up with her weeping. He'd miss her. She was an all right sister. And he'd miss the baby, too. Hell, he'd even miss cranky old Morgan, though he doubted the feeling was mutual. Morgan would be damned glad to see his dust, so he and Norah could spend more time in that big brass bed.

Mickey studied his shoes. Norah had made him polish them to a high sheen. He was glad to be leaving, glad to be off to school and find a direction for his life. Like Morgan told him, this was the best opportunity he'd ever get, so he intended to make the best of it. He'd show people what a Kelly could do!

He realized that even if he was a bit tight in the throat, he was glad to leave Norah and Morgan to themselves. They were just starting off and they deserved some privacy. One thing for certain, if he had a new bride, he'd hate like hell to have some pesky kid hanging around all the time. He'd want her all to himself. He was getting to an age where he understood such things.

Father Riordan turned to Mickey. "Well, Michael, are you ready to go? This will be quite an adventure for you."

"Yes, Father." He picked up the battle-scarred satchel that held his belongings. Since the reward from the robbery was paying for his school, keeping the old leather bag seemed appropriate.

"Good-bye, Mick." Morgan held out his hand. "And good luck."

"Thanks." Mickey wasn't sure what else to say to his fearsome brother-in-law. He didn't know how to tell Morgan he was his hero. "Maybe I'll come back someday and be a deputy."

Morgan shook his head. "Go to school, Mick. Learn to use your brain. That's what you'll do best.

Then you can be the man you were meant to be."

The boy nodded, even if he didn't quite understand. He hugged his sister, blinking back huge tears, and headed blindly for the train.

"Mickey!" Morgan called. "We'll see you at Christmas."

Burt Adams was everything Morgan could have asked for in a deputy. He was serious, single, and sober. A dedicated lawman, he expected to work a full shift with only one day off a week. It didn't occur to him that Morgan wouldn't also have time off.

For the very first time, Holbrook's law enforcement reached the standard Morgan wanted. He was a satisfied man.

Norah, too, was pleased with Deputy Adams. She immediately arranged her life so she and Morgan could spend their free day together.

"You don't need to take Bruna's dress home," Dolly protested. "I know you and Morgan plan to ride up to the mesas. We'll have everything finished by Saturday night."

"I'm going to take it. Something unexpected will crop up at the last minute. It always does. Since this is the most complicated frock we're doing, I want it finished early, just in case she wants some alterations."

"A bale of hay is a bale of hay," Dolly said cryptically.

"Dolly!" Norah couldn't help laughing. Bruna did have a difficult figure to fit.

"We perform miracles," Dolly said reasonably.

"Nobody knows better than me." She paused to snip a thread. "Did I mention I have an escort to the ball?"

Norah stared. "No, you did not. I would have remembered if you had."

Dolly had never been courted before. Nor had she ever expected to be. She was filled with girlish excitement, yet she was trying to be very casual about it.

"It must have slipped my mind."

Norah threw a spool of thread at her. It didn't even come close. They both burst out laughing.

"Who?" Norah yelled.

"Tod Willis."

"Tod?" The cabinet maker. "Oh! He's a nice man, Dolly."

"Yes, he is." Dolly sounded a little bit defensive.

"So, when did he ask?"

"Last night." Dolly thawed. "He brought me a flower."

"I don't believe it." In Holbrook flowers were as rare as gold nuggets.

"A rose." She giggled, unable to control herself. "I think he stole it from Winnie's rosebush."

Norah laughed. "I always did admire a man with ingenuity."

By Saturday evening, Holbrook was buzzing with excitement. According to Frank's article in the *Critic*, the Grand Ball was to be the spectacle of the year.

The well-publicized dance would start precisely at eight, with Mayor Whitehall and all the members of the town company and their ladies leading off the festivities. Frank Reed had hired two society reporters to collect the details on what every woman wore. The town had employed not one but three bands to play for the all-night event.

Around midnight there would be a huge buffet. And finally, before the party ended, a sunrise breakfast. Nothing in Holbrook's history had been so elaborate. It would certainly be a night to remember.

After a long discussion with his deputy, Morgan decided to attend the dance. He wanted the pleasure of dancing with Norah. The two men agreed to make their rounds at ten and after the midnight buffet. Since nearly everyone within thirty miles was attending the ball, they weren't expecting trouble.

The wool warehouse, just north of the depot, was empty for the time being except for a few odd broken bales and some tufts and strands clinging to the walls and rafters. The spidery fibers hanging from everywhere gave the inside a ghostly appearance.

One hundred and fifty thousand pounds of wool had been shipped out of Holbrook since the warehouse was built. To the cattlemen of the area, that was an insult.

"Stinkin', filthy sheep," Henry Copper muttered, leaning over to spit on the ground. "I jist hate 'em!"

Crom Rogers, Jed Oaks, and Henry stood inside the warehouse at 11:35 P.M., looking at the wisps of white wool. Crom held a candle, and Jed had a container of kerosene in his hands. He'd spent some time down in the Pleasant Valley, after a brief stint in jail, and now he was fired up with anger against anything connected with sheep.

"Jeeezz, it stinks in here," Henry muttered.

"I say we torch it," said Oaks.

Crom Rogers hadn't said a word since they left the Bucket of Blood. They'd purchased the kerosene and half a dozen candles from the dumb guy at the mercantile. Because of the Grand Ball, nobody else was around.

Rogers's hand shook. He wasn't as drunk as the other two, having arrived at the Bucket of Blood only an hour before, and he was having second thoughts about this plan. For one thing, he was afraid of fire. For another, he was scared to death of Morgan Treyhan.

"Henry, climb up in that loft and throw down some of that loose wool. Crom, split open that there bale. Pile it around these support beams. Watch that candle! Yer burnin' this damned shed, not my coat!" Oaks began to splash kerosene on the walls.

Several minutes later, Oaks was satisfied with their progress. "Come on down, Henry. Before you get your feathers singed."

Eldon morosely wiped the mahogany bar with a dirty cloth. He just hadn't been the same since Jewel died.

Three men came in and plunked themselves down at a table, but he didn't pay them any attention. If they wanted a drink they could come to the bar. Eventually, one did approach the bar for a bottle. Eldon put it and three glasses on the wooden bar without so much as looking at the fellow.

It thundered so loud outside that the windows rattled.

A medicine drummer who was drinking cheap whiskey in the corner coughed and told Eldon his lamps were smoking. Eldon didn't give a twaddle about the lamps. He poured himself a beer. He didn't drink much, had never much cared for the stuff. But tonight he was bored and lonely.

It thundered again. The lightning outside the window seemed to glow forever.

Suddenly Willie Wilson burst through the swinging doors. Eldon glanced up from his beer.

"Eldon! Eldon," Willie shouted. "Look outside."

"Go home, Willie. I ain't in the mood for lookin' at lightning."

"There's a fire!" Willie screamed. "At the warehouse."

Eldon dropped the mug and ran to the door. "Oh, God," he shouted. "Oh, good God!"

The drummer followed him to the street.

The other three looked at one another and smiled.

"Crom, what's that stuff you got all over you?"

Rogers looked down at his shirt. "Oh, hell, that's wool. It's all over you, too. We better get outta here before Treyhan sees us."

Jed Oaks refused to leave with them. He was proud of torching the warehouse. Goddamn sheep! He wasn't leaving Holbrook till he got to see the ashes.

Willie began to ring the depot bell moments before Eldon reached the steps of the Holbrook House. The band was playing "The Bells of Ireland." The melodious sound of the music mixed sweetly with the crooning of the wind.

"The wool warehouse is on fire!" Eldon told the men who were outside jawing on the porch. "Where's the sheriff?"

"Inside," Digger said as he started for the corner to look up the street. "The deputy just took a drunk to jail."

Sheriff Treyhan was on the dance floor with his wife, who was resplendent in emerald green velvet. Mayor Whitehall was gracefully twirling Mrs. Clarabelle Rose. Quinton Rose danced with Bruna Schriener. Every lady over the age of twelve was dancing, and men waited in line to lead them out.

Eldon ran onto the dance floor. Within seconds the Grand Ball had ended. It was not yet midnight.

"Fire!" men screamed, and people in their fancy dress clothes flooded out the doors and into the streets.

A makeshift fire brigade assembled within minutes, gathering every available bucket and barrel, as the town had no other fire equipment. Though Holbrook was small, the men were strong and determined. They would save the warehouse.

And then a train whistle blew.

And blew, and blew.

It came streaking through the night, down the straight stretch of track, like a powerful thundering force of nature.

Unable to stop because of its speed, the freight train barreled through town, separating the townspeople and their water buckets from the burning building. Several men risked their lives to run in front of the speeding train, but they could do nothing to save the warehouse when they got to it. Nobody could. The fire was too hot, and the wind was blowing too hard.

"Oh, my lovely house," Winnie whimpered as she and Nathan waited with the others. "It's so close to the fire."

"We're not in it," he said, holding her tenderly. "That's all that counts."

"Look," Clarabelle gasped, grabbing Quinton's arm. "Fire is flying over the train."

"That's burning wool and wood," her husband said. "The wind is blowing it this way."

They were helpless for a brief time, a whole town standing powerless on one side of a railroad track, seeing glimpses of an inferno on the other. With every gust of wind, more cinders and fiery debris floated over the rumbling freight train toward them and toward their homes.

"Norah," Morgan said. "Take the baby on home. Then wrap whatever clothes and personal items you want to save in a sheet. Set them out on the porch. And be ready to run."

"Do you really think . . . ?" She couldn't finish the sentence.

"You better be ready." He kissed her hard, then turned away. Right now the people needed a leader, and Mayor Whitehall was a fool.

He looked around to see Quinton Rose talking to Clarabelle. Tears were running down her rosy cheeks. She nodded, kissed him quickly, and turned back down the street to the fancy goods store. Dolly had already turned up the lamp in the sewing shop and was quickly gathering her things.

The caboose finally thundered past.

Then the men ran across the track, only to see what the daredevils had discovered earlier. The warehouse was engulfed in flames. For all practical purposes it was gone.

"The Red Rock Saloon is on fire!"

Morgan looked back across the street, and his heart sank. The warning he'd given Norah had been simple common sense. Now it looked as if they'd all be fighting the unthinkable—every building in Holbrook could go up in flames.

The roof of the Red Rock was burning. Lily Mae was throwing her clothes out the window a piece at a time, while the owner and the bartender dragged their precious mirror out the door. Several cowboys ran into the saloon, loading up their arms with whiskey bottles, certain they'd hit a gold mine. Deputy Adams was waiting for them, his shotgun resting in the crook of his arm.

"Just put those right over there with the mirror," he said quietly. "Then go back and help get another load. You steal even as much as the brass spittoon and I'll put a hole in you."

From where she sat on her porch across the tracks, Norah watched Holbrook catch fire. She'd packed their clothes and a few precious things, including several dime novels that had belonged to Cal. Then she'd moved the baby cradle onto the porch and sat down to wait. Colleen slept like an angel.

Norah saw the Red Rock catch first, and then Wilson's Mercantile. They were both two-story buildings. The depot and its warehouse went next, then the Bucket of Blood flared, and finally the livery stable behind the alley from the Red Rock. Building after building went up in blazes.

In the night sky thunder boomed and lightning flashed. Yet not one drop of rain fell. Other trains passed, blowing their whistles but unable to help. The wind whistled and keened, and the flames boiled and grew, whipping from one building to the next.

Norah watched in horror and fascination. Primordial elements challenged one another—wind and fire, lightning and flames. Wrestling and twisting, churning and burning.

She moaned when she first saw the orange glow at the dress shop. That little building had been Cal's dream, and then her salvation. A silent tear slipped down her cheek. She saw Dolly walking toward her with huge bundles in both arms.

"I saved the sewing machine," she said when she sat down on the step beside Norah. She, too, was crying.

Building after building caught on fire. Men fought the impossible. Women began to cross the tracks, carrying their possessions, to sit and watch with Norah. From the way the wind was blowing, her house might be spared, but little else would be.

At three in the morning it began to rain, though not the pounding, drenching torrents they'd had through the summer. This rain only lasted a short time, but it washed them and cooled them.

It was too late to save the town. With the exception of the adobe Brunswick Hotel, everything on the south side of the track had burned to the ground. The Ralston house, so recently shot up by gunfire, didn't even have the paint blistered. Winnie was the only one who spent part of the night in her own bed.

Dawn spread its first rays of light over the ashes, cool and gray. Morgan was sickened at the smoldering mess that had only hours before been a thriving, growing town.

He looked eastward toward the horizon and stopped. Enormous majestic clouds dominated the sky, gold and mauve and bright pink. They were breathtaking. And beams of light shone down from their heights, touching all the way to the earth.

It was beautiful. It was hope.

He heard a murmur and saw other men watching the sky, some with tears running down their smoke-stained cheeks. And he felt maybe all was not lost. As horrible as the fire had been, not one person had been badly hurt—not even Eldon, who at the last moment had rushed into the Bucket of Blood to try to save the ghastly

painting on the wall. He wasn't able to, but only
his eyebrows got singed.

Morgan started to walk toward his house.
They'd saved some of the food from the Grand
Ball, as well as things from the butcher shop and
the bakery. At least they'd all eat this morning.
Before they did, he wanted to wash his face and
hands.

A train whistle blew. A freight train was coming
in from Winslow.

"Ah, hell. Some things never change."

He stopped to wait for the train to pass, but
then he realized it was slowing down, preparing
to stop. Within minutes, the train crew was
unloading food and blankets and tents.

"From the people in Winslow," the engineer
shouted down to Morgan. "More is coming in
from Flagstaff. Your deputy had telegrams sent—
even before the other trains brought the news."

"Thanks," Morgan said, overwhelmed.

Digger said a prayer of thanksgiving before
they ate. For an uneducated man, he was sur-
prisingly eloquent.

Willie Wilson saw Morgan standing alone. He
hesitated, then walked over to talk to him. It
wasn't easy. Since he'd let Putney escape from
jail, Willie had been afraid of Morgan.

"Sheriff?"

"Yeah, Willie?"

"I think somebody mighta started the fire."

Morgan had his own questions about the
warehouse. Tensions between cattle and sheep
people were worse than ever, but he had no
proof. "Why is that, Willie?"

"'Cause three men bought some kerosene and candles last night when I was alone at the store. And—" he took a deep breath, "and 'cause I saw 'em come runnin' back across the railroad track a little before I saw the fire."

"Do you know who they were?"

"Yep. Jed Oakes and two cowboys. Henry—I can't think of his last name—and Crom Robbers."

"You mean Henry Copper and Crom Rogers? I know them both. Thank you, Willie. I'll have a talk with those men in a day or two. I appreciate you telling me."

Willie flushed and ambled away.

Before they had all finished eating the strange meal that was their breakfast, wagons from miles around had begun to arrive. Men and women were coming to help. Holbrook was going to rebuild.

When the passenger train arrived, Beatrice Wilson announced she was leaving town.

"We put everything we had into this uncivilized place. And now we've lost it all!" she said loudly. "I won't stay here another day. Jed, get our things. We're going back East. My family will take us in."

Jed, as usual, did what she said, but Willie refused.

"I'm not going," he told his mother.

"Get on the train, Willie." Beatrice lifted the hem of her once-elegant ball dress and strode off.

"No. I like it here—I'm staying."

Beatrice and Jed Wilson were the only ones to leave that day. Everyone else chose to stay.

"We'll build bigger and better places," Mayor Whitehall announced that evening when they'd all gathered at a torch-lit town meeting down by the river, where the air smelled of water and willows. "We'll build out of sandstone this time—buildings that will last a hundred years."

And people cheered, because that gave them hope.

At the back of the crowd, Morgan stood with his arm around his wife. Her head was on his shoulder and in her arms lay the sleeping baby.

"Will we make it?" she murmured, her voice hoarse with exhaustion.

His arm tightened on her. "We'll always make it, Norah, my love." His lips brushed her temple. "And I think Holbrook will, too."

Epilogue

October 1897

Morgan Treyhan gazed down at his sleeping wife and the tiny bundle in the crook of her arm. It amazed him how Norah still looked like a young girl, not a woman of thirty-one. Certainly not the mother of four. It was hard to believe she'd stayed so beautiful despite the life they led.

The baby whimpered in his sleep and Norah's hand brushed protectively over him. He settled down immediately, knowing he was safe. Morgan felt his throat tighten. Heaven help her, she'd do anything to protect her own.

And he'd do anything for her. She was the main reason he'd retired from being sheriff to take up ranching. She deserved a lot more than a part-time husband and the daily fear of some thug putting a bullet in his back. Besides, he'd grown weary of long days and longer nights on the job, of drunks, roughnecks and whores, of missing meals with his family. His heart no longer belonged to his badge.

And so on the last day of September 1897, Morgan had turned in his silver star to the town company. He and Norah had bought a small place in the Verde Valley from Ferdie Wattron, who'd moved there and was selling land.

Being a reasonable man, Morgan had intended to stay in Holbrook until after this baby was born, but Norah insisted they leave immediately.

"All my best moves have been in October," she told him, "and I don't want to break a lucky streak."

And like a lovesick boy, Morgan agreed.

He looked at the red spikes of hair on his son's round head—his son, Chad Michael—and grinned. He remembered the shock he'd felt at his first sight of the baby. This son whom he'd delivered only hours before.

The other boys, Chris and young Cal, were dark like Morgan. They were fine-looking boys with happy dispositions. And, of course, Colleen's coloring was dark. They'd all been beautiful babies.

He touched a soft red strand with his weathered finger. God, he hadn't been prepared for this!

This one arrived three weeks early, in the back of the damned wagon, five miles from their new home, squalling his head off and completely put out with the world. All his terrified father could think when he saw the kid's sunset red hair was that there must have been a mistake.

Norah was thrilled with her howling off-spring. "Isn't he beautiful!" she kept saying.

It was not a question. She meant it! And Morgan was smart enough to make all the right responses. Yet, as he sat beside her on the bed and studied the baby, Morgan couldn't help thinking that even now, when he was all cleaned up, the kid looked like an orange-haired monkey.

"Takes after the Kellys," he muttered, as he stroked Norah's soft cheek.

He'd met a half dozen of the Kellys so far, and he was sure he'd meet more. The young ones all saw the Arizona Territory as the land of opportunity, mainly because Norah was there and took them in so they could get away from their dad.

They were a hardheaded lot, from the old Irish reprobate on down. Young Mickey turned out just fine in spite of his yen to be a desperado.

Katie taught school for a year in Holbrook and then surprised them all by eloping with Burt Adams, Morgan's stalwart deputy. Meg and Nell came together, married shopkeepers, and now owned a mercantile down in Phoenix.

And little sister Evelyn, who was nearly as pretty as Norah, had taken Holbrook by storm last summer when she'd come just for a visit. Jimmy, who'd become Morgan's deputy after Adams retired, married her two months later.

Norah's parents now had sixteen children and another expected. Yet Morgan still thought Norah was their best effort.

God, she was beautiful. He could hardly believe that eleven years had passed since she'd stepped off that train. So much had happened to them, and to Holbrook, in those passing years.

Morgan sighed, thinking it was almost a shame they'd moved, since the town had finally begun to settle down. *Almost.* But he did not regret hanging up his guns. His responsibility was to Norah and their children. They had his heart.

Besides, Holbrook wasn't the same. Most of their friends were gone now. Myrtis moved to Phoenix last fall. She and Digger bought a big old Spanish hacienda and took in boarders, mostly old folks like themselves who had no place else to go. Clarabelle and Quinton Rose and their twins, who were the same age as five-year-old Calvin, sold their store and moved to Prescott to be closer to Ferdie and his family.

Dolly married Tod Willis, the cabinetmaker, after she divorced Mordecai Smith. Three years later, Tod was shot by a stray bullet one afternoon as he passed the Red Rock Saloon. The man with the gun had just murdered Lily Mae. Dolly and their son, Patrick, who was two months to the day younger than eight-year-old Christopher, now lived outside Flagstaff with her third husband, Thor, a huge, good-looking logger from Wisconsin.

Mordecai Smith had a run of bad luck after Dolly divorced him. His young pregnant Indian wife hemorrhaged to death of unknown reasons in her seventh month, and her younger brother Joseph walked in front of a westbound train the following week. Mordecai seemed to lose his spirit after that and got old. He had a stroke a year or so later, to remain an invalid for more than two years.

Cephus, his oldest son, took up with a Catholic girl from Concho, and eventually moved to Phoenix. The other boys split up the property, married, and cared for their mothers.

Winnie and Nathan Ralston left Holbrook two months after the big fire of '87 and settled in Globe, where the climate was more moderate. Nathan never completely recovered from the bullet wounds Bunky Lindstrom gave him, but he and Winnie seemed happy together. She wrote to Norah several times a year.

Mayor Whitehall embezzled the town company's building fund and was last seen hopping a freight train heading west. Frank Reed had a heyday with that. Frank was still in Holbrook, still stirring up trouble. But he'd recently confided to Morgan that he was thinking about heading up north to Alaska because Holbrook was getting so dull.

The cattle trains had all but stopped. The big companies didn't make the high profits they'd expected from the thousands of head they'd shipped in. They'd discovered the land couldn't support such a volume of animals. Their experiment in greed had forever altered the landscape. The flowing grasslands were gone. With little grass left to stop the relentless wind and violent summer rains, great washes and gullies eroded away the rich topsoil. And the river was full of mud.

Morgan's hand tightened on Norah's.

"What's the matter?" Norah asked softly.

Morgan looked down at her and his face softened. "Nothing important. I was just thinking. I didn't mean to wake you."

"I'm rested. What were you thinking about?" She stroked his palm with her fingertip.

He closed his eyes against tears that threatened and squeezed her hand. "I love you, Norah," he whispered. "With my heart and soul."

"I know," she told him, her own love showing in her eloquent eyes. "I've known from the very first day."

Author's Notes

Holbrook, Arizona, still exists today. Both of the authors lived there for quite a few years. During the time period of this novel Holbrook was the second town in Arizona Territory that was known for being "too tough to die." The first was Tombstone.

Sheriff Morgan Treyhan is based loosely upon Commodore Perry Owens, who was the sheriff of Apache County at that time and had his office in the county seat of St. Johns. He was nicknamed "Ironman" because many believed he lived a charmed life and could not be killed. He was a dead shot with the twin .45s he wore tied down, and he carried a rifle and a shotgun in his saddle scabbards.

Norah Kelly Welsh Treyhan is based loosely upon the grandmother of one of the authors.

The only character in this book based upon himself is Frank Reed, the editor of the *Apache*

County Critic. Many of our historical tidbits come from old copies of his newspaper.

The landmarks of Holbrook are authentic, although we changed the names of the occupants. The shoot-out at Winnie Ralston's house is our version of the Blevins shoot-out on April 4, 1887. On that day Commodore Perry Owens went to the Blevins House to arrest Andy Cooper. In a matter of moments he had killed Andy Cooper and Sam Blevins and wounded John Blevins and M. B. Roberts, who died a couple of days later.

The earthquake actually happened—on Tuesday, May 3, 1887, at 3:14 p.m., according to Frank Reed.

The "Invitation to a Hanging" was actually issued by Sheriff Frank J. Wattron on December 8, 1899. The guest of honor was a cattle rustler by the name of George Smiley. We couldn't pass up such a wonderful bit of historical color so we incorporated it into our story. We figured George wouldn't mind.

The big fire actually occurred on June 26, 1888. We simply changed the date to better fit our story. The facts remain. The town burned to the ground, but its staunch residents wouldn't let it die.

Navajo County was created in 1895. Holbrook became the county seat, and the courthouse was completed in 1898. Owens was appointed the first sheriff and assessor of Navajo County. In the first election, however, he was replaced by his deputy Frank J. Wattron, the same deputy he'd had to fire because the town company decided they couldn't afford two lawmen. Owens went down into the Verde Valley and became a rancher.

Soon after, Wattron hired a deputy by the name of Burton Mossman. Mossman, who had been the manager of a large ranch in Bloody Basin on the Verde River for a number of years, had just been hired by the Aztec Land and Cattle Company to take over as manager of the Hashknife outfit.

For fourteen years, between 1884 and 1898, the Hashknife outfit had not been able to get a conviction for horse or cattle stealing. Mossman promptly changed that. He kept the jail full of cattle thieves, but George Smiley was the first convicted cattle rustler.

Even Mossman's efforts were not enough to save the Hashknife outfit, though. In 1900 he was ordered to liquidate the last of its fluid holdings and turn over the management to Frank Wallace, who in turn sold the last of the cattle empire's holdings to the firm of Babbitt and Stiles in 1901.

The old Hashknife outfit was dead. Its demise also ended the violent era of Holbrook's history. It settled down to become a fast-growing western railhead town, where the residents could walk the streets without fear of being shot down.

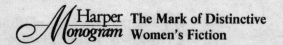

COMING NEXT MONTH

DREAM KEEPER by Parris Afton Bonds

The spellbinding Australian saga begun with *Dream Time* continues with the lives and loves of estranged twins and their children, who were destined to one day fulfill the Dream Time legacy. An unforgettable love story.

DIAMOND IN THE ROUGH by Millie Criswell

Brock Peters was a drifter—a man with no ties and no possessions other than his horse and gun. He didn't like entanglements, didn't like getting involved, until he met the meanest spinster in Colorado, Prudence Daniels. "Poignant, humorous, and heartwarming."—*Romantic Times*

LADY ADVENTURESS by Helen Archery

A delightful Regency by the author of *The Season of Loving*. In need of money, Stara Carltons resorted to pretending to be the notorious highwayman, One-Jewel Jack, and held up the coach containing Lady Gwendolen and Marcus Justus. Her ruse was successful for a time until Marcus learned who Stara really was and decided to turn the tables on her.

PRELUDE TO HEAVEN by Laura Lee Guhrke

A passionate and tender historical romance of true love between a fragile English beauty and a handsome, reclusive French painter. "Brilliant debut novel! Laura Lee Guhrke has written a classic love story that will touch your heart."—Robin Lee Hatcher

PRAIRIE LIGHT by Margaret Carroll

Growing up as the adopted daughter of a prominent Boston family, Kat Norton always knew she must eventually come face-to-face with her destiny. When she travels to the wilds of Montana, she discovers her Native American roots and the love of one man who has always denied his own roots.

A TIME TO LOVE by Kathleen Bryant

A heartwarming story of a man and woman driven apart by grief who reunite years later to learn that love can survive anything. Eighteen years before, a family tragedy ended a budding romance between Christian Foster and his best friend's younger sister, Willa. Now a grown woman, Willa returns to the family island resort in Minnesota to say good-bye to the past once and for all, only to discover that Christian doesn't intend to let her go.